# You Can See Me

# A.E. VIA

*You Can See Me*
Written by: A.E. Via
Copyright © February 2014 A. E. Via
All Rights Reserved
Cover art by Clarissa Yeo © February 2014
Interior Design & Formatting by Fancy Pants Book Formatting

No part of this e-book may be reproduced or shared by any electronic or mechanical means, including but not limited to printing, file sharing, and e-mail, without prior written permission from A.E. Via.

No part of this book may be reproduced in any form or by any electronic or mechanical means, including information storage and retrieval systems, without the express written consent from the author, except in the case of a reviewer, who may quote brief passages embodied in critical articles or in a review.

Trademarked names appear throughout this book. Rather than trademarked name, names are used in an editorial fashion, with no intention of infringement of the respective owner's trademark.

The information in this book is distributed on an "as is" basis, without warranty. Although every precaution has been taken in the preparation of this work, neither the author nor the publisher shall have any liability to any person or entity with respect to any loss or damage caused or alleged to be caused directly or indirectly by the information contained in this book.

The characters, locations, and events portrayed in this book are fictitious. Any similarity or resemblance to real persons, living or dead is coincidental and not intended by the author.

A.E. VIA

# Disclaimer

This is a M/M Romance and contains graphic content. It's not intended for readers under the age of 18.

# YOU CAN SEE ME

# Dedication

To my husband and children, thank you so much for understanding the many long nights.

To the potential authors who aren't sure if they can do it...don't think. Just write.

YOU CAN SEE ME

# Acknowledgments

A special thank you to the LaSalle Sisters (Cheryl, Stephanie, Iza) of Man2Mantastic.blogspot.com for all their help and support. Ladies, you did a wonderful job writing the synopsis and creating a title for my next release, *Nothing Special*. I've sincerely enjoyed working with you talented ladies and look forward to a very productive 2014.

# YOU CAN SEE ME

# Contents

**Disclaimer** ............................................................. 3
**Dedication** ............................................................ 5
**Acknowledgments** ................................................ 7
**Prologue** ............................................................. 11
**Chapter One** ....................................................... 13
**Chapter Two** ....................................................... 15
**Chapter Three** .................................................... 21
**Chapter Four** ...................................................... 27
**Chapter Five** ....................................................... 33
**Chapter Six** ......................................................... 39
**Chapter Seven** .................................................... 43
**Chapter Eight** ..................................................... 47
**Chapter Nine** ...................................................... 53
**Chapter Ten** ........................................................ 61
**Chapter Eleven** ................................................... 71
**Chapter Twelve** ................................................... 79
**Chapter Thirteen** ................................................ 87
**Chapter Fourteen** ............................................. 101
**Chapter Fifteen** ................................................ 111
**Chapter Sixteen** ................................................ 117
**Chapter Seventeen** ........................................... 123
**Chapter Eighteen** ............................................. 129
**Chapter Nineteen** ............................................. 135
**Chapter Twenty** ................................................ 141
**Chapter Twenty-One** ........................................ 151

| | |
|---|---|
| Chapter Twenty-Two | 159 |
| Chapter Twenty-Three | 161 |
| Chapter Twenty-Four | 167 |
| Chapter Twenty-Five | 171 |
| Chapter Twenty-Six | 177 |
| Chapter Twenty-Seven | 187 |
| Chapter Twenty-Eight | 193 |
| Chapter Twenty-Nine | 201 |
| Chapter Thirty | 205 |
| Chapter Thirty-One | 209 |
| Chapter Thirty-Two | 213 |
| Chapter Thirty-Three | 221 |
| Chapter Thirty-Four | 231 |
| Chapter Thirty-Five | 233 |
| Chapter Thirty-Six | 241 |
| Chapter Thirty-Seven | 245 |
| Chapter Thirty-Eight | 255 |
| Cha[ter Thirty-Nine | 259 |
| Chapter Forty | 265 |
| Chapter Forty-One | 279 |
| Chapter Forty-Two | 285 |
| Chapter Forty-Three | 293 |
| Chapter Forty-Four | 299 |
| Chapter Forty-Five | 301 |
| Chapter Forty-Six | 305 |
| Chapter Forty-Seven | 311 |
| Epilogue | 321 |
| Coming Soon | 327 |
| About the Author | 340 |
| Also By A.E. Via | 341 |

# Prologue

Prescott sat in bumper-to-bumper traffic on Interstate 664 on his way home from the James Beard Culinary Awards ceremony in Richmond, Virginia. At only twenty-seven years old, he was one of the youngest chefs to receive the prestigious honor. Prescott had known he wanted to be a chef since he was ten years old. His mom had pictures of him—as young as the age of five—in the kitchen beside her, watching and learning.

He reached into the box and picked up the trophy. For the tenth time he read the engraved inscription on the shiny gold plate of his award and smiled at memories of himself and his mother.

*I should call Angie, let her know I'm on my way home.* It was thirty degrees outside, and the bridge had accumulated a lot of black ice. The traffic advisory had warned everyone to stay off the highways if they could, but his fiancée had wanted him to come home right after the ceremony.

Pres hit the speed dial on his cell phone to call his beautiful fiancée.

"Hello."

"Hey, baby. I'm on my way home," Pres said with a wide grin on his face. His cheeks were still burning from all the smiling he'd done that evening at the banquet.

"Oh good, you left right after the ceremony."

"Yeah, I left right after, just like you begged me to do. I don't know why I couldn't just stay in a hotel and drive back in the morning. I'm sure I'll hit traffic coming back this late," he said.

"I'll make it worth it, baby," she purred in that sexy voice that drove him crazy.

Pres pushed down on his rising cock. "How are you gonna make it worth it, huh? Tell me what you're gonna do to me."

"I can show you better than I can tell you," she replied.

Pres was crossing the bridge and saw the rear taillights light up on the car in front of him as traffic slowed to an idling crawl. *Great, here comes the traffic already. Might as well do something to keep me entertained.*

"I'll be home in a few hours, and the first thing I want you to do is get on your knees so I can fuck your pretty mouth," he moaned while squeezing the head of his dick.

"Pres, stop it," she whined. "You know I can't talk dirty. I always feel stupid."

Pres laughed. His fiancée was so old-fashioned, he was surprised she even gave him head. "Okay, baby. I'll let you show me later. I'm already hitting some traffic, so keep the bed warm for me."

"I will. I love you, Pres."

"I love—"

Pres's words were cut off as he heard the screeching sound of tires skidding behind him. He looked in his rearview mirror and saw a tractor trailer had hydroplaned on the ice. The driver lost control and barreled toward him at a terrifying speed, and Pres's mind went into overdrive. His cell phone slipped from his hand. He couldn't jump out of his vehicle because the trailer had turned at a ninety-degree angle. He would have to jump over the railing and into the bay in order to avoid it. With below-freezing temperatures in the water…it was probably not a good idea. Pres tensed every muscle in his body, slammed his eyes shut, and tried to brace for the crash. He said a silent prayer as he felt a split second of impact before everything went dark.

# Chapter One

After six excruciatingly painful months in the hospital, Prescott was released to go home. The surgeries to his limbs were successful, but when he woke in recovery from the extensive brain surgery…his vision was completely gone. Prescott had never prayed so hard for anything in his life, but he begged for weeks for his vision to return.

The neurologist explained in detail the severity of the injuries he sustained from the accident. Although it would be highly unlikely in his case, there was a ten percent chance that he'd recover his sight. He softly advised Prescott that he should come to terms with the fact that he was now blind and would be for the rest of his life.

But he refused to believe that he'd never see again. He didn't know how he would function as a blind person. He was a chef and a damn good one, too. He was finally being recognized for his skill and art in the kitchen. He'd just accepted a one-in-a-million opportunity to go to Paris and work shoulder to shoulder with his idol, only to have it all stripped away in a matter of minutes. Cooking was all he'd ever known. He'd never prepared a contingency plan if anything were to ever happen and he couldn't cook anymore.

Prescott was in a state of depression he'd never thought imaginable. His doctors gave specific instructions for him to continue physical therapy and enroll in a school for the blind.

He did neither. He went home, closed himself in his bedroom, and sealed the dark drapes. He was nobody now.

# YOU CAN SEE ME

## Chapter Two

His fiancée, Angela, tried so hard in the beginning to be there for him both physically and emotionally. She waited on him hand and foot, preparing his food, picking out his clothes, even bathing him. He fussed at her constantly for doing everything for him, and then he'd turn around and fuss at her for not doing enough. He'd get extremely angry if she even hinted about them going out of the condo and having some fun together. He didn't want to leave the house because then people would see him…but he wouldn't see them.

He hadn't cooked in months despite her persistence. Whenever she'd mention the school or counseling for his depression, he'd yell at her. She finally had enough and called on both of their parents to come and help her.

Pres was asleep in bed when he heard his mother come barging through the door, cursing up a storm.

"Get your ass out of the bed this instant, Prescott Montgomery Vaughan, or so help me God, I will kick the shit out of you—blind or not!" she yelled so loud she could've woken the dead.

"Mom, get outta here," he groaned weakly.

"Right the hell now! Get up…or else!" she screeched as she ripped the covers off him.

"Mom, cut it out!" Prescott rose up in the bed. He turned his head in the direction of the crazy woman in his bedroom and tried to put a hard scowl on his face. Pres kept his eyes closed tight. He never wanted to open them again, knowing that would be useless.

"Or else what, Mom? What are you going to do, huh?" He flopped back down lazily on the bed. "I'm gonna call Pop and tell him you're acting insane. He wouldn't stand for this," Pres threatened angrily.

"Sure, have it your way," she replied casually.

*That's right. Just leave.*

Pres thought maybe his mom was losing her mind. She was nothing like this in the hospital. All she could do was whine, sniffle, and coo at her poor, sightless baby. Now, here she was acting like a goddamn drill sergeant. *What the hell?*

Pres lay there for a couple more minutes before he felt a blast of freezing cold water hit him in his chest.

"Auggh! Shit!" he screamed right before another gush of cold water hit him dead in his face. He coughed and sprayed water out of his mouth. "Jesus Christ! Mom, what the hell are you—"

Another violent splash to the side of his face abruptly cut off his yelling.

"All right, all right…damn it! Just stop. I'm getting up!" He threw his hands up in surrender.

"Better. Now, get up and go to the bathroom and clean yourself up. You smell horrible. Everything is in the bathroom already set out for you, including some clothes. After you're done, I want you to come into the kitchen. I'll be waiting." His mother sounded completely composed, as if they were discussing the weather and she hadn't just waterboarded him.

"Tell Angela to come and help me get into the bathroom," he hissed angrily at his mother.

"No. Angela is busy right now. You've been living here for two years. Go to the bathroom yourself."

On that note, she left the room.

Pres managed to get to the bathroom and get himself cleaned up with very little difficulty. As he let the hot water cascade over his tired body, he realized that he'd been making Angela do everything for him, including leading him around like an invalid.

He was able to adjust the hot and cold knobs to the temperature he wanted. He cleaned his body, using the soap that was always in the soap holder. His shampoo and conditioner were always kept in the far left corner of the shower, on the upper shelf. Pres reached his hand out of the shower and grabbed a fluffy towel from off the towel rack on the wall above the wastebasket.

He didn't want to attempt to shave with his wet razor, so he used his dry electric one. He was again surprised at the simplicity of the act. He put on his clothes by feeling for the tags to make sure they were turned in the right direction. He grazed his fingers along the polished wood, pulled out the top right-hand drawer underneath the sink, felt around for his deodorant—locating it immediately—and smiled. Even though the act was so minute, he'd still done it himself, and it was the first time he'd actually done anything on his own in a while.

Pres made his way out of his bedroom and into the main living area and heard several sets of voices. He recognized Angela talking to her parents. He stood there for a few seconds when everything went completely silent.

*Well, it sounds like they see me. Is anyone gonna say shit?*

He stood there a few more seconds at the continued silence.

*I guess not.*

"Angela, can you help me?" he asked, with a little more annoyance in his voice than he'd intended.

"No, she can't. Do it yourself," his mother answered coldly. From the proximity of her voice, it sounded like she was in his kitchen.

*Might as well get this over with. The sooner she talks, the sooner I can go back to bed.* Pres tamped down his anger and thought for a second before he took a couple of tentative steps toward his large kitchen. He didn't bother to acknowledge his future in-laws, since they didn't speak to him.

"Honey, you look better. Come here toward my voice." His mother spoke softly but clearly.

Pres figured she had to be standing by the wraparound breakfast bar, so he moved in that direction. "Mom?" he called out timidly.

"Right here, Prescott," his mom said directly in front of him, and it made him flinch violently.

"God. Don't do that, please," he admonished.

"Sorry."

She embraced him in a warm, tight hug. At first he just let his arms rest at his sides as she squeezed him. He realized that it felt really good to be in his kitchen again, and his mom was the one who had gotten him there. He slowly brought his arms up around her waist and hugged her back. He felt her sigh in his ear as she noticeably relaxed against him.

"There, are you satisfied? I'm up now." He tried not to sound too pissed with his mom. He could never truly be mad at her for anything. His mother always had his best interest at heart, and he did love her.

"Well, you smell better, but no, I'm not satisfied. Come here." She put his hand in the crook of her elbow and brought him to stand in front of the wide island in the center of his kitchen. "Feel around," she said quietly.

He lifted his hands and began to pat around on the cool surface. Suddenly feeling foolish, he growled and slammed both his hands down hard on the marble top.

"Knock it off!" she fired at him immediately, obviously not fazed by his little tantrum. "Feel around, damn it." This time she was more aggressive.

*What has gotten into my soft-spoken mother? Before today, she would cover her mouth and giggle if she accidently swore. Now she's cursing like a sailor.*

He huffed an exasperated breath and brought his hands back up to feel around again. The tips of his fingers on his left hand bumped into something. He grasped his fingers around it, feeling it more thoroughly, and realized it was a bowl.

"A bowl," he growled. "You want me to guess what the objects are? Is that what I'm about to do? Well forget it. I'm not interested in a kitchen utensils lesson for the blind today. Do you really think I can't figure out what a bowl is, or a fork, a plate, a spoon, for crying out loud? I'm blind, not dumb!" Pres's voice had grown deep with anger.

"Damn straight you're not. Now lift the bowl up to your nose and tell me what's in it," his mother demanded.

Pres didn't move. He kept his eyes closed tight and his lips parted slightly at the increase in his breathing. He slowly brought the bowl up to his nose and inhaled deeply.

"Scallops," he replied dryly.

"Scallops, huh?" his mother stated coolly. "Sure. But tell me about them."

Pres scrunched his face in confusion, but brought the bowl back to his nose again. He took several deep inhales before replying, "They're not fresh. At least a few days old, and previously frozen."

He heard his mom let loose a victorious laugh, and then she slung her arms back around his neck again.

"That's right, honey. I unthawed those scallops exactly two days ago. Oh, Prescott, don't you understand what I'm trying to do? You can keep cooking, honey. It's just going to take work and practice. You have to be willing to learn again. I've been doing a lot of research. I've read about schools and jobs for blind people with a culinary background. Just come talk to the admissions counselors with me and Angela. They can show and teach you how to live a fulfilling life."

# Chapter Three

Pres's mom stayed with him and Angela while he swallowed his pride and went to school to learn how to live life as a blind person. He even learned how to cook again. He knew how to cook, but he didn't know how to cook without using his sight. He relied on his other senses in the kitchen, which were now all heightened. His palate was more refined and sensitive than ever. He could name just about every ingredient in a dish, down to the allspice.

He was doing wonderfully in school. It'd taken him only a year and half to learn how to read Braille. His settlement and monthly annuity from the accident allowed him to pay off his condo and buy the amenities needed to make living life as a blind man a little easier, like paying for a maid service, purchasing a beautiful Labrador retriever seeing-eye dog, and hiring a full-time personal assistant and a driver.

He was just gearing up to open his own food critiquing business and feeling like life was still worth living, when his fiancée of four years dropped her bomb.

"I'm sorry, Pres, but I just can't do this anymore. You've overcome so much, and I'm so proud of you, but we are not in the same place anymore. I stuck by you through your recovery, and I really tried to make it work in my mind…but I want children, Pres. I wanted to go to Paris with you. I want to travel and see the world…" Angela stopped short at the realization of what she'd just said.

*I want to fucking see the world too.* Pres felt his heart explode into a thousand pieces. He'd tried so hard to be a complete man for her. He'd apologized repeatedly for how he'd treated her in the beginning. To his knowledge, she'd understood and forgiven him. There wasn't a day that went by that he didn't try to do something special for her. He tried to stay enthusiastic and adventurous by taking her out places and showing her that he'd never be embarrassed again.

Since the day his mom barged into his bedroom and dragged his ass back into his kitchen, he'd never given up hope on once again becoming successful in his field. Although he couldn't cook in anyone else's kitchen, he could still cook like Emeril Lagasse in his own. He cooked for her every night they didn't go out. She raved about his dishes. Now she was saying everything he did wasn't enough for her to forget his disability.

As far as his appearance was concerned, he was always dressed impeccably and stayed groomed to perfection at all times. He had a stylist who kept him looking "breathtaking"—her words, not his. Prescott was a good-looking man, always had been. The accident hadn't changed that. He'd never really cared about his looks because he kept his face in a pot or pan all the time. However, he prided himself on staying attractive…for her.

She'd been his best friend, lover, and companion for six years. Now, without even giving Prescott a hint that there was a problem, she was leaving. Even though he was in the dark now, he still had a small sliver of light in his Angela. If she could leave him, then what hope did he have of meeting a woman who would fall in love with a blind man? No matter how rich or gorgeous he was, obviously his impairment wasn't something a woman could overlook.

"Angela, please don't do this. I can't live without you. Baby, please…are you looking at me?" Prescott held her small face in his hands. He remembered her beautiful green eyes. He squeezed his eyes shut harder and visualized her sharp nose and high cheekbones. He let his thumb trace her perfect Cupid's bow lips and worked desperately to hold in his sobs, but the tears were flowing freely.

"Yes, Pres. I'm looking at you. It's not you. It's me," she said.

"What the hell, Angela? What is that supposed to mean? I...I...I don't even know how to take that," Pres stuttered as confusion and anger barreled to the surface.

"Pres, you will find someone better for you. I know you will," she said as she tried to wiggle out of the grip he had on her face.

"No! No, I won't, Angela! I won't find someone. I can't fucking see, remember!" he yelled in frustration. He heard her let out a shocked gasp, so he took a couple breaths to try to rein in his rage.

"You were ready to get married in a month before the accident happened. That's why I was rushing home in terrible road conditions, right after the awards ceremony, instead of staying the night in a hotel. You'd set the date and wanted to start ironing out the details right away. Remember?"

Pres knew he was hitting below the belt on that one, but he was desperate now. She was leaving him, and if he had to lay on a little guilt trip to get her to reconsider, then what the hell.

"We've made it through the hard part together. I need my best friend with me, baby." Pres was trying hard to make her understand. There was no way he could be without her. He couldn't fathom being alone in the dark all the time. "Honey, the food critiquing business is almost under way. I'm going to give you anything and everything you've ever wanted. We can still travel, have kids, and go to—" He stopped short when he heard her suck in a sharp breath at the word "kids."

He placed a shaking hand over his mouth at the realization.

"You don't want to have kids with me. Is that what this is about? You can't see yourself raising kids with a blind man, can you?" *No wonder she never wanted to make love.* They'd only made love once or twice a month, and even then she was stiff as a board. Pres almost felt like he was raping her. They didn't have any foreplay or pay special attention to other areas.

Pres had thought she was tired and overworked at her job. All the while, she was being overconscious of not getting pregnant since they didn't use condoms. *Jesus Christ.*

He didn't know if he could handle this level of rejection or not. He wished he could just fall down right where he was standing and go to sleep forever. The pain in his chest was that deep and awful. This was the first time in months that he actually wished he had his sight back. He wanted to see her face one last time.

"I'm so sorry, Pres. It's just…this is not what I signed up for." Her voice was weak and strained. It sounded to him like she was crying.

Prescott didn't move from where he stood. *Not what you signed up for.*

He felt exposed and raw. His silk tie was like a noose around his neck. He silently prayed it would get tighter and cut off his air supply. Pres's heart went into last-chance-full-on-desperation mode when he heard her scuffling with her bags as she moved through the condo.

"Oh God. No, no, no, no. Please don't leave me, baby…I'm begging you. Please don't go. We can work this out. We just need to sit down and talk." Pres held both hands out in front of him, without words, asking for her to take them and hold them. She never did. "Sweetie, I need you so much. We can go to counseling if you want. I can fix this. I can, if you give me a chance."

"Bye, Pres," she whispered.

He numbly listened to her heels click-clack across the French-style hardwood tiles in his entryway. The definitive clank of the closing door boomed through his apartment like a jail cell slamming shut. That was it... She was gone. As much as he wished otherwise, he knew she wouldn't be coming back.

He slid down the wall and dropped his head between his knees.

"Angie, please. Come back. Come back. Come back," he whispered repeatedly as if he could will her to return to him. He sat there alone and sobbed quietly for hours into the empty room...the very dark, empty room.

YOU CAN SEE ME

# Chapter Four

*Five years later*

**P**rescott took the starched white napkin from his lap and dabbed the corner of his mouth. "Simply divine, Chef Molly. Your use of saffron in the lemon caper sauce is unique but absolutely refreshing. The scallops have nice searing on both sides and are cooked to perfection. Nicely done."

"Thank you, Chef. Is there anything else I can get for you? Perhaps another glass of Chardonnay?" Chef Molly replied elatedly.

When Prescott showed up unexpectedly, the excitement and nervousness in her voice told him she was completely taken by surprise that he'd chosen to critique her new harborside restaurant off of the Chesapeake Bay.

Pres was the most sought-after food critic by every chef and restaurateur on the East Coast. His palate was the most refined of any reviewer ever heard of, according to *Food & Cuisine* magazine. If Prescott Vaughan gave your food a good rating, then your restaurant's clientele would surely increase exponentially.

"You're most welcome, Chef, and no, thank you, I don't think I can eat or drink anything else. I've enjoyed everything very much. My business partner will be in soon to rate the appearance of the restaurant and the overall ambiance.

"However, I must say, I've enjoyed breathing in the salty ocean air coming through your open bay doors. The sound of the boats coming in and out of the harbor even puts you in the mind frame to order seafood. You made an excellent decision on the choice of location, Chef."

"Again, thank you, Chef Vaughan. Tell your partner, Mr. Carbone, whenever he's available would be fine for me."

"Well, I'm going to get out of your way. I'm sure your dinner rush will start soon." Prescott placed his napkin neatly beside the almost-empty plate. He pushed his chair back easily and bent down to feel for his cane.

"Let me get that for you, Chef."

He felt Chef Molly place his retractable cane in his hand. As she did, her fingers lightly grazed over his, making goose bumps prickle on his forearm. It was the touch of a woman, not just any woman, a highly regarded chef. His cock immediately took notice.

"Thank you, Chef Molly. When I've finished the written review for *Fine Cuisine of Hampton Roads* magazine, I'll have my assistant forward you a copy."

"I'd appreciate that. Do you need any assistance with getting to your vehicle, Chef?" Her voice was timid and unsure.

He liked that most people still called him Chef, even though he hadn't worked as one since the accident.

"No, Chef, my driver is out front. I can manage just fine." Prescott could feel her breathing. Her warm, Shiraz-scented, erratic burst of breath made the fine hairs on his neck stand up. She was close to him…very close. He stuck his hand out in her general vicinity and waited for her to grasp it. When she did, she held his hand lightly and gave it a couple of soft rubs with her other hand.

Her skin was silky soft, and Prescott silently wished he could hold on to it a little longer. However, he was a professional and renowned food critic. It would be completely unethical to get involved with someone he'd critiqued.

"Take care, Chef Molly."

"It was a pleasure, Chef," she replied, sounding winded. After a few seconds of uncomfortable silence, she added, "Chef Vaughan, I hope I'm not out of line by asking you this, but do you think you'd like to get a drink sometime...uhh...with me?"

Prescott wanted to say yes so badly. However, he was not a cheater or dishonest.

"I'm flattered, Chef Molly, but I'm currently in a relationship," he replied softly.

*If you could call it that. Shit. I haven't seen my girlfriend in weeks, and it's been longer than that since we had sex.* Prescott shut off his internal rant, letting his mind drift back to when he last saw Chef Molly's face. He remembered her deep blue eyes with thick tan lashes, and long blonde hair that she kept pulled up into a tight bun when she was in her kitchen. He'd had the pleasure of hosting a charity food rave with her a few years ago...before his life changed forever. She was gorgeous inside and out. He hoped she hadn't taken the rejection badly. He tried to listen to any changes in her breathing to gauge if she was upset.

"Oh, I'm sorry. I didn't realize. Well, you take care." Her voice faded as she moved away from him, sounding slightly embarrassed.

*Damn it.*

"Good-bye, Chef." Prescott started toward the entrance. He mentally remembered the overall steps he'd taken to get to his table and through the entrance, but he still needed to use his long cane. He didn't want to trip on a chair leg and fall flat on his face. *Been there...done that.* He made it to the front door and heard the hostess bid him a good day.

When he got outside, he heard his personal driver, Scott, whistling a little tune as he waited for him. Prescott knew it was his driver's personal way of letting him know where he was without drawing too much attention to him by yelling his name as soon as he appeared.

Prescott made his way to the curb and waited as Scott opened the back door to his sleek black Lincoln Town Car.

"Damn, I hate rush-hour traffic. They already reported a five-car pileup on the Chesapeake Bridge. Dang-on. You sure you don't wanna drive, Pres?" Scott asked playfully.

"Shut the hell up." Prescott popped Scott in his midsection and climbed into the backseat. He loved that Scott was able to joke with him about his disability, unlike so many others who treated him like he was either five years old or completely stupid. Prescott was the same man he'd always been…sort of.

"So, back to the office, Pres?" Scott asked while climbing into the driver's seat.

"You got it." Prescott made himself comfortable as the car smoothly pulled into traffic. He ran his hand down his silk tie and pulled his cell phone from his suit jacket pocket. He thought of giving Victoria a call, but paused mid-dial. *She's probably still at work.* He called his business partner instead.

"Hey, Pres. How'd the critique go?" Adam Carbone greeted him the same way every time he picked up the line.

"It went great, Adam," he replied. "I'm giving the food and service three out of four stars. Chef Molly looks forward to you critiquing the interior at your convenience. What else is on the schedule for today? I'm hoping it's light. I really want to get caught up on some review writing." He listened as Adam rustled some papers, which Prescott assumed meant he was checking the schedule.

"We're good, Pres. I'm going to accept some requests for critiques on the Eastern Shore and then write my review on that little bed-and-breakfast in Williamsburg. You gave the food a three-star rating, but I had to give the interior a one-star. I can't believe they thought I'd overlook mouse traps behind the furniture, or dusty windowsills," Adam said, annoyance lacing his strong Italian accent.

"Damn, you're getting tough, partner. You couldn't give them a thirty-day extension to make improvements? I've noticed you've become very intolerant lately. Everything cool?" Pres asked, wondering why his partner had been so on edge the last few months. He didn't cut anyone a break anymore, and even in the office, the staff was starting to give him a wide berth when he came through. Prescott had worked hard to build his reputation after his accident. He didn't want them to be seen as the asshole critics everyone dreaded to see enter their establishment.

"No, man, I'm fine. Just our critiques need to be spot-on and reliable. Just because they don't know exactly when we're coming to do our review, doesn't mean that they should get extra time if something isn't right. Their restaurant should be immaculate at all times. Am I right?" Adam countered.

"You're right, Adam. Consumers rely on our reviews, so we do want them to be accurate. Sorry, man, I wasn't trying to imply anything."

"It's cool, Pres. Go home and do something fun, man. The reviews can wait another few days…it's the weekend."

"Actually, that doesn't sound bad. I got quite a few books I've been meaning to catch up on," Pres thought out loud casually.

"Oh, for shit's sake, Pres. Don't go home and listen to goddamn audio books. Go to a bar, or have Captain get your yacht ready and take it out for a couple days. Maybe take Victoria to your vineyard in Fishersville. Well, no, don't do that because her ass is too ungrateful." Adam balked at saying Victoria's name.

Pres let out a deep chuckle. "You really don't like her, do you?"

"What's to like, Pres? She treats you like shit. You're a human being, not an ATM."

"Calm down, my friend. I may go to a lounge and enjoy some live music or something. I'll talk to you later." Pres disconnected the call before his partner could go on any further. "Change of plans, Scott. I'm going home, buddy." Pres adjusted his black-and-chrome Burberry aviator sunglasses and pressed the button to let the window down. He listened to the sounds of traffic, silently missing the visual of Hampton Roads as Scott drove him to his condo.

# Chapter Five

 **P**rescott gave Scott a nice tip on top of his weekly salary and told him to enjoy his weekend. If he needed to go anywhere over the next couple days, he'd call a cab. He went through the lobby doors, let out his cane, and used it to get to the bank of elevators. He'd been living in the luxury oceanfront condominium's building for seven years, and he knew the layout, but he never knew if some furniture would be moved around or if a display would be set up.

 Last thing he wanted to do was run into a brand-new grand piano in the middle of the lobby. *Been there...done that.*

 He got to his floor, stepped into his apartment, and immediately disarmed the alarm. The spacious twenty-five hundred square-foot condo had a large, state-of-the-art gourmet kitchen, two master bedrooms, and an office. The large living room had been masterfully designed by a decorator, but Pres spent most of his time in the cozy den if he wasn't in his kitchen. The dining room was not overly spacious, which was fine, because it was rarely used. Pres liked to eat at the large wraparound breakfast bar.

 He dropped his briefcase by the table next to the door and whispered into the empty condo, "Honey, I'm home." *Yeah right.* No one was ever there to greet him when he came home, not a human anyway. Josey would jump up and lick his hands and bark at wanting to go for a walk, but even he was not there tonight. He was at the groomer's. His assistant would be back with him any minute. Josey accompanied Pres only when he was out and about. He never took him with him to work.

Making his way into his kitchen, Pres could smell the lemon citrus disinfectant the cleaning lady used on his counters. He was sure his condo was spotless. He'd been told that enough times. The maid service he used was wonderful. Not only did they never miss a week or forget to do a task, they also did little things for him to assist with his disability.

His regular cleaner took the initiative to learn how to use his Braille labeler and labeled his groceries when they were delivered. She would put everything away in the places he specified. All the boxes and canned goods in his pantry were organized and labeled as well. She even went as far as labeling his DVDs and CDs.

He went to his wine rack on the wall next to his refrigerator and ran his fingers along the raised Braille labels, wanting a bottle of Merlot. When he selected the one he wanted, he pulled a glass from the cupboard and used his finger to measure his pouring. He put a wine cap on the bottle and tucked it into the crook of his arm to bring with him. *Why keep getting up?*

His feet didn't make a sound on the plush carpet as he walked into his den and dropped down in his brown leather La-Z-Boy, releasing a soft sigh. He should've gone to his bedroom to remove his pin-striped Ralph Lauren suit to get more comfortable, but he was feeling a little too lazy for that right now.

Setting his wineglass down, he picked up the cordless phone to call Victoria, wondering what she was up to.

"Hello," the sweet voice purred into the receiver.

"Hey, babe. How was your day?"

"Oh…hi, Pres. Sorry, I thought you were someone else."

*Someone else, like who?* "Who did you think it was?"

"Never mind. My day was fine. I was actually just getting ready to go to happy hour with a few coworkers, and I'm trying to finish freshening up. Did you need something?" The way she spoke sounded as if he was bothering her with his call.

"Well, honestly. I was thinking maybe you'd like to come over tonight. I haven't seen you in a couple weeks. I understand that your work keeps you busy and—"

She cut him off. "Work is busy, Pres. I just want to unwind with friends sometimes."

"So how about coming over after happy hour. It is still an hour, right? I could really use some company." Pres winced at how desperate he sounded.

Victoria sighed loudly into the receiver. "Sure, Pres, I'll come over, but I can't guarantee that I can stay the entire night, okay?"

Pres felt like complete shit. He had a girlfriend but constantly felt lonely. He was starved for affection, for real feelings, for compassion…for love.

"Okay. Yeah…uhhh, I understand, Vikki. Have fun, and I'll see you later, around…?"

He let his sentence trail off, hoping she'd fill in the time for him. She never responded.

"Do you know what time you're coming? I can make you a really nice dinner. I know how much you love my lemon-butter langoustine lobster over linguine." He smiled, remembering how she'd moaned at the succulent flavors of his popular dish.

She let out an exaggerated huff before finally responding, "I don't know, about ten, I guess."

Pres's head snapped back. He felt the hands on his watch. *It's four thirty. What the hell kind of happy hour lasts until ten? Well, I guess it's one for dinner again.*

"Okay, now bye. You're gonna make me late," she said angrily.

"Hey, wait," he rushed to say before she could hang up, and then lowered his voice seductively. "Tell me what you have on right now."

His voice went deep while he simultaneously loosened his now too-tight slacks. He palmed his growing erection and moaned shamelessly.

"Do you have on the lacy panties I like, baby?" Pres asked, figuring maybe he could coax her into a little phone play to assist him with some much-needed release. All he needed was for her to say a couple dirty words and he'd blow like a geyser.

"Pres, grow up," she sneered before disconnecting the call.

*What the fuck?*

Pres felt like a damn idiot, and what was even worse was he still wanted to ask her to cancel her plans and come to him instead...but he knew that wouldn't happen. Most of the lights in his condo were on. He always flicked on a few when he came in, but he was in the dark and now on his third glass of Merlot.

Pres picked the cordless back up and called the only person he knew who might be happy to hear from him.

"Hello?" the deep voice answered. "Is this who I think it is? No, It can't be the gorgeous Prescott Vaughan that stole my heart in college and then hightailed it out of my life with a class-C beauty queen."

Prescott let out an indignant chuckle. "It's been too long, Frat."

"That it has, my friend. So what's been good with you? I think the last time we talked was at Tom's bachelor party eight months ago."

"Yeah, something like that. I'm surprised you remember that night at all." Prescott laughed again, reflecting back on that crazy night.

"Oh, I remember, love. Do you?" His friend let his voice drop to that husky whisper that always made Pres's cock take special notice.

Pres was silent. He wouldn't go there with the tall, handsome blond who was his frat brother and roommate their last two years in college. He'd shown Pres things that should only be done during the hour of the wolf.

"Talk to me, man."

Pres took in a deep breath. He had no clue what to say. *Why did I call him? So he could listen to me gripe about my lack of a sex life and desperate plea for affection? Right. I called the one man that couldn't possibly relate. The one man that has no shortage of female or male company.*

"I'll be there in two days."

"No, wait. Leo. Leo."

The line disconnected.

Pres couldn't help but smile. Leo was coming.

Pres didn't have a regular rotation of visitors. To everyone on the outside looking in, it appeared that Prescott Vaughan had his shit together. He'd opened his own successful business and authored four cookbooks. Two of them he'd had translated into Braille, which won him six different awards and a shitload of recognition. He'd even made several guest appearances on a couple of highly syndicated television shows.

Everyone believed that even though his sight was taken from him, it hadn't changed him. But it had. He was not the same. He'd lost so much more than just his sight.

YOU CAN SEE ME

# Chapter Six

**P**res didn't want to think about being lonely anymore. Last night he'd eaten his langoustine lobster alone when his girlfriend never showed up after happy hour. He'd called her a couple times, but it went straight to voice mail.

The next morning he'd done his usual Friday morning workout with his personal trainer and worked on some reviews since he didn't go into the office. In the afternoon, he did meaningless organization in his kitchen pantry and marinated some pork tenderloin for dinner.

Cooking always made him feel better. He only wished he had someone besides himself to enjoy it too. He'd even gone as far as giving his neighbors Jeff and Cindy a couple dishes, just to hear a few compliments. How pathetic.

While he waited a few minutes to cook his meat, he sat at the kitchen island and listened to an audiobook his dad had given him. Josey came over and whined at him, laying his heavy head on his knee.

"Sorry, boy. You need to go out, huh?" Pres got up and moved quickly and effortlessly to his bedroom to change into something a little more comfortable. Josey whined some more. "Okay, okay. I'm coming, Josey."

Pres slid into his Jordan flip-flops and grabbed a plastic doggie-poop bag and the leash from out of his hall closet. He took his keys off the hook, grabbed his long cane, set the alarm, and left his condo. He didn't need to put Josey's harness on. They'd walked this path for over three years now, and he knew it well.

As Pres waited for the elevator, he felt a presence next to him. It was a male presence because the scent was spicy with a sweet undertone. Just when Pres prepared to speak, his visitor spoke to him first.

"Hello," he said in a deep, sultry voice.

"Good evening," Pres responded.

"Going for a little stroll, huh? He's a beautiful dog. May I pet him?" asked the good-smelling stranger. His accent was slightly northern but not overly pronounced. Listening to him speak made Pres think about what the man's mouth might look like. If a person had a strong voice, he immediately pictured a warm, inviting smile covered by full lips.

"Yes, go right ahead. He's very spoiled. Any attention he can get, he's more than willing to take." Pres lifted Josey's leash, making him rise up off his belly.

"Awww. So handsome. You're a good boy, aren't you? Yes, I can tell you're a good boy," the stranger crooned to his dog.

Pres could hear the man ruffling Josey's scruff underneath his collar as he scratched him.

"So do you live on this floor?" Pres figured he'd spark a little conversation since the elevator was taking forever.

"Yep. Actually, just a few doors down from you," he replied happily.

"You know where I live? Well, now I have to kill ya," Pres joked, hoping his neighbor had a sense of humor, which he did because he heard him let out a genuinely deep laugh.

With a laugh like that, he definitely has a nice smile.

"Funny guy, huh? My name is Rickson Edwards, but everyone calls me Ric. I'm sorry I haven't introduced myself sooner, but I'm fairly new to the building, and every time I see you, you're either just getting on or off of the elevator."

He felt Ric take his hand that wasn't holding Josey's leash and slide his into it during his introduction. Damn, he has a strong handshake.

Pres returned the firm grip. "I'm Prescott Vaughan. It's a pleasure to meet you, Mr. Edwards."

"How respectful of you, but there is no Mr. Edwards, just Ric…Mr. Vaughan."

Pres mocked him right back. "How respectful of you, but Mr. Vaughan lives in Richmond with my mother, just Prescott, or Pres, if you like."

"I do like…I mean the name. I like your name," Ric stammered.

Pres smiled as he imagined a slight blush creeping up on the man's face.

At its arrival, they both stepped into the elevator, leaving the introduction awkwardness in the hallway. Neither said another word. There was only the humming of the elevator gears as it descended its way to the lobby.

Pres was overly aware of Ric's gaze on him, and it made him smile.

"Why are you smiling?" his neighbor asked.

"Why are you staring at me?" Pres retorted.

"Because you're—" He stopped quickly.

"Because I'm what?" Pres questioned, wondering why Ric didn't finish his sentence.

"Nothing. Didn't mean to stare, and I'm not even going to ask how you knew that I was, either." He laughed.

"It's within my power," Pres joked back.

Pres found himself trying to imagine what Ric's face looked like. If the appearance matched the voice and humor, then he probably had light brown hair and light green or hazel eyes. His cheekbones could probably make a woman envious, and he didn't breathe heavily, so Pres assumed he didn't have any weight issues. His voice came from slightly above Pres when he spoke, so the man was taller than him, making Ric probably six foot two or three. Being closed in the small compartment had Pres's sensitive nose filled with Ric's unique scent. It had him feeling dizzy and a little disoriented. That spicy, sweet combination was like nothing he'd ever smelled before. He liked it…a lot.

That thought did not freak out Pres at all, and liking the man's smell was an interesting feeling for him. He wasn't squeamish that a man had given him such a sensual reaction. If he was going to be totally honest with himself, everything he did when he was in his fraternity didn't scream hetero from the word go, but that was over twelve years ago. Pres had not met a man he was attracted to since…until now.

The elevator doors opened, and Pres extended his hand, telling Ric to go ahead and exit first.

"Thank you, Pres."

"You're welcome. It was nice meeting you, Ric. Have a good evening."

"Likewise," Ric said.

Pres walked through the lobby having a nagging urge to turn around and look back. But that was fucking pointless…right?

# Chapter Seven

**C**hef Prescott Vaughan. *Holy hell, the guy was fucking stunning.* The pictures of him in the food magazines did not do him justice. Ric didn't think he'd ever met anyone that beautiful in his life. The man looked casually comfortable in his worn blue jeans and light blue North Carolina Tar Heels T-shirt. His Jordan flip-flops showed his manicured feet. Ric found himself enticingly wondering how groomed the man was everywhere.

He'd seen Pres leaving and entering his stylish black town car on more than one occasion. He didn't know if the man had a girlfriend or not, but he knew he wasn't married because he lacked a band on his finger. Ric would be sitting in the bar off the lobby and notice him come into the building solo, oftentimes looking slightly melancholy, and he wished he could put a smile on that beautiful face.

It didn't matter to him that Pres was blind. Hell, he'd dated a deaf guy for almost eight months during his residency until the asshole cheated on him. It really caught Ric off guard, too. He didn't know why he thought a deaf person wouldn't be unfaithful. The more that he thought about that, the more stupid he felt.

*There is no way that Prescott is gay anyway.* Ric put his duffel bag over his right shoulder and started his two-mile walk to the hospital, putting Mr. Vaughan to the back of his mind.

"Dr. Edwards, the patient in exam room three is ready for discharge, so can I get your signature on the release forms and his scripts, please?"

"Sure, Maggie." Ric pulled his pen from his white lab coat and scribbled an illegible signature on the forms, then wrote the patient's prescriptions for pain medicine and an anti-inflammatory. He watched the petite nurse saunter off, then turn and look over her shoulder seductively. Ric turned quickly toward the doctors' lounge, avoiding more eye contact. He hated when the nurses flirted with him, which was all the damn time.

No one at this hospital knew he was gay. He'd transferred to Chesapeake General Hospital after a nasty allegation was made that he'd exhibited inappropriate behavior with a male nurse. As soon as Ric had come out at his other job—after getting tired of turning down advances from the female nurses, doctors, and even paramedics—his character was immediately attacked. A couple of vindictive nurses had gone to human resources saying they saw Ric touching himself while watching a male nurse perform his duties—which was complete bullshit.

Ric had thought the staff at Beach Leigh Memorial were his friends. He'd been there for over six years after he'd graduated and done his internship and residency. Ric's primary focus for the last ten years had been school and becoming a doctor. He'd had a few lovers, but nothing he'd call a serious relationship. The few friends he'd had in undergrad school were no longer around, having moved on with their careers. During his last year of med school, he didn't have time to hang out and meet people, so then he had no friends, or family, for that matter. His parents died in a car accident a couple years ago, and his one and only sibling didn't want anything to do with his older, faggot brother. So the hospital staff had become his friends and family...or so he thought. He was invited to parties and family functions all the time, but when he told them of his sexual preference, he was outcast. Only a select few still spoke to him.

Now he was in a new city and at a new hospital starting all over again. One thing was for sure. He'd have no choice but to put up with the women's advances, because he wasn't coming out again.

Ric sat in the doctors' lounge reading this month's *Journal of Modern Medicine* waiting on his shift to end. He saw Nurse Sheila come into the lounge and pour herself a cup of coffee. He tried to appear overly engrossed in the magazine, hoping to discourage her from wanting to interrupt him. *No such luck.*

"Dr. Edwards, a few of us are going to a new bar that just opened next Friday after second shift gets off. Think you'd want to go?" She looked at him expectantly.

*Here we go.*

"I'm sorry, Sheila, but I'm already involved with someone," he lied. Ric tried not to look at her with annoyance at being asked out, when he heard her crack up with laughter.

"Ummm, conceited much, Dr. E?" She gave him a teasing look. "I'm glad you're involved with someone. So am I. About fifteen of us are going to this new bar next week, and anyone who wants to come is invited. My boyfriend says that he wants to go, but he doesn't want to be the only man there. So I'm asking a few doctors to come along. Also, some of the staff from the second floor are coming too…should be fun." She grinned from ear to ear. Probably because Ric's face was burning hot from embarrassment.

He didn't have plans for next weekend, of course. He was going to work out in his building's gym and catch up on his DVR recordings. *Fun times.* Maybe he'd see Prescott in the workout room with his personal trainer again.

"Sorry, Sheila. I guess that was pretty presumptuous of me. What time are you guys going?" Ric tried to recover.

"It's cool, Dr. E. I understand how you could've thought I was putting the moves on you. Lord knows a lot of the women around here talk about wanting you." She smirked. "But trust me when I say I am happy with my boyfriend." She looked at her watch. "Well, my break is over. We'll be there about nine o'clock next Friday night. Hope to see you there. Oh yeah, and bring your girlfriend. I'd love to meet her," she said and bounced out of the lounge.

*Good luck with meeting someone that doesn't exist.*

Ric changed out of his lab coat and scrubs and put on black slacks and a collared shirt. He rolled the sleeves up and unfastened the top two buttons, not wanting to appear too dressy.

On his way down the hall to the parking lot, he saw that several nurses were in the nurses' station having a little powwow with Sheila. He silently prayed that she wasn't telling them about his embarrassing assumption.

"Good night, ladies," he said in his deep and calm voice.

"Good night, Doctor," they said almost in unison, some of them flashing him a hint of lust in their eyes.

He just smiled and waved as the emergency room doors opened to the damp night air. It was Virginia Beach in May, and the weather was unseasonably warm and—you know what, forget that. It was fucking hot. It was so humid and sticky that it made him want to jump in the nearest pool and cool his sweaty skin. Ric preferred the fall over any season—cool, brisk breezes, cashmere sweaters, soft butter-leather jackets, and sweat suits.

On his way home, Ric grabbed a bottle of Merlot at the grocery store around the corner from his building in preparation for a long weekend of solitude. *Maybe I should go out next week. This staff could be different. I just won't be feeling up any guys on the dance floor...yet.*

# Chapter Eight

It was Sunday afternoon. Pres took a cab to his parents' house to visit with them for a few hours. He and his mom made grilled salmon and pasta for lunch. Pres always loved cooking with her. She made cooking fun and exciting. She played games with his sense of taste, always challenging his unique ability.

He told her about the new restaurant on the harbor that he'd critiqued, how great the food was, and offered to take her and his father there whenever they had some free time. He hoped his mother didn't pick up on how desperate and lonely he was…again.

He played a couple games of chess with his father before leaving. Although his father didn't go to the vision-impaired school with him like his mother did after the accident, his father found his own way to bond with him. He showed him how blind people play chess. Before the accident, it was their favorite thing to do, a battle of wits between him and his old man. It hurt him very much when he thought they'd never have that time again. But his father really shocked him. It was difficult to grasp at first as he listened to his dad call out his movements, but after lots of practice, he was able to really compete with his dad again.

The cab driver announced they were in front of his building. He opened his wallet and reached for the bills with the right corner folded down—those were his hundred-dollar bills. He grabbed three of them and told the driver to keep the change. Richmond was a three-hour drive.

He slowly walked through the lobby and heard the piano player in the lounge. It didn't sound as if there were too many people in there, so he figured a drink was a good idea. Besides, there wasn't anyone waiting for him upstairs.

He barely used his cane as he made his way across the carpeted floor to the entrance of the lounge.

"Will you be dining in tonight, Mr. Prescott?"

"No, thank you, Jules. Just a drink at the bar." Pres didn't know what the young lady looked like, but her German accent was unmistakable. She didn't work here before his accident, but he'd come to know her a little over the last two years. She was always courteous and polite, but not annoyingly helpful. She didn't do stupid shit like try to help him sit on the barstool like the other hostess had. Why would she think Pres didn't know how to fuckin' sit down? *Whew. Some people.*

He'd been at the bar for over an hour and was on his third round when he caught a very familiar spicy scent. The scent just lingered around him for about thirty seconds, never fading or getting stronger.

"Well, are you going to sit down, Ric, or just stand there staring at me?" Pres said matter-of-factly.

Pres heard a deep chuckle come from the man before a broad shoulder brushed against him as Ric took the stool next to his. "How the hell did you know it was me?"

"Don't think this is strange…but your scent gave you away. My nose is a little more sensitive than others'. I remembered your cologne." Pres smiled, hoping that Ric was smiling too and not thinking he was creepy.

"I don't think that's strange at all. But let me ask you this. Do you remember most people's scent?" Ric asked, his voice dropping a couple octaves.

Pres smiled a little wider. "No, not most people. Why?" he asked, intrigued.

"Well then, I'm flattered that you remembered mine. It's good to see you again, Pres," Ric said in his deep, manly voice.

Pres felt a light tap from Ric on his right hand so he lifted his and gripped the tall man's hand for a friendly shake.

"Nice to talk to you again, Ric. Can't exactly say it's good to see you, now can I?" Pres laughed, and surprisingly, so did Ric. Pres was immediately relieved that the man could laugh with him about his disability. He picked up his drink and drained the rest of the glass.

His shades were still on even though he was inside. He tried not to do that too often, but after having three drinks and a beer, it was probably safe to assume his eyes looked like shit. His mom always said his eyes were bluer than the Mississippi, but they looked as red as the devil's when he got drunk.

"What are you drinking, Pres?" Ric asked him.

"Whiskey sour," Pres replied.

"Sounds good."

Pres heard Ric ask the bartender to make them another round. "Thank you for the drink. I'll get the next one," Pres said.

"I'm not going to refuse that."

He heard Ric shift on his seat and felt their knees come into contact. Pres made sure he didn't jerk his leg away.

"So it looks like you're trying to wind down from a difficult week," Ric said.

Pres smirked at Ric's weak attempt at small talk. "I guess you could say that. More so tiresome than difficult."

"Tiresome, huh? Not sleeping well, Prescott?" Ric asked, his voice now lower…softer.

"Guess you could say that," Pres replied as he picked up his fresh drink now back in front of him.

"Sorry to hear that," Ric replied cooly, his knee still touching his.

"Are you now?"

"No. But it's the nice thing to say, right?" Ric chuckled.

Pres laughed, too. "Say what you mean, Ric. I prefer the direct approach." He smiled as he felt Ric shift a little more, their knees still touching, and then Ric was leaning closer. Pres found himself holding his breath.

"All right then. You not sleeping well means that there's no one in your bed making sure that you do. Which suits me just fine. How's that for direct?" Ric asked, dangerously close to Pres's cheek.

Pres let the air whoosh out of his mouth at Ric's statement. *What am I getting myself into here?* He found himself smiling and replied, "Better."

After a couple more rounds, Ric suggested they get more comfortable at one of the low tabletops in the far corner on the other side of the bar. It wasn't complete seclusion, but it was just private enough that they didn't worry about others eavesdropping. Pres lost himself in an easy give-and-take banter with Ric. The man was witty and funny...and they flirted the entire time. Pres was extremely relaxed several drinks later and immensely enjoying Ric's company as he tried to explain to him why instant mashed potatoes from a box were not the same as homemade.

"It's faster and easier, and tastes just as good. I've gotten rave reviews on a few of my dishes, too, Chef Vaughan, and don't get me started on how my Hungry-Man meals never have ice chunks in the middle...all evenly warmed," Ric boasted.

Pres had a hard time containing his laughter. Ric was like a breath of fresh air. Pres had been so bummed after leaving his parents' house, and now he was sitting here with this awesome guy, and maybe even a new friend, wiping the tears from his eyes as he cracked up with each new joke Ric told.

"Yeah, those dishes sound one of a kind, Ric," Pres responded sarcastically.

"Thank you very much. Now I can say that the most popular food critic on the East Coast endorses my easy mashed potatoes."

Pres paused with his drink halfway to his mouth and asked, "Wait. How did you know I was a food critic?"

"I have my ways," Ric responded slyly.

Pres felt his face flush with heat. Ric's voice had dropped two octaves lower. His scent was right up under his nose, and Pres had enough alcohol in him that his cock was no longer under his command. Last thing he wanted was to stand to leave and have a large bulge with a wet spot for all to see.

Pres stumbled on his wording. "It—It's not exactly top secret. I just didn't know you knew who I was."

"Yeah, I know who you are, handsome," Ric whispered against the shell of Pres's ear.

*Oh fuck.* Pres didn't move, and neither did Ric. *What am I doing? I have a girlfriend.*

"Um, I—I should get going now. I—I have an early morning tomorrow," Pres stammered.

"Didn't mean to scare you off." Ric pulled back.

"No, it's not that at all. I'm not scared," Pres said a little too loudly and chastised himself for sounding like a first-date virgin.

"You're calling it a night at seven thirty?"

Pres's mouth kinda hung open at the realization of the early time. *Shit, no one goes to bed at fucking seven thirty.* "I just got some work to finish up, and Josey needs to go out now."

"Sure, I understand. Well, it was nice talking to you."

Pres could hear Ric sliding his chair back, the disappointment clearly evident in his now monotone. He didn't want Ric to leave with bad thoughts. He knew he wanted Ric as a friend and maybe even…

"Have a good evening, Pres. Hope you get all that work done," Ric said before Pres heard him push his chair in.

Pres stood abruptly. "Wait! Ric, hold on. I was wondering if you'd like to come by my place this week and let me prove to you that homemade is better than instant." Pres smiled.

"I'll let you know. I actually keep a pretty busy schedule myself. To be honest, I rarely have time to even sit and eat a meal…but thanks for the offer. Good night."

Before Pres could say another word, Ric's footsteps were loud as he walked away. *Goddamn it.* Pres yanked his wallet out of his back pocket and made his way to the front side of the bar to pay the tab.

"It's already taken care of, Mr. Vaughn," he heard the bartender say after he tried to hand the man his credit card.

*Fuck.* He'd blown Ric off for no fucking reason, and the man had paid both their tabs. *Shit.*

# Chapter Nine

Pres made his way out of the lounge, trying desperately not to stumble or wobble. It was a little unnerving to see a blind man drunk and falling all over the place. Pres made his way to his apartment with very little trouble, and as soon as he opened the door, Josey was there wagging his tail.

"All right, boy. Come on." Pres grabbed the leash off the hook and turned around, heading back to the elevators. He caught a faint whiff of Ric's cologne that still lingered in the hallway. Pres's brow creased with frustration.

*Ric probably wouldn't want to escort a blind man around town anyway. Forget it. I'll probably never have a real friend again.*

The thought pained him more than he wanted to admit. The fact of the matter was he was lonely and miserable eighty percent of the time. His girlfriend barely came to see him…let alone made love to him. *Maybe she'll come by tonight…right.*

Thirty minutes later, Pres returned from his walk with Josey and let himself into his condo. Josey let out a low, menacing growl, and Pres's footsteps halted in the foyer at the sound of his shower running.

*What the fuck?*

Pres smelled a subtle cologne fragrance lingering in the entrance to his home. He began to move toward his bedroom when Josey began whimpering and pulling on his pants legs. He bent down and gave him a reassuring rub.

"Calm down, boy. I don't think a criminal is going to wash up first before he hurts me."

Pres unhooked Josey's collar and continued into his bedroom. He pushed open his bathroom door and was bombarded with steam and the scent of his favorite body wash.

"You're a detective. You should know breaking and entering is a felony." Pres leaned against the wall and pulled a fluffy towel off the rack. He heard the shower door slide open.

"You should have a better lock on that door, sexy. Anyone can get in here." Leo's husky voice penetrated right through Pres's intoxication.

Pres sucked his teeth, but couldn't stop the smile from forming on his mouth. "What are you doing here, Leo?"

"I told you I was coming, remember? Have I ever not done something I said I was going to do?" he asked while taking the towel from him.

"No, I guess not." Pres huffed tiredly as he began to walk out the bathroom. He felt Leo reach out and grip his arm.

"Hey," he whispered.

"Hey," Pres whispered back. He let his frat brother and longtime friend pull him into his wet, solid chest. Pres held on to the rock-hard body. He couldn't help but remember back to how Leo looked when he lay underneath him so many nights in their senior year. Pres would stare at the tribal tattoo on Leo's left pec before tonguing and tugging on his nipple piercings, exactly how Leo instructed. Back then Pres still didn't consider himself gay. "Just doing typical college experimenting," he'd tell himself.

Pres let Leo intertwine their hands and pull him into his bedroom.

"Get comfortable. I'm going to grab us a couple beers."

Pres began to do just that. He swapped out his shirt and slacks for a pair of soft, threadbare sweatpants and no shirt. He pulled back the heavy comforter and flopped down tiredly on his large bed. He grabbed the remote and turned on the television. The channel was still tuned to CNN, and he heard a commentator speaking on a recent scandal uncovered in a politician's campaign. Pres immediately tuned it out.

"Are you hungry, Leo? I could whip you up something quick if you want?"

"Nah, dude, I'm good, but if you twist my arm, I'll let you make me eggs Benedict in the morning. I can only stay for tonight. We're on a big case, and if I don't show up by tomorrow evening, my partner will never let me hear the end of it. I barely got out of there today," Leo voiced from the kitchen.

Pres felt Leo drop his lithe frame onto the other side of the bed. "You drove ten hours to stay for one night?" he asked his friend.

"No. I caught a federal prisoner transport flight into Williamsburg, and then I drove one hour to see you. But I would've driven ten hours for even a half of a night, because you needed me to, whether you're going to admit it or not." Leo situated himself more comfortably on the bed. "What's going on, Pres? I call you. I e-mail you. If you do finally respond, it's always a few sentences and a bunch of shit about how busy you are."

Pres's voice was low as he tried to keep his emotions in check. "Yeah, I know, Leo. I'm sorry. I just don't want to be a burden on anyone." He took a large gulp of his beer and leaned back against the leather-padded headboard.

"Have I ever given you the impression that you're a burden…fuckin ever, Pres? Don't give me that bullshit. I don't know what type of people you've been around lately—obviously the wrong kind if that's the feeling you get from them. But don't you put me in there with those assholes. You have been and will always be a very important part of me, Pres, and you know that. So, why the cold shoulder on me, man?"

Pres knew he had only a few real friends left in this world, and one had flown over six hundred miles to ask him what's wrong. *I better take advantage.*

Over the next three hours, Pres purged his soul. He told his friend everything. He told him about his so-called girlfriend and how he knew she was basically using him. He told of the many solo dinners and lonely nights. He explained that his worst fear was he'd never have a normal relationship again and would most likely grow old alone, all of this until his mind could no longer stand his dismal existence. By the end of his confession, Pres couldn't hold in the tear that fell down his cheek.

"It's so fucking dark in here, Leonidis." Pres harshly tapped the side of his temple with his beer bottle. "It's killin' me, man."

Leo took Pres's beer from him and laid it on the nightstand before pulling him into a strong hug. "Fuck, Pres."

There was nothing more Leo could say. He couldn't change Pres's situation, and the man wasn't a therapist. Pres let Leo do the only thing he could do… He let Leo hold him until he fell asleep.

According to the raised hands on his watch, Pres woke a little after five in the morning. Leo still had his strong, muscular arms around him, and Pres took a deep inhale and let his friend's delicious scent invade his sensitive senses. He felt Leo stir and let out a sexy moan as he turned further into him and tucked his face into the crook of his neck. Pres groaned. His cock was hard, locked, and loaded. *What girlfriend?*

Pres's hips began to move instinctually, almost on their own. He maneuvered himself completely on top of Leo, all the while remembering exactly what his friend looked like and how much he used to like it when Pres would grind hard on top of him. Leo's body was taut and firm with muscles, but not overly huge. He had blond hair that he used to keep in a buzz cut, but Pres could feel the length on it now as he rubbed the soft curls against his cheek. Vibrant green eyes used to stare up at him, pleading for Pres to do more. They would lick, rut, and rub against each other like wild animals until they both got off. Pres dipped his head and aimed his mouth for Leo's barbell in his nipple. He could feel that Leo was fully awake now...but he wasn't responding.

Pres stilled his thrusting. He sucked in a sharp breath and rolled off of a stiff, unresponsive Leo. *Oh my God.*

"Pres, I'm sorry."

Pres sat up and swung his legs over the side of the bed. He was humiliated. He dropped his head and let his forehead rest in his palm. "It's cool. I'm sure you didn't come here for that. My bad."

"I'm in a relationship now, Pres, have been for about six months. I've wanted to tell you, but—"

"I never fucking answer the phone. I know." Pres cut Leo off before he could say it.

"Pres, don't think—"

Pres stopped Leo again. "I'm not upset." He couldn't see Leo's face, but he'd come to recognize the tone of pity in a person's voice—matter of fact, he'd heard it so much, he was a damn master at honing in on it.

Pres had always told Leo that he wasn't gay. That's why every time he'd asked Pres for something deeper when they were in college, Pres refused him. Now here he was years later practically begging Leo for something deeper...how ironic.

After whining and crying on Leo's shoulder last night, he couldn't take hearing that sorrowful tone right now. It might be best to get Leo fed and out of his damn condo before he had a mental breakdown.

"I'm going to get cleaned up and make you some breakfast." Pres jumped up and damn near ran into the bathroom. He heard his friend whisper, "Damn it," right before he closed the bathroom door.

Pres was dressed in his business suit although his critique wasn't until noon. He set the plate of eggs Benedict and country fried potatoes in front of his friend while he sipped on his glass of juice at the breakfast bar.

He had the worst fucking headache, but he made sure to keep his expression neutral while hiding his watery eyes behind his dark shades. The tension in the room was palpable. They were both so damn quiet, you could hear a pin drop.

"I didn't mean to make shit worse, Pres. I just wanted to talk to you, dude. I've missed you."

"I know. It's cool, Leo."

"Stop saying it's fucking cool, Pres, when it's not!" he yelled.

Pres jumped at the tone. He gritted his teeth. "I don't know what the hell you want me to say, Leonidis! You want me to say how desperate I am, that I'm so fucking lonely I'd try to fuck my best friend, even though I'm not gay!" Pres threw up air quotes when he said the word "gay."

"All right, yeah…if that's the truth. You can still talk to me. I'm still your brother."

Pres jerked his head back and grimaced at the term. They would always be frats, he knew that, but the term "brother" almost made him sick. *I just tried to fuck my goddamn brother.*

Pres needed some air, and he needed it fast. "I appreciate you coming, Leo, but I got to go, or I'm going to be late. Finish your breakfast, and don't worry about locking up when you leave."

"Wait, I thought you said your critique was at noon," Leo argued, his frustration evident.

Pres was eagerly grabbing his keys, wallet, and cell off the breakfast bar. "Yeah, uhh, I know, but I forgot I got some important errands to get done before then." He knew Leo could tell he was lying. The man was a highly skilled Atlanta detective. It was what he did for a living. "I'll call you later."

Pres moved fast through his condo before Leo could say anything else. He almost had the door closed when he heard what had to be Leo's breakfast and entire damn place setting crashing to the floor. "Pres, goddamn you!"

He closed the door and hightailed it down the hall, bypassing the elevators and taking the stairs. His heart was heavy with the realization that it would probably be the last time he talked to Leo.

## YOU CAN SEE ME

# Chapter Ten

**P**res had just finished with his evening chores of walking Josey, sanitizing his already spotless kitchen, and listening to some notes from one of his reviews. He was sipping a glass of Merlot when he picked up his cordless phone and dialed his girlfriend.

"Hello."

"Hi, Vikki, how are you, babe?" Pres put one hand behind his head as he reclined in his favorite chair.

"Oh, hiya, Pres. I'm fine. I was actually getting ready to call you," she replied casually.

"Really?" Pres replied, feeling a little silly at how happy that made him.

"Yeah, my credit card bill came today, and they said because I missed the last two months' payments that they were going to start collection activity soon. I don't know what I'm going to do," she huffed.

"It's all right, honey. I'll make your last two months that you missed," Pres replied.

"Thanks, Pres. I appreciate that. Well, I gotta go. I'll talk to you later."

"Babe, wait!" Pres yelled. "I was wondering, if you weren't busy tonight, then maybe you'd like to come over."

"And do what, Pres?" Her mood immediately switched to irritated.

"I don't know…maybe watch a movie or—"

"You can't watch movies." She cut him off, stating the obvious.

"I actually still like listening to movies, Vikki...but whatever. We don't have to do that if you don't want to. We can listen to some music and talk instead. What do you say? I really miss you."

Pres was getting tired of begging her all the time to be with him, especially after he paid one of her many bills. Leo had told him to dump the high-priced hooker, but that was real easy for him to say. Leo had a warm body in his bed every night. He pushed down the thoughts of him and Leo. He'd done enough pining over that horrible fiasco for the last few days and refused to let his mind wander there again.

"I'll call you back later, Pres. I got to go. I have another call coming through."

Pres heard the definitive click of the line disconnecting before he could say another word. He let the cordless drop and sat there in silence, wishing he had some company. Automatically, his thoughts went to Ric and the wonderful time they'd had in the lounge last week...and how it'd ended.

He replayed Ric's words. *"I don't really have the time to eat a real dinner anyway."*

Pres jerked upright. *Hmmm. Maybe you don't have time to cook you a real dinner...but I sure as hell do.* He jumped up from his couch with a newfound determination.

Pres first turned on his favorite classic rock station and swayed his hips to the music as he grooved his way to his gourmet kitchen. *Hmmm. What would Ric like to eat tonight? He mentioned mac 'n' cheese and mashed potatoes. You're a startchy kind of guy, huh, Ric?* Pres moved around in his pantry feeling the Braille labels on his boxes of pasta. *Let's see...fusilli, ziti, cavatappi, linguine.* Pres found the one he wanted. *Bingo, ditalini. I'm thinking, thinking...* Pres tapped his chin with his finger. It came to him quickly.

"Mini Swedish meatballs over parmesan ditalini pasta," Pres whispered to himself as if he was in awe of his conclusion.

Feeling the hands on his wrist watch, he figured he'd have this all done in two hours...*and special dinner delivery at seven.*

Two and a half hours later, Pres was popping the last Tupperware lid over the pasta and tucking it into the insulated thermal food bag. He cut a thick piece of fresh parmesan from his block and sealed it in another container. *Oh, don't forget the grater.*

Pres immaculately cleaned his kitchen. A real chef never left his kitchen dirty. Since he'd shaven and washed up while the meatballs baked, he was all set to go. He positioned the bag on his shoulder, grabbed his cell, and locked up his condo. He casually dragged his fingers down the wall of the wide hallway to guide him to the fourth door on his right. He tapped lightly and waited. After a few seconds, he tapped again a little louder and waited. *Oh shit.* For some reason, it never dawned on Pres that Ric might not be home. He never even asked the man what he did for a living.

"Goddamn it," he whispered as he turned to go back to his place.

"Looking for me?" Pres heard the baritone voice ask from what sounded like almost at the end of the hall.

Pres stopped midstride and couldn't stop the flush that rose up in his cheeks at the possibility that Ric probably heard him curse his disappointment at him not being home. He cleared his throat. "Yeah, actually, I am. I had all these leftovers from last night's dinner and thought you'd like to have it."

"Leftovers, really?" Ric's heavy steps came closer, and Pres was again treated to the man's delicious spicy scent that lingered underneath...*perspiration?*

"Yep, would hate for it to go to waste," Pres responded coolly like it was no big deal.

"I see. That's awfully generous of you." Ric was speaking in a suspiciously husky whisper, and it felt like he was right over top of him.

Pres didn't respond for a few long seconds. "Are you busy? I can just leave this with you. I didn't mean—"

Ric interrupted him. "You're fine. Come on in. I just came from the gym. Do you mind if I freshen up some first?"

Pres could hear Ric jingling his key in the lock. "No, I don't mind at all. If you direct me to the kitchen and get me a plate, I'll whip it up for you." He hoped Ric didn't tell him to just leave it on the counter. Pres lived for feedback on his dishes.

Pres barely contained his startled reaction when he felt Ric place a firm grip on his elbow and lead him into his home. He silently wished he could see Ric's kitchen. It didn't feel like the man had very many amenities, as Pres was able to lay everything out on the very bare countertop. He was hyperaware of Ric's musky male scent lingering close by.

"That's an awful lot of food to be leftovers. Did you have a party or something?" Ric asked while standing directly behind him.

His hot breath ghosted over Pres's neck as he tried desperately to concentrate on not making a mess while plating Ric's pasta. His hands shook nervously when he pulled out the small block of parmesan and tried to get it inside the grater. *Fuck.* Pres knew this food looked freshly prepared and not from a damn leftover meal. *Why did I tell that stupid lie? Just tell him you want to be friends.*

**R**ic watched Pres make him a large plate of some type of small pasta rings with meatballs and cheese. Damn, it looked fucking delicious. He'd been working out for the past three hours…more like working off long–pent-up sexual frustration and was shocked to see the sexy chef standing at his front door, looking more than a little pissed that he wasn't home. After Pres blew him off in the lounge last week when Ric turned the flirting up a notch, Ric wasn't sure if he'd get to talk to him again.

But now the man had cooked a meal especially for him. Ric didn't believe that leftover shit for one second, and he wasn't letting Pres off the hook either. Ric was skating toward thirty-five years. He was too damn old to play games. He had told himself it was time to settle down…five years ago, but opportunity had not presented itself. Pres was a pretty awesome guy from what he could see, and they definitely had some awesome instant chemistry. Ric wanted to explore that, but he had to see where Pres's head was at first.

Ric needed to go shower, but he wanted to get the truth out of Pres first. "Pres." Ric grabbed on to Pres's shaking hand that was trying unsuccessfully to grate some cheese over top of his dish. Pres didn't answer. He turned Pres toward him so he could stare into the man's gorgeous face. "Did you make me dinner, sweetheart?" He heard and felt the hard breath the beautiful man sucked in, obviously at Ric's choice of endearment, but he wouldn't hide the fact that he was very much attracted to this man…and not in a buddy-buddy sort of way. "Prescott, I asked you a question."

Pres didn't try to tear himself from Ric's hold. "Yeah, uhh, I guess I did. You said you didn't get much time to cook, so, you know…"

"No, I don't know." Ric persisted. He wanted to know what Pres thought.

"I didn't like the idea of you not eating," Pres huffed.

"Why?"

"Why what?" Pres sighed, almost exasperated. "Why are you making this difficult? Just eat the food—that happens to be getting cold now, thank you very much."

"Oh, barking orders now, too. Tsk,tsk,tsk," Ric teased and released Pres's wrist, deciding to lighten the mood. Regardless of how things had come to an abrupt halt in the lounge last week, he knew Pres was feeling the chemistry too, and right now he didn't want to apply too much pressure too soon and risk the man leaving without Ric having made at least a couple more moves. "All right, I'll eat now, if you promise to stay and talk with me a little while after I'm done and not run away."

"I'm not gonna run aw—"

Ric gently put his hand over Pres's mouth to stop the man's protest and noticed that his eyelids shuttered at Ric's touch. *Duly noted, beautiful.* Ric brought his hand down, but crowded into Pres's space so that their chests were just barely touching. Ric dropped his voice and purred sensually in Pres's face, "I'm hungry. Feed me."

Ric ate the delectable meal and was not short on the compliments he bestowed on the renowned chef, and Pres seemed to eat it up.

"I can't remember having a meal that good. Thank you so much, Pres. You saved me from ramen noodles and strawberry Pop-Tarts." Ric laughed and rubbed his stomach as he brought two beers into the living room and dropped his large frame down beside Pres on his couch. After taking the fastest washup ever, he'd hurriedly thrown on some comfortable shorts and a T-shirt, making sure his company didn't miss the time he was gone.

Pres sat comfortably on his couch, looking more relaxed than Ric thought he would. "It was nothing, really…but you're welcome," Pres replied.

"So how has your week been?" Ric asked. He saw a variety of emotions flash across Pres's features. *Regret…no, hurt.* Ric wondered what had happened to him, but if Pres didn't volunteer, then he wouldn't push.

"Fine," Pres stated simply.

"Not sounding too convincing," Ric responded. He wanted to scoot closer, but thought to play it cool for now. He'd make his move soon enough.

"Just had a falling-out with a friend, and my girlfriend's been a little difficult lately."

*What the fuck…girlfriend? You've got to be goddamn kidding me.* Ric mentally kicked his own ass for thinking that Prescott Vaughan might be gay. Maybe Ric had seen something in the lounge or in Pres bringing him dinner that wasn't there to begin with. None of those actions had to mean that Pres was interested in him sexually. Ric had found himself really wanting to explore more with the sweet man. Now that did not appear to be possible.

"You have a girlfriend?" Ric practically spat the phrase out like it was venom.

"I guess you could say that," Pres said drily.

*Wait, I might can work with this. Doesn't exactly sound like wedding bells are about to ring.*

"Could say that or it is that?" Ric asked boldly.

"Like I said, she's becoming difficult. It might be coming to a screeching end very soon," Pres said easily before taking a deep gulp of his beer.

Ric observed Pres as he spoke about the potential breakup like it was no skin off of his back and definitely no love lost there.

"But I don't want to talk about her. Let's talk about anything else…sports, work, food—hell, the weather," Pres said hurriedly.

Ric let out a throaty chuckle and had no problem turning the conversation from the future ex-girlfriend to something that would work out more in his favor…like getting Pres a little tipsy and flirting with the man some more.

True to form, three beers and two mixed drinks later, Pres was practically leaning against Ric on his small couch while he slurred on about his business partner giving him a difficult time on his recent reviews. Ric was enjoying the various conversations and found that Pres was the type of man he'd like to have around for a while. He was fun and easy to talk to, and the fact that he smelled wonderful made Ric want to keep leaning in and subtly sniffing the man. When Pres steered the conversation back to his "rigid" girlfriend—that's how he described her—Ric wasted no time telling Pres how he'd treat him if he was his.

"She's a damn fool," Ric purred. He wasn't drunk, but he was damn sure relaxed and feeling uninhibited.

Ric watched Pres roll his head on the back of the couch to face him as if he could see him. "What makes you say that?"

"Because if you belonged to me, then sex wouldn't be something you'd have to beg for." Ric leaned into Pres's ear. "At least not that kind of begging...maybe begging me to not stop."

He had taken the step again and kicked up the flirting to see how Pres would respond. Ric was shocked to see a wistful expression on Pres's face appear and disappear just as quickly.

Pres shifted a little, and Ric realized that over the course of their conversations, he'd slouched down low, spread his legs wide, and was almost sprawled out on the small couch with his throat bared as his head rested on the back of the cushions. "You wouldn't make me beg, Ric?"

"Only when you're being bad...but I would always give in to you," Ric said. He was inwardly pumping his fist at this small victory. Pres was definitely interested. No completely straight guy would ask that type of question and listen to Ric's flirtatious dialogue if he wasn't curious. *He's bi-curious at least...I can work with that too.* Ric thought it was well worth the effort to woo Prescott Vaughan, regardless of his disability. The man was sex on a stick, smart, funny, capable, and cared whether he ate a decent meal.

"I need to be getting back." Pres sighed hard, sat up higher on the couch, and let his head drop for a few minutes while aggressively rubbing what looked like a million knots on the back of his neck. Ric brought his own hand up to take over and do it for him while effectively breaking the touch barrier. Pres didn't pull away either.

Ric used one strong hand to knead the stubborn knots on Pres's neck and heard the man let out the sexiest motherfucking moan he'd ever heard. *Oh fuck.* If Pres could see, he'd know that Ric's cock was hard as steel and his thin basketball shorts couldn't contain the rod that was straining to get out.

"That feel good, Pres?" Ric whispered.

"Fuck yeah."

"Turn around," Ric instructed hoarsely.

Pres didn't put up a fight. He turned so that his back was to Ric, and he let his chin rest on his chest, giving Ric's fingers complete access.

Ric crowded in close behind Pres, letting the man practically lean into him. Ric used both his hands and oh so slowly began to caress Pres's solid shoulders before taking the pads of his thumbs and moving them in long, fluid strokes up the back of his neck. Pres moaned again, and Ric had to stifle his own groan. He also had to make sure Pres didn't come into contact with his eager erection. Pres was at Ric's complete mercy. He could see the man's fists balled up and resting on his thighs. *God, what the hell are you going through, sweetheart?* Ric went after each and every kink in Pres's upper region until he was satisfied that Pres was more relaxed. He slowed his massage and leaned in to rest his forehead on the back of Pres's soft hair.

"Feel better?"

"Damn. Yeah, Ric. I didn't realize how much tension I had." Pres was talking, but he was completely still, maybe because of Ric's closeness. He turned his body and whispered a soft thank-you before moving to stand.

Ric stood and let Pres get a light grip on his elbow so he could lead him to the front door. "Can I walk you home?" Ric let loose a soft laugh.

Pres's million-dollar smile flashed at him. "I think I can manage."

"Okay, then." Ric didn't want this man to leave. He wanted to take him to his bedroom and see if he could relieve some tension Pres may have had in other places as well. Ric decided right then and there that this man would be his. "Thank you for dinner, Pres." He unlocked the door and slightly cracked it open.

"You're welcome. I had a good time tonight, Ric. It...It..." Pres stalled in his confession.

"It what?" Ric urged. He wanted to hear what Pres thought. He'd refuse to let him run from how Ric made him feel.

"It was nice," Pres said, his voice sounding like he was out of breath.

"Yes, it was."

Ric brought his hand up to squeeze Pres's shoulder and watched him drop his head again at his touch. Ric slowly let his grip move around to the back of Pres's neck, giving the man time to pull away if he wanted to. But Pres was patiently waiting on Ric's next move.

"Com'ere," Ric purred while he carefully brought their faces together. He bypassed Pres's twitching mouth and let his scruffy cheek rest on the gorgeous man's soft face. He gently rubbed their skin together before pressing a ghost of a kiss on Pres's neck. He heard him inhale deeply and turn into the touch. *Damn, this man is starved for affection.* Ric insisted on playing this safe, though. If Pres wanted more, he'd have to come and get it. Ric let his lips linger a second longer before saying, "Good night," his lips brushing the shell of Pres's ear when he spoke.

According to the rapid rise and fall of Pres's chest, he'd definitely lighted a fire in the man, but Ric released Pres and watched him walk slowly down the hall until he was at the door to his own condo. He'd decided Pres needed to process what he was feeling before he would move this further...and most of all, Pres needed to dump that fucking so-called girlfriend, too. One thing Ric didn't do was share.

# Chapter Eleven

It was Friday night, and Pres had come home early to get a few chores done and to take Josey for an extra-long walk in the park. The last couple of days his mind had been filled with Rickson. Goddamn, that man knew how to use his hands. Pres just wasn't sure he wanted to be labeled gay, or if he was willing to get sex from any damn body since it'd been forever since he'd been laid. It wouldn't be fair to Ric to use him, just like it wasn't fair to Leo all those years ago. Look what it had done to a friendship that had meant a lot to him.

Pres didn't know if he could really be just friends with Ric since the man was so attracted to him and wasn't afraid to show it. But, no matter how many times Pres tried to reason that starting a thing with Ric might not be a good idea, all he kept hearing in his head was the sound of Ric's gruff voice when he was turned on and the way the hot fucker smelled. *"I'd only make you beg if you were being bad...but I'd always give in to you."* Ric's sexy words echoed in Pres's mind over and over again.

Pres was sipping on a glass of Merlot and listening to an audiobook when he picked up the cordless and called his "girlfriend." *I need to fuck.*

"Hello," Vikki said in that sweet voice that immediately made Pres sit up.

"Hey, Vikki. What's going on? I haven't heard from you all week. How you been, sweetie?" Pres said quietly while rubbing his palm over his heart. Why was it that whenever he spoke to

Victoria, his chest seemed to start hurting? *Probably because you know she doesn't want you, just like your fiancée didn't.*

Pres shut those thoughts down immediately. He just needed to reconnect with Vikki again. She'd been sweet as pie when he first met her eight months ago in line at his bank. She immediately struck up a conversation about Josey as he led Pres through the line. Pres liked her forwardness and couldn't resist asking her to dinner after he was sure not to be mistaking her flirting as simple kindness. But the way she brushed her hand over his as he held Josey's leash was not easy to mistake. Pres enjoyed her company so much, and he felt alive again. Only problem was, over time, the visits to Pres's home, and their dates, became less and less regular, but the phone calls for money were endless.

"Nothing's going on, Pres. I've just been busy is all," she said in a bored voice.

"Well you sound like you could use some fun. Hey, I just had a great idea. How about you and me get together tonight? I'll make us a gourmet meal…the one that gets you real hot, baby. Remember my bourbon shrimp flambé? Then we'll pack a weekend bag and go out on my yacht. Just us and the salty ocean breeze, good food, and good loving." Pres moaned, already getting excited, because who could say no to that suggestion?

"I've already made plans to go meet some friends at this new bar on the beach tonight."

"Okaaay. Do you mind if I come too? I mean, are you able to bring your significant others?" Pres tried to keep the hope out of his voice, but it'd been a while since he and Vikki had gone somewhere together.

She let out a long, exasperated sigh before finally responding. "Fine, Pres, you can come. We're meeting there at ten."

"Vikki, can you come and pick me up? If it's on the beach, then you have to come past here, right? It's just I gave Scott the weekend off."

"Jeez, Pres. All right, fine, I'll pick you up. Just don't try to make me late." *Click.*

*What the fuck?* Vikki was really going out of her way lately to make him feel like shit. He didn't remember doing anything to make her act like such a bitch toward him. However, Pres was finally getting to go out on the town for a little while, so he didn't ponder the negative thoughts for too long.

He had only forty-five minutes to shower and get dressed. All his clothes were labeled and color coordinated. His stylist put together complete outfits for him. All he had to do was feel the raised Braille label on the garment bag, unzip it, and voila! He was dressed like a Calvin Klein model.

Pres knew he was wearing dark denim jeans and an untucked cream-and-blue striped collared shirt. He pushed up the sleeves of the light-colored Kenneth Cole blazer, just like he'd been taught when he was going for sexy casual. He put a couple dabs of his most expensive cologne on his neck and waited for his date. He was lightly sipping his fourth glass of Merlot and feeling a slight buzz when he heard a persistent tapping at the door, not with a hand but with an object, probably her key fob or cell phone.

"Coming," he called out and hurried to answer her impatient knock. *Damn. Let the whole building hear your knocking.* He opened the door with a wide smile on his face. "Hi, babe."

He heard her huff and step past him into the apartment.

"Well, can I have a hug, Victoria? Jesus, I haven't had you over in weeks."

He stood there in his entryway with his arms outstretched, feeling slightly foolish. After a few too-long seconds, she was in his arms. He hugged her tight, basking in the embrace. He turned his lips toward hers and felt her draw back before he was able to make contact.

"I can't have a kiss?" he asked, sure that his forehead was creased with a ton of frowns.

"I don't want to smear my lipstick, Pres. Besides, we're gonna be late. So come on."

"We don't have to be there right at ten on the dot, do we? I mean, it's not a surprise party or anything. Maybe we can have a little pre-cocktail cocktail right here before we go…if you know what I mean." He moaned and reached for her small waist.

"Pres, no. I don't want to get my clothes all messed up," she said as she pushed his groping hands away.

"Describe to me what you're wearing, baby." He spoke in sexy groan as he rubbed his aching cock.

"Oh, come on, Pres, Jesus. Can't you control yourself?" she practically yelled.

"Damn it, Vikki! Control myself for what? I thought we were together. You know, a couple. And is it so bad that I want to be intimate with my woman?" Pres was so frustrated he thought his head might explode…both of them.

"We are a couple. I'm just trying to unwind with a stress-free weekend after working hard all week. I didn't come here to be fussed at. Just forget it, Pres. I'll go out alone."

He felt her breeze past him, slightly knocking him in the shoulder as she went. He reached out fast and grabbed her arm.

"Babe, I'm sorry. Don't go, okay?" Pres released a shaky but frustrated breath at the obvious lack of affection he was going to get. "Look, I still want to go and meet your friends, if that's all right with you. I didn't mean to pressure you or fuss at you, okay? I just miss you so much." He gently massaged her arms and heard her let out another breath.

"Fine. Let's just go," she said.

"All right, just let me use the bathroom real quick and—"

She turned and opened his door to leave. "What! No!" she screeched. "We're already late. Dang, what are you, five years old? Use it when you get there. It's a short ride."

"Whatever," he mumbled. Pres didn't bother to reach for her hand. He grabbed his long cane off the shelf by the front door.

"Oh no. Leave that cane here. I'm not going to have you hitting me in my ankles all night with that damn thing," she scoffed. The disdain and disgust in her voice made Pres's neck jerk back so hard it cracked.

Pres stood there numbly with his mouth hanging open. *I've never fucking hit you with my cane. Damn, that shit was mean. Fuck. Am I that damn desperate? There's gotta be a woman out there that will treat me better than this…or maybe a man.*

"Pres, leave it, or else I'm leaving…alone," she threatened.

"Vikki, how the hell am I not going to run into something if I don't have it? Are you going to help me if I need it? I don't want to burden you every time I need to move around, go to the bathroom, or whatever."

"Just leave the freakin' cane, Prescott," she hissed. "If you need help, I or someone else will help you. Now come on. You're making me late…like I knew you would."

*This is a bad idea. Shit.*

Pres stepped out into the hallway minus his cane. He made it to the elevators and paused when he smelled spicy cologne again. He smiled just a little.

**R**ic had to bite his tongue when he walked by Pres's open apartment door. There was an extremely attractive blonde witch fussing at him about not taking his cane with them. Ric wanted to push her out of the way, fold Pres into his chest, and tell him it was okay and that he'd never be embarrassed by him.

When Ric walked by and caught a glimpse of the man's hurt expression, it almost crushed him. How could someone be so goddamn insensitive? Regardless that that beautiful creature was blind, he was still a person with feelings.

He didn't know where the couple was going for the evening, but it didn't look like she'd be providing him any assistance with the way she turned her back and made her way to the elevators without even a backward glance. Maybe Pres was going to break up with her and she knew it.

Ric was waiting for the elevator when he looked up and saw Pres slowly making his way to the elevators. He squeezed his eyes shut at the sight. Prescott looked stunning in his evening attire. The pin-striped shirt was untucked from his expensive-looking jeans, making him appear dressed up but casual at the same time. The blazer looked expensive, too, and so did his shoes. Everything matched and went together so perfectly. Ric found himself wondering if the mean lady had dressed him.

Although Pres was blind, he didn't move his head back and forth like Stevie Wonder or gaze off into space. If it wasn't for the obviously custom-made, sleek black-and-chrome cane, then you probably wouldn't even know he was blind. When he removed his designer shades, his beautiful blue eyes appeared focused as if he was looking right into you.

Pres walked down the hall with one hand casually in his pocket, looking like he owned the world. The man had so much finesse to be blind it was ridiculous.

Pres was only a few feet from the elevator when Mean Girl turned and gave Ric a seductive once-over. Ric immediately turned up his lip in disgust, making her suck her teeth at him and turn her head away. He heard her murmur to herself, "Now I'm stuck babysitting him all damn night."

Ric didn't wait for Pres to reach the elevators. He opened the door to the stairwell and began to walk down the twenty flights of stairs so he could calm himself down.

He didn't know why he was reacting so defensively when it came to Prescott Vaughan, but something inside of him wanted to protect the gorgeous man…and make him his.

… YOU CAN SEE ME

# Chapter Twelve

"Vikki, over here!"

Pres heard a female yelling his girlfriend's name, even over the loud music. The music wasn't blaring like in a club, but it was still loud. Pres's other senses went into overload. He smelled many scents: sweat, liquor, beer, cheap cologne, and lots of bad breath. The bass from the music made his chest vibrate. He tried to hold on to Vikki's hand as she moved them quickly through what felt like a thick crowd. He was thrust into people and stumbled a little over a chair leg, when he finally pulled on her hand gently to get her to turn around.

"What!" she yelled directly in his ear, making him cringe at the pain that caused in his head.

He placed his hands on her waist and put his lips on the shell of her ear. "Please slow down, baby. I know you don't mean to, but you're knocking me into people and making me stumble. I think I may have knocked someone's drink over back there." He kissed her ear tenderly, enjoying the smell of her sweet perfume.

"All right, fine. There's a barstool right behind you. If you're tired, just sit there and buy a drink while I find my friends," she ordered.

"Wait. I'm not tired at all. I can go with you to look for your friends. I was just saying you were kinda dragging me back there." He tried not to sound too needy, but he didn't really want to be left alone sitting on a barstool.

"It's all good. Sit tight. I'll be right back."

"Vikki...Vikki!" he called out, but got no answer. She'd left him on the barstool, and he couldn't fucking get up or leave. He didn't have his goddamn cane or Josey. He had his cell phone, but he couldn't call his driver or his assistant because he'd specifically told them they had the entire weekend off. He wasn't going to call them at midnight and say, "Stop what you're doing and come and get me from a bar." He'd have to wait for her.

"Hey, want a drink, buddy?" a male voice called from in front of him.

Pres hoped the bartender was talking to him as he nodded his head. "I'll have a Bud Light." He figured he shouldn't drink too heavily since he was still buzzing a little from the almost entire bottle of Merlot he'd consumed earlier and he didn't know if he was going to be on his own for getting home. He reached into his wallet and felt for the bills that were folded longwise, his ones. He counted out five and reached out to hand it to the bartender when his knuckles hit a glass and sent something—probably his beer—crashing to the floor.

*Fuck me.*

"What gives, dude? That was my drink, man. What the fuck are you? Blind?" An extremely pissed man was close to his left side, yelling at him for knocking over his drink.

"Actually, yeah, I am," Pres replied drily.

*Why the hell was your drink so damn close to me in the first place?*

"Oh" was the man's only response.

"It's all right. I'll buy you another one. If you could signal the bartender for me, I'll buy you whatever you were drinking." Pres tried to reason with the drunk man. His breath was foul, and as he spoke to Pres, little pieces of spittle hit him on his cheek. Pres desperately wanted to get off this fucking stool, now.

"I was drinking a bottle of Cristal," the man stated boldly.

*Bull-fucking-shit! There's no way you were drinking a two-hundred-dollar bottle of champagne.* Unfortunately, for Pres, his supernose was immediately able to detect the man's foul breath and knew exactly what the man was drinking. It was vodka, and it wasn't even premium.

"Look, man, I'll buy you a double shot of Ciroc vodka with a Corona back. How's that?" Pres said, hoping the man didn't push this ridiculous issue.

"Whatever, man." The guy accepted his drinks and moved on. *Thank God.*

*Where the hell is Vikki now?* Pres felt the raised hands on his platinum Cartier watch. *I've been sitting here over an hour.*

Pres had had three beers sitting on his lonely stool, and coupled with the drinks he had before he left home, he really needed to use the bathroom.

*I knew I should've brought my cane. This is crazy. She can't pretend I'm not blind.* It wasn't like he could just ask some stranger to take him to the men's room. He pulled his cell phone out of his pocket and speed-dialed Vikki. It went straight to voice mail. *Fuck, fuck, fuck.*

Pres waited for the bartender to come back and ask him if he wanted another drink. He politely refused and asked him to direct him toward the men's room.

"Dude, I'm not gonna help you take a whiz, man," the bartender laughed.

"I don't need help. Just tell me which way it is," Pres hissed.

"To your left," was all he said.

"And..." Pres prompted, but the man was gone.

*Goddamn it.*

Pres hadn't felt this stupid in a long time. He'd let his idiot girlfriend talk him into doing what he knew he should not have. Pres slid off the stool and immediately bumped into someone.

"Sorry," he tried to apologize over the music.

This was ridiculous. He had to put his hands out in front of him to keep from falling over something. He knew he looked crazy, but what else could he do? People were bumping into him as he walked extra slow through the crowd. Some were not so polite in moving him out of their way.

He ran smack into a stool that was occupied by a woman. "Sorry," he murmured as he heard a recognizable giggle. *What the fuck? Vikki.*

"Vikki!" he yelled angrily over the pop music.

"Better watch where you're going, Pres." She laughed hysterically, and so did several of her friends who were in close proximity.

*Watch where I'm going?* Pres was humiliated. She'd probably been watching him the whole time, knowing he wouldn't be able to move without her.

*I'm done with this bitch. I'd rather be alone the rest of my life than put up with this.*

"That's it. Take me home right the fuck now," he growled in her ear.

"Hey. I'm not going anywhere. I told you you wouldn't like it here, but you begged to come with me. Now, you can wait until I'm ready to go," she slurred.

"Well at least show me to the bathroom." He held her shoulder and spoke sternly in her ear, not wanting anyone else to hear his request.

"Awww. Poor baby needs to go to the bathroom and can't." She mocked him.

"Hey, man, I'll take you to the bathroom and help you hold it up too," a man purred very close to his ear, making Pres jerk away. His feminine lisp told Pres that he definitely didn't want his kind of help.

"Okay, Vikki. Fine. You've succeeded in humiliating me, and rest assured, I will not bother you again…ever. Will you just show me to the bathroom and walk with me out of this bar so I can hail a cab, and you'll never see me again."

Pres could feel the heat in his face, he was so angry. He didn't want to go to the bathroom on himself, and he feared if he didn't get there soon, then those four beers and glasses of wine were going to come out whether he liked it or not.

"I don't know why the hell you're treating me like this. Why would you treat anyone like this? I thought we were togeth—" Pres stopped talking. "Forget it. That doesn't matter anymore. Just show me to the bathroom, and I'll call a cab."

"Oh, go on with Danni. He'll take good care of you." She laughed some more.

"I don't fucking know him, Vikki. And I sure as hell don't need him to hold my dick while I piss. Look, don't be a bitch, okay? The least you could do—"

His angry sentence was abruptly cut off by a hard slap across his face.

"Augh. Fuck!" Pres yelled as he held one side of his face waiting for the ringing in his head to subside. Vikki had hit him so hard across his cheek that he saw bright lights as his head snapped to the side.

"Don't you ever call me a bitch! Find your own way home. I hope your blind ass left a trail of bread crumbs. Don't think I didn't see that you canceled the payment on my Visa this month. I have no further use for you, Pres. Now get out of my damn face!" She shoved him backward—hard—sending his arms windmilling wildly. He couldn't recover fast enough as he toppled over a low table a few feet behind him, knocking himself and all of its contents to the floor.

He heard people gasping, but no one came to help him. He was in a heap of broken glass and alcohol. He put his right hand on the ground to pick himself up and felt a sharp piece of glass go into his flesh. He yanked his hand back quickly and could feel the blood running from the very tender gash. He wanted to call out for help, but figured it futile.

"All right, buddy. Out ya go. You've caused enough trouble in here for one night." Pres felt a beefy hand wrap around his arm and haul him off the floor.

"Are you shitting me? I was just assaulted. I want to press charges," Pres argued. He was angry and so embarrassed for being beat up by a woman he could scream.

"Did anyone see this man get assaulted?" The bouncer's deep voice bellowed into the room.

There were several nos, and one person nearby yelled, "He actually assaulted her." The insults and rants rang out of the crowd as Pres was shoved toward the front door.

"Get the hell out of here, and don't come back. We don't take kindly to men assaulting women in this fine establishment."

*I have to be dreaming this nightmare.*

The man shoved Pres again, making him hit the side of his head against the entrance to the door as he stumbled out onto the busy sidewalk.

"Goddamn it! Take it easy. I can't fucking see, man." Pres turned his head back toward the club. The once-blaring music now sounded muffled. It was safe to assume the bouncer had closed himself back inside.

*Shit.*

Pres didn't know how big the sidewalk was or how far he was from the curb. So he put his hands out a little in front of him and moved forward. He took a couple steps and felt a burly man stumble over his feet and holler in his face.

"Hey, watch where you're going, dipshit."

*Shit, shit, shit.*

Pres's injured hand was throbbing. The part of his head that had come into contact with the club door was surely showing a nice bruise now. He didn't know if the glass was still in his hand or not. All he knew was that it hurt like hell. The tears were flowing down his face from anger, but he still felt like a pussy. No matter what, he couldn't stop them. And worst of all, he knew he was going to piss himself any minute now, right here on the extremely crowded oceanfront strip. He could hear so much activity going on around him, but was too afraid to stick his hand out and beckon someone to help.

*Oh my God.* Pres put two nasty, alcohol-drenched fingers in his mouth and whistled, hoping to signal a cab, while he clutched his bloody hand to his rapidly beating chest. He raised his hand to his mouth and whistled again, this time a lot louder.

Before he could process the deep growl, he was shoved forward violently. "Thanks for doing that in my ear, asshole."

*Fuck! Where the hell am I...in Brooklyn?*

"It was an accident...I—I—I didn't see you!" Pres stammered. He assumed the guy had said his piece and moved on because he didn't hear anything else.

Now after that shove, he really didn't know how close he was to the street. He took another couple steps and stumbled off the steep curb. Horns blared and tires screeched as he jumped backward, running right into a rock-hard chest.

Pres ducked and shivered violently as the warm urine ran down his pants leg and pooled around his feet.

*You got to be fuckin' shittin' me.* Pres put his one good hand out in front of him to hopefully ward off the attack he was about to get. "Please don't hit me. I'm sorry. I didn't see you, I swear. Just...don't hurt me, please."

"I'd never hurt you, baby. Com'ere. Hold on to me."

*Baby?*

A very masculine, rich voice was in his ear as a strong arm took Pres's good hand and wrapped it around a narrow waist as the man held his limp, bloody hand up in the air. "Keep it elevated, Pres. Jesus. I'm so sorry. It's all right. I'm gonna take care of you."

*This person just said my name. Okay...so it's someone who knows me.*

Pres's keen senses had shut down because of the surge of fear coursing through him. He couldn't figure out who this kind stranger was.

Pres heard a shrill whistle as the deep voice yelled, "Taxi!" The man had one thick arm around Pres's back as the other kept his throbbing hand up in the air.

"I got you, gorgeous. Just hold on to me." The deep voice was smooth and soothing.

Pres was in no condition to fight that it was a strange man holding him like this and calling him "baby." He'd never been so terrified and abused since he'd lost his sight. He'd never been abused, period. He lost the fight at trying to hold on to a small amount of dignity and buried his head in the strong chest and let his tears fall quietly. He felt himself being ushered into a car, a taxi, he presumed.

"Chesapeake Hospital," the deep voice told the driver.

# Chapter Thirteen

**R**ic had been in the VIP room on the upper floor of the bar. He'd decided to take Nurse Sheila up on her offer and come out to hang with a few of his new coworkers. After seeing Pres leaving with that witch tonight, he really needed a couple drinks. He'd actually been having a good time, when he'd come out of the bathroom and saw several people blocking the stairs. So he went back to the VIP room and asked Sheila's boyfriend what the ruckus was about downstairs.

The short man just shrugged his shoulders. Ric went to the railing and looked down to the lower level. He could see there was some type of commotion going on at a few tables by the bar. They were all the way on the other side of the club, and Ric could barely make out their faces in the dim lighting. He got ready to turn around when he noticed a chick slap this man across his face.

*Wow! That look like it hurt.*

Ric saw the man fly back over the top of a table and crash to the floor, like he was a stuntman in an action movie. The bar lights were flashing wildly, and there were so many people standing around that Ric could hardly see what was going on.

It wasn't until the bouncer hauled the man to his feet that Ric took in the man's outfit and that dark wavy hair.

*Pres.*

The bouncer was manhandling him roughly. He was slinging Pres around tables while pushing him toward the exit. Ric's heart ached terribly, and he saw red.

"Stop pushing him, asshole!" Ric yelled as loud as he could as he took the stairs two at a time. At the bottom, the stairs were blocked by people standing around trying to get a better look at the commotion. "Let me through!" he barked, but nobody moved.

The rap music the DJ was playing was deafening, and there were too many people gathered around cheering. You would've thought it was a UFC championship match, not a blind man getting assaulted.

By the time Ric was able to get through the large crowd and onto the sidewalk, Pres was being shoved toward the street by some punk. He raced forward to grab him, but Pres fell back into him instead. The man was crying and shivering terribly. His hand had a thin sliver of glass sticking out of it, and blood was running down his arm and into his shirt sleeve. Ric wrapped him in his arms, surprised that he came willingly. Pres looked so relieved that someone wasn't trying to kill him, he probably would've wrapped himself around the devil at that point if he was offering help.

Now he was taking the beautiful man to the hospital to get him stitched up, and then he'd safely take him home.

**P**res rode in silence while his savior pulled him in and held him to his massive chest. One heavily muscled arm was wrapped tight around his shoulder, while the other still held his injured hand. Pres's other arm was around the man's waist. He was being held by a man—he just didn't know who. As they rode, Pres could hear the man whispering softly to him as he tried to get control of his emotions.

"I'm so sorry, Pres. I tried to get to you, baby. I tried. I'm not gonna let anyone hurt you again."

He felt the man place a soft kiss on his forehead. It felt...it felt...fucking wonderful! Then he smelled that warm, spicy scent, and the familiarity hit him like a ton of bricks.

"Ric," he whispered quietly.

He heard the man chuckle softly. "Yes, it's me, Pres. I see you can still recognize my scent. I'm taking you to my job, and I'm gonna fix your hand. Then I'm gonna take you back home...okay? Don't worry."

"Thank you. I was so scared." He spoke quietly into Ric's neck and felt the tears building. "I pissed myself," he whispered. Then there were the tears again. He felt like such a whiny bitch.

"I know, baby. It's all right. You don't have to be scared now. I got you." Ric squeezed him harder. It was more comforting than anything he'd felt in a long time.

"Hey, you're gonna clean that up back there! I'm not cleaning some grown man's piss," the taxi driver yelled into the backseat.

"Shut the fuck up and drive!"

Pres could feel the rumble in Ric's chest from his growling words.

About ten minutes later, the taxi driver slammed on his brakes, causing them both to wrench forward. "We're here. Now get the hell out!" the driver barked.

"Here, asshole."

Pres felt Ric throw some bills over the seat.

"And keep the change to buy yourself a new fucking attitude."

"Ric, please, let's just get out," Pres whispered against the side of Ric's face. He could feel the heat and anger radiating off of the big man.

"I'm sorry, baby. Okay, come on." Ric gently eased him out of the back of the car.

"My hand is killing me," Pres hissed. "Ric, I don't want to walk in there like this. Is it really busy in there right now?"

"Yes, it's busy, but I'll take you straight to the back, okay? I'm not gonna make you wait in the waiting room." Ric put his arm back around Pres's shoulder and pressed him closely against his chest, moving them forward.

Pres walked stiffly. He was overly conscious where he stepped, not wanting to trip on a curb or any stairs.

"It's okay. I wouldn't let you fall, Pres…ever. There are two steps at the entrance about fifty feet ahead, and then it's a flat surface all the way to the back of the emergency room," Ric informed him.

Pres immediately felt better at the direction and started to move a little faster. He never removed his arm from around Ric's waist. He counted to forty-five, and was prepared to step up, when he felt Ric turn him toward him and cup his face tenderly.

"When we get inside, don't say anything, and don't stop walking, okay?" Ric was very close to his face, and he could feel the man's breath blowing into his own parted lips. He smelled so spicy and sweet, like the best Galliano liqueur he used for his favorite flambé, a sexy, aromatic blend of anise, vanilla, and honey with rich, spicy overtones. Pres had to admit that he loved the man's scent and would recognize him in any crowd.

"Okay, Ric," Pres whispered back.

"Step up twice," Ric instructed.

Pres followed the directions and heard the automatic doors open up. The noise was pretty loud, but it was an emergency room on a Saturday night. Pres was glued to Ric's side as he ushered him through the noisy lobby. Ric was fairly tall, because Pres was able to slouch some and tuck his face into Ric's armpit. He didn't want anyone looking at his face—which they probably weren't since he had a huge wet spot down lower for them to focus on.

Ric did as promised and moved them quickly across the linoleum floor.

"Well, hello there, handsome. I thought you were off tonight?" a female asked. The soft voice held a bit of desire in it as she spoke to his protector.

His.

Pres concentrated on not turning his head and scowling at the woman.

"I am off, Sandra." Ric didn't slow his steps, not even for a second. "Send Maggie to private room sixty-three," he called over his shoulder.

"Okay." The woman had to yell back at them since they were already turning the corner. No doubt she was wondering why the hell they were practically running down the hall.

"Right here." Ric took his arm from around Pres and turned him to the left.

Pres heard the door squeak open, and he assumed it was dark because he heard Ric flick a light switch.

"There's a chair ahead of you. I want you to sit while I help you take off your clothes. After that I'm gonna—"

"You don't have to do that, Ric. I'm sure you have—"

Pres's words were cut off. "I know what I have and don't have to do. Now sit down, Prescott," which he immediately did. He heard the door squeak open and raised his head to listen.

"Nurse Maggie, can you first get me a suture kit, a ten-milligram syringe of morphine, and two IV bags of fluids." It was spoken as a demand, not a question. "Bring them stat, please, Maggie. Then, I'll need some size-large scrubs from the doctors' lounge." Ric was busy removing Pres's soiled clothes while he issued the instructions.

"Sure thing," the warm voice quickly responded and was back out the door.

"Are you going to stay here while the doctor does the stitches?" Pres questioned, his voice still shaking from the night's horrific events.

"Nobody touches you but me, baby. I am your doctor. I'll be doing the stitches. Then I'm gonna get you cleaned up myself. After you've rested a little and I'm comfortable that the knot on the side of your head is not a problem, I'll take you home." Ric spoke with so much assurance that it made Pres want to beg the man to stay with him forever. It'd been years since someone besides his parents cared so much for him.

"You're a doctor, Ric?" Pres asked, the shock evident in his tone.

Pres didn't get an answer because the nurse walked in right at that moment.

"Do you want me to start a chart, Dr. E?" she asked nicely.

"No. I don't want anyone coming in here besides you, okay, Maggie?" Ric said.

"Of course, Doctor. I'll go get the scrubs. Did you want me to assist with your sutures?"

"No. I'll be fine. Just keep this room clear for me."

"Will do, Dr. E." The young voice left without another word.

"I didn't know you were a doctor," Pres remarked again as he was ushered to the bed.

"You didn't ask," Ric's stated easily, his voice hinted with humor. He concentrated on cleaning the outer part of Pres's hand with alcohol-soaked cotton balls. "Now hold still. I'm going to give you a shot of morphine in your arm, and then I want you to sit back and relax. I'll numb your hand real good and remove the shard of glass. Once it's clean, I'll give you a shot of antibiotic before I start the sutures. You shouldn't feel anything, okay, but if you do, just speak up. I don't want you to hurt at all." Ric rubbed Pres's bare thigh as he spoke the details of his treatment.

Pres sat there on the side of the hospital bed with a cool sheet draped over his privates. He wasn't feeling the least bit uncomfortable around the sweet doctor.

"I'll be fine. Go ahead, Ric. Believe it or not, I'm tougher than you think. I know all evidence points to the contrary...but it was an unusual night." Pres tried to sound surer of himself. He felt the needle pierce the crook of his arm.

"I know you're strong, baby. I can't imagine how it felt to go through what you just went through. I'm just sorry I couldn't get to you in time." Ric sounded genuinely hurt.

"Hey. Why do you keep saying that? Were you watching me?" Pres had to know why Ric kept saying he tried to get to him.

"Not really. I was at the club, in the upper-level VIP room with some coworkers, when I came out of the restroom and saw everyone watching the commotion. I didn't notice it was you until the bouncer was pushing you toward the door. There were so many damn people blocking my way, and I couldn't reach you before you were tossed out. I'm so sorry, Pres."

"Shhh. Hey, it wasn't your fault. And it's not your job to protect me. I shouldn't have been out with that crazy broad in the first place. It's just been pretty lonely over the last few years...ya know? Well, you probably don't know."

"No. Believe me...I do know," Ric said before he went back to working.

They fell into a comfortable silence. Ric was already done with his sutures and wrapping a bandage around his hand. Pres didn't feel any pain.

"Feeling okay?" Ric questioned.

"Yep. I'm just peachy." Pres chuckled.

Ric laughed too.

Pres was feeling pretty good with the strong narcotic flowing through his system. Ric informed him he'd been given a double dose to ensure he stayed comfortable. Now he was high as a kite. The previous intoxication from the liquor he'd consumed earlier added to his now-euphoric condition.

Ric was wrapping some kind of plastic cover over his entire hand so Pres couldn't get the fresh bandages wet while he showered. "All done, baby. Now let's get you cleaned up."

He felt Ric helping him off the table, when Pres suddenly stopped short. "You keep calling me 'baby.'" he slurred a little, his eyes half closed from the drugs.

"It's just a term of endearment. Am I offending you?" Ric asked carefully.

"No. I think I actually like it." Pres smiled.

Ric moved Pres slowly to the bathroom.

"So you're gay, Ric. I mean, like…not bisexual…completely gay?" Pres stopped their movement and waited for Ric's answer.

"I am gay," Ric admitted surely.

"Oh. Well, that's fine. I'm fine with it…really." Pres held on tighter to Ric's arm. "You're attracted to me, Ric?"

"Fuck yes," Ric answered without hesitation. "Is this going to bother you? I mean helping you in the shower…because I can be professional."

"No, Ric. I can use your help. I'm feeling a little woozy, to be honest," Pres said.

"Good," Ric responded. "Ummm, are you bisexual, Pres? You seem pretty comfortable with me…and, you know, the other night at my place."

"I did some experimenting, I guess you would say, in college. But, I haven't been attracted to another man in a very, very long time. I can't see you, Ric, but you sound handsome. Your voice is very rich and masculine, and your scent is intoxicating," Pres whispered against Ric's neck. "Will you describe yourself to me, Ric?" Pres silently hoped that Ric didn't think that was weird, or too much, but he really wanted to know.

"Of course I will, beautiful. But let me get you cleaned up and dressed first, okay?" Ric took Pres into the small bathroom and started the stand-in shower. "When I get you home, I'll let you see me."

"Okay, honey." Pres smiled warmly, teasing the gentle man.

"You asshole. Get in there." Ric laughed. "Keep your hand up on the wall so it's out of the path of the showerhead."

The small shower was only the size of mini closet, with a small bench protruding from the back of it and a detachable showerhead.

Pres heard Ric unwrapping the soap. He felt him try to press the washcloth in his hand, but Pres didn't take it. Instead he turned around and put both hands up on the wall, assuming the position.

**R**ic concentrated on not letting loose moan after moan as he watched Pres turn around—showing off that perfect ass—spread his legs, brace both hands high on the cool tiles, and drop his head down to his chest.

*Jesus fucking Christ. He wants me to bathe him. God, give me strength.*

He started on Pres's long tan neck and began to make slow but firm circles. He hoped he could keep his hands from shaking long enough to finish the job. Pres lifted his head slightly, and Ric washed his throat. He dropped his hand to Pres's defined abs and couldn't resist using two hands to clean in between the ridges and valleys there. It didn't appear that Pres was uncomfortable with this, even though Ric's other hand was lathered and sliding along Pres's body without a rag.

He wanted to step inside that shower—clothes and all—and press his body up against this man's wet, slick form. For Ric there wasn't anything more stunning than the image he had in front him right now. If nothing ever came of him and Prescott Vaughan, he would always have this moment to jerk off to, for many years to come.

Ric abandoned the rag and used just the bar of soap to wash Pres's strong back. He quickly came back around the front to his chest. Pres's head lolled on his shoulders and fell back, baring his throat, and Ric had the urge to lick the suds running down his Adam's apple. He took a deep breath and let his hands glide down the slick patch of hair on Pres's abdomen and into his neatly trimmed pubic hair surrounding his—

*Fuck. He's hard.*

Ric said he would be professional, but this was ridiculous. His touch had aroused Pres. How could he just ignore it now? Ric figured he'd take his cues from Pres and see what he wanted.

Ric moved in a little closer to Pres but still stayed out of the spray of the hot water. He wished he could get a good look at Pres's cock, but that would be impossible to do without getting soaked. He took one hand and ran it under Pres's balls in every effort to appear that he was only cleaning them, but he couldn't resist rolling them an extra couple of times when he felt Pres shiver.

"Oh my God, Ric," Pres whispered into the steamy bathroom.

Ric moved up to gently run the bar of soap along Pres's weeping cock head and was rewarded with a fierce shiver.

"Ric, please," Pres moaned.

"Say it," Ric ordered. He massaged Pres's shoulder with one hand to keep him relaxed and pliant, while he moved the other back and forth around the base of his cock. "Say it, baby. Tell me what you want."

"Make me come. Please, make me come," Pres begged.

Ric wrapped his large hand around Pres's cock and gave it a hard squeeze around the head. He then set a steady up-and-down rhythm along the entire length of the beautiful dick. Pres's legs were trembling, his head was tilted back, and his eyes were closed tight in the throes of passion. Ric picked up the pace and let out a groan at the painful feeling of his own erection confined in his tight jeans.

"Ric, fuck. I'm not gonna last," Pres whispered harshly. "Feels so fuckin' good…God, don't stop."

"I got you, baby. Come for me."

Ric tightened his grip and couldn't resist dropping his other hand from Pres's shoulder to his tight ass to rub in between his seam. When he ran across that tight bud, he felt Pres clench his finger and let out a hoarse shout as his come shot out of him like a bullet from a gun, spraying the tile and coating Ric's fist.

"Fuuuuck. God, Ric," Pres groaned as Ric milked the last of his seed from his sated cock.

Ric couldn't take it any longer. He scrambled with one slippery hand on his jeans zipper to free his angry cock from its prison. The first feeling of the shower's steam on his dick made Ric cry out in sheer bliss. He removed his come-coated hand from Pres's cock and used it to stroke his own. He placed a hand in the middle of Pres's back and commanded him, "Don't move, you gorgeous fucker."

Pres gave a slight whimper that made Ric almost lose his mind.

Ric knew he wasn't going to last but a few seconds, too. He kept his eyes trained on Pres's muscular lower back that curved into his round ass. He had to have another touch. He jerked himself fast and hard, his grunting filling the small space, and spread one side of Pres's ass cheek to get a better look at his hole. He gasped at the wrinkled star that fluttered at him when he rubbed across it. He wished he could step all the way in and shoot his load on that perfect fucking ass, but he couldn't leave the hospital with soaking wet clothes.

Ric threw his head back and yelled Pres's name before spraying rope after rope of his load onto the shower floor. His knees almost buckled as he came down from one of the best orgasms he'd had in years.

Ric took deep breaths to get himself back under control. He rinsed his hand and tucked his limp cock back into his pants, then quietly finished cleaning Pres off and helped him out of the shower. Ric was slightly nervous at Pres's now-withdrawn demeanor, but figured he wouldn't say anything just yet. He'd give Pres some time to think about what they'd just done while he rested.

Ric watched Pres drift in and out of consciousness, carefully watching him for any signs of a concussion. He never left the room the entire time. He knew Pres was feigning sleep when Nurse Maggie came back in with his lab results and went over them with Ric.

"He seems to be just fine, Dr. E," Maggie said quietly, thinking the patient was sleeping.

"Good. I'll get him out of here as soon as he wakes again." Ric breathed a soft sigh of relief. "Thank you so much for helping, Maggie."

"You're very welcome, Dr. E." The woman paused and turned back to look at Ric. "Umm. Would you like to get a cup of coffee or something tomorrow night…if you're not busy?" she questioned timidly.

"I thought you were married, Maggie." Ric raised one eyebrow.

"I am, but my husband doesn't look like you do, Doctor. Besides we have sort of an open relationship." She giggled, blushing terribly.

*What the hell happened to the sanctity of marriage vows? Jeez.*

"Thank you for the compliment, Maggie. But sorry, I don't date married women."

*I don't date any women.*

He smiled to soften the rejection he had just given the petite adulterer.

"Sure. Just thought I'd ask." She gave a slight smile and walked out the door.

"All right, come on, faker. Let's get you home." Ric stood next to the hospital bed and squeezed the center of Pres's thigh, making him jerk and laugh loudly. "Ahh. So you're ticklish. Good to know, Pres, but I knew you weren't asleep."

"So, Mr. You Look So Much Better Than My Husband, do I have a clean bill of health?" Pres grinned from ear to ear, showing him how much he liked to tease.

"Oh, shut up, and come on." Ric popped Pres on his ass, making him jump in surprise. He was hopeful that Pres was feeling so much better now and not squeamish about their hot shower scene.

He liked seeing Pres smile and laugh. He was willing to do anything to make him happy.

# YOU CAN SEE ME

# Chapter Fourteen

By the time they got to their building, Pres had sobered some from the pain medicine, and his hand was feeling a lot better, probably still numb from the lidocaine. He felt Ric reach for his good hand and lead them through the lobby.

"How's your hand feeling?" he asked when they were in the elevator.

Pres looked in Ric's general direction. "It's still fine. I can't thank you enough for helping me."

"Yes, you most certainly can," Ric whispered.

"Excuse me?" Pres raised one corner of his mouth, intrigued.

"Grilled salmon with orange fennel sauce," Ric said and laughed. "What did you think I meant, beautiful?" Ric inched closer to him.

"I think it means someone's been Googling me," Pres stated. How else would Ric know of the recipe that had won him so many awards?

"I sure have," Ric said boldly.

Pres thought if he leant forward even a little bit that he'd probably end up kissing the man right on his neck. He could feel Ric's body heat in the small space and was not turned off. He couldn't wait to get to his apartment. He wanted to know what Ric looked like. He remembered a nurse called him handsome...actually a couple nurses. Hell, one was willing to cheat on her spouse with Ric.

The mental image he was conjuring up in his head was taking a turn for the wicked and naughty. He couldn't stop picturing some of the male models he'd seen in a charity calendar of Doctors Without Borders years ago in Angela's old apartment.

"You think I'm beautiful, Ric?"

"You're breathtaking, Prescott. Why don't you know that?" Ric whispered seductively in his ear.

Ric's hot breath was doing funny things to his body, unfamiliar things. Things he hadn't experienced in too damn long.

Pres had to consider if he was gay now. Would being in a relationship with a man really be any different? His disability had really done a head trip on him, thinking he had to settle for whoever was willing to give him a little affection. Dark thoughts crowded Pres's mind. He'd dated women, he'd tried to make friendships with other guys, but ultimately everyone left him—woman or man. Ric probably would too…eventually. *Maybe he just wants to know what it's like to fuck a blind guy.*

Victoria's words tonight replayed in his head: *"I have no further use for you."* Pres shook his head, trying to dislodge those depressing thoughts, only to have them be overtaken by another one: *"This just isn't what I signed up for."* Pres's fiancée had said that before she slammed the door on their relationship. His heart still ached when he thought about her walking out on him. Pres put his good hand up to Ric's chest and again was astonished at how solid and muscular he was. He took a hard gulp and pushed the man back a few steps.

"Don't try to make it seem like you're interested in me…I mean really knowing me. All you see is a weak little blind man that can be taken advantage of. Well, I'm not some stupid weakling, Dr. E, and I'm done with letting people walk all over me," Pres spat and stormed out of the elevator as soon as he heard it open.

"What the hell? Hey, don't you even think about it. Don't you dare walk away from me like that, Prescott!" Ric yelled down the hall.

Pres hoped no one was in the hall or sticking their heads out of their apartments. Ric had a deep voice that carried. Pres pulled his key out and struggled one-handed to stick it in the lock, when he felt solid pressure slam against his back.

"Augh. Get off me," Pres hissed with his cheek flat against the cold metal door.

"Open the door," Ric growled in his ear, his voice thick with anger.

Pres was hoping that Ric wouldn't turn violent, but deep down, he knew he wouldn't. Pres grew angrier, and damn it, there was another lump forming in his throat at the possibility of never being able to have a real friendship…or relationship.

"Don't try to pretend like you want something with me. You probably want to see if you can turn out the hopeless straight guy—jerk him off, make him come and beg for more. Get cool points if you can bang the blind man and brag about it to all your suave doctor friends."

"Open. The. Goddamn. Door. Prescott." Ric pushed so hard against his back he could barely turn the knob. When he did, he fell into the apartment, but was grabbed by Ric before falling face first onto the hard tiles in his entryway. Ric put a death grip on both his arms, spun him around, and pulled him hard against his chest.

"Tonight I got a good glimpse of the relationships you've been in, Prescott Vaughan, and I refuse to let you place me right alongside those other assholes that have hurt you in the past. You don't know what my fucking intentions are because you didn't ask. Don't assume that I have some ulterior motive for wanting you. I don't know why I'm so drawn to you, Pres. I just am." Ric's voice was raw and strained as he spoke.

Pres suddenly felt bad for saying what he'd said in the elevator. He was so screwed up inside that even when a good thing presented itself, he didn't know how to receive it. Pres began to think that maybe he was destined to be alone. He closed his eyes tight as the tears started to fall. The last couple of weeks began to catch up to him, and Prescott was so emotionally drained that he couldn't even think straight.

"Look at me, Prescott." Ric held his arms tight. His breath brushed across Pres's face with every word he spoke.

Pres kept his eyes squeezed shut and bucked against Ric's tight hold.

"Look at me, damn it!" Ric yelled.

"I can't see you!" Pres yelled right back as he tried to force his way out of Ric's punishing grip.

Ric's voice lowered to barely a whisper. "Yes, you can, baby." He wrapped his arms around Pres's waist and squeezed him tight. "Yes, you can. Come here."

Pres was pulled into his den and positioned to sit on his couch. He thought Ric was going to sit next to him, but he didn't. To Pres's surprise, Ric dropped down to his knees and wedged himself between Pres's legs. He felt Ric lift his uninjured hand and place it gently on his face before he dropped his hands to rest on the top of Pres's thighs. Pres instinctively moved to the edge of the couch, his groin pressed against Ric's hard abs as he began to explore every inch of his face.

**R**ic let the beautiful Prescott Vaughan have a look at him. He felt Pres's shy fingers start in his hair. He ran them all way through to the ends at the nape of his neck. Pres finally opened his pretty blue eyes, his long, spiky eyelashes wet from his tears.

"What color?" he whispered so softly that Ric barely heard him.

"Light brown," Ric answered. "It's too long. I need a haircut."

"I like the length." Pres smiled at him.

*God, he's so damn pretty.*

Pres brought his hand back up and ran it through Ric's hair again, his fingers gliding easily over his soft brown locks. He leaned in to have a smell as well.

"Feels so soft," Pres said while rubbing his cheek against the waves. It was as if he wanted to linger there longer but chose to continue his exploration instead.

He grazed his fingertips over Ric's smooth, average-sized forehead, not staying there for long, then stilled his fingers at Ric's open eyes. He tenderly felt the thin eyebrows and fingered his long lashes. Ric let his eyes flutter close and open again so that Pres could see how long his eyelashes were. He must've liked them because he stayed there for a while. His fingers grazed lightly over his eyes.

"What color?" Pres whispered again.

"Green, baby. My eyes are green."

Pres sucked in a quick breath at that description. Ric could feel Pres's erection get firmer against his stomach, making him let loose a moan before he could control it.

"Ric." Pres was breathless.

Pres moved away from his eyes, and those timid fingers traveled to his strong Roman nose and then to his high cheekbones before venturing lower. Pres cupped his stubbled chin in his soft palm as if he was about to kiss him. Ric held his breath and closed his eyes as Pres's fingers danced over his lips oh so gently. Ric's lips were soft and full, according to what he'd been told. His bottom lip was slightly fuller than the top one, and he felt Pres give it a gentle squeeze, making him smile.

Pres gasped, "I can see your beautiful smile, Ric." He raked his fingertips across Ric's straight white teeth.

Some people said his eyes were his best feature, but his mom always said it was his smile. He only hoped that Pres liked it.

Pres's hand was still skittering over his lips, his eyes half closed as if he was mesmerized by his mouth. Ric pursed his lips and kissed Pres's tender fingers. To Ric's surprise, he didn't pull his hand away. Pres's mouth was slightly open, and his breathing picked up.

Ric rubbed up and down Pres's thighs as he waited for the man to process what he was feeling. He could tell Pres was so starved for affection. There was no telling the last time he'd been touched with love. Ric's heart ached at the realization that no one wanted this wonderful man only because he was blind. To Ric, it only made him all the more wonderful.

"Please let me kiss you, Pres. Please, baby. I have to know what you taste like." Ric realized that he was begging, but he didn't care. He wanted to show Pres that he was what the man was missing in his life, and Ric believed he could show him that with just one kiss.

Pres only nodded his head yes and waited, assumably for Ric to close the distance between their mouths.

Ric came in slowly and just let his lips brush across Pres's mouth. He'd take it slow just in case the man got freaked out. Ric saw that Pres had closed his eyes and was inching forward some more. He figured he could move in a little more as well. Ric brought his hand up to cup Pres's jaw and felt the man moan into his mouth. He swallowed the sexy sound and slanted his mouth to deepen the kiss.

"Ric, please," Pres begged.

"I know, baby."

Pres was floating, he felt so high. He was kissing this man, a very generous and kind man. He'd done a thorough feel of

Ric's face and loved every minute of it. Ric was right, he could see him. He saw that soft brown wavy hair that had enough length to grip and pull, gorgeous green eyes fanned by long, sexy lashes that lay seductively on his cheek when he closed his eyes. His skin was flawless and smooth. His five-o'clock shadow wasn't coarse like his. It was soft.

*Oh my God. This kiss feels so good. It's been so long since I've been kissed. Mmmm, more, more, please. Awww. God, so good. I forgot it could feel like this. Ric, don't ever stop...please.*

"More please. Feels so good." Pres released all his nervousness and inhibitions and just allowed himself to feel something that he hadn't felt in years. He felt affection.

Pres wrapped his arms around Ric's neck and gave it everything he had. He drove his tongue in to explore this wonderful man and relished the flavors that exploded in his mouth. Pres didn't know why this felt so right...It just did. Ric felt like sunshine in Pres's very dark world.

Ric was one hell of a kisser too. He was giving it to Pres real good, and he didn't stop, just like he'd begged him not to. Ric moaned passionately into his mouth as if he was enjoying it just as much as he was.

"Baby, wait a minute."

Ric pulled back a little, and Pres immediately chased his mouth. He heard Ric chuckle as he held him back by his shoulders.

"Mmmm. You feel so damn good, but I want us to stop for a minute. I don't want this to go too much further. I want you to know that I'm serious about wanting something deeper with you. So if you keep kissing me like that, sexy boy, then it could easily lead to other things...nasty things." Ric accented his words by popping Pres on his hip and nipping his jaw, making him smile. Ric was still on his knees in between his legs, and Pres vaguely realized that he was grinding his hard cock into the man's stomach.

"Oh, shit. I'm sorry, Ric. It's just been a really long time." Pres knew his face was bright red.

"Don't you dare apologize. I loved every minute of it. Believe me, beautiful, I want so much more. But I want us to get to know each other first before I make slow, sweet love to you and make you mine. I don't need a one-night stand, Pres. I can get that from anyone. If that's all I wanted, then I would not have been celibate for the last two years." Ric pressed his forehead against his.

Pres took the time to calm his rapid breathing so that he didn't throw this gorgeous man on the floor and ravish him.

"Jesus Christ. It's been two years since you've had sex with someone, Ric?" Pres questioned unbelievingly with his mouth hanging slightly open.

"Yes, baby. Actually, it's been a little longer than that, but who's counting?" He smiled into Pres's mouth. "I vowed a long time ago that the next time I made love it was going to be with someone I loved and respected. I'm too old to be bed-hopping now. That's why I got so upset with what you said in the elevator. I would never just try to bed you and leave you, Prescott. Number one: that would hurt you…and I'd never hurt you. Two: that would be irresponsible and immature, and I'm neither one of those, baby." Ric cupped Pres's jaw, and he instinctively leaned into the embrace.

"I'm so scared, Rickson. Everyone always leaves me, and I'm in the dark here…alone."

"I know, baby. But you're going to have to trust me for no reason. Just leap with me. We'll fall together, okay?" He placed gentle kisses across Pres's cheek.

"Okay. But can I ask one more thing?" Pres spoke quietly.

"Anything." Ric caressed his face.

Pres was glad that Ric could already tell he needed constant contact.

"Will you kiss me again?" Pres asked shyly. He was embarrassed at appearing so desperate, but he didn't care. He needed this so bad.

"Of course." Ric smiled.

Then he kissed Prescott to within an inch of his life.

# YOU CAN SEE ME

## Chapter Fifteen

"Show me your place, baby. It looks beautiful in here." Ric got up off the floor and adjusted his hard cock before helping Pres off the couch.

"Okay. I think I have enough blood back in the head on my shoulders now." Pres grinned wide and started walking toward his showpiece—his kitchen.

Ric was impressed with Pres's spotless condo and how gracefully he moved through it without his cane. Needless to say, everything was organized and orderly. The furniture was large and spacious but left enough walking room. There was nothing protruding out into the floor or scattered objects that could cause Pres to trip and fall. He turned the corner and was floored at the luxury gourmet kitchen.

The floor was a polished mahogany wood. All along the borders of the kitchen were neutral-colored bricks, giving the room an earthy feel, though all the appliances were stainless steel and state-of-the-art.

The wraparound breakfast bar had a brown marble top. There were four stools on the opposite side, and each seat had a small but elegant place setting with a fluffed napkin hanging out of the coffee mug.

The stove was equipped with a grill and six gas burners. In a separate section was a large microwave set atop a double convection oven. All the cabinets were the same mahogany brown as the floor and reached almost to the ceiling except for the bright green ferns that hung over the edges. The wrought-iron chandelier overhead cast beautiful warm lighting throughout the room.

Ric had a feeling that Pres would show him this room first. His man was a chef, and from what he'd read, a damn good one. Ric walked around looking at all the gadgets as Pres poured them two glasses of water. He spotted a neat little appliance that was shiny and had a lot of buttons.

"Hey, Pres, what's this do?" Ric asked while pressing a neon green button on the machine. It came to life with a loud, shrill buzzing sound. Ric jumped, and repeatedly pressed the button, but nothing happened. "Shit, shit, shit!"

The sound was loud and annoying in the quiet condo. He looked at Pres and saw the man was cracking up as he casually leaned against the refrigerator, sipping his water.

"Can you turn this thing off, please?" Ric yelled over the noise.

Pres curtly walked over to the little noisemaker and pressed a neon blue button, ceasing the noise.

"Thank you. Goodness. What is that thing?" Ric continued staring at the contraption.

Pres laughed harder. "It's a juicer. You load the fruit up here." He lifted a long cylinder and pointed into the hollow opening. "Then the juice comes out of here." He pointed to the wide opening on the other end.

"I see. What happened to good ol' fashioned—"

"Squeezing it by hand?" Pres interrupted Ric and rolled his eyes at him.

"No…buying it in a carton at the supermarket." He grabbed Pres around his waist and dropped a chaste kiss on his lips.

"Oh right, of course, what was I thinking? You go to the grocery store for fresh-squeezed juice." Pres shook his head in amazement and smiled. "Are you hungry? I can make you something to eat. I know it's late, but I can whip up something real quick."

"No. If I eat this late, then I'll never get to sleep. Besides, you really should take a pain pill and get some rest. Your hand will be very uncomfortable in a few hours after the numbing completely wears off. I wouldn't mind taking you out to breakfast, though," Ric said into Pres's ear, smiling at his shiver.

"Okay, that sounds nice," Pres admitted.

Ric could see that Pres really wanted him to stay, and his face wasn't hiding his disappointment.

"Hey." Ric raised Pres's chin and kissed him again on his lips. He kissed his cheek, his forehead, and both his eyes. "I will be back in the morning. If I get in your bed with you, Prescott, I can't be sure I'll control myself. Believe me, baby, I don't want to leave you right now…but I think I should. I don't want you to doubt my sincerity."

Ric led Pres to the back of his condo, toward his bedroom. "I want you to seriously consider if you can have a relationship with a man. I can understand you being nervous about being hurt, but honestly, I'm more afraid of you than you are of me. I haven't taken the chance to fall in love in over eight years. If you suddenly decide you don't want to be gay, or a pretty woman advances on you, how do I know I won't be tossed aside like yesterday's trash?"

Pres reached his hand up toward Ric's face. Ric met his hand halfway and rubbed his cheek in his palm. "I guess we both have some trusting to do," Pres said and opened the door to his bedroom. "Good night, Sunshine." Pres closed his door.

Ric let himself out of Pres's condo and locked the door behind him. As he walked the four doors down to his own condo, he realized that Pres had called him "Sunshine," and it made a warm smile spread across his face.

He desperately hoped that Pres could love him because he believed he was already falling for this sensitive man. Ric hadn't felt this strongly about a man since his high school sweetheart.

*God. I've watched this man come and go for weeks. It's just something about him.*

Ric knew he was taking a large gamble by falling for a straight, or at minimum bisexual, guy. The fact that Pres was blind only meant that Ric had to be extra careful that Pres wasn't entertaining the thought of being gay only because he was lonely.

It was four in the morning, and Ric was exhausted. He took a very quick shower and flopped down on his king-sized bed. Ric was a tall man, standing at six two, and his feet were touching the footboard. He thought he would fall right asleep, but his mind was occupied with thoughts of the intriguing Prescott.

Ric thought about how sexy Pres sounded when he came in the shower at the hospital, then the hot and heavy kiss they'd shared in Pres's den. The rock-hard cock that had been pressed into his abs told him Pres was just as turned on as he was. Ric remembered Pres's soft tongue, so scared and shy at first and then becoming bold and adventurous as he explored every inch of Ric's mouth.

It was the most action Ric had had in months. He'd refused to sleep with the few men he'd dated over the last couple of years. All of them were only interested in his looks as they paraded him around their friends.

*I hope I'm not dating a blind man only because I don't want a man that's hung up on my looks.*

"Hell no." *Why would I even think that? There's no way I would do something like that. I'm just crazy about him...plain and simple.*

Ric was glad he'd made the decision to go home and not stay at Pres's house. He could clearly see the man wanted him to stay...but not for the right reasons. Pres just didn't want to be alone tonight, especially after what he'd gone through.

*Fuck. But I want him so goddamn bad.*

Ric tossed and turned for another fifteen minutes, his mind replaying the kiss over and over. He brought his hand up to his lips and rubbed them the same way Pres had. Ric stuck his tongue out and wet the tips of his fingers and dug his hand inside his pajama bottoms to caress his balls. "Aughhhh... Fuuckkkk," he drawled slowly.

Ric rolled his balls around in their sac so torturously slow that his legs anxiously moved up and down on the soft sheets. He reached over to his nightstand with his unoccupied hand, grabbed his lube, and applied a small amount to the head of his blushing cock and the sensitive skin underneath his balls. He didn't rush it. Ric hadn't had good jerk-off material for a long time, and right now, his head was full of Prescott Vaughan.

Ric raised one leg up and took his lubed middle finger and pressed into his aching hole all the way to the knuckle. His strong back bowed off the mattress.

"Pres, mmmm, want you to fill me up so bad, my sexy man," Ric moaned into the empty room. He took his other hand and gave his fully erect cock one long, slow stroke from base to tip. "Mmmm. Fuck. Damn, been too fucking long. Aughhhh."

Ric set a slow rhythm as he stroked his cock and pushed his finger in a little deeper. He wanted to use his dildo but didn't want to waste time pulling it out now. He wasn't going to last much longer anyway.

Ric wished he could've left Pres's scent on him. Lord knows after the man had showered in the hospital, he smelled so good. Ric wanted to suck on his neck until he was forced to stop. He found himself wondering if Pres was jerking off to thoughts of him as well. When he pictured Pres stroking his own cock and yelling out his name, Ric's muscles tensed, and streams of hot white come shot out of him before he could even react.

"Aughhhh. Gawdddd!" Ric yelled and aggressively milked the last of his orgasm.

He prayed that Pres would learn to trust him quickly because he needed Pres to fuck him, like, yesterday.

# Chapter Sixteen

**R**ic finally dozed off after his much-needed release. He was sleeping like a rock when he heard a loud, piercing siren in his head. *Damn. Did I forget to turn off my alarm clock?* Ric pulled his plush down pillow over his head and squeezed his eyes shut tight at the irritating noise. His brain was too sleep deprived, and he was not thinking clearly. The shrieking alarm was so loud that Ric raised his head suddenly while glancing at his alarm clock. It read seven forty-five in bright green neon. His dark drapes were pulled closed, but he could see the sunlight filtering in through the cracks. Then, as if he was knocked over the head with a cast-iron skillet, he jumped out of the bed at the sound of the building's fire alarm.

"Shit. Pres!" he yelled.

Ric stumbled out of his bedroom, shirtless, and ran full speed to his front door. He unlocked the locks and slung the door open so hard the knob hit the wall and went into the drywall. Ric noticed the entire floor's tenants were moving quickly to the ends of the hallways. More than a few people were panicking and knocking others over as the sounds of the fire engines came into range. Both ends had elevators and stairwells, but Ric was focused on four doors down.

He moved quickly, trying not to knock anyone over in the process. He got to Pres's door, arm poised to pound on it at the same time Pres opened it.

"Pres." Ric pulled the man into his arms. He closed them back inside Pres's apartment, letting the other people scurry through the hall.

"Ric, what's going on? Is this a drill?" Pres said around a yawn as he stood there rubbing his tired eyes. His hair was smashed to one side of his head, and he only had on tight black boxer briefs.

Ric thought he looked adorable. But now wasn't the time. This was no fucking drill, as Ric heard the sirens get louder.

"No, Pres, this is not a drill. Hurry up and get something on. We need to go, now." Ric watched Pres take off to his bedroom, cutting and running around the corner effortlessly.

Ric ran after him. "Where's Josey?" He raised his voice to be heard over the building's alarm.

Pres threw on a T-shirt and sweats that were neatly arranged in an armoire at the far side of his room. "My assistant picked him up at seven. He's at the groomer's."

"Okay. Let's go. We need to leave now, Pres," Ric said hurriedly.

They moved back through the apartment and opened Pres's front door. Ric grabbed Pres's cane from off the hook and pressed it into his hand. "Just in case you need it, but hold my hand, okay?"

There was no one in the hall now, and Ric's heart hammered inside his chest. What if the lower floors were on fire and he'd waited too long to get Pres out?

Ric led them to the stairwell, knowing better than to use the elevator. He didn't smell smoke or feel any heat.

Pres spoke up. "I smell smoke, Ric."

"You do? I don't smell anything." Ric pulled Pres up close behind him. He quickly counted the stairs. "Let's just go. Twenty flights, babe. Ten steps, then turn left on the landing, then ten more steps, and turn. Got it?"

"I got it," Pres stated and fell in step behind Ric.

Pres was actually sleeping better than he had in ages and dreaming about him and Ric being in a relationship, when he heard the horrible piercing in his ears from the damn fire alarm. He thought about not even getting up, figuring it was just a false alarm. Then he heard all the scurrying and panicked voices moving quickly in the hallway. His thoughts immediately went to Ric, and he slung his door open and was smacked in the face with the man's warm, spicy scent. Ric had come for him…shirtless.

They moved quickly down the stairs, Pres counting as he went, not wanting to trip and fall into Ric. Ric had a firm grip on his hand and was reading off the floor about every three levels. Ric stopped suddenly at level four, causing Pres to run into his back.

Ric turned and whispered in his ear while stroking his back tenderly. "Sorry, I didn't mean to do that. There are about forty people on the stairs, and they're moving very slow."

"Why?" Pres's brow creased. He could hear a few people grumbling and urging people to "Move faster!"

"Do you still smell smoke, Pres?" Ric asked.

"No. I smelled it stronger on my floor. Then it faded as we got lower. Probably someone had a small kitchen fire." Pres talked into Ric's bare shoulder. He was standing on a stair above him, putting them at just about the same height. Ric smelled so good. Pres turned his mouth into the crook of Ric's clean neck and licked him before he could think better of it.

"You sexy boy," Ric growled while turning his lips to Pres before kissing him lightly on the mouth. "You miss me, sweetheart?" He nuzzled Pres's face.

Ric turned back toward the crowd and saw a man in about his early forties appearing disgusted at their display of affection.

"What's wrong, Ric?" Pres asked. He could feel the tightness in Ric's shoulders. Something had him upset.

"There's an asshole staring at us like we both have glitter thongs on."

Pres chuckled at Ric's twisted humor. "What?"

"We're in the middle of an emergency. Can't you wait to do that nasty mess when you're back in your own apartment? I didn't even know we had queers in this nice building." The man's rude comment drew a few gasps from other people.

This man had chosen to butt into someone else's business that didn't have a damn thing to do with him. *Great. Bigoted asshole.* Pres tightened his grip on Ric's arm.

"Do you have dental insurance?" Pres heard Ric ask the man in a manner that was too calm for Pres's liking. He was sure the man had a seriously perplexed expression on his face at Ric's off-the-wall question.

"What…dental insurance? W-w-why?" the man stammered.

"I was wondering if you could get your teeth replaced when I knock them down your fucking throat." Ric bristled with anger, his voice a snarling whisper.

Pres was glad he wasn't yelling. He didn't want Ric to draw too much more attention than they already had.

"Ric, please, don't hit him. I don't like violence." Pres spoke quietly against Ric's ear. His hand was on Ric's large bicep, and he could feel it flexing with the man's growing anger. The concern and worry in Pres's voice must have had an effect, because Ric immediately took it down a notch.

Pres lifted his head in the direction of the man who had insulted them. "Sir, I suggest you turn your head in the future if our display of affection is too much for you to stomach. Otherwise, next time, neither he nor I will be very forgiving of your derogatory comments."

"I disagree. I think you should knock his lights out," a lady's voice chimed in a few steps below them. "We don't want any bigoted jerks in our building. As a matter of fact"—the woman spoke even louder—"what's your apartment number? I'm going to report you to the committee."

Pres heard several others agreeing with her.

"Look, I'm sorry, okay? Calm down." The man hurried to recover, his surrender obvious. "I'm sorry, sir. I didn't mean to offend you. Let's just get out of here safely. I don't want any trouble."

Ric turned to embrace Pres. "Nicely done, baby. I'm sorry I got so upset. I just don't want anyone mistreating you. I'll try to be a little calmer, okay?"

"Okay, Sunshine."

# YOU CAN SEE ME

# Chapter Seventeen

An hour later, everyone was let back into the building. A woman had indeed started a small fire in her kitchen, when the dish towel caught and she panicked. Her husband was able to get it out quickly, but not before the fire alarm sounded.

Ric walked Pres back to his apartment and promised him he'd be back in an hour to take him to breakfast. Ric went home and showered with Pres's obviously favorite body wash and used a dab of his Giorgio Armani on his neck. He decided to wear his most comfortable Levi jeans and a well-worn Duke University T-shirt. The thin cotton material was soft to the touch, and he had a feeling Pres would like it. He didn't put any product in his hair since he'd spent a couple extra minutes conditioning it in the shower so that it was delicate and fluffy.

Ric couldn't help but smile at the thought of how much his regimen was revolving around Prescott already. Pres was all about touching and feeling. Ric would put as much time and effort into preparing himself as needed to please him.

Ric knocked on Pres's door. A couple seconds later, Pres opened the door, and Ric saw the man was groomed head to toe. His hair was just cut, but still tousled like the models wear it. His face was freshly shaven, and there wasn't a nick in site. His man was dressed in a white short-sleeved Polo collared golf shirt. The trim around the collar was a light tan, which matched perfectly with his tan cargo shorts. He didn't wear socks with his white-and-tan canvas boat shoes. Prescott looked straight out of a Ralph Lauren beach photo shoot.

"Holy shit! Baby, you look delicious." Ric wrapped both arms around Pres's thin waist. They embraced for a while, neither man wanting to let go. Pres's fingers gently skimmed over Ric's face, lightly touching his cheeks, his eyes, his lips.

"You don't mind me touching you like this, do you?" Pres asked him nervously.

"I love you touching me like this. You can always touch me. Anytime and anywhere that you feel like it, I want you to do it. Do whatever you feel."

Ric didn't give Pres time to respond to his words because he captured his mouth in the most tantalizing, erotic kiss he'd ever given. It was all tongue as Ric tasted every inch of Pres's mouth that he could reach. He cupped Pres's jaw affectionately as he walked him backward until he was cornered between his chest and the door.

The kissing got hot, fast. Ric's cock was hard and leaking as Pres ground his erection against his thigh.

"You feel so fucking good," Ric breathed into Pres's mouth.

"I need you, Ric. I need you now," Pres groaned.

"Need you too, baby."

Ric worked his hand to the back of Pres's head until he was gripping his neck and controlling the kiss. He wedged one hand inside Pres's shorts, needing to feel the firmness of his ass under his large palm. He slowly rubbed up and down Pres's seam, basking in his man's reaction to his touch.

"Oh, Ric," Pres groaned, his eyes squeezed shut at the intensity of his pleasure.

Pres's moans were turning Ric on to no end. It wouldn't be long before Ric lost complete control.

*I swear. I'm going to take his ass right here in his entryway if he fucking moans like that again.*

Ric took two blunt fingers and applied a little pressure on Pres's tight bud, wanting to breach him so bad it hurt. "Feels good, Pres, huh? Tell me how it makes you feel, baby." Ric licked Pres's neck and dipped down to nip at his Adam's apple while keeping him pressed firmly against the door with his bulk.

"My goodness. There's about to be a fire in here now." A women's voice, full of amusement, broke into their kiss.

Ric jumped so hard he practically knocked Pres over. When they both parted, they were completely out of breath. Ric couldn't help but let out an embarrassed laugh at getting caught making out like a horny teenager.

Ric took Pres's uninjured hand and kissed it gently. He leaned down and whispered against the side of his face, "You didn't tell me you had company."

"I, uhh, forgot. Fuck. Ummm, this is my…" Pres was completely flushed and still panting for breath as he pointed to the snickering woman standing in front of them, boldly eyeing their large bulges in their pants.

"Oh, allow me, Prescott, while you gather your bearings," she giggled. "I'm Janice Boggs, Prescott's stylist. I do all his grooming and some wardrobe styling. But he has another girl that is responsible for his clothing. I've only been here an hour, but I already feel like I know you, Dr. Edwards. Pres has been going on and on about his new boyfriend," the eclectic woman teased as she stuck out a thin hand with long fingernails covered in intricate designs.

"Janice, damn. What ever happened to confiding in your hairdresser? Isn't there, like, some unwritten confidentiality clause with our relationship?" Pres feigned anger.

Ric laughed and shook Janice's hand, careful not to squeeze too hard as he took in the woman's appearance. She had bright red spikes of hair sticking up on her head in many different directions. Her dark eyeliner and extra-long fake lashes hid her beautiful brown eyes.

Ric lost count of how many holes and studs she had pierced in both ears. She was average height for a woman, but had about twenty extra pounds on her around her midsection. However, her smile was warm and inviting, and Ric could tell right off that she was happy to see Pres smiling the way he was in Ric's arms.

She pulled out a business card from her classic hairdresser smock and handed it to Ric. "You have gorgeous hair. I'd love to style it for you. Give me a call if you're looking for a hairdresser. Though I must say, the natural run-your-fingers-through-it look is really working for you." She stopped and clapped her hands together loudly. "I could put some gold-toned highlights in your hair, give you a Ryan Gosling–type look, you know. What do you think?" she asked with a crazy sparkle in her eyes.

"I think, hell no," Ric said.

Pres doubled over laughing at Ric's response, when Janice, surprisingly, walked up and reached her arms up high to hug Ric around his neck.

"Wow. Not that I'm complaining, but what was that for?" Ric was confused at the sudden gesture. He saw Pres stop laughing and look in his direction, and he clued him in. "She just gave me a huge hug, and now she's tearing up."

Janice continued to stare at Ric in awe. "I've been Prescott's stylist for three years, and I haven't seen him laugh like that since I've known him. Bless you, Ric. Please keep making him happy." Her tears flowed down her round face. She turned to Pres, wrapped her arms around his neck, and kissed his cheek. "Happy really suits you, Pres. I mean you really wear it well." Janice pulled back and looked at the two of them as if they were England's royal couple. "I'm sure you all want to start your day, so Pres, I'm going to pack up my things, and I'll see you again in a few days."

"Okay, Janice. Thank you, sweetie." She walked into his bedroom and started packing away her large travel hair salon.

Ric took Pres's bandaged hand and caressed it softly. "How's your hand feeling, baby? Is it sore? I can give you something for the pain if it is." He placed a light kiss on Pres's knuckles as he inspected the bandage.

"No, Ric. It's fine. Doesn't really hurt at all. You're a really good doctor. I still need to thank you for taking such good care of me last night…and this morning. I'm about to have you fitted for a cape if you keep rescuing me," Pres said jokingly.

Ric laughed. "You really are something else. Just let me take you to breakfast, okay? Then we can work on a proper thank-you." He held Pres around his waist and dipped low so he could nip him on his chin.

"My goodness, you two. I'm gonna have to start announcing myself when I'm about to come into the room. Your naughtiness can really make a wholesome lady like myself blush." Janice hefted her large duffel bag over her shoulder as she shuffled to the front door and pulled it open.

"Wholesome, my ass," Pres admonished. "I've heard some of your phone calls to Stanley the Stallion." He laughed again.

She laughed hard. "Hey! Stylist-client confidentiality, remember?" They heard her giggling as she closed the door behind her.

"She's a character," Ric said, watching Pres gather his keys and wallet off the breakfast bar.

"You have no idea. But she's really good at her job."

"Yes, she is. You look gorgeous today. Did she pick out your outfit?" Ric came up behind Pres and wrapped his strong arms around him, nuzzling his neck.

"Yes, she did, actually. I had on jeans and a T-shirt, but she wasn't having it. Not for my first date, she said."

Ric deliciously held Pres from behind and watched him put on another custom-made, raised-hand sports watch. He grabbed his Kenneth Cole sunglasses and turned around in Ric's arms.

"All ready." He grinned.

"You have the most beautiful smile. Has anyone told you that?" Ric whispered.

"Not in a long time," Pres confessed seriously.

"You don't mind if I tell you how attractive you are to me...do you?" Ric asked before kissing Pres on his cheek.

"No. I guess not," Pres responded shyly.

"Your smile was the first thing I noticed about you when I saw you a couple months ago in the building parking lot, standing next to your driver."

"You've watched me before?" Pres asked, shocked.

"Yes. Not only once. Just this particular time is branded in my head. The sun was shining on your beautiful face as you stood beside your car. You had one hand propped up on the hood, and you were talking on your cell phone. I think you had more blond in your hair at the time because I noticed how much it glowed in the sunlight. You had on a very expensive-looking suit, and it made me want to rip it off of you. Everything except the tie...you could've kept the tie on," he whispered seductively and licked the shell of Pres's ear. "Everything about you screams style. That's what attracted me to you right away. Your physique is spectacular and well taken care of. I've seen you in the gym with your trainer. I want to be the first to let you know that the workout sessions have paid off well. You are fucking fantastic."

Ric gave Pres a big hug. He was sure Pres appreciated the description he was giving him, as he realized he probably didn't get it very often. It had to be frustrating to never see yourself after a new haircut, or dressed up for a party, or even wearing a new outfit. People take those types of things for granted.

"Thank you, Ric. That felt really good," Pres said into their hug.

"You're welcome. Come on. Let's eat. I know you are practically starving by now." Ric moved them toward the door. He let Pres lock up and prepared to take his new boyfriend to breakfast.

# Chapter Eighteen

**R**ic picked a little bistro on the oceanfront for breakfast. He was trying to be the perfect gentleman by opening and closing Pres's door and pulling out chairs for him. He hoped that Pres didn't take it the wrong way, but he was trying to be chivalrous.

Ric picked up the menu and started perusing through the selections. He didn't look up for several minutes while he made his decision.

*Yes, the T-bone and eggs over easy. Sounds good.*

Ric was smiling hard on the inside. He felt great. He was on a date with a beautiful, sweet man. It was Sunday, and he didn't have to work again until Wednesday. Things were looking up. Ric's lack of a social life had really begun to put him in a rut.

"What are you gonna have, bab—" Ric slammed his mouth shut so hard it made his teeth click. When he looked up, he saw Pres sitting quietly with his hands in his lap, his menu never touched.

*Of course, dumbass. He's not going to pick up the menu.*

"Pres. Oh man. I'm sorry. My brain just completely shut off for a minute."

*Shit, he's mad. I was insensitive.* Ric watched Pres's brow crease with anger, or was that confusion? He couldn't tell.

"Do you want me to read the menu to you?" he asked.

"Ric, calm down." Pres chuckled. "Do you think I'm mad? Do I look upset or something?"

"Well, I don't know. You look kinda…" Ric's words trailed off.

"Why are you apologizing? I was just waiting for you to make your decision before I tell you mine."

Ric let out a sigh of relief.

"Ric, I know this menu like the back of my hand. I helped make it. I come here a lot. George, the guy who owns this place, makes the best eggs Benedict I've ever tasted. His restaurant is considered to be one of Hampton Roads's hidden gems for dining."

"I'm sorry. I assumed..." Ric stopped again. He didn't know what to say. He'd thought Pres needed his help, again.

"Look, Ric. Some people think that because I'm blind that I need constant, twenty-four-hour assistance. Maybe that's why I don't date much, because people assume that I'll be their burden. Well, I'm not a burden. Anyone that I need assistance from, I pay them to do the job. I don't want to pay for a date. Or, if I do manage to get a date, I don't want to make going out with me so tiresome that the person never wants to see me again. Please don't feel like you have work to do if we go out."

"Pres, I'm sor—"

"Stop apologizing, Ric! I'm not a goddamn kid. My fucking feelings are not hurt because you can read your damn menu. I don't need you to pull my chair out for me like I'm a helpless broad, or help me decide what to eat, or cut up my food, and I sure as hell don't need you to order for me. I didn't think I was going out with my damn PA...because I sure as hell don't want to fuck my personal assistant." Pres had just managed to keep his voice to a dull roar.

Ric let out a shaky breath. He was going about this all wrong and royally fucking up this date. He couldn't blame Pres for being upset...and boy, was he looking upset right now. Ric was treating him like a baby. Pres didn't want a babysitter. He didn't want another employee. He wanted a partner, an equal.

Ric reached out and grasped Pres's trembling, unbandaged hand that now sat on top of the polished wood table. He didn't say another word. He just stroked Pres's hand for a minute hoping his touch could calm him. He thought carefully about what he was going to say next. Whatever it was going to be, it damn sure wouldn't be another apology.

"I'm being stupid, and I guess a little self-conscious, too. You are a capable man, Prescott. I saw that in you when we first met at the elevators in our building. That's why I was so attracted to you in the first place. If anyone is making this date tiresome..." Ric snorted indignantly, "...it's me right now. I'm just silently praying you're not ready to throw up your hands with me already."

**Pres's** angry eyes were still hidden behind his dark sunglasses. Ric was being so overanxious, it was driving him crazy. They hadn't been out in public for an hour, and already Ric had on the kid gloves. Pres began to doubt whether he and Ric were going to work.

Maybe if Ric wouldn't have had to rescue him that night at the club, things would be going differently. He'd been beaten up by a woman, shoved into the street, and pissed himself. *Now he's thinking poor, helpless, blind little Pres.* He'd just basically told Ric to shut the hell up with the damn apologies, and now the man was deathly quiet.

*Well, here we go. Back to square one again. No company, no companionship, and no fuckin' sex. Shit.* Pres groaned inside. *Back to cooking for my little old neighbor just so I don't eat alone every night.* He figured the date was over now since he'd had his tantrum.

Then, he felt a strong hand grip his own, interlocking his fingers. The hold tightened, and Pres released a small breath.

"Maybe dating a blind man is not something you could see yourself handling," Pres said quietly. He focused on controlling the gut-twisting ache he now felt deep inside him. *Things finally seemed brighter in my world. No more sunshine. Damn it!*

"You're wrong. Don't tell me what I can handle, Prescott. I will admit that that was stupid of me to apologize for not asking you if you wanted your menu read for you, and for trying to pacify you. But, Jesus, Pres, that was only five minutes that we've disagreed on something. Otherwise, we've been having a good time in each other's company. Are you telling me that you can't have a fucking five-minute dispute in a relationship without you wanting to bail out? Because honestly, if we do pursue this further, I'm going to fuck up some more. Not just with being a little overprotective of you, but I hear that I have some idiosyncrasies that may drive a significant other to wanna shoot me."

"Like?" Pres said, amused.

"Like," Ric drawled, "I heard that I can be a dick when I'm tired. I sometimes let my job frustrate the hell out of me, and I accidently take it out on others. As far as the little things…let's see. I drink directly out of the milk cartoon, and then I'll leave a swallow at the bottom and put it back in the fridge. I also leave my wet towel on the bathroom floor. I'll leave my bed unmade or not clean my apartment for weeks. And, oh yeah, if I throw my briefs toward the hamper and I miss, I don't worry about those motherfuckers being on the floor until laundry day."

Pres chuckled lightly.

"Mmmmm. There's that smile." Ric paused before adding, "I'm gonna screw up, baby. But, you being blind doesn't have a goddamn thing to do with what I can and can't handle." He brought Pres's hand to his lips and kissed his knuckles tenderly. "Just give us a real chance, beautiful, before you say we don't work together."

"Okay. You're right about that. I have enjoyed you very much. It's frightening how much I like you already. Guess we both have to lighten up, huh?" Pres said. He took his other hand

and placed it on top of Ric's before adding one request. "Just treat me like a man. That's all I need."

"Oh, I plan to treat you like a man, gorgeous," Ric said seductively.

Pres moaned. *Better.* He did like Ric—more than he wanted to admit right now, not wanting to jinx it. They'd had a little spat. It happens. This was already starting to feel like a relationship. Pres was still smiling when he heard the waitress approach the table.

"Have you gentleman decided on your orders?" she asked cheerfully.

He put his hand out in front of him, gesturing for Ric to go ahead and order. Ric continued to caress his hand while he spoke. "I'm going to have the steak and eggs. My steak cooked medium rare, with Heinz 57 too, please."

"And the usual for you, Mr. Vaughan?" she bubbled excitedly.

"Yes, Cindy. Thank you."

Pres felt Cindy whisk their menus off the table and walk away.

"Okay, Mr. Vaughan, you've proven your point. I was stupid for assuming. Can we forget about the other stuff and have a nice breakfast and evening?" Ric said very close to Pres's face. Pres could feel his warm, coffee-scented breath ghosting over his cheek. He turned in to press a small kiss on Ric's plump lips.

"I'd like that more than anything right now," he sighed into Ric's mouth.

"Good."

"Hey, Ric?"

"Yeah, babe?"

"Why do you need Heinz 57?"

"For flavoring for my steak. You know…so it will taste good," Ric said matter-of-factly.

"Oh, babe, I'm going to show you what your taste buds have been missing," Pres teased.

"Don't wait. Why don't you show me right now?" Ric groaned.

Ric kissed Pres right there in the restaurant, full-on tongue, teeth, and moans.

"Kissing was not what I meant. I was talking about food. But starting there is good, too." Pres laughed.

# Chapter Nineteen

They'd had a great day after the sticky wicket at breakfast. Ric was really showing him a great time, and the conversation, chemistry, and teasing banter flowed naturally. But, Pres still wanted to show Ric his independence. After walking along the beach and enjoying the ocean breeze, he asked Ric to go for a small cruise on his yacht that was docked just a few miles away.

He needed Ric to know that he could be an equal partner in this relationship. Taking control of the date would also show Ric that he didn't have to bear the responsibility of always having to show Pres a good time.

When he asked Ric to accompany him for an evening on the bay, he was met with a few seconds of silence before Ric simply said, "No."

"You don't like boats, Ric?"

"They're all right, Pres. I just don't think…uhh…ummm…I just thought…ya know. I didn't want you to go out of your way," Ric stammered.

Pres could hear more behind Ric's hesitation. But, he really wanted to show Ric a good time, so he thought he'd give it another try.

"Come on. I promise you'll have a good time."

He heard Ric let out a very quiet sigh before he responded, "If it makes you smile like that, then sure. I'll go. But don't let it inconvenience anyone. Do you have staff on there all the time or something?"

"No, they're not on there all the time, but I'd asked the captain earlier this week to have it ready to go this weekend. I was going out alone, but now I don't have to." Pres hugged Ric.

"Okay. I just want you to be careful." Ric hugged Pres tightly.

Now Pres understood. Ric thought Pres was too delicate to sail. He found himself being more amused than angry at that thought. He'd show him.

**R**ic let Pres talk him into sailing on his yacht this evening. He was not excited at all. In fact, he was damn near terrified. He never would've suspected that Pres had his own fucking yacht. Jesus. What he told Pres about boats being "all right" was not a lie. It was the water—the very large body of water surrounding them—that he hated.

While they rode the few miles to the harbor, Ric held Pres's hand. He softly caressed him and placed quick, chaste kisses on his cheek. Pres looked so beautiful, and he smelled so fucking good. Ric silently wished they could just go back to one or the other's place and finish this date correctly. It was too late to change it now, though, as the taxi parked in the mostly empty parking lot adjacent to the dock.

Ric looked around at the view. It was really nice. The sun was slowly setting over the horizon. The vibrant orange ball sat amid beautiful streaks of blue, purple, and red. Despite his insecurity of the ocean, the water looked so peaceful and serene. It was as if the ocean, and its inhabitants, was its own entity, and it slept peacefully until it was disturbed by man's vessels, rigs…and yachts. When you woke the peaceful ocean from its slumber, that's when it showed its power. Ric desperately did not want to see that power again.

Ric closed his eyes and took a calming breath. He had to stop thinking like that. The negative thoughts would only make him more nervous, and Prescott was too insightful not to pick up on it immediately. He just needed to relax and trust that Pres would remain safe in his arms.

Ric leaned in close to Pres and whispered a detailed description of the sunset in his ear, not forgetting to lick and caress his earlobe in between descriptions of every color.

"We can do more of this on the water. Come on. Cap's waiting." Pres gave him a slow, sexy kiss on his mouth before exiting the cab.

The yacht's name, *Sees the Day*, was written elegantly in black on the lower part of the stern. The fifty-foot motor yacht was cloud white with a cobalt-blue boot stripe, and she was a beauty. It wasn't a flauntation of wealth. It was tasteful in size, classy, sleek, and sexy… It was Prescott Vaughan. Ric grinned broadly.

As they walked, he took Pres's fingertips and put them to his lips, showing him that he was smiling and liking what he saw. The smile Pres gave him in return was Kodak perfect.

Ric could see the captain giving them a slight salute from the raised pilothouse. Two men in starched white uniforms greeted them as "Mr. Vaughan and his guest" as they boarded portside. Ric stood back and let Pres greet some of his staff as they made their way to the spacious salon inside. It was bright and very tastefully decorated with dark brown leather furniture. The fully stocked bar was at the far side, in the corner, adjacent to the fifty-inch television mounted on the one solid wall. The rest of the sidings were windows to gaze from. Ric ran his hand along the polished cherry wood-grain table.

Pres talked to a young guy in a white coat and checkered cotton pants, whom Ric figured must be the chef, because Pres was questioning him about the evening's menu and inputting a few ideas of his own. Ric decided to give them privacy and looked out the window at the sparse furniture on the stern instead. The three white high-backed deck chairs sat behind a table large enough for dining comfortably. Ric immediately noticed that the stern of the boat was void of any guardrails. He made a mental note to stay far away from there.

"Ric," Pres called out after the chef left to return to the small galley below.

"Right here, babe."

"So, what do you think?" Pres came up behind him and wrapped him in tight arms. It was nice to feel strong arms securing him right now.

"It's beautiful. It suits you. It's not too big, and it's not too small… It's perfect. Like you," Ric said.

"I'm glad you like it. Why don't you come down to the master stateroom with me? I want to put on my trunks and get comfortable before dinner. I have an extra pair for you too," Pres said against his neck.

"Trunks…for what?" he asked.

"Just to get comfortable, enjoy the view, the weather, ya know. We can eat out back and talk. I'd love to get to know more about Dr. Rickson Edwards." Pres ground his growing erection into him and slowly licked his way down his neck.

Ric completely forgot what he was worried about and let himself feel what Pres had to offer. He turned around in Pres's toned arms, gripped the back of his neck, and took over the kiss. He loved Pres's mouth. His lips were so soft and supple.

Pres wrapped him up tighter and kissed him back with fervor. Ric hadn't felt this passion and urgency from him yet, and he loved it. He lowered his hands and gripped two round, firm cheeks—man's cheeks. He squeezed hard, and swallowed the moan Pres released into his mouth.

"Mmm. I like that. Like your hands on me," Pres groaned, his voice low and thick with lust.

"You do? Good, because I love touching you. Need to touch you, baby." Ric spoke before licking the inside of Pres's mouth.

He felt Pres pull back, and Ric sucked in a much-needed breath and opened his eyes. Pres still had his sunglasses on, so Ric removed them and set them on the nearest surface. "Look at me. You can see me."

Pres brought his hands up to Ric's face. He started at the top of his forehead and slowly worked his way down to his scratchy chin, his five-o'clock shadow already present. Pres touched him in places that many past lovers never did. He touched his brow and his eyelids, gently fingering his long lashes. Pres leaned in and kissed his eyes. Ric felt his soft, warm tongue on his eyelids, and it made his cock weep with pre-come, it was so fucking sexy.

Pres ran his fingers through his wavy hair to the base of his neck, stopping only briefly to massage at the nape before bringing his hands back around to his cheeks. His cheekbones were raised slightly because of the smile he wore whenever this beautiful creature looked at him...truly looked at him.

"What are you smiling about?" Pres purred, his hot breath scorching the skin on Ric's face.

"You. You make me smile." Ric cupped Pres's face and returned some of the same tender gestures Pres was doing to him.

"You make me smile too, Sunshine. It's something I haven't done in so damn long," Pres confessed.

"Mmmm. Com'ere," Ric said. His emotions were all over the place. He felt so much for Pres at that very moment that he didn't know how to put it into words, so he didn't. *Damn. How can I feel like this already?* He let his forehead rest on Pres's and rocked them back and forth in a slow dance, just relishing the joy of finding each other.

They kissed, and rocked, and moaned so long that Ric didn't feel the captain pull away from the dock and coast smoothly into the bay. He was navigating them toward the departing sun and deeper into the Atlantic. He held Pres in his arms and kissed the man until all the tension and anxiety about being out on the ocean faded.

# Chapter Twenty

**P**res felt like he was in a bear hug while being kissed. Ric felt so wound up that Pres thought maybe he'd get sick if he didn't relax.

*I'll relax him.*

"Come downstairs with me now." Pres's voice sounded deep and raw with desire. He needed this man like he needed his next breath.

"Okay," Ric breathed heavily.

Pres led them down the narrow stairway into his large stateroom. The room was equipped with a gorgeous king-sized bed that took up most of the middle of the room. Along the wall were two midsized burgundy side-by-side dressers. The opposite wall held another fifty-inch flat screen television that was already turned on to the Weather Channel.

Pres didn't waste time. He stripped off his shirt and tank top and tossed them in the direction of the bathroom. He spun Ric around in his arms and attacked his mouth.

"Need to feel you, Sunshine. I can't wait. I have to know what you feel like. Fuck me, baby. Oh God. Please fuck me," Pres begged.

Ric took over at hearing Pres's needy moans. He pulled Pres to the bed, but laid him gently atop the burgundy-and-gold comforter.

"Need you too, so damn much, more than I've needed anyone in a very long time," Ric confessed to him. "But, I want to feel you inside of me, Pres. Claiming me. Making me yours."

Ric ground their still-confined erections together, making Pres gasp at the contact and his request. He wanted Pres to top him. Pres suddenly felt his nerves kick into high gear. His few encounters with other men were mostly kissing, dry humping, and jerking off. Pres had never actually fucked a man before, nor had he been fucked. Ric was so damn large and alpha male, Pres just assumed that he'd be the bottom.

After shutting down his nervous stomach, Pres thought about what it would be like to fuck this big, hulking man, overpower him, and make him come. He thought about shoving his dick inside Ric and making him scream out his name. He'd push in balls deep and grind his tight ass until Ric blessed whatever God he worshipped. Pres's dick jerked and leaked in his shorts.

"Fuuuck," he groaned. His internal fantasy needed to be made a reality, right fucking now.

Pres had lost his true self after his fiancée walked out on him. He'd become someone he despised...a needy man. He let his disability change him, change who he truly was. He'd convinced himself that because he was blind, he'd have to settle for whomever was willing to give him a chance, and therefore he'd let Vikki walk all over him. Being with Ric made Pres's dominant side reappear with a vengeance for being tucked away so long.

Ric continued to deliciously grind and writhe on top of him, and Pres reached inside of Ric's slack jeans and grabbed a handful of his lightly furred ass. It felt overwhelmingly erotic. Ric turned him on so damn much. He let one unbandaged hand graze along Ric's seam and hissed between clenched teeth when Ric pushed his ass out more, craving a deeper touch. Pres didn't hesitate to give it to him.

Pres licked and gnawed at Ric's throat as he unbuttoned Ric's pants and inched them down over his ass. Ric was grinding him into the mattress, and he bathed in the thoughts that his touch was making Ric lose himself. Having been with women all these years, Pres had forgotten the strength and feel of a man when in ecstasy. He admitted to himself right then that he'd missed that feeling.

"Pleeease," Ric whispered.

Pres spread Ric's cheeks and inched one finger down his hot seam until he got to that tight star.

"Oh fuck!" Ric bucked. "More, please."

"Shhh. I got you, Sunshine," Pres whispered back. He applied more pressure this time, feeling the tight bud quiver and dance under his fingertip. *Holy fuck. That's hot.*

Pres rubbed and massaged Ric's outer rim until the man began to growl and bite at Pres's cheek and lips.

"In. Fucking put it in," Ric spat while trying to impale himself on Pres's finger.

"Don't we need lube first, babe?" Pres questioned. He was not an expert on anal fucking, by far. But, he'd watched enough porn in college and remembered the man using lube before fucking a woman in her ass.

Ric grabbed Pres's hand and sucked two fingers into his hot mouth. Pres's mouth formed a perfect *O* as Ric tongued in between his fingers. Ric moaned and sucked until the two digits were nice and wet.

"Fuck me with your fingers, baby. Get me ready, fast."

Pres moved his wet hand to Ric's hungry hole, then timidly pushed one fingertip in and waited for his reaction.

"More. More, Pres. Don't be afraid. You're not gonna hurt me. I use a dildo all the time," Ric assured him.

Flashes of light danced behind Pres's closed eyes at the image of Ric fucking himself with a dildo, and that was all he needed. He reversed their positions, flipping Ric onto his stomach and working his way on top of him, which was not as easy as it sounded, but Pres was operating on pure erotic adrenaline. He felt for the top drawer of the nightstand, pulled out the Vaseline he used when he jerked off, and made quick work of greasing up his fingers.

Pres was nestled snugly between Ric's muscular thighs. He felt the man spread his legs like a wanton slut and thrust his ass up for the taking. Pres's senses were flooded with Ric's masculine, spicy-musky scent. It made him want to forget about the prep and mount him right then and there.

Instead, Pres knelt down and licked the furry globes while pushing one finger in to the first knuckle. Ric's guttural moan vibrated through his back, and Pres could feel it under his tongue. He rotated his finger in and out, just like he remembered in the flick. He assumed it was right because Ric's legs began to tremble.

He gave Ric what he needed. He pushed his finger all the way inside him, pegging his gland on the first try, and felt Ric hiss and arch his back. Pres pumped his ass again and again, wanting to hear Ric call his name and beg for his cock.

"Yeah, fuck, right there. Fuck, right there," Ric yelled.

Pres knew there was some deckhand wondering what the hell Pres was doing to his guest, but it only made him smile and push his finger in even deeper. He was glad he hadn't shut the windows first. He wanted Ric's cries to ricochet off the waves and crash against the surf.

"Like that, honey? Is that what you need?" Pres licked and sucked, making pretty red marks on Ric's perfect ass while he finger-fucked him. Though he couldn't see them, the idea of Ric wearing his passion marks was enough for him.

Ric gripped the sheets and thrust his ass back into Pres's hand, shamelessly taking what he needed. Pres had reduced him to a whimpering, blubbering mess on his wide bed. He listened to Ric's unintelligible sentences. Ric mewled and growled like a sexy tiger, and Pres heard him twisting and pounding his fist into the comforter.

"I know. Gonna give you more right now. Gonna spread you open and give you my cock," Pres whispered in Ric's ear. He sucked his earlobe, never pulling his fingers out. One, two, three fingers inside Ric's tight channel had Pres clenching his teeth in concentration of not coming all over himself.

Pres had his entire body covering Ric's from head to toe, needing the full body contact. His forearm was wrapped around the front of Ric's chest as he pressed his face into the back of his neck. He slowed his movements and ground his hips in time with his three fingers still stretching Ric's ass.

"I'm ready, Pres. Fuck, I'm ready. That's enough. Fill me up, baby. Need you to fuck me, now," Ric cried. He stopped meeting Pres's thrusts, and he felt Ric's body fully relax and melt into the soft blanket.

Pres slowly removed his fingers, grabbed a generous amount of Vaseline, and spread it down the length of his cock. "Fuuuuck," he moaned, gripping the base of his dick hard. Pres didn't think he'd ever been that damn hard or so ready to fuck in his life. He wanted to last and make it good for Ric. He remembered his man hadn't been fucked with an actual throbbing cock in over two years. Pres felt the pressure, but he'd make it good for Ric no matter what.

He pushed the aching head of his cock inside Ric's beautiful body and was met with the tightest squeezing sensation he'd ever felt around his dick. *Oh my God, this is too fucking much.* It would take every ounce of willpower Pres had not to blow his load as soon as he sank halfway in. Ric's ass was hot, and tighter than a virgin on her wedding night.

**R**ic couldn't believe how Pres was making him feel. The man's fingers were magic. He'd stroked Ric's prostate so many times that his eyes had rolled into the back of his head and his mouth hung open. He'd thought he'd need to give Pres some coaching, but he was terribly mistaken. The man had him humping the bed and crying to be fucked in a matter of minutes.

For some bizarre reason, the fact that Pres couldn't see him and operated solely on Ric's physical reactions had his cock leaking even more. *This is insane.* It was fascinating that Prescott could so easily anticipate what his body wanted.

Ric thought he may have been having an out-of-body experience. He couldn't talk, he couldn't move, all he could do was wait and see what Pres was going to do to him next. Pres aggressively massaged his ass while rubbing his slippery dick up and down his seam.

Then he felt it. Pres's bulbous head was pressing against his well-lubed hole. Too many feelings attacked all his senses at once. Pres's thick bicep wrapped around his throat, his hot breath on his neck, his sweaty forehead pressed against the back of his head all made Ric swoon like a cheerleader getting ready to get fucked by the captain of the football team.

"Babe," was all he'd managed to get out when Pres's head breached his outer ring.

It went in easily thanks to the careful preparation. Pres slowly rocked his sexy hips back and forth, not giving him another inch, letting Ric get used to the feeling.

"Don't you fucking tease me, Prescott," Ric growled.

"Motherfucker," Pres hissed in his ear and pushed all the way in, in one long, smooth stroke.

"Augh. Fuck!" Ric yelled. His screams weren't cries of pain. They were vocal releases of unadulterated pleasure.

Pres's balls were cradled between Ric's thighs, and he felt Pres heave in a few breaths before willing himself to move. He pulled out almost to the tip and drove back in deep again.

"Oh, honey, you are tight. Jesus. Squeezing my cock so fucking good."

Ric instantly liked that Pres loved to talk dirty, and his body responded beautifully to every word he moaned into his head.

"So full, baby," Ric said. "Give it to me. I'm ready. Fuck me, Pres. Fuck me hard. Want to still feel you tomorrow."

Pres didn't wait for another invitation. He reamed Ric's ass until he was begging for Pres to make him come.

Ric was cursing and spurring him on. He could feel Pres working double time on not shooting first, his brow clenched with concentration.

"Fuck me. Fuck me. Fuck me," Ric hollered in between Pres's hard, deep thrusts. He lifted his ass even higher and jerked his dick in time with Pres's pumping. *Make me come, you gorgeous fucker.*

Pres abruptly stopped his thrusting without warning, and Ric couldn't help but growl at the too-sudden cease of pleasure. Pres pulled out of Ric's needy channel, and Ric immediately reached back and grasped at his hips, scratching Pres's skin as he tried to pull him back inside of him.

"You bad boy," Pres teased Ric as he manipulated him to turn back over onto his back, "scratching me up like that. You love my cock that much, honey? Can't wait for me to fuck you, huh?" Pres settled himself back on top of Ric and pulled one heavy leg up onto his shoulder, opening him up nice and wide. "Want you to watch me come in you. Want to kiss you hard when you scream my name."

Pres positioned his cock and pushed back in to the base. "Augh, fuck! Not gonna last much longer, want you to come with me."

"Yes. Need to come, now. Fuck. Make me come, Pres. Make me come so hard," Ric groaned.

"Jerk that thick cock for me while I fuck you," Pres ordered.

Pres piston-fucked Ric's ass until he felt Pres's sweat hitting him on his chest. Pres dropped down and shoved his tongue deep into Ric's open mouth, forcing his submission. Ric's fist flew up and down on his own cock, wrestling with the urgency of wanting to come and wanting to keep being fucked.

He felt Pres thrust in until his balls were snug against his tight, muscular ass and ground against him viciously.

"Come now, Ric."

"Pres! I'm fuckin' coming! Augghhh. Fuuuucckk!" Ric yelled into Pres's mouth and sucked his tongue hard as he shot his thick load all over his hand, chest, and his lover.

Pres managed to thrust in one, two, three more times and stilled his hips deep inside as he released rope after rope of his seed into Ric's ass. "Fuuuuuck, Ric," Pres groaned low and deep in his throat, his body jerking spastically with his orgasm.

Ric caught Pres's weight as his arms gave out on him. He cradled him under his chin and rubbed drowsy circles in the center of his sweaty back while he caught his breath.

"Jesus. That was like nothing I've ever felt before." Pres breathed heavily

"It was wonderful, baby. Just what I've waited for, for so long." Ric kissed the top of Pres's head. "Now, I need sleep," he yawned.

"Oh no you don't. I'm ready for dinner." Pres licked Ric's ear and rubbed his cheek against the side of his sweaty face.

"Come on. Just half an hour, tops." Ric whined like a spoiled child. "Baby, you can't fuck me like that and expect me not to go to sleep… I'm a man…remember?"

"Yes, I can fuck you like that and then tell you to get your ass up and come on, let's eat. I'm starved." Pres let his sated dick slide easily out of Ric's still-clenching hole.

Ric hissed at the odd sensation.

"You okay, honey?" Pres asked with concern.

"Yeah. Fine," Ric growled. "Fucking tired as hell, though. I just got rode like Seabiscuit, and now I'm being kicked out of this warm, comfortable bed for no good reason." Ric pushed Pres playfully in his chest, telling him to get off him, then bitched and griped all the way to the bathroom.

He could hear Pres laughing hysterically at his expense before yelling through the closed bathroom door, "Oh, my big, strong doctor gets grumpy if he doesn't get his nap after sex!" Pres used his best baby voice.

Ric was glad Pres couldn't see him, because he was doing everything he could to stifle his laugh. He was falling for this man fast, and he liked it.

# YOU CAN SEE ME

# Chapter Twenty-One

Finally, Ric was loosened up. After the lovemaking, he appeared not to have a worry in the world…until they got back on the upper deck. Pres had no idea why the man was so wound up over being on his yacht. Why live in a city surrounded by a beautiful, vast ocean, and littered with countless bays and rivers, if you didn't like water? It made no sense to Pres, and he couldn't fathom it. He just figured it was Sunshine being his usual overprotective self and thinking Pres wouldn't be safe.

*I'll show him… Oh, this is going to be so funny.*

They were sitting outside at the large white marble table on the boat's stern as the staff placed a vast seafood feast in front of them. Ric had on a spare pair of Pres's trunks and a white tank top. They almost matched, except his trunks were blue and Ric's were red with large white strips weaving an intricate pattern around his groin.

The chef prepared everything wonderfully, and they ate comfortably. The water was peaceful, and the air was crisp and salty, just like he liked it. He bet the water was seasonally warm too. The conversation was wonderful, of course. He discovered even more of Ric's sense of humor. The man could be downright hilarious. Pres was still cracking up at Ric making fun of the cougars he worked with, when the chef personally brought out their desserts.

"Mr. Vaughan, if I may be so bold, it's such a pleasure to hear you laugh, *cher*," his chef commented in his rich French accent.

Pres blushed hard. He was sure the whole damn boat knew why he was so happy, but he thanked the chef for the compliment and the wonderful meal. He didn't think he could eat another bite after the succulent oysters Rockefeller, shrimp-and-lobster bisque, filet mignon, and braised seafood with vegetable noodles. However, the smell of Chef's famous chocolate lava cake was making his mouth water. It would be almost a sin to refuse it.

"Chef, you can retire for the evening...but leave the dessert." Pres laughed again when Chef swatted him on his shoulder. He knew the chef was a petite Frenchman, but he'd never tried to touch the man or ask what he looked like. He was only needed for his brilliant cooking skills, and Pres adored French-influenced food.

Pres's thoughts went back to his staff and if they were wondering what the heck was going on with him getting down and dirty with a man now—but to be honest, he didn't give a damn what they thought. They worked for him. It wasn't like any of his staff came by to keep him company on any given night. It wasn't like Cap invited Pres to his every-other-weekend barbecues the man hosted, followed by whatever sports event was on television that afternoon. Pres didn't take it as hard as he used to, but he wasn't going to worry about their opinions of him or his chosen company.

"Of course, sir. Enjoy your evening." After the chef's retreat, Pres and Ric were alone to share the delicious dessert.

"Open up, Sunshine." Pres scooped up a generous helping of the cake and some of its warm, gooey chocolate center and aimed it toward Ric's mouth. He felt Ric close his soft lips over the prongs of the fork before he eased it out slowly.

"Mmmm. Damn, that's good," Ric moaned.

Pres's dick jerked at the erotic sound. *Oh my God.*

"You got chocolate on my chin, handsome. Fix it," Ric purred.

"My pleasure." Pres could feel Ric's closeness. The man was practically sitting on his lap on the soft, cushion-covered bench they shared. He cupped the back of Ric's neck and pulled him to him until his lips met his. He didn't slip his tongue inside Ric's eagerly parted lips. Instead, he gently licked the rich chocolate off his lips and chin. Pres felt Ric's panting, warm breath as he continued to nibble his way to Ric's earlobe. Ric chuckled and returned Pres's kisses, chasing his mouth and silky tongue.

"Why do you call me Sunshine, baby? I gotta know. It sounds..." Ric trailed off when Pres stopped his kisses.

Pres's face stayed buried in Ric's warm neck. He tried to still his racing heart as he gauged his answer carefully. *Please let him understand.*

"You're a ray of bright light in my very dark world, Ric. It's like when I step outside and take my sunglasses off to let the sun shine on my face. It gets a little lighter in here." Pres gently tapped his pointer finger against his temple. "When I'm in my office...there's no light. When I'm in my bedroom alone...there's no light. When I sit in my kitchen, eating my very carefully prepared meal—for one—there's no light. But, when I'm around you, wrapped in your arms, kissing you, laughing with you, making love to you, everything's so goddamn bright...like sunshine," Pres whispered.

"Oh baby, I understand. You have no idea how you just made me feel," Ric confessed, turning his face towards Pres's and nuzzling him out of his neck.

"I'm not freaking you out?" Pres flushed, slightly embarrassed at his Hallmark confession.

"No. I'm not easily freaked out."

"Really?"

"No, I'm not. You wanna hear what type of shit freaks me out? One time I had to remove a completely consumed ten-inch vibrator out of the vagina of a four-hundred-pound woman in the ER—now that freaked me the fuck out." Ric shivered violently.

Pres laughed harder than he'd ever laughed in his life. *Sunshine.*

After sipping on after-dinner cordials, Ric held his man in his arms and gazed up at the millions of stars while the boat swayed on the dark water. It was peaceful, he had to confess. His eyes were drifting lazily when he felt Pres wiggle his way out of his embrace. He stood and stretched like a lazy lion, making Ric smile and shake his head at him. Pres began to move from around the table to the edge of the stern, and Ric felt his heart kick up a notch...or a thousand notches.

"Hey, baby. Where you going?" Ric was already rising from his reclining position.

"Nowhere," Pres replied lazily as he stumbled a little, moving closer and closer to the edge of the yacht that dropped off into the now-pitch-black ocean.

Ric watched Pres fumble over his feet again. He had only had two drinks. Ric knew he wasn't drunk. He frowned. *Maybe he's sleepwalking. Fuck.*

"Pres, baby, watch where you're goi—"

Ric's words were cut off as he watched Pres take five more quick steps and flail his arms wildly before falling headfirst into the dark water.

"Pressss!" Ric shouted to the top of his lungs as he lunged to the rear of the boat where Pres had fallen in. He looked frantically around the disturbed water. Pres didn't resurface. "Help! Someone, help! Please! Prescott fell in!"

Ric's heart was trying to burst through his chest and leap into the dismal water to search for his love. He was yelling so loud for assistance that his head throbbed with an instant migraine.

"Somebody, help me!" Rick wanted to jump in and swim all the way to the bottom and grab Pres himself. But there was one big fucking problem with his rescue plan.

Ric couldn't swim.

He stood there, paralyzed with fear of the ocean. Hell, Ric couldn't even doggy-paddle, a result of having stayed away from any water that was over one foot deep. Every second that went by that Pres didn't resurface felt like hours.

"Where is everyone?" Ric shouted as he continued to look down into the dreary mass of water. It seemed to be taunting him, teasing him, daring him to come inside. The drop was over eight feet. Ric's entire body shook with horrific fear. "Pres! Pres! Pres! Someone help!"

Ric didn't want to, but he was gonna have to take his eyes off the water and run to get help. As soon as he turned around, he ran smack into the captain, his velocity knocking the man to the cold deck.

Ric didn't have time for apologies. He yanked the thin man up by his arms. "Help him, help him, please! He fell in! I can't swim! Just help him!" Ric practically pushed the man to the edge, would've probably pushed him in if the captain hadn't yelled at Ric to calm down.

"He's drowning! He's been under for almost a full minute!" Ric shouted, his tears falling rapidly down his face. He was completely baffled by the captain's composure. Then Ric registered that there was a slight look of humor on the man's pale face.

*What the fuck?*

"I'm sorry, but I think Mr. Vaughan is playing a joke on you," the captain said softly as he wedged his bruised arms out of Ric's death grip. "Obviously, not a very funny joke."

"What? No, he fell. I saw him. He fell right here."

Ric ran back and pointed over into the water at the precise place Pres had fallen and was stunned into silence at the sight he saw. Pres was casually floating on his back as if he were in a resort hotel swimming pool in the middle of the afternoon.

"What the fu...?" Ric didn't even finish his sentence as he watched Pres casually backstroke around the boat in the dark water.

"Mr. Vaughan can hold his breath for almost three minutes and swim like a dolphin. I'm sorry he did that to you, but he always dives off the back end. One time I actually drifted several miles away from him before I realized he'd gone for one of his impromptu swims. He really thinks it's funny. Are you all right, sir?"

"I...I... He l-l-looked like he tripped," Ric stuttered in complete awe of the whole situation. His tears were still falling, and his body shook against his will. Or was he now shaking with rage? *Why would he do that to me? Why? Who does that to someone?*

"Mr. Vaughan, I think you better get back up here. You may have a little problem," the captain yelled over the side.

Ric watched Pres drop his legs under the water and easily navigate back toward the end of the yacht and pull his soaking wet body up the ladder.

"Hey, Sunshine!" Pres chuckled while grinning like a Cheshire cat. He was completely and utterly oblivious to Ric's scowl and his tear-streaked cheeks.

"I'll just leave you two alone," the captain stated while making a very safe and hasty retreat.

"Why didn't you join me, honey? The water is fabulous." Pres grinned wider.

"Have you lost your fucking mind? What the hell is wrong with you? Do you have the slightest fucking idea what I just went through right now?" Ric bellowed, hoping he could keep his hands from around Pres's neck.

He'd never gone from relaxed, to excited, to bone-chilled fear, to rage all in a matter of minutes. His mind vibrated with contained heat. He was so damn angry, his body temperature had to be a sweltering one hundred and fifty degrees.

"Ric, what's wrong? I was only playing around. You do know I can swim, right?"

*How the hell would I know that?*

"Why would I have a fully staffed yacht and live five minutes from the beach if I couldn't swim?"

To Pres that probably seemed like the obvious thing to assume, but Ric was a surgeon…he didn't assume things. Anyway, Pres was blind, and he'd flailed his arms before he went over.

"Why'd you make that fucking show of falling? Why didn't you just dive in?" Ric spit out angrily. He knocked Pres's arms down when he tried to reach out for him. He must have hit Pres a little harder than he'd intended because he immediately saw his concerned demeanor change to something that resembled sorrow and fear.

"Sunshine, I'm s-s-sorry," Pres stammered. "I guess I didn't really think. I thought you'd feel more relaxed if you knew I could swim and take care of myself."

"That's bullshit. Who the fuck fakes a man overboard! How the hell would that make me calm?" Ric fumed. He had to get off this boat. He was feeling too out of control, and the water all around him was threatening to make him lose his nice dinner. "You wanna play Russian roulette with your life, fine. Do it without me around. I don't have the stomach for these types of near-death games you like to play, Prescott."

If Pres got his jollies by fighting in bars, scrapping with massive bouncers, and jumping off the back of yachts in the middle of the night into shark-infested waters, then Ric felt he was with the wrong guy. He was too damn old to play childish games. He wasn't trying to fall in love with Ashton Kutcher, where he'd go through the relationship getting punked all the time. As bad as it was going to hurt, he'd rather take his loss and mend his broken heart over time rather than go through losing a lover to the hands of death…again.

# Chapter Twenty-Two

Ric couldn't get off the yacht fast enough. He'd locked himself in the guest room until the captain docked. Pres waited for him to open the door, but as soon as he did, Ric's words stopped him in his tracks before he could utter another apology.

"I thought I could, but I just can't do this. I won't watch you kill yourself, Pres." Ric moved quickly past him.

"W-w-what? Kill myself? Ric, I would never…" Pres stuttered, completely baffled by Ric's comment.

"Bye, Prescott."

With those stinging words hanging in the air, Ric left. Pres gripped the railing as he listened to Ric's heavy but determined footsteps walk up the dock. An engine came to life and faded as it got farther away…taking his light away from him.

*Not again. God. Not alone again.* The darkness came fast, and Pres shivered at the coldness of it.

Pres's head was foggy and disoriented when he felt strong hands lift him off the floor.

When had he fallen?

"Ric?" He grasped at the hands on his shoulders.

"No, *cher*. He's gone." His chef helped him to stand. "Come on, sir. Let's get you to your room. You've been lying here for almost six hours. I thought to give you a little space, but it's time for you to get up. I'll help you."

Chef led Pres to his stateroom and helped his limp, tired body into his freshly made bed. He stayed with him while Pres cried into the pillows.

"What did I do? I didn't know," he moaned painfully. "I didn't know he hated jokes so much."

"Oh, *cher*. I don't think he hates jokes. He liked to laugh too much to hate jokes. I think he has a phobia of the ocean. The captain said he was frantic he couldn't jump in when he thought you were drowning, because he can't swim," his chef informed him.

"What have I done?" Pres whispered into the large room.

"You didn't know. You were just having some fun with him. Maybe he had a family member or a friend that drowned, or perhaps even a boating accident. Just give him some time, *cher*. He'll come around. I watched him while you were together. He's crazy about you. You just frightened him, is all. Let him calm down, and then talk to him. You'll see."

After countless unanswered calls to Ric, Pres decided to stay on his yacht for the rest of the week. He didn't leave the bed. The chef would bring him healthy dishes, but he'd only take a few bites. The staff was going to be off for the upcoming weekend, and he had a restaurant to critique in Roanoke the following Monday. He couldn't hide any longer.

# Chapter Twenty-Three

As soon as Pres stepped off the elevator onto his floor, Ric's spicy scent hit him hard. His knees buckled at the intensity of the pain in his heart. He'd most likely just missed him. He'd been telling himself over and over that Ric would stop overreacting and forgive him. He and Ric had been on an amazing date, shared meals, shared laughs…and made passionate love. There was no way it could end like this.

It'd been two weeks since Ric dropped him like a bad habit. Pres left more messages than he wanted to admit to, apologizing over and over for his stupid joke. He'd even apologized for his insensitivity if Ric had lost a loved one to drowning and Pres accidently dredged up painful memories. On another message, he swore he wasn't mocking Ric because he couldn't swim—he simply didn't know. He begged for Ric to pick up and give him a chance to explain, but he never did. After message number twenty-five, the computer-generated voice told him Ric's mailbox was full. Ric didn't return a single message.

When Pres came home one evening last week, he stepped inside his entryway and heard the sound of bubble wrap pop under his feet. He bent down and picked up the thin envelope with the small square of bubble wrap taped to it. He knew right away it was from his Ric…who else? His heart leapt at the possibility of having his light back.

Thank God his maid was still there because he immediately had her open the letter to read to him. He didn't care how personal or private it was. He had to know, now.

She told him it was a copy of Ric's negative HIV test results, and nothing else. Pres's mouth dropped open and his fingers shook with sadness when he took the single piece of paper back from her.

At first his brow creased with confusion. Then he remembered they'd made love without protection. Pres had filled Ric with his life's seed without a second thought. This was the final straw, the last nail in the coffin. Ric was saying he was done with him, but he still had to do what was responsible. Maybe Ric was the one who was worried, since he thought Pres was so careless.

The next week, Pres spent hours preparing his famous salmon with orange fennel sauce. Unfortunately, he had to leave it on Ric's doorstep when he refused to answer the door. Attached was a copy of his negative test results and a note saying: "I still owe you this meal. Please enjoy. I'm thinking of you."

Ric still didn't call. It killed Pres just a little bit more every night as he waited in the dark for the phone to ring or for a knock at his door. He imagined Ric coming to him in the middle of the night—because that's the time he thought about Ric the most—and kissing away his hurt.

It was Friday night, and Pres was coming up from the bar in their building when he got off the elevator and was again attacked by Ric's scent. It was after eleven at night, so Ric had to have just gotten off a shift at the hospital.

With four drinks coursing through his bloodstream, Pres was feeling pretty brave. He bypassed his door and counted down to the fourth door on the right and stopped. He poised his hand to knock but froze.

He dropped his forehead to the cold door and laid both palms flat against the smooth surface. After several minutes, he heard footsteps moving around inside.

With newfound energy to come face-to-face with Ric again, he tapped gently. The steps got closer and stopped right at the door...but it didn't open. He figured Ric could either see him through the peephole or just knew it was him and didn't open the door.

"Please open the door." Pres meant to ask boldly, but it came out as a mere whimper. "I'll give anything if you'll just open the door and talk to me, honey." Pres spoke quietly.

He waited a minute. No movement. No reply.

He huffed with frustration. "I swear. I never meant to hurt you, or scare you. I admit it was stupid, but come on," he said, building confidence. "Can't you get upset and talk about what the problem is instead of just walking away? You begged me to not quit on us so fast and to give this a chance, but at my first mistake, you storm off."

Pres was getting worked up, and he checked his tone when he heard one of his neighbors' doors open and close again.

"You at least owe me the chance to apologize face-to-face."

He waited. No movement. No reply.

Pres was suddenly hit with the realization that Ric never wanted to see him again. He sucked in a deep breath as an agonizing wail threatened to break through his chest and retch out of his mouth. The tears fell silently. His body shook with the sobs. He didn't care who may have been listening now. He was heartbroken, and he wasn't handling it well. That short week with Ric was the happiest he'd been since his accident. How was he supposed to go back now? Back to lonely dinners, quiet rooms, solo trips to the bar...back to total darkness.

*God, please.*

"I swear on everything that I don't have a death wish. If I kill myself, then I'm taking myself away from you. I'd never choose to do that." Pres waited. Still no reply. "How could you do this? You asked me to open up, and I did. You said you wouldn't hurt me. What do you call this? You know I didn't mean to hurt you, Ric. Just give me a chance to fix it. Please," he whispered into the crack of the door.

This was it. Either Ric truly wanted him or not. It was now or never.

Pres put his lips right up against the doorjamb and spoke in a hushed, desperate tone. "Sunshine, please. You're the only thing in this world I can see...I'm begging you. Please open this door and let me back in. Let me keep falling in love with you." He held his breath.

After fifteen torturous minutes, Pres heard Ric's footsteps walking away from the door. His heart seized in his chest, and for a minute, he thought he might be having a heart attack. He squeezed his eyes shut and tried to will his head to stop pounding. He kept his forehead pressed to the door, still desperate to hear any movement inside the condo. His right hand that Ric had cared for and stitched tenderly stroked the surface of the door. After countless more minutes, he accepted defeat. Ric wasn't going to let him in...not now...not ever.

He slowly made his way back to his apartment. Josey met him at the door, surely needing to go for a walk by now, but Pres was too drained. "Just go on the floor, boy," he groaned on his way past his kitchen.

He shucked his clothes, went to his pantry, grabbed a bottle of vodka, and closed himself in his bedroom. Typically he'd turn on the lights in his home, just because, but not tonight. *Why fuckin' bother?*

"Fuck."

Ric dropped his exhausted body onto his bed and let his heart bleed for the desperate man at his front door. God knows he wanted to open that door so badly. But every time he got ready to turn the handle, he saw Pres's arms flailing wildly before splashing into the water. *That sound.* The same fucking sound Aaron made when he fell in.

Damn, he wanted to yank that door off the hinges and pull the pleading man into his arms…but he just couldn't. He couldn't go through life being scared for Pres's safety. He was reckless. Ric should've known he lived a little too carefree when their building's fire alarm went off and the man barely bothered to get out of bed.

Maybe Ric's job had him a little more paranoid than the average person should be. As an ER trauma surgeon, he'd seen it all. Gunshot victims, car accidents, boat accidents, drownings, stabbings, bar brawls gone terribly wrong, and that didn't even include the diseases and ailments of older patients. It was always the careless young ones who were his worst trauma cases, many of them under thirty and never making it out of the operating room, leaving their families torn and grieving forever.

"Pres," he whispered painfully, "I just can't watch you die like I did Aaron. I wouldn't survive this time, baby." Ric would rather be alone the rest of his life than suffer like that again. However, the pain he was feeling now, by leaving Prescott on his doorstep begging for light, was killing him slowly.

Ric tried to rest, but he hadn't been able to acquire more than two to three hours of sleep a night. The chief had taken him off the surgery schedule until he got his shit together. Ric was actually shaking with fatigue in the operating room. There was no way he could cut into someone's body with unsteady hands.

It was two in the morning, and again, he was restless. Ric dragged himself off his unmade bed and went to his refrigerator. There it was. The leftover salmon dish Pres had made for him. It was delicious. He'd damn near wept the entire time he ate it, until he finally decided to put it away. This was supposed to have been eaten with the beautiful man, preferably by candlelight and while being serenaded with soft music in the background.

He pulled the rest of the dish out of the fridge and ate it without even reheating it in the microwave. It was just that good. As he sat at the table eating a cold dinner and surfing the Internet on his laptop, his fingers instinctually typed "Prescott Vaughan" in the search engine. He saw thousands of hits from Pres's various stages of his career. There was a multitude of sites showcasing his award-winning dishes and cookbooks, pictures of him teaching seminars at culinary academies all over the country. Ric read an article about him being the youngest chef to win the Beard Award, and raves all the way up to his very sought-after food-critiquing business.

*So wonderful.*

Ric clicked on another link and saw news footage of Pres's accident on the bridge that left him blind for the rest of his life. He slammed his laptop closed and scrubbed his hands over his tired face.

## Chapter Twenty-Four

"Pres, it's been a month, honey. You have to let the doctor go now. I never would've thought things would go south so fast, but that's the way relationships are. It's hit-and-miss until you find the right one. There's someone out there for you. You're too wonderful for there not to be." Janice patted his legs.

She came over—or more like kicked his door in—when he started ignoring her persistent calls after he'd canceled his last eight appointments with her. Janice would not have him walking around with an overgrown beard and wild, unkept hair. She'd dragged him to his bathroom and begun roughly taming his wild appearance.

"Why don't you come over for my Halloween extravaganza this weekend?" she asked cheerily as she began edging his sideburns. "It's going to be so much fun. There will be plenty of fine men and women there. My friend still wants to meet you. She's a thirty-five-year-old woman, and she's drop-dead gorgeous. She owns her own chic beauty salon and spa on Pacific Avenue. Ever since she saw your picture in the *Fine Cuisine* magazine, she's been begging me to set up a date for her," Janice said while nudging his back with her wide hips. "What do you say, hon?"

Pres winced at being set up on a blind date.

*No pun intended to me.*

He cringed even more at dealing with another high-maintenance woman. Owner of a chic spa? He didn't think so.

"I'll think about it. Thank you for the invite." Pres spoke softly, his voice sounding raspy from hardly talking. There was no one to talk to. He went to his assignments, ate alone, recorded his reports from home, and sent them to his assistant by messenger. He hadn't been into the office or seen his business partner, Adam, since he and Ric split. They also didn't come to see him. They weren't his friends—they were his colleagues. As long as Pres did his work and his name was on the letterhead, their business would be successful, and that was all his partner cared about.

Every blue moon, the little old lady who lived in the next apartment over would bring a bone for Josey. That was the only company Pres got.

"Okay, Pres. Well, just let me know if you want to come. Maybe bring that handsome driver of yours. He can definitely come. Tell him he doesn't even have to dress up. Just wear his uniform. Yum-my," she crooned, trying to coax a smile out of him. She eventually gave up and put the finishing touches on his hair.

Pres was sure his slight smile he tried to give her never quite reached his lips. "I'll see," he said again with even less enthusiasm than the last lie.

"Okay, all done. You look fabulous, of course. I put together some new pieces in your closet if you want to go out on a special occasion…or a date." She sighed while hugging his neck.

Pres took the contact. He wouldn't mind a hug or kiss—hell, anything—but Janice was under his employ, so therefore off-limits.

Pres raised one hand and patted his smooth face and trimmed goatee. "Thanks, Janice. This feels a lot better." He spoke softly into her spiky hair.

"You're welcome, honey. I'll see you next week. If you try to cancel, I'll do the same thing I did today," she yelled on her way out the door.

Pres heard the door click shut. He went to the pantry and pulled down a bottle of tequila and closed himself in his bedroom.

# YOU CAN SEE ME

# Chapter Twenty-Five

It was Halloween night, and of course Pres didn't go to Janice's extravaganza, which was probably in full swing since it was almost nine o'clock. He was sure it would've been nice, since Janice didn't do anything half-assed, but Pres just wasn't into it.

He was nursing a Jack and Coke and stewing in his sorrow when a commercial on the television caught his attention. Actually, two words caught his attention.

*Male escorts.*

Pres didn't play his television too often, but the daily silence was eating away at his sanity. He reached for the remote and turned up the volume.

*Looking for a night of fun company? Call us to set up a date with one of our hundreds of escorts. Male or female are available right now to come to you. Give us a call. 555-344-5535.*

Pres didn't know why, but he picked up his receiver before he could talk himself out of it and called the number.

A cheerful female voice answered on the second ring. "Hello. Thank you for calling Illustrious Escorts. How may we satisfy you this evening?"

Pres froze. He thought he'd get some kind of irritating recorded prompt first. Who actually gets a live person on the phone anymore?

"Hello?"

Even though he was on his fourth drink, he had to clear his now-dry throat before finally speaking. "Yeah, uh, how much for one evening?" Pres squeezed his eyes shut at his forward question and hoped he didn't sound like a horny weirdo.

"Well, depends. What city are you in?"

"Virginia Beach."

"Are you wanting company to go out to a function or staying in?"

Pres thought about it for a couple seconds. "Staying in."

"Male or female?"

*Oh shit. Male or female.* Pres hadn't thought about that. *This is fucking nuts. What am I going to do? Invite a complete stranger to my home and sleep with them and then pay 'em? I'll feel like a loser. What if they try to rob me or someth—*

Pres's internal argument was interrupted by the woman. "Sir, male or female?"

"Umm...female... No. No. Male, please." He rushed to correct himself. *Jeez, I'm an idiot.*

"Oh, sure. We have a beautiful variety of men. I want you to go to our website and take a look at the men we have available and see what you like. I can give you the password to access the webs—"

Pres cut in. "I can't do that."

"I'm sorry. You can't?" she questioned uncertainly, sounding confused. "You don't have Internet access?"

"I'm blind." Pres waited for her response, but nothing came. He wanted to scream at the silence he was met with on the other end. He huffed in frustration. "You know what, never mind. I'm sorry to have bothered you." Pres moved to press the "end" button on his cordless, when he heard her shouting for him to wait.

"Sir, I can assist you. I can set up a profile with you over the phone. What day and time were you looking for company?"

Pres took a deep breath, and after a few seconds, he replied, "Your commercial said 'escorts available now.' Is that accurate?"

"Yes, of course." Her demeanor picked up again. "Tell me your name first, and then I want you to tell me a little about yourself."

Pres gave the lady all of his information, and she set up a profile with his likes, dislikes, hobbies, et cetera.

"If I may be so bold, I think I may have someone perfect for you. He's thirty-four and has very similar likes and interests," she replied jovially.

Pres gave himself a mental kick in the ass while he gave the bubbly receptionist the approval number on his Black Visa, and she gave him a date for the evening.

*I'm fucking worthless...paying for a goddamn date.*

Apparently, that perfect someone lived in the area and was set to arrive in one hour.

Forty-five minutes and three shots of tequila later, Pres was still a mess. He'd walked Josey first and gotten him settled in his room. Then he showered and dressed in casual black slacks and a charcoal cashmere V-neck sweater. He was going for sexy but comfortable—at least that's what it said in Braille on the hanger he pulled. He was pacing back and forth in his spacious den when he heard a soft knock at the door.

*Oh shit, oh fuck, oh damn, oh hell,* he fired off in one long run-on statement. *What am I doing? There's a complete stranger at my door that I paid five hundred dollars to come and keep me company. Am I that desperate now? Damn you, Ric, for reducing me to this.*

He was still facing the unopened door and almost jumped out of his skin when he heard the tapping again, this time a little louder.

Pres slowly opened the door and was instantly met with a deliciously clean soap-and-water fragrance.

*I did ask for a man, didn't I?*

Pres didn't have to question the gender of his company any further when the man finally spoke up in a slow, sexy baritone drawl.

"Well hello, darlin'."

*Damn. That's one hell of an accent. He must be from the very Deep South.* It did funny things to Pres's deep south.

Pres cleared his throat. "Hi. I'm Prescott Vaughan." He stuck out his hand, and it was grasped in a firm grip. His company's touch was sure, and bold, and when the shake was over, he didn't release Pres's hand.

"Yes, as I live and breathe. I know exactly who you are, handsome. I am a huge fan, Prescott Vaughan. I'm Blair McKenzie."

Damn that drawl. Pres was kind of hoping he didn't pop wood right there in his damn hallway.

"You know me?" Pres questioned while working on keeping his erection under control.

"I most certainly do. I've followed your entire career. I'm just finishing up my master's in contemporary French cuisine at Le Cordon Bleu. I'm actually doing my thesis work now. This is my fifth year, and I'm about to graduate in a few months," he stated with pride.

"Wow. That's impressive," Pres responded, overly aware that they were still holding hands.

"May I come in, darlin'?"

Pres jumped at the question. He realized he'd been standing there mesmerized by the man for several minutes. "Oh. Of course. I'm sorry." Pres stepped to the side and allowed the man to come in. He moved to close the door, but paused mid-action when he heard a slight grumble from out in the hallway.

Pres froze and listened intently, but was taken aback at being hit with none other than Ric's spicy-sweet fragrance.

"Ric," he called out before he could stop himself. He hadn't had the opportunity to face the man in over a month, not since he'd stormed off of his yacht.

It amazed Pres that the man could avoid him so easily when they lived on the same floor…just four doors down. Either Ric had turned into goddamn Houdini or Pres was not as sharp as he thought he was. No matter what he tried to do to catch Ric, it never worked.

"Ric, wait, please." His date of the hour forgotten, Pres trotted down the hall, behind Ric's determined steps that had sped up when Pres gave chase. "Don't be a fucking coward. Face me," he growled, coming to a stop at the elevators.

"I'm not a coward. Go back to your date, darlin'," Ric sneered nastily, clearly mocking Pres's date.

Was that jealousy Pres heard in the man's voice? He sounded jealous, but more than that, he sounded tired.

"I'm not on a date, Ric. He's a…" Pres didn't dare finish that sentence.

"Looks like a date to me," Ric stated casually now.

Pres could hear Ric repeatedly pushing the elevator button. *He can't get away from me fast enough.*

"Ric, please. I'll send him away right now if you'll give me five minutes."

"I'm late for work."

"After work."

"Won't you be busy?"

"No, I won't, Ric. I told you I'm not on a date."

"I'm not a fool, darlin'." Ric spit his harsh words through clenched teeth.

"Stop calling me that, Ric. That's not what you call me." Pres felt his emotions betraying him. He would not cry right now. He'd cried enough to last him a lifetime. "Ric, I'm just asking for a couple of minutes. Is that too much?" Pres begged. He heard the elevator doors open. "Ric."

"Bye, Prescott."

# Chapter Twenty-Six

**P**res stood stock-still in front of the closed elevator doors. He wasn't sure how long until he felt a warm hand rub across his tense shoulders, making him jerk violently back to reality.

"Come on, Prescott," said the smooth voice.

*Oh yeah, my illustrious escort for the evening.*

Pres didn't know what to feel now: angry, sad, depressed, raw, or cheated. To be honest, he kind of felt all of it. Ric really wasn't going to give him another chance. He'd played a joke that had cost him a chance at real love. *How does that happen?*

Pres was back in his condo. He went straight to the pantry and removed the closest bottle of liquor he touched. He'd find out what his numbing elixir was for the evening after he took his first gulp.

He wouldn't be choosy. He just wanted the pain in his chest to subside enough for him to maybe get a few hours of sleep. He poured one glass—not bothering to offer a drink to his expensive rent boy—and slammed the bottle on the marble breakfast bar before dropping his weary body onto one of the four stools.

"So. He's the one that got away, huh?" Blair asked softly. He was standing a few feet away from Pres, probably staring at him pathetically as he gulped the strong…

*Hmmm, so gin is my poison for tonight.* He winced at the intense burn moving down his throat and settling into his empty stomach. Pres didn't respond to Blair's observation. He just took another gulp.

"Don't do this, Prescott. You'll regret it in more ways than one in the morning."

Pres felt Blair place his hand over top of his to prevent him from pouring another glassful from the bottle. Pres jerked his hand away. He didn't want to discuss "the one that got away," and he damn sure didn't want to stop drinking. Not until he was so sick that the pain in his stomach overrode the pain in his chest. He'd drink until his ears rang so loud that it drowned out the breaking sound of his heart.

"This is a beautiful kitchen you have here, and that stove belongs in a magazine," Blair stated out of the blue, referring to Pres's forty-eight-inch all-gas professional range.

Pres still didn't respond. He slowed down on the drinking, but didn't cap the bottle just yet.

"I mean, I've seen some beautiful kitchenware, but this is gorgeous." Blair continued to fawn over Pres's amenities. He knew his kitchen was one hundred percent state-of-the-art with any and every appliance needed to make a gourmet feast. On top of that, it was superbly decorated. He'd done it himself, years ago.

"Thanks," Pres finally mumbled. He heard his refrigerator open, then the rattling of pots and pans from inside his cabinets.

*Make yourself at home.*

"What are you doing?" Pres couldn't disguise the slur.

"How about I cook a little something for you? Your fridge and shelves are fully stocked. I could whip us up something real quick if you want," Blair said while continuing to explore his kitchen. "That is if you want me to stay. I really don't mind. You asked for company. I like to think of myself as pretty good company."

"I thought you came to have sex." Pres frowned at his crassness. He wasn't a rude man, and he didn't want to make Blair feel bad. It wasn't his fault that Ric had put him in a sour mood. "I'm sorry. That was unnecessary. I just thought that escorts…you know. Fuck. Never mind. You don't have to cook. It's, like, eleven at night, and I'm a mess now. So here." Pres reached for his wallet, but at lightning speed, Blair's hands were covering his when he attempted to withdraw some money.

"Hey, some escorts just have sex. Some actually provide companionship. Tell me what you need, Prescott, and I can provide you with it." Blair's hot breath fanned across his face as he spoke.

Pres was stunned at the close proximity. He took both his hands and ran them up Blair's torso. His chest was lithe and rock solid. He had chiseled abs that twitched beneath Pres's touch. Pres reached for Blair's face, but stopped short at the man's sharp intake of breath.

"I'm sorry," Pres gasped.

Before he knew it, he was being pulled into a tight hug. Blair's entire body molded to his, from chest to shins.

"It's okay. The way you touch me feels good," Blair said, sounding winded.

Blair stroked Pres's back tenderly and kind of swayed them back and forth a little as if there was a slow song playing only in their minds. He whispered sweet nothings in his ear, and it felt good. Pres held on for dear life. He wanted to purge, to release the emotions, to scream, to buck and fight, but he'd done enough of that. He didn't have any more energy to do it, even if he wanted to. So he gripped Blair's small waist and let himself get talked down.

"He's a stubborn jackass," Blair whispered to him, his lips brushing the shell of Pres's sensitive ear with every word he spoke. "I could see it in his eyes, he's hurting just as much as you are."

Pres groaned at hearing that. Blair had watched him grovel and beg Ric for another chance. Pres tried to pull out of the embrace. His face felt hot, and his pride felt wounded. He'd practically fallen at Ric's feet, even said he'd send Blair away in a heartbeat for five minutes of Ric's time.

*Oh my freaking God. That was shitty, and he'd heard it.*

Blair gripped him tighter. "You are one of the most talented men in the world, darlin', and if you were mine, I'd worship you every day." Blair's southern drawl was doing it to him again. However, he found himself wishing that Ric was saying these things, instead of a man who was paid to say them.

*Or does he mean it? Fuck. I have no idea. Is he playing out a fantasy for me? Saying all the things I yearn to hear from someone? Damn it. I have no clue.*

"Sure, you can cook," Pres said. It was the only thing he could think of to break the intimate moment.

"Cool," Blair said simply.

Pres sipped on the espresso Blair made him as he rattled around in his kitchen for the ingredients for his dish. He didn't mind it. It actually sounded pretty nice. Someone was cooking for him. It was a welcome change. Blair hummed a little when he really got comfortable, and the pleasant aromas started to permeate Pres's greater senses.

Pres spoke up after fifteen minutes of silence. "Making strawberry crepes, huh? Smells like you used the cinnamon sugar instead of plain cinnamon…nice technique."

"Wow. Are you serious? So it's true what they say about your senses, huh?" Blair questioned, sounding truly shocked at Pres's impressive skill.

"My sense of smell is sharper since I lost my sight. Over time, I've concentrated on my other senses to keep me going hard in the kitchen," Pres said matter-of-factly, as if everyone could tell the difference between cinnamon and cinnamon sugar by scent alone.

"I bet you are all kinds of hard, Chef Vaughan," Blair purred.

Pres blushed, and a slight grin actually made its way to the surface of his face.

"Mmmm, nice. When you smile…you're stunning, darlin'."

Pres couldn't help it. Blair's deep voice was wonderful to his ears, and his seductive banter was even better. This was probably the best he'd felt in a month.

"Open up, handsome."

Pres was grinning so, he hadn't heard Blair turn off the burners. His meal was ready, and it smelled heavenly. He opened his mouth and let Blair feed him. It was affectionate and nurturing, but not in a mommy/daddy sort of way. It was nurturing in a "I'm your partner and can be there for you" kind of way. Pres moaned at the wonderful flavors that burst on his tongue.

"Blair, your sautéed berries are caramelized to perfection, and the thin French-style pancakes are as light and delicate as rose petals. Well done, Chef. You've prepared this masterfully. Le Cordon has trained you well."

"That means everything coming from you, Chef Vaughan," Blair said, sounding truly appreciative of the compliment.

"Did you know I love everything strawberries?" Pres asked Blair with a knowing smirk dancing on his mouth.

"Yes. I think I may have read that somewhere." Blair laughed. "And I believe I've tried to master every one of your favorite strawberry dishes." He paused for a minute before adding, "I hope you don't find that weird."

"No, actually I'm flattered." Instinctually, Pres began to give Blair some pointers on incorporating new flavors and ingredients for various crepe dishes. He found out that Blair had studied with some of the best chefs in the world while receiving his master's in French cuisine.

They talked until it was time for the sun to come up. It was amazing how much they had in common, and not just culinary arts. They had the same taste in music, art, authors, and even shared a love of old Westerns. Pres teased Blair mercilessly when he confessed to loving reality television.

Pres really enjoyed Blair's company. What he thought would be a disastrous evening after the encounter with Ric turned out to be pretty great. He was not disappointed Blair had been there.

"Well, I can see you need to get a nap now, darlin'. I've kept you up way past your bedtime," Blair said in a hushed tone during the early morning hour. They'd been sitting on the couch for five hours just talking and enjoying each other's company. "Would you let me tuck you in?" Blair's whisky voice was laced with lust.

Pres laughed at that request. "Excuse me? I don't need tucking in. I'm not a little boy."

"No, you most certainly are not…but humor me. Let me tuck you in." Blair was an inch away from Pres's face now.

"I think I'm too tired to argue this. Sure, tuck me in." Pres rose off the couch and felt Blair intertwine their fingers and lead him to his bedroom.

Pres did a quick washup in the sink and brushed his teeth before heading back toward his bed.

Blair met him halfway. "You're amazing," he whispered. He took his strong hands and put them around Pres's naked waist.

Pres was glad he'd chosen pajama pants instead of just his black boxer briefs like he usually slept in. He didn't want to give Blair the wrong idea…or did he?

"Fuck, darlin'. You even smell like strawberries." Blair moaned. "I wonder if you taste like them, too. Earthy and sweet," Blair drawled sexily, sending all kinds of heat down Pres's bare torso that landed with a thud in his drawn-up sac.

It'd been too damn long since Pres had had any type of intimate contact and even longer since he had relief that wasn't self-inflicted. God never meant for man to be alone.

"Oh my goodness. Blair, I can't do…" His sentence wavered. "Fuck, that feels good," Pres whimpered.

Blair continued to nuzzle Pres's cheek before placing the most delicate kisses along his jaw. He nipped at Pres's collarbone and oh so slowly licked him from the base of his neck to the tip of his chin.

"I'm trying so hard to behave here, my sweet strawberry, but I'm losing. Believe me. This doesn't have a damn thing to do with money that you paid the agency," Blair said, completely breathless. "After it hit me that I was indeed seeing the Prescott Vaughan that I've followed my entire career, all I've thought about is tasting you since you opened your front door."

"Blair, please. I don't know if I can…" Pres's words tapered off. He was breathless, too, at Blair's ministrations. He was horny and in need of attention, but he didn't want to give Blair the wrong idea. As much as he hated to believe it, his heart still belonged to the man four doors down the hall on the right.

"Shhh. I know, Strawberry. I know you're still raw from your breakup, and I'm not trying to complicate things. I just think you are so fucking special. I ached for you this evening. I just want to make you feel good. Can I do that for you?" Blair held Pres in the most comforting way.

"I know you love this other man, but you deserve to be cherished like the precious dish you are. Before I leave, I just want to make sure you are sated and comfortable. Will you trust me to do that? I'm not going to try to have sex with you. I just want you to lay back and relax. Don't think about anything but the pleasure," Blair said and laid Pres down on his king-sized sleigh bed.

Pres sank into the plush down comforter as Blair's words sank deep into his soul: precious, sated, pleasure, comfortable. These were feelings Pres craved to have. He would let Blair do it. He fucking deserved this after the months of hell he'd been through.

He felt Blair climb up his body like a sultry predator. He had to weigh only about one hundred and eighty pounds. He wasn't overly muscular or hairy. He was sleek and smooth, almost soft and hard at the same time. His erection was snug against Pres's left thigh, and it had Pres moving his leg back and forth, wanting to give Blair some pleasure too. It must have worked because the man's moaning increased tenfold. Pres let his hands caress what he could reach as he dared to learn this man's body.

"Relax, darlin'. This is all about you," Blair said.

Then it happened all within a matter of seconds. Pres's back arched off the bed as Blair took his entire eight inches of hard, aching cock all the way down his throat.

"Ahhhhh. Fuck!" Pres shouted.

Blair's mouth was so goddamn hot, he thought his dick was being branded. Pres would've blown his load in five seconds if Blair hadn't had a death grip on his nuts. Blair didn't move. He just let Pres stew in the ecstasy. He kept his nose buried in Pres's pubes for several seconds. He felt Blair swallow a few times, his throat constricting around Pres's blushing head. Then that tongue…oh, that tongue began to do some kind of figure eights around his length.

"Fuuuck," he moaned as his body vibrated from all the pent-up lust he'd harbored inside for so long.

Blair reached both hands up and simultaneously pinched both of Pres's erect nipples, making him jerk violently.

"So good. Yeah. Fuck, Blair, just like that, honey."

Pres had been reduced to putty as Blair stroked his burning tongue up and down his cock, amazingly not missing a single inch of his manhood. No nerve was unteased, no skin unsinged. Blair's mouth should be considered lethal and dangerous. A man could make all kinds of promises with that talented mouth on his cock. Pres's eyes rolled to the back of his head at the care, skill, and sheer wickedness of this act. Blair was a motherfucking professional, but it had chilled Pres to the core when Blair said this had nothing to do with what he paid.

"Ssssssss…damn it, Blair," Pres hissed like a snake when Blair pulled up his length in a tortuously slow combination of sinful tongue, sharp teeth, and plush lips. "Blair, you're killing me, honey."

Right after Pres's confession, Blair let out a loud, tormented groan that deliciously vibrated around Pres's dick head as he felt Blair's hot come run down his thigh. Blair's body shook with his orgasm, but he never released Pres's cock.

The pressure started in Pres's balls and rocketed up his shaft. There was a split second of complete stillness before Pres slammed his head back into the pillow and let loose the first thick rope of his essence inside Blair's mouth.

"Blair!" Pres managed to shout before burst after burst of creamy goodness was swallowed eagerly. Blair didn't falter. He gripped the base of Pres's cock and milked him with slow, steady strokes all while sucking painfully hard on the head of his dick, making sure Pres would remember him and this orgasm well into the evening after he awoke. He'd have a fucking hickey on his cock head for the next two days. Pres squeezed his eyes closed at the erotic pleasure-pain of Blair's intense sucking.

"Aughhh. Shit." Pres gripped both sides of Blair's head and wrenched him off his sensitive, spent dick with a hard pop from the bastard's evil mouth. "Augh. You motherfucker." Pres's chest heaved up and down. *Damn, that was intense.* Pres rubbed his deliciously abused cock and winced at the tenderness. He concentrated on getting his heart rate back to normal. "Fuck, Blair."

Blair let out a deep chuckle that quickly turned into an erotic moan as he licked the last remnants of Pres's come that ran down his soft cock.

"You are fuckin' phenomenal when you come unhinged, Strawberry."

Pres smiled at the "Strawberry" endearment. He found it kind of cute now, or maybe he was just too relaxed to care.

He'd been dozing off when he heard the water start running in the bathroom. Blair came out with a very warm rag and gently washed his spunk off Pres's thigh. Then there was the telltale sign of his company getting dressed to leave. Pres felt a few different feelings about that, but chose not to overanalyze it and enjoy his current serenity.

Blair leaned down and gave Pres a slow, tongue-less kiss on his slack mouth.

"I can walk you out," Pres managed to say through a stifled yawn.

"Sleep, Strawberry. It's almost five in the morning. I'll lock up when I leave." Blair pecked Pres on his forehead. "Can I call you?" he whispered against his skin with a little uncertainty in his country drawl.

"I'd like that a lot." Pres reached his hand up to stroke Blair's cheek and felt him lean into it. "And Blair, thank you for a wonderful evening."

"My pleasure, darlin'."

Pres was already drifting into a peaceful slumber when he heard the chirp of his alarm and his front door open and close shut. After months of agony, he finally drifted into sleep with a smile on his face and without the assistance of alcohol.

# Chapter Twenty-Seven

**R**ic was one hundred percent exhausted. Even though he was still off the surgery rotation, he was swamped down in the ER handling small traumas. Halloween night was one of those nights the hospital dreaded…along with every other unofficial holiday. Every one of the hospital staff was either there or on call, andRic handled everything from sugar overdoses to gunshot wounds.

*Jesus Christ, the damn bar fights are the worst. Assholes getting drunk and pummeling each other—in silly-ass costumes—until they are either pepper-sprayed by the cops or one of them gets brutally injured.*

Ric was in deep thought as he made his way into his building. Everything about the shift had royally gotten under his skin. His coworkers had steered clear of him and his foul mood. He'd barked and growled at the nurses and orderlies for everything, whether it was their fault or not.

If he hadn't run into Prescott and his smoking-hot date, then perhaps things wouldn't have gone so bad. It'd never dawned on him that Pres would eventually move on. Ric was the one who had sworn off relationships since he stormed off Pres's yacht.

*How could I be so stupid? Of course he would move on. I just didn't expect it to be with a man. Sure as fuck not one that looked like a six-foot-two Texas god.*

Ric got pissed every time he thought of that man's face or that sexy accent. His body shook, and his hands clenched. Ric couldn't say for sure if his panic attacks hadn't gone undetected by his coworkers tonight or not. However, if Ric was being totally honest, he couldn't care less.

It was five in the morning, and all he could think about was crashing hard. He didn't even stop and get breakfast at his favorite diner for fear of falling asleep at the counter.

Ric trudged through his building lobby and tried to give smiles to some of the staff, but doubted he managed to pull it off. He decided to bypass the stairs, which he usually took in his continuous effort to avoid Pres, but today he just couldn't make the trek. He was bone tired.

Ric leaned his head back against the elevator paneling and watched the numbers light up all the way to floor ten before his eyes drifted shut for the rest of the way. When the doors opened, he came face-to-face with Prescott's Texan.

*Fuck me.*

Instead of the gorgeous prick getting on the elevator and leaving, the cocky bastard took a couple steps back and leaned against the wall on the opposite side of the hallway and stared openly at him as if he hadn't a care in the world. His hazel eyes scanned Ric up and down, taking in his disheveled, stressed-out appearance.

"Do you have a fucking problem?" Ric growled, refusing to pretend to be cordial to the man even though he was a complete stranger and had done absolutely nothing to him.

The man had the nerve to smirk at him and shake his head as if pitying Ric, or perhaps throwing it in Ric's face that he'd definitely had a better night than he had. Ric did try to hide his anger at knowing the man had slept with his Pres. Why the hell else would he be leaving at five in the damn morning? Unless he delivered newspapers or milk, he had absolutely no reason to be on this floor this time of morning. *Bastard.*

"No, I don't have a problem," he drawled slowly, making sure to put extra enunciation on the "I" part of his sentence.

"But, obviously, you do. Or else you wouldn't be scowling at me for no reason."

"Fuck you," Ric snarled, stepping just a little closer. He wanted to tear the man's lips off for talking with that accent. Then he wanted to rip his hands off for daring to touch his Prescott. *The man's probably a male gold digger.*

"Did you enjoy taking advantage of Prescott? Did you get what you came for?" Ric growled like a rabid animal three inches away from the man's face, but he'd be damned if the asshole didn't even flinch at his showcase of fury. No reaction whatsoever.

The Texan had one hand casually tucked in his jeans pocket, kicking back one side of his stylish blazer, while he lazily rubbed his other hand over his taut chest and washboard abs that showed through the thin material of his untucked dress shirt. Ric hated to admit it, but the man looked well fucked, and he wore it well.

"How could you do that to someone like him?" Ric fumed, and it took everything in him to control his rage.

*If I hit him, no one would know. There's no one around, no witnesses. It'd be his word against mine.*

"I knew I'd peg you in less than five minutes." The man spoke with one dark brown eyebrow cocked up. He ran his fingers through his bed-tousled dark brown hair and let out an exasperated breath.

"Excuse me?" Ric blinked.

"Now I know why you were too stupid to hold on to Prescott Vaughan. You were too busy feeling sorry for him. Instead of you seeing a brilliant man, a world-renowned, accomplished chef who happens to be one of the most talented men to ever set foot in a kitchen, you see a needy, helpless man. Ahhh. Now it makes perfect sense."

"Don't try to act like you know me because you don't," Ric growled, still trying to be mindful they were in the hallway of the floor that he lived on.

The Texan pushed off the wall and closed the few inches between them. His six feet, two inches of height had him eye to eye with Ric, and the man showed no fear. His handsome face was now a mask of furious anger.

"I saw you treat him like shit on the bottom of your shoes last night. I watched him beg you for five fuckin' minutes of your time, and you spat in his face. Now, you have the audacity to say I'm mistreating him? Fuck you," he snarled right back at Ric.

Just as fast as the man's anger came, it disappeared, and he composed himself to reveal that smirk that Ric selfishly rejoiced Pres couldn't see, because it was sexy as fuck…and the man knew it.

Ric watched his competition push the elevator button as he rubbed his hand over his morning stubble before speaking again. "You know what they say, don't you, Doc? One man's trash is another man's treasure, and Prescott Vaughan is definitely a rare, precious treasure."

The Texan inched in even closer, which surprised the hell out of Ric since they were practically nose to nose. Ric was smacked in the face with a faint soap-and-water fragrance that made his eyelids flutter and his own dick jerk to life. Ric's half-lidded eyes were riveted to the Texan's plush lips as he leaned in and whispered directly into Ric's open mouth.

"If you don't pull your head out of your ass and claim Prescott Vaughan like he wants, I won't stop until I've fucked the sexy strawberry ten ways to Sunday and there's not a single trace of your existence left in his mind, because with or without you, he needs love, and I was the one there last night to lick his sweet tears when you walked away."

The elevator doors opened at his final words, and the smooth Texan took a few graceful steps backward into the elevator and gave Ric a sexy wink right before the doors closed.

*Fucking asshole,* Ric thought.

# YOU CAN SEE ME

# Chapter Twenty-Eight

Pres was waiting in the lounge in his building for Blair to come have dinner with him. The man had called Pres just like he'd said, and then every day after that for weeks. Before Pres knew what hit him, Blair had become very important to him. He still worked as an escort, but he always made Pres a priority, and he swore to him that he wasn't fucking his clients.

They had at least three to four dates a week. He took Pres to a comedy show, where he'd laughed until his stomach hurt. They went to several restaurants all over the city, and he even took Blair with him to a French bistro he had to critique last week.

Pres was shocked when Blair surprised him one evening by taking him to a food rave. He hadn't been to one in years, and the greatest part was how all the young chefs knew him and were chomping at the bit for his culinary expertise. The women swooned at his spectacular smelling sense and super-sensitive tasting palate. It made Pres feel like he was on top of the world, and Blair had done it all for him.

Spending time with Blair had shown Pres what he'd been missing his entire life, even during the small amount of time he'd had with Ric. He enjoyed the company of men, and he wasn't in a constant state of bending over backward to please and satisfy all the time. Pres didn't like the weakling he'd become after his fiancée left and while dating Vikki.

Pres was falling hard for Blair, and they both couldn't deny what was brewing between them, but there was something missing, and they had yet to put their finger on it.

"Hey, Strawberry." Blair's deep voice reached him before he made it to the table.

"Hey, sexy. Sit your ass down and stop drawing attention." Pres smiled wide, loving their sexy jeering. Pres felt Blair give him a soft kiss on his lips.

"Mmm. You taste good." Blair leaned back in and licked Pres's lips.

"You'd better stop before your sinful mouth gets you in trouble." Pres laughed. "You hungry, babe?"

"Maybe just an appetizer, I had a big lunch," Blair stated as he read the menu. "So what do you suggest, Chef?"

"The Mexican egg rolls," Pres said without hesitation.

"Is it your recipe?" Blair asked.

"Yep. They're really good, too."

"I'm sure they are, you brilliant man. So hey, before I forget, do you want to go to another comedy show next weekend? My dad got me free tickets."

Pres felt Blair grip one of his hands that rested on the tabletop and rub it lightly.

He reached over and lightly brushed Blair's face with the backs of his fingers from his temple to his chin. Since their first meeting, Blair had picked up on Pres's constant need for intimate contact, and he never let Pres down.

"Sure, that sounds like fun. You want me to have Scott drive us?" Pres flipped his hand over and linked their fingers together.

"No. I'll come and get you. Then we can walk down on the beach. There's not much time left before it's too cold to enjoy—" Blair suddenly stopped speaking.

"What's wrong, Bl—" Pres froze at the spicy-sweet scent that wafted over their table.

"I'm gonna go make a phone call, Strawberry. Looks like someone has something to say," Blair stated calmly.

"Okay. You want me to order for you?" Pres asked as Blair continued to stroke his hand.

"Sure, darlin'. I'm your man. You know what I like."

Pres heard Ric let out an indignant snort at Blair's obvious verbal sucker punch.

**R**ic stood at the entrance to the lounge and watched Pres and his Texan fondle all over each other. The man looked smooth, and Pres looked mouthwatering in his sleek business suit. The bastard said he would step aside and let Ric have a chance to fix his mistake, and a mistake he did make. He loved Prescott Vaughan, and he was ready to be what he needed in a partner...not a nagging parent.

*I'm just gonna be bold as fuck and say my piece right there in front of his new beau.*

Ric sat down opposite of Prescott and tried not to let his tongue wag out of his mouth at the man's stunning appearance or let his anger show at the Texan's pet name for his man. Ric blurted out, "What the fuck is a strawberry?"

"It's a sweet, soft red fruit with a seed-studded surface," Pres replied coolly.

"No shit. I mean, why the hell does he call you that?" Ric asked.

"Why does that matter to you, Ric?"

"It... I... Well, I was wondering is all." Ric wanted to kick himself at his fumbling over his own words. "Never mind. I wanted to maybe talk to you, if you had some free time."

"Some free time?" Pres retorted.

"Yes, Pres. I think I made a mistake," Ric said in an extremely low tone.

"You think...you made a mistake." Pres threw up air quotes when he said the word "think." "So what exactly am I supposed to talk to you about, Ric? I tried—no, I begged—to talk to you for months, and you were sure that you'd made the right decision, no matter how much I tried to argue…through your fucking apartment door, because you wouldn't open it," Pres spat. Ric could see Pres's anger bubbled just below his exterior.

This was not going at all how Ric had thought it would go. How was he going to explain this to Pres and get him to come back? He was sure that Pres still loved him enough to allow him to apologize and give him a second chance.

"Pres, I wanted to apologize. I was going through something very toxic to my heart, and I got scared. I saw you go into that water, and it just paralyzed me. A wound that I thought was healed wasn't. I needed to heal. I should have just talked to you about it, but I was so scared of losing my heart again."

Ric saw Pres's face lighten and the scowl disappear.

*Oh, thank you, God.*

"You are my heart, Pres, and believe me, the thought of losing you tragically still makes my head pound instantly. But, I will not shelter you, or constantly hover over you either, if you give me another chance. There was not an hour that went by these last few months that I didn't think about you."

Pres didn't speak any more. His beautiful eyes were hidden behind his sleek Gucci shades, and his face was a stony mask.

"Baby?"

"Don't," Pres snapped angrily. "Don't you fuckin' call me that. I need to think about this, Ric, but I honestly don't feel like you deserve another second of my time."

"Are you in love with the Texan?" Ric wanted to bite his tongue at blurting out his thoughts, but it was out now, and he really wanted to know.

"First off, his name is Blair. Second, yes, I do love him," Pres answered without a bit of hesitation.

Ric wanted to run out of that lounge and throw himself in front of the next vehicle that was barreling down the street at over sixty miles per hour. Pres had moved on and was in love with another man. Ric had waited too long.

*How the hell did I let this happen? I was in love, and this man loved me, and I threw him away. Now he's another man's treasure, just like the Texan said he'd be.*

"As much as it hurts, baby, I hope he treats you good, because God knows you deserve it." Ric got up and placed a soft kiss on Pres's cheek. He meant to pull away quickly, but he lingered. Pres smelled so good…fuck…like a ripe, sweet strawberry.

Ric almost let a sob escape, but he controlled it. He couldn't pull away. He let his lips dwell on Pres's soft cheek after he noted that Pres wasn't pushing him away.

Pres turned his lips toward Ric's mouth, but didn't kiss him. He whispered softly, "Blair is my very special friend. He was there for me when I was drowning in depression. I do love him, Ric, but he's not my lover."

"Oh… I thought… The way you two look together, you look very friendly," Ric admitted with a little more venom in his voice than he intended.

"That's just his nature—"

"Yeah, being an escort and all, I'm kind of a natural flirt." Blair's deep voice interrupted Pres's last statement.

"A w-what?" Ric stammered, pulling back from Pres's cheek. He was sure he hadn't heard what he thought he heard.

*There are male escorts that look like you? I thought all those commercials were false advertisement.*

"You heard me right, Dr. Hottie."

*Uhhh, that fucking accent is driving me up the fucking wall. Does he have to make everything drip sex?*

Blair laughed deep in his chest. "Oh, Strawberry, his face right now. The phrase 'fish out of water' comes to mind."

Pres laughed, and Ric immediately turned his attention away from the sex fiend. He hadn't heard Pres laugh in so long.

As much as he wanted to hate the guy, he had been good for Pres. Now that he knew what Blair did for a living, his mind couldn't help but drift to some of the things that southern mouth of his had done to his Pres...or could do to Ric.

*What the hell? Don't think about him. He's the enemy.*

"Blair, the waitress didn't come take our order yet. You want another drink?" Pres asked the Texan nicely. Ric found himself wishing that Pres would turn a little of that kindness on him.

*Why? I don't deserve his kindness.*

"No. I'm going to head out. I finally got a hold of my elusive professor, so I'm going to go meet him while he's still in his office. I'll catch up with you at the end of the week for the show."

"Okay, honey. Will you call me later?" Pres grinned at the dark-haired beauty.

"I most certainly will. I gotta go. Give me a kiss, darlin'."

Ric clamped his large frame to his chair to keep from bolting up and wrapping his hands around the smug bastard's throat. *Pres would be pissed if you killed his new BFF by asphyxiation.* He gripped the armrest as he watched the Texan put on a show. Blair placed both hands on the arms of Pres's chair, securing him in. He seductively licked his lips, locked eyes on Ric, and slowly bent down to bring his pretty mouth in contact with Pres's slightly parted lips, never breaking eye contact with Ric.

*He's fucking daring me. Don't let me find out where you live, you cocky asshole.*

Ric couldn't take his eyes off the two men, one of them being his man, the other a pain in his ass. The bastard had the nerve to let his tongue just barely graze Pres's lips before he began to pull back slower than humanly possible. Pres admonished him for the stunt.

"Behave, honey. Don't goad him," Pres whispered against Blair's still-lingering lips.

"Yes, my treasure." With that said, the Texan winked at Ric and walked out of the lounge like he owned the entire damn building.

YOU CAN SEE ME

## Chapter Twenty-Nine

Pres couldn't believe how nervous he was. He'd agreed to let Ric come over to his place to plead his case. Pres was by far still in love with Ric. He knew that for a fact when Ric sat down beside him and he got a whiff of that scent that went straight to his cock so fast, it made his head spin. Yes, he still had it bad.

However, Ric had still hurt him like crazy. At one point, Pres didn't know how he would go on again. If it wasn't for Blair, things probably would've turned out a lot worse for him. He remembered the countless midnight conversations he and Blair had had and went about putting his plan in motion.

Pres put the small hors d'oeuvre tray on the living room table and jogged back into the kitchen. *Damn it, he'll be here any minute.* He scurried to put the crackers on the dish and accidently knocked over the jar of olives he was trying to arrange for his cheese crudité. He heard the loud shatter of glass and olives scattering everywhere across his hardwood floor.

"Fuck, fuck, fuck. Of all the damn tea in China. Fuck! I do this now!"

Pres had to get this mess up fast. He hated cleaning up spills, obviously. However, he didn't want Ric to come in and see him scrubbing a floor, or be overwhelmed by the now-powerful scent of Calabrese olive juice everywhere.

Pres tried to be mindful of where he stepped. He was barefoot and didn't want to try digging out a shard of glass from his foot, too. He tried to sidestep the spill altogether, but still ended up losing his footing on a patch of juice, making his legs fly up from under him. He fell back, and his eyes shot wide open at the horrific sting of the corner of his kitchen island coming into contact with the back of his skull.

Pres could hear a muffled dog bark sounding far off in the distance. There were various colors dancing around behind his eyelids. The pain was too much. Pres let the darkness surround him.

**R**ic had just closed his condo door when he heard a dog barking frantically like he was trying to get out of a burning apartment. It was a big dog's bark, not like the little Yorkiepoos everyone seemed to have on this floor.

*Everyone except Pres. Shit!*

Ric raced down to Pres's door and banged hard on it. He tried the knob and was surprised but relieved to find it unlocked. Ric didn't waste time on the hysterical retriever barking and whimpering at his heels.

"Pres!" he yelled, but got no answer. Ric ran into the kitchen, and his knees buckled at the sight—Pres unconscious on the floor, bleeding from the back of his head, and broken glass everywhere.

Although it was Pres, Ric went into trauma surgeon mode. He pulled out his cell and dialed 911 while trying to asses Pres without moving him, ultramindful of a possible neck injury as well. He rattled off the address, brief patient history, and seriousness of the injury to the operator and let the phone drop to the floor. He didn't need her instructions. He knew what to do.

Damn it, Ric's medical bag was in his apartment, and he'd be damned if he was leaving Pres's side. Pres was still alive, he was breathing, but his pulse was weak, and all the color had drained from his beautiful face. He got all the way down and spoke directly into Pres's ear. He'd have no choice but to wait for the paramedics. It wouldn't be wise to move him to try to check the head wound. The blood that had pooled around Pres's head was enough to scare the shit out of Ric, but he would be strong for Pres this time and not run.

"Hang in there, baby. They're coming. I'm right here with you. Stay close to my voice, Pres. Stay focused on that. I'll be by your side the entire time. You're going to be okay. Oh God, please be okay." Ric wept quietly.

He was coming over today to win his man's heart back. He'd had a well-thought-out plan and everything. There was no way God could be this cruel. Hadn't he suffered enough loss? Hadn't Pres suffered enough for ten lifetimes?

Ric kept a firm hold on the pulse point on Pres's wrist as he concentrated on the faint drum of his man's lifeline. "We're gonna make it through this together," he whispered on the shell of Pres's ear before kissing his cheek tenderly. "Me and you, baby, that's how it's going to be, forever. I'm not going to run ever again. No matter how scared I am...like right now."

Ric squeezed his eyes. The endless forming of tears was clouding his vision. Pres's pulse was weakening.

"Noooo," Ric groaned. "Don't you dare, Prescott. Fight, goddamn it. Do you hear me? Fuckin' fight, baby... Fight for us."

Ric whispered harshly now, desperation taking over. He stopped talking to concentrate on finding the pulse and this time felt a firmer beat underneath his fingertips, making him gasp at the realization. Pres was listening to him, and he was fighting.

"That's it, Pres. Fight harder. Fight harder. Me and you. I love you, Pres, so fucking much. You can't go until I've shown you how much you mean to me." He kissed Pres's cheek again, letting his tears slide down both of their faces.

Ric barely registered the firemen and paramedics bursting into the apartment or Josey going crazy at all the activity. He was focused on the firm pulse beating under his fingertips now.

"Sir, please let us help. Sir, let us get to him to help him." A paramedic was yelling at Ric, but all he could do was feel, feel

Pres's pulse. A second later, several sets of arms were lifting him away from the floor.

"Dr. E, let them do their jobs," a deep voice spoke in front of him. Ric was still locked on Pres and his pale, motionless face. Ric finally looked up and recognized the fireman and two of the four paramedics. All of them frequented his ER. "You can ride with him in the ambulance, Dr. E. Come on. We're moving now."

They had Pres on the gurney and wheeling out of the apartment so fast that Ric had to jog to keep up.

*I'm here, Pres. Keep fighting.*

## Chapter Thirty

They wouldn't let Ric in the back with Pres, because he was too emotionally involved. He knew this already. He'd told countless family members who were medical professionals the same thing before he went into the OR to play God on their loved ones.

Pres was currently getting a full neuro work-up by the best neurosurgeon in the country. The brilliant doctor was here consulting on a clinical trial at the university when Ric called him in for a favor.

*Thank God Dr. Brown was still here. If anyone can save Pres, it's him.*

Ric was staring out the window debating if he'd done the right thing by going through Pres's contacts on his cell phone and leaving a voice mail for Blair. Blair was Pres's best friend now, so he believed it's what Pres would've wanted, despite the fact that the sexy Texan grated on Ric's last nerve. He also contacted his parents. They were driving in from Richmond as Ric waited alone—but not patiently—for Dr. Brown to come out with some answers. It'd been hours already. Actually, it'd been one hour, fifty-two minutes, and thirty-three, thirty-four, thirty-five…Ric's counting was interrupted by Nurse Maggie.

"Here, Dr. E. I went and got this from the cafeteria before they closed for the shift change." The small woman handed Ric a steaming cup of coffee. Her hands were so small and timid as she lightly brushed his fingertips in a comforting gesture.

"Thanks, Maggie. You didn't have to do that. But thank you very much." His voice couldn't hide the despair he was feeling, and it was obvious Maggie caught it too, her light brown doe eyes taking on a sorrowful look.

"I'm so sorry about your friend, Dr. E, but he's in good hands. I'm on another case, but Dr. Brown is working frantically at his computer. That's always a good sign from him. It means something has him very intrigued."

"Really? How long's he been at his computer?" Ric's voice was rushed, and he jumped back when Nurse Maggie's eyes got as wide as saucers. He vaguely realized he'd grabbed her by both arms. "Oh, Maggie, I'm sorry. I didn't mean to do that. It's just I worked on a trial with Dr. Brown four years ago. I know what it means when he's intrigued." Ric dropped his chin to his chest.

Regarding Dr. Brown, "intrigued" meant one of two things. Either Pres actually had developed something that Dr. Brown couldn't figure out, which was extremely farfetched. The man had been all over the world studying the human brain. He knew it all. Well, he knew a hell of a lot. Or two, Pres was exhibiting symptoms that Dr. Brown had rarely seen. Either instance would have the smart doctor working nonstop until he found a solution.

"God, when is he coming to get me?" Ric whispered more so to himself.

"Do you want me to go get him?" Maggie asked as she began to turn to walk away.

"No! Please, let him work. It's why I called him. Please, don't disturb him." Ric spoke hurriedly to stop her in her tracks. He took a few calming breaths and tried to give Maggie a little smile. He hoped he'd pulled it off. Maggie was always so sweet to him, a little flirty, but sweet nonetheless. "Just, talk to me okay? A little distraction might help."

She smiled warmly. "Sure, Doctor." She gestured for Ric to sit as she sat next to him and jumped right into distracting him. "So, the clinic's kid's charity bazaar was yesterday, and we raised over five thousand dollars for the children's wing."

Maggie excitedly rattled on about the hospital's charity events, her new book club that she'd joined, a chick flick she saw over the weekend, and her husband's inability to cut the grass every week or take out the trash when needed. This time Ric did smile. She never expected him to input any thoughts. She just released irrelevant story after story. After a good while, he realized he wasn't holding his breath anymore in anticipation of a "code blue" being called over the PA system.

"Dr. Edwards."

Ric jumped at Dr. Brown's sharp tone, and Maggie immediately shut her mouth. Ric rushed to the counter where Dr. Brown was handing the nurse a few faxes.

"Send these now, please," he ordered.

The man was no-nonsense all the time. Ric had sensed that Dr. Brown liked him from the first time they'd met, when he'd promptly requested Ric to work with him on one of his trial studies. When Dr. Brown asked, you accepted, because it was indeed an honor.

"How is he, Clark?" Ric looked into Dr. Brown's intellectual eyes for any fraction of sorrow and saw none.

"Come on back, Rickson. I have something to show you." Dr. Brown led them back to a small family waiting room in the neurology wing that was empty and waited for Ric to join him at the small four-person table.

"Is the family coming?" he asked first.

"Yes, I called his parents and his best friend. The parents have to drive in from Richmond, so they'll be here in about another hour or so, I guess," Ric answered. He fidgeted nervously while Dr. Brown scrunched his wise brown eyes at some results on Pres's CT scan. Ric didn't dare interrupt him. Finally, Dr. Brown raised his head to speak.

"When I looked at the CT scans, my first concern was blockages, or clots, in his brain, specifically because of his previous surgery from his car accident. Then, Mr. Vaughan woke about fifteen minutes into his angiogram exam, and we had to immediately put him back under. However, when he was awake for those few minutes, he was screaming about bright light, Rickson, and his eyes were wide open." Dr. Brown looked at Ric as he processed what he'd just said.

"Wait. Clark. Are you s-s-saying that Pres..." Ric's voice trailed off as his hands shook violently.

"I believe Mr. Vaughan may have regained a portion of his vision from the head trauma he just sustained."

*Holy shit.*

## Chapter Thirty-One

Pres could hear beeping and footsteps all around him while he lay as still as he could on the most uncomfortable bed he'd ever felt in his thirty-plus years. He had to concentrate on not moving an inch, because even wiggling his toes required a command sent from his brain, and any use of his head hurt like hell.

Pres was hopeful, because at least he remembered what had landed him in the hospital, so he believed that meant no serious brain damage.

*Maybe I just have a big knot on my head.*

He didn't remember too much else. He'd dreamed of a blinding light and loud knocking sounds. There were frantic voices yelling his name and telling him to calm down.

*Maybe I was closer to death than I thought. Man, so it's true. You do see bright lights before you die.*

Pres was just pondering that thought when he registered a gentle touch on his thigh and then someone grasping his hand.

"You should be awake by now, baby. They stopped the medicine an hour ago."

*Ric?*

Ric was there and talking to him, and oh God, he sounded so sad. Pres could hear him as clear as day. He desperately wanted to open his mouth and tell Ric he was fine, but his mouth didn't work, and it scared him shitless.

*I can't talk. I can't talk.*

The fear gripped and seized his brain, and he fought not to throw up at the intensity of the pain. He felt as if he couldn't breathe, and he began to shake fiercely.

"Pres, calm down." Ric squeezed Pres's hand hard. "I'm right here, baby. Try to relax. You're okay. You're actually better than okay. Please calm down."

*Like hell I'm okay!*

Pres heard the door burst open and a man's voice barking at Ric to step back.

"Mr. Vaughan, can you hear me? Mr. Vaughan, I'm your doctor, and I can give you something for the pain, but I need for you to calm down. You're having a panic attack. I need you to concentrate on my voice and breathe in through your nose and out through your mouth."

Pres tried to follow the orders that he could hear so clearly, but he still couldn't speak.

*Why can't I speak? Fuck! Fuck! Fuck!*

"Rickson, get over here," Dr. Brown commanded. "The monitor shows that he's wide awake, but he's not responding to me, and I don't want to give him a sedative until I've had the results from his EEG on his vision. Help him to calm down. Talk to him."

Ric leaned down to whisper in Pres's ear. "Pres, we need you to calm down. You are not critically injured. I don't know what has you so upset, baby, but you're going to be just fine. I have the best doctor taking care of you. But, if you don't calm down, then he'll have to sedate you, and we don't want that. I know you can hear me. Just concentrate on my voice, and slow your breathing."

Ric's deep voice was warm and soothing on Pres's neck. It felt so good and familiar, as if it'd been there all the time. Pres remembered how scared Ric could get, so he tried very hard to do what he said. He squeezed his eyes tightly and fought through the pain in his head. Pres sucked in a shaky breath through his nose and coughed and sputtered when he tried to release it through his mouth.

"Ric," he managed to croak out.

*I can talk.*

"Yes, I'm right here. That's it. Breathe again. Just like that, gorgeous."

Ric was squeezing Pres's hand with a harsh grip, but the soft, whispered words in his ear contradicted the paralyzing fear Pres assumed Ric would be feeling. Pres faintly registered the decreasing beep of the machines as he focused on Ric's breath so very close to his face. He breathed in again—this time a little slower—and got a large whiff of Ric's scent.

*Ahhh. Smells so good.*

He wanted to nuzzle Ric's scratchy jaw, but refused to move his head, which would surely result in another jolt of pain. So, he just breathed in that beautiful fragrance and felt his body untense.

Dr. Brown spoke up. "Well done, Rickson. All right, we're back to normal. Mr. Vaughan, can you verbally respond to me?"

*Why is he yelling? Goddamn it. If he's such a brilliant doctor, doesn't he know I have a damn headache the size of Blair's ego?*

"Yes, I can hear you, but the pain… It's too much." Pres managed to finally find his voice, but every syllable that he spoke was like someone whacking him in the head with a steel hammer. He couldn't even remember feeling that kind of powerful pain after his accident.

*Oh, well, maybe that was because I had a doctor nice enough to give me morphine.*

"Well done. Yes, I know the pain is intense. You have twenty stitches in the back of your head, but otherwise, and very luckily, there were no additional internal injuries. You just have a local anesthetic right now for the discomfort. I'll give you something stronger for the pain as soon as I get the results of your last test that will hopefully tell me what I suspect has occurred as a result of your recent head trauma," Dr. Brown said.

"What result occurred?" Pres asked to whoever was in the room.

"I'll let Dr. Edwards explain that to you, since he's more than capable. I just got a text that your results are ready. Let me go have a look, and I'll be back in a few."

Pres heard the man's heavy footsteps leave his room.

*What results? Am I even more blind?*

"Ric, what results?" Pres squeezed Ric's hand. He really didn't want to talk, but Pres hated surprises. He just wanted Ric to rip it off like a Band-Aid and tell him the bad news.

"Pres, Clark—I mean, Dr. Brown—thinks that the fall you had in your kitchen, the impact of a precise location of your skull to the corner of your counter, may have affected your vision…for the better, not worse."

*This is so stupid. I can't see shit. Can I just get some pain medicine, please?*

"Jesus. You say this guy is the best there is," Pres huffed, not meaning to sound so annoyed, but he felt this was all very unnecessary and pretty cruel. "How can it be better? It's still pitch-dark, Ric."

Ric leaned in and pressed a soft kiss on Pres's forehead before responding, "You have bandages over your eyes, baby. That's why it's dark."

Pres jerked his hand up to lightly graze the featherlight bandages covering his eyes. *How the hell did I not realize that?*

# Chapter Thirty-Two

Ric was still in shock at the results from Pres's neurology tests. It was true. Pres had regained some of his sight back. It was a medical miracle, a miracle that Pres had hit his head in the exact location that could alter his vision loss when only point two percent of those cases ever occurred. A doctor rarely saw one in his entire career, but of course, Dr. Brown had seen a few. They wouldn't know how much sight was regained until they removed the bandages.

Dr. Brown had postponed his trip to stay and work with the ophthalmologist after Pres's bandages were removed. However, every test that was run and rerun showed significant vision recovery. It wouldn't be long before there were news cameras wanting to interview Pres on this phenomenon, and countless neurologists who would want to read Dr. Brown's journals on this case. Needless to say, the hospital was buzzing about Ric's miracle boyfriend.

Ric didn't correct them on the use of "boyfriend" either. Regardless if Pres and Ric never got a chance to hash out their breakup, he had no doubt he'd win Pres's heart back.

After scanning the cerebral angiogram for the hundredth time, Ric felt a buzz in his left pants pocket. It was Pres's cell phone with a message from the tasty Texan.

*Is he all right, Ric? I'm going out of my mind. I'm at school in Richmond and just got finished with presenting my thesis, so my phone was off. I'll be on the next thing smokin' back to the beach. But first tell me he's okay.*

Ric hit reply, but stopped short. *Thesis? I thought he was an escort. Do they give out master's degrees in sexual manipulation now? Whatever.*

Ric replied: *He's better than all right. You'll see when you get here.*

Ric pocketed the phone and scrubbed his tired eyes. Pres was sleeping after visiting with his very emotional parents. He and Dr. Brown had sat them down as soon as they arrived and explained what happened to Pres, from slip-and-fall to finish.

Pres's mother was crying so hard by the end of their consultation that she couldn't manage to ask her questions. Pres's father, however, was the epitome of calm. He was a rock for his wife. Pres looked very similar to him and favored a lot of his mannerisms, but the striking blue eyes he got from his mother. Pres's father only wanted to know one thing: "When can I see my boy?"

Ric had to say he wasn't looking forward to the Texan's arrival. He was sure his appearance would stir the gossip mill and sound the horns with all the single—and probably even the not-so-single—nurses. Ric could hear the overhead PA system now: "May I have your attention, please? The sexiest gay man in the world is on level five. Attention all staff, the sexiest man alive is on level five." He mentally rolled his eyes.

Ric tried unsuccessfully not to think of Pres's reaction to seeing the man either. He had to believe that he had love on his side. To him, Pres was the sexiest man alive. The Texan had too much self-appreciation. Pres was so beautiful, but had no idea that he was, which only made him even more breathtaking.

Pres was eating and conversing fine, but it was obvious he wanted the bandages off…like now. Dr. Brown wanted to wait until Pres's headaches were manageable, but somehow Pres had talked him into taking them off tomorrow. They had all agreed to no news cameras. Only the doctors, the hospital's media correspondent, Pres's personal assistant, and immediate family would be present. A ton of flashing lights and gawking faces in the eyes of someone who has been in complete darkness for the last five years probably wouldn't be a good idea.

Ric was nervous as shit. He wanted Pres to be happy, and he was so happy for him, but he selfishly wanted Pres to be happy with him and only him. He needed to talk to him before Pres's unveiling. It was after ten at night, and Pres's parents had gone back to their hotel a few hours ago so they could be here first thing in the morning.

Ric tiptoed into Pres's room and was surprised to find him sitting up, twirling a strand of loose thread from his blanket around his forefinger.

"Hello, Sunshine," Pres said softly in the quiet room.

Ric stopped short at hearing his endearment name on Pres's lips. He concentrated on finding his voice. "Hi, baby," he whispered back. He saw Pres pat the side of his hospital bed a couple times, asking Ric to sit next to him.

Ric sat down gently and leaned over to kiss Pres on the side of his mouth. He let his mouth hover there on Pres's smooth cheek. He was freshly washed, shampooed, clean shaven, and minty fresh, courtesy of Nurse Maggie.

Ric couldn't help but rub his lips against the now-soft surface. Pres turned his mouth toward Ric, seeking him out, obviously wanting something deeper from him.

"Kiss me, Ric," Pres moaned.

Ric didn't make Pres ask twice. He placed his hand on Pres's cheek and very softly urged him forward, mindful of his headaches. He kissed him first with just lips and breath. He inhaled Pres's scent, basking in his sheer presence.

Pres deepened the kiss on his own, and Ric couldn't help the guttural moan that worked its way out of his chest. Pres swallowed it up and continued to ravish Ric with everything he could give, and Ric gave right back to him.

Ric pulled back at the sound of a throat clearing loudly in the doorway. Both of them were so consumed with passion that neither one had heard the door open.

"Dr. Edwards, my patient needs his rest." Dr. Brown's stern voice was like a bucket of ice water thrown over top of them.

Ric knew he was a deep shade of crimson at being caught kissing a patient, especially by his mentor, but he'd never pass on kissing Prescott Vaughan, no matter where he was.

"I just came to talk with him before tomorrow's events, sir."

"I'm no brain surgeon, but that didn't look like talking to me," Dr. Brown replied, his knowing eyes twinkling with humor.

"You are a brain surgeon…aren't you?" Pres scrunched his eyebrows in confusion.

"Don't mind him, baby. Clark has a really weird sense of humor. His attempts at jokes are only funny to him."

Ric grinned at the man who had taught him everything there is to know about the human brain, so much more than any textbook ever could. Ric immensely respected this man, not only as a colleague but as a friend. When Dr. Brown dropped everything at Ric's call, he'd found out just how honorable and loyal the wise man truly was.

"Rickson, can I speak to my patient alone, please?" Dr. Brown asked, his humor quickly replaced with exemplary professionalism.

"Sure, Clark." Ric got up to leave but was stopped by Pres's grip on his forearm.

"Dr. Brown, anything you have to say can be said in front of Ric. I will withhold nothing from him anyway. So whether you tell him now or I tell him after you leave, he's going to know," Pres stated confidently.

Ric wanted to burst. Pres was his again.

"Of course, Mr. Vaughan. I just wanted to be sure you're okay with it." Dr. Brown moved closer to the side of the bed. "I just wanted to reiterate how things are going to go tomorrow.

When I remove the bandages, I'll want you to keep your eyes closed. Dr. Stevens, your ophthalmologist, will lift your lids to administer the eye drops. These drops will eliminate any grit or residue that may cause discomfort when you take your first look around. Try to look at only one thing or person. Don't try to scan the entire room. I also wanted to check with you again that you're positive about not speaking to a psychologist before we remove the bandages. Seeing again after so long can be hard on the mind. Even seeing loved ones' faces after so many years can be disturbing, Prescott."

"No, Dr. Brown," Pres said with finality, "I'll be fine. I know when to ask for help. I've had to do it before. If I need it, I will accept it then. Okay?"

"Very well. Rest, Prescott, and I'll see you in the morning." Dr. Brown patted Pres's thigh and left the room.

"You okay?" Ric asked.

Pres let out a huff before speaking. "Yeah, I'm fine, Ric. Just a little weirded out, for lack of a better word. What if the bandages are removed and it's still dark in here?" Pres tapped the side of his head with his finger.

Ric took both of Pres's hands in his own and kissed his knuckles. "It won't be. I've seen the scans, Pres. I've studied them for hours. You definitely have visibility. You just have to be willing to accept whatever level of visibility you have. Images may be blurry or distorted, just like Dr. Stevens said, but it's all how you perceive it. Don't be afraid, baby. Even being able to see a sliver of light is a blessing, right?"

"Yeah, you're right. Even if I can only see light and not actual objects, it's more than I'd ever dreamed I would have again." Pres hesitated before speaking again. "The first thing I want to see is you, Sunshine. I'll focus on your face. Are you okay with that?"

Ric couldn't swallow for the large lump that was lodged in his throat. He took Pres's hands and brought them to his face. He wouldn't hide his emotions from him.

"Yes, Pres." He choked up. "Does this mean, you know…?" Ric hesitated on the wording.

"Yes, Ric. Hopefully you forgive me and I forgive you, and we move on after this."

"What about the Texan?" Ric didn't want to, but he had to ask. He had to be sure that he didn't have competition.

Pres held a serious expression. "Blair means a lot to me, Ric. There will be some things that we'll need to discuss when I'm outta here. If you care for me, then that means you're gonna have to trust me."

"Of course I trust you. It's him I don't trust."

"Well, you should trust him, because he's been rooting for me and you all along. When I accepted your invitation to come over and talk before all this"—Pres waved his hand around in the air—"Blair told me to be open about letting you in again. He told me about your talk by the elevator and how miserable you looked every time he saw you in the building. He said eventually you'd be back, and I needed to hear you out and not hold a grudge at the pain I felt."

"Wow. I wasn't expecting that. It seemed as if he was waiting for you to agree to be with him, and anytime he saw me, he threw you guys' relationship in my face."

"That was just his way of baiting you. He knows how I feel about you. When he arrives tomorrow, you be nice to him, and I mean it. I want everything that happened to be in the past," Pres demanded.

"Pres, I'm so sorry I lost it on you that day on your yacht. I was coming over to your place the other day, before you fell, to give you an explanation. I was coming over to tell you that I lost my partner of five years to a boating accident. He was my high school sweetheart, and we were supposed to get married after we finished medical school. We'd planned out our entire lives."

Ric felt Pres squeeze his hand a little tighter, giving him silent support while urging him to continue.

Ric took a deep breath as he recalled the painful memories. "We'd just finished finals and were looking for a way to release a little steam. After hitting up several bars, we ended up on my friend's small cabin cruiser. It was only a few of my friends from med school. It was dark, we were drunk, and my friend decided to open up the engine.

"We were in full speed when Aaron went over the side on a sharp turn. My friend tried to turn around as fast as he could, but Aaron never resurfaced. It was so fucking dark, and I was so scared of never seeing him again, that I jumped in without even thinking. I almost drowned myself before my two friends could pull me back into the boat. The police and coast guard searched for fifteen straight hours before giving up."

Ric was silent for a few minutes. Pres never said anything, patiently waiting for him to keep going. He appreciated the comforting circles Pres rubbed on his back, because he desperately needed the touch of the man he loved now.

Ric continued, "I prayed for days, but I knew he was gone. After five days, Aaron's body washed up on a shore sixty-two miles from where he fell into the ocean. It was like the ocean swallowed him up and spit him out where it saw fit.

"I grieved hard, for many years. What was most difficult was that Aaron's parents blamed me for his death. They said I didn't take life seriously, and now my joking around had killed their son."

Ric leaned his forehead against Pres's. "I shouldn't have let those memories into what we had. I just couldn't figure out how to separate it. Please forgive me, baby. I promise you, I'll never let anything like that happen again. Aaron is gone. I won't make you live your life in a protected box because I'm scared of losing you."

"I understand, Ric. I truly do. I don't want you to be afraid for me. But I promise you, you don't have to worry about me playing silly pranks again."

Enough had been said. Ric laid butterfly kisses on Pres's face until he was sleeping soundly.

# Chapter Thirty-Three

Pres's room had only seven people in it, but it felt full to capacity. He was the major attraction, and he was beyond nervous. The only thing keeping him grounded was Ric's scent. His man was right there with him, holding his hand, as Pres listened to Dr. Brown's instructions for the tenth time.

"Are you ready, Prescott? Dr. Stevens is going to remove the bandages now." Dr. Brown's imposing voice was loud in the quiet room.

"I'm ready," Pres said, his voice quivering from the nerves.

"Nurse Maggie, dim the lights, please."

"Sure, Dr. Brown."

Ric picked up Pres's hand and sat down on the side of the bed. He turned his entire body to face him as Dr. Stevens peeled back the tape on the left eye and then the right. Pres didn't open his eyes, just like instructed. He felt the doctor just barely lift his eyelids to drop the cold solution into his eyes.

Then he had to wait.

Ric leaned down to his ear and whispered just loud enough for him to hear, "I love you, Pres."

After fifteen minutes of silence in the room, Dr. Brown instructed, "Open your eyes slowly, Prescott."

Pres's heart was trying to beat out of his chest. This was it. He would see his man, his parents, and Blair. He couldn't bring himself to open his eyes. His chest heaved up and down, and he began to break out in a cold sweat.

*Fuck. Fuck. Fuck.*

Pres's entire body shook with fear.

"I can't breathe," he croaked, his eyes tightly sealed shut.

"Prescott, please calm down," Dr. Brown said. "Nurse, get me two milligrams of midazolam."

"Yes, sir," she responded.

Ric intervened. "No. He doesn't need to be sedated."

Pres felt Ric lean in and use his heavy upper body to cover him, blocking him from everyone in the room.

"It's okay. I'm right here. Need you to calm down. Slow breaths now." Ric's deep voice was in his ear. Ric wasn't panicking. He was being strong for him, so Pres needed to be strong too. "That's it."

Ric peppered kisses along his jawline until he got to Pres's lips. He laid several gentle kisses on his panting mouth before easing his moist tongue inside. Pres kissed him back. Whoever else was in the room could be damned if they didn't like it. By the time Ric finished kissing him with so much love and emotion, he was a lot more relaxed.

"Now, open your eyes and look at me, beautiful," Ric whispered in the sexiest voice Pres had ever heard him use.

Pres took one last deep breath and began to very slowly open his eyes.

Nothing was moving. He could see dark shadows of figures in the room but no faces. Then he remembered what the doctor said, *"Focus on one thing."* He turned his head to look in the direction of the sweet scent drifting up his nose from his left side.

Pres's excitement began to fade. He could only see shadows, and even they were blurry. He wanted to see Ric's face so badly. He wanted to see Blair, too. He blinked again and again, but he never turned his head. Ric's face became clearer and clearer. Soon he was staring into grassy green eyes.

*Green, his eyes are so green. Oh God, he's…he's…so handsome.*

Pres didn't speak yet. He just blinked the beautiful image—the very large image—in front of him into better focus.

*Sweet Jesus. His shirt…brown…it's brown. Oh God. I can see.*

This was better than Pres could've ever dreamed. He thought he'd only see spots of light, but this was not even close. He could actually see fairly well, and it kept getting better with every few blinks. He saw Ric raise his hand toward his face, and it made him flinch back.

"No moving, Rickson," Dr. Brown barked, making Ric jerk his hand back.

"Oh shit. Pres, did you see my hand?" Ric smiled, but also looked very concerned.

*That smile is amazing.*

"Sunshine"—Pres barely whispered the endearment—"you have a beautiful smile."

Pres heard collective gasps from around the room. His mom's cries could be heard—no, actually, he could see her sobbing into his father's chest.

"Pop, your hair is so gray." Pres beamed at his father's wide smile.

Pres saw his dad's tears falling down his cheeks as he squeezed his wife tighter to him. "Yeah, son. Well, that's your mother's fault." He winked back at his son.

"I saw that, too," Pres whispered in awe. He actually saw his father wink at him. It'd been so long. His father used to always wink at him.

Dr. Brown spoke up. "Prescott, take your time, please. You can see colors as well as details on our faces?"

"Yes, I can see details and colors, but it's still a little blurry," Pres responded. He felt Ric squeeze his hand, making him turn his attention back to him. "I can see you, Ric. Jesus, your shoulders are huge, and your eyes… Jesus."

Pres watched those toned shoulders rise and fall with Ric's deep laugh.

"Okay, so enough compliments for Rickson. We need to run some vision tests, Prescott. We don't want you to overexert your eyes, so I want you to close them back now and let them rest before the tests," Dr. Stevens requested.

"Damn. Okay." Pres groaned a little. "I have throbbing behind my right eye, Dr. Brown."

"Headaches, sometimes even migraines, are going to be expected, Prescott. That's why it's important to look around in small time intervals until you can get used to seeing again," he said.

Pres closed his eyes and immediately felt the throbbing lessen. "Ric."

"Right here, Pres. You did so good. I'm so proud of you." Ric sounded so emotional that it was making Pres get emotional too.

"Let's leave them alone for a while, everyone. Prescott, Dr. Stevens and I will get everything set up for the tests. It's going to take several hours to complete them, so try to relax a little while, and keep your eyes closed, please. We'll be back in an hour." With that, Dr. Brown and Dr. Stevens left with everyone except Ric and his parents.

"Pres, honey, I'm so happy for you. This is God's work. He's blessed you in the most wonderful way. I can't wait to cook with my baby boy again. I know we never technically stopped, but it's going to be different. I'm so excited." His mom was crying all over his chest as Pres gently stroked her soft honey-blonde hair.

"Me too, Mom. I love you."

"Come on, dear. Prescott needs to rest a bit." His father's calm voice was so comforting at that moment. He felt his dad prying his weeping mother off of him before patting him on the shoulder. "I'll take your mom down to the gift shop and let her look around so you can rest. Rickson, take care of my boy, son, and see that he follows the good doctor's orders," his dad requested of Ric, and it pleased Pres that his parents had completely overlooked the fact that their son was now with a man.

"I will, sir," Ric responded respectfully.

Pres waited for his room door to open and then click shut before he abruptly rose up and gripped the back of Ric's neck, slamming his mouth over top of his. He kept his eyes closed and hungrily swallowed Ric's shocked gasp and sexy moans. He clung on to the beautiful man for dear life. Now that he'd seen the broad shoulders, large chest, emerald-green eyes, and wavy brown hair, Pres was a hot, horny mess. He needed Ric in the most animalistic way. He released Ric's supple lips with a moan.

"Fuck, Sunshine. I didn't want to say this in front of my folks, but damn, you are delicious. Jesus. You're the sexiest man I've laid eyes on in the last ten minutes." Pres chuckled at his blind joke.

Ric huffed breathlessly against his mouth. "Thank you, honey. Wait until you get a look at yourself." He let out a nervous sigh against Pres's neck as he hugged him.

"What's wrong, Ric?" Pres pulled back, but kept his eyes closed.

"I think there may be someone that has me beat in the looks department, baby." Ric sounded exasperated.

"Blair," Pres said simply. Thinking about the enticing man who had become his best friend over the last few months, and who he was very much in love with, too, brought a slow smile to his face. Pres couldn't wait to see him.

"Damn it. That's what I'm talking about. How can you say you love me and then smile like that when you speak that man's name on your lips?" Ric spat as he rose up off the bed to pace the length of the room.

"Ric. I do love you, honey. I love Blair, too. I don't know what to do. If it wasn't for Blair, I don't know where'd I'd be right now. Honestly, I know for a fact that I wouldn't be here. I was thinking about moving away, because of my depression of knowing you were right down the hall from me but I couldn't have you.

"I was drinking and self-medicating, and he didn't let me do it anymore. He cooked with me, went to my assignments with me, took me out, bragged about me to his friends and family. He was falling in love with me, all the while knowing that I love you. He never once spoke badly of you. He just waited…He's still waiting. I'm not the type of man to mistreat someone, especially someone that loves me so much. However this goes, I need you to understand that."

"What are you saying? That you want us both…as lovers? What the fuck, Prescott? Are you asking me to let you cheat? I don't fucking share!" Ric growled.

Pres couldn't believe how he was feeling right at the moment: powerful, turned on, elated, scared, excited even. Ric was growling and being all possessive of him, and it had him rock hard. The thought of Ric and Blair snarling and rumbling over the right to claim Pres had him dizzy with want and lust, or maybe it'd just been too long since he'd had release.

*I want both of them in my bed.*

"I'm saying we should take this slow. I need you, Sunshine. I've made that clear. All I'm asking is, if you really love me, you'll be open and understanding. To answer your question, no, I will never cheat on you, or anyone that I love." Pres made sure to put emphasis on the word "cheat." If both men were his and they were together, then it wasn't cheating.

"You need to rest, Pres, and I need to think about some thi—" Ric's sentence was cut off by Pres's hospital room door bursting open.

"My sweet Strawberry, how are you?"

Blair's bass-filled drawl was beautiful music to Pres's ears. He'd missed him so much while he'd been away at school. Paired with Pres's accident, they hadn't seen each other in a week. That was a long time for them, but Blair was on his final preparations to graduate, and Pres knew all too well how demanding that was. He had spoken to Blair several times on the phone and insisted that he was okay, and to just come when he was finished with his finals.

Pres felt Blair lean down and place a slow kiss on his lips. Blair smelled like Cool Water cologne, and his skin was scruffy like he hadn't shaved today.

*I have to look.*

Blair pulled back, and Pres slowly opened his eyes for his first look at the other man he loved. Once he had his eyes wide open, he gasped at the heavenly vision.

"Darlin', what's wrong? Are you in pain?" Blair took Pres's hand and pressed it to his cheek. He always made Pres touch his eyes, lips, and cheeks so that Pres would know his facial expressions. Blair had no clue that he didn't need to do that now. Pres could see the concern on the man's handsome face.

"Ric, why are you staring out the window like that? What's wrong with him? What aren't you telling me?" Blair turned his angry hazel gaze from Ric's back and focused on Pres.

"Talk to me, darlin'. What's going on? You said you fell, but it wasn't life threatening and you had to get stitches. I'm not a doctor, but that doesn't require a four-day hospital stay. So, don't bullshit me."

Pres couldn't stop the smile on his face. His best friend never lost his cool. He was demanding but composed at the same time. His attitude, coupled with the sexy drawl, made him a lethal combination of provocative seduction that no man or women could resist. No wonder Rickson was nervous, but Pres didn't believe he needed to be. Ric was in a class all by himself, and Pres loved him just as much as he loved Blair.

*I'm screwed.*

"Honey, I'm fine." Pres held Blair's face with both hands. He took in the light brown eyes, the long, dark lashes that he'd always loved to finger, and the plump, soft pink lips in the center of a trendy five-o'clock shadow.

Blair had a two-inch black barbell in his left eyebrow.

*Hmm. That's new.*

Pres rubbed the two sparkling one-carat diamond studs in each of Blair's ears. Damn, the man was all style. His tight denim jeans hugged his tight ass to perfection, and his thin "I Can Burn in the Kitchen and the Bedroom" V-neck T-shirt was so damn tight, it looked wet.

Pres lowered his voice. "You can burn in the bedroom too, huh?"

"You're fuckin' right I can. Maybe you'll let me sh—" Blair jumped back from Pres's bed so fast that he knocked the flowers that he'd just placed on his tray to the floor with a loud crash. The realization that Pres had read his shirt was all over that beautiful, stunned face.

Blair's wide eyes bounced from Ric's back, to Pres, to his shirt.

"D-darlin'," he stammered, "did you just read that? Tell me I'm not fucking crazy." Blair looked like a deer caught in headlights.

"Ric!" Blair growled. "Fuckin' turn around."

**R**ic gritted his teeth as soon as he saw the Texan barrel in like a tornado, but with an astonishing amount of finesse and swagger. In with him came the most erotic smell, and it pissed Ric off that his dick jerked happily under his scrubs.

Ric kept his back to them as the man kissed and swooned all over his Prescott. He wouldn't act like a jealous prick. He'd just gotten Pres back, and he'd be damned if he was going to walk away again. If he had to go to war with the longhorn, then he would.

He could hear Blair's cool disintegrating as he tripped and knocked shit over in the room at the realization of Pres's sight. The man was growling and snarling at Ric's back like Ric had done something wrong.

Ric rolled his eyes. He knew Pres was surely gushing over the Texas god, because Lord knows the man was stunning.

"Ric, fuckin' turn around." That suave southern drawl had been replaced with the anger of a speared bull.

Ric felt strong arms jerk him around by his shoulders, and he snapped. He gripped the Texas model by his small biceps and slammed him against the wall.

"Don't fight!" Pres yelled at them.

"Stay in the bed, Pres," Ric barked.

Ric smothered the pretty man with his bulk, daring him to fight back.

"How dare you put your fucking hands on me?" Ric was two inches from Blair's shocked face. "Yes, Pres can see now. He can see everything, including you, you gorgeous prick. But, the last thing he needs is you coming in here starting drama," Ric snarled and bared his teeth in intimidation.

The damn man was just too fucking fine for words. His long lashes fluttered over his piercing fair-colored eyes, and his fuckable mouth was open and panting out cinnamon-flavored breath. He could see what Pres was talking about.

Ric froze and clenched his teeth together as Blair began to do a slow grind on the leg he had pinned against the man's—*what the fuck?*—hard cock.

"You son of a bitch," Ric growled, completely breathless.

He watched Blair lick his lips and close his eyes. Ric was so torn. He had this sexy southern incubus attached to him, and he was slowly becoming hypnotized by Blair's slow dance. He needed to fight this, fight him. He could destroy what he was trying to have with Pres.

"Give him what he needs, Ric." Pres sounded winded as he spoke into Ric's lust-filled haze.

"What?" Ric gasped.

*Jesus. Pres is watching this.*

Ric had to stop this. They were in a hospital where he worked, not a brothel. Ric released Blair, and the man's feet dropped back to the linoleum floor. Blair in a full state of submissive arousal was too damn much.

"I can't," Ric whispered as he darted out of the too-hot room.

## Chapter Thirty-Four

**P**res had never been so turned on in his entire life. Ric completely dominating Blair was a sight his brand-new eyes couldn't look away from. Ric was stunning, his bulging biceps and massive chest rendering Blair completely helpless and under his authority.

Blair's naturally wanton ways reacted instinctually to Ric's alpha side. Pres only wished he could've gotten up and joined in, but he wanted them to connect so badly. This was exactly what he'd been dreaming about the last couple of months.

Pres finally spoke into the silent room. "Com'ere, honey."

"I think I just blew it." Blair sulked over to Pres's bed, his breathing now under control.

"No, you didn't. He just needs a minute." Pres moved over and let Blair cuddle up next to him in his bed. "I was just telling him that I loved you both, when you came in looking good enough to eat."

"Speaking of"—Blair shifted against him—"you can fucking see now…like, everything? How the hell does something like that happen? This is unbelievable, darlin'. How are you feeling about all this, and more importantly, why didn't you tell me?" he admonished.

"Honey, I don't know. One minute I'm making an olive-and-cheese crudité. I slip and fall, busting the back of my head on my kitchen island. The next thing I know, Ric and two other smarty-pants doctors are telling me that I basically knocked something back in place that was jarred during my accident."

Pres kissed Blair's smiling lips. "Now I'm looking at your stunning face and feeling like my life has just begun."

"Mmmm. I love you, Strawberry."

"I love you too, babe." Blair and Pres kissed for a long time before he pulled back and stared at him some more.

"What are we going to do? You saw what just happened, too." Blair hid his face in Pres's neck. "Leave it to me and my slutty self to completely lose focus on why I'm here. Are you mad at me for upsetting the Bear?"

Pres chuckled at Blair's pet name for Ric. He'd been calling Ric "Bear" since they met at the elevators in Pres's building and he described how Ric was growling in his face.

"Oh yes, I saw it. I thought I was going to spontaneously combust. Jesus, you two are smokin' together."

"You're not mad?"

"No. Goodness. Why would I be mad? We've talked about this. We've talked about being together…all of us. You told me about his reaction to you in the hallway, and how he looks at you. I know he will be all right with it, as soon as he wraps his logically thinking head around it. I saw him with you just now." Pres grinned wide at being able to even say something like that. "You looked beautiful, honey, and I thought he was going to throw you on the floor and take you right then and there."

He held Blair's face in his hands and latched on to his mouth, showing the unsure beauty just how "not upset" he was.

# Chapter Thirty-Five

**R**ic was in the surgeons' private lounge, brewing in his anger.

*That sneaky bastard. Seducing me in front of my man.*

Ric was steering clear from everyone, from all the nurses, Dr. Brown, Pres's parents, and especially Blair. Pres was undergoing his vast array of vision tests. Though he'd been paged several times by Dr. Stevens with an invite to sit in on them, he just couldn't face Pres right now with all the crazy feelings swimming around inside him—especially his lower parts.

No doubt that Blair was probably walking around looking for him, and the surgeons' lounge was the safest place he could think of to cower and hide.

He couldn't believe he'd just read Pres the riot act about not sharing or cheating, and before he could blink, he had Blair pinned to a wall while he imagined devouring his sexy body from head to toe.

"What did I do?" he whispered.

"Only what Pres and I have fantasized about for months," Blair's husky voice answered him.

*Fuck. How did he find me?*

Ric refused to turn around, no matter how much he wanted to visually feast on the man. Instead, he stared out the large double-paned window, down into the near-empty parking lot.

"What the hell are you talking about?" Ric asked after registering what Blair just said.

"Are you mad at me?" Blair asked.

"Yes," he said simply. "More than anything, I'm mad at myself. You're not mine. I have no right to touch you."

"I can be…yours, I mean. Yours and Pres's." Blair spoke confidently as he inched closer to Ric.

"I don't want a whore." Ric inwardly flinched at his harsh choice of words before he could think better of saying it.

"I'm not a whore!" Blair yelled. "Don't you ever fuckin call me that, you self-righteous, judgmental bastard."

Ric was shocked at the man's loss of composure. Blair was cool and relaxed. He didn't get rattled. However, Ric was able to get under his smooth outward appearance. He didn't want to hurt the gorgeous man in order to get a rise out of him. His mother always told him if he didn't have anything nice to say, then don't say anything at all.

Ric cocked one eyebrow up at Blair's name-calling.

"Not a whore, huh? Don't people pay you money to sleep with them? Or did I misunderstand the job details of an escort?"

*Shit.*

Ric was really on a roll with the verbal vomit. The hurt in the Texan's voice was making Ric's chest hurt. He really didn't want to be mean to him, but he should have left Ric alone so he could process what was going on between the three of them.

"No, I'm not paid to sleep with people. Escorting someone on a date, to a wedding, or a formal function doesn't require fucking. I think you want to think the worst of me because hopefully it will quench some of the desire you have for me. But I got news for you, big guy. I happen to be one of the most highly regarded chefs to come through the Le Cordon Bleu Academy in twenty years. Being an escort while I studied for my master's paid the fucking bills, and I will not apologize for it.

"Now that I have my degree, you have your back turned on the youngest executive chef to ever manage a five-star restaurant right out of an academy. So turn around and face me, you son of a bitch."

Blair grabbed Ric's arms again to spin him around exactly like he did in Pres's room. Ric surged forward and came face-to-face with Blair's rage.

*Jesus Christ, he's exquisite.*

Ric growled and scooped up the small man in one swift move.

"Why are you doing this? What is it you want from me?" Ric again had Blair's significantly smaller frame up against the wall, wedged between the window and the coffee vending machine. They were alone, the lights were dim, and Blair's seductive lashes were fluttering again at Ric's strength.

"I want you to take what you want, and stop fighting it," Blair panted.

"I want Pres," Ric replied with little conviction.

"You want me, too." Blair lifted both dangling legs and wrapped them around Ric's waist.

*Fuck.*

"I won't cheat on Pres," Ric moaned, his mouth pressed against Blair's long, slender neck. He wanted to bite him, he was so pent up and in need of release.

"Believe me. Cheating on Pres would be the last thing you're doing." Blair ground his hard cock into Ric's. "We both want you, darlin'. In our lives. In our bed. The three of us. One relationship." He accented each statement with a torturously sensual roll of his hips. "Pres and I haven't slept together, because we're missing our other partner." Blair's sexy winding hips and that deep baritone drawl did Ric in.

Ric hissed at the pleasure and gripped Blair's round ass in a ferocious grip. "Motherfucker," he growled.

"That's it. Growl for me, my sexy bear," Blair purred like a nasty kitten, and Ric damn near lost his mind.

"This is what you both want? How do I know you're not tricking me into messing around with you, only to go back and tell Pres that I'm a no-good cheating rat?" Ric asked.

Blair didn't dignify Ric's suspicious question with an answer. Instead, Ric watched him pull an ultra-thin cell phone from his back pocket. He sent a single-sentence text to Pres's phone and turned the screen around to Ric. The text was simple: *I'm with the Bear.*

Ric gave Blair a sexy smirk. *Bear, huh?*

Ten seconds later, Blair's phone vibrated with a return message. The sexy Texan looked at the phone and let a devious smile play across his fancy face. He flipped the phone over and showed Ric Pres's response: *Be done with testing in an hour. Make him ours, honey.*

Ric stared at the phone. He couldn't believe Pres wanted to be in a ménage relationship.

"You heard Pres in the room when you had that delicious body pressed up against me. He said to give me what I want. Do it, Ric," Blair urged before licking and biting at Ric's jaw.

Ric ground his aching cock into Blair with complete and total abandon, but he needed more. The dry humping wasn't cutting it. He was not in high school. He walked them both into one of the small adjacent rooms. There was a small bed where surgeons could rest in between surgeries. He dropped Blair onto the thin mattress before covering him with his large body.

Blair lifted Ric's shirt and licked both of his nipples, making him arch his back and pray the man never removed his mouth from his body.

"Turn over, Bear. I need to finally taste you. I've jerked off to this fantasy for months. I'm not letting that sweet load of yours get wasted in those fucking pajama pants you have on."

Ric reversed their positions, letting Blair situate himself on top of him. He gave Blair a hard slap on his ass. "They're not pajama pants, smartass. They're OR scrubs."

"*O R* they?" Blair laughed at his own joke and then reined it in just as quickly when he saw the feral look in Ric's eyes.

"Fuck, you are hot." Blair got comfortable between Ric's thighs. "Just lie back and enjoy what's yours now."

Ric let Blair remove his shoes, socks, and scrubs, never taking his eyes off the god. The Texan was so damn handsome. The thought of being in a relationship with him and Prescott simultaneously had Ric's cock leaking like a broken faucet.

Blair didn't let his essence go to waste. Ric watched his pink tongue lap at his dick like it was a lollipop. He licked and licked until Ric thought he'd lose his load without even getting to the suction.

"Get it in your mouth, baby," Ric groaned. He needed relief, now.

"Tsk, tsk, tsk. Patience, love. Good things come to those who beg," Blair drawled lazily before he lapped at Ric's balls.

"Augh, fuck. Yeah, that feels so good." Ric was thrashing helplessly on the small bed. Blair was making him his slave. He'd beg the man, all right, if that's what it took. "Please…"

Blair took Ric's cock into that hot, sinful cavern and buried his nose in Ric's bush. He swallowed around his throbbing head so many times that he lost count. Ric was so overwhelmed with pleasure he damn near levitated them both off the bed.

*Fuuuckk. I can't hold it.*

"Blair!" His eyes rolled in their sockets as he shot his load, over and over, into Blair's perfect mouth. Ric's hips jerked violently from Blair's tugging.

*He's gonna yank my fucking dick off.*

The Texan was moaning and grinding his own cock into the thin mattress as he milked Ric dry.

"Blair…enough. Fuck!" Ric had both hands on Blair's face, desperately trying to get him to release his viselike suction from his spent cock. Blair finally unlocked his jaw and released his aching dick. "Shit! Fuck!" Ric roared.

"You'll only make me suck harder when you growl, Bear. Turns me the fuck on." Blair pushed the come leaking down his chin back into his mouth. He climbed up Ric's body and molded himself to him.

Ric had to admit he liked the way they fit together. He imagined Pres's sexy body plastered to his other side.

*Oh hell yeah. Now, this I think I can do. Damn socially unacceptable.*

He'd have to set some ground rules for Tex. Ric meant it when he said he didn't share. If Pres and Blair were his, then that's exactly what that meant. They would sleep with each other and no one else, and Tex would definitely not be escorting no-fucking-body anywhere else.

"Listen up, Tex."

Blair laughed against Ric's chest. "Tex…really? I can't get a sexier name than that, Bear?"

Ric shook his head in awe and kissed the top of Blair's head at the man's conceit. "What do you want me to call you, fancy face?"

"Ummm, not that either, it's too feminine." Blair tilted his head as if deep in thought. "I don't know. How about 'lover' or 'slut'?"

Ric gasped at the names. "You're incorrigible." He gripped Blair's chin and tilted his face up to look him in his erotic hazel eyes. "You wanna be my slut?" he asked, letting his voice go as deep as he could, knowing now that Blair liked his growling voice.

"Yes. More than anything," Blair said without an ounce of hesitation.

"You can be my slut, baby…but only me. Do you understand? I will not tolerate you and Pres with anyone else. I've lost a lot of time with Pres over my insecurities. Now that I have him"—Ric licked his lips and took Blair's mouth in a sensual kiss—"and you, too, I won't share."

"We'll be everything you need us to be. I'll be everything you need me to be," Blair promised with his words and his eyes.

"No more escorting," Ric commanded in a tone that said there was no negotiating.

"I'll quit tonight."

"I'll take care of you, if you need me to."

"Wow. You are protective, aren't you? That's good. It soothes my submissive side. But, I don't need a sugar daddy. I need a partner, and so does Pres." Blair stroked Ric's large chest as he spoke seductively. "I'll be starting my new job in two months. I can take care of myself, Doc."

"I know you can, and Pres can, too. I'll work on the overprotectiveness, but I make no promises." Ric pulled Blair in closer, thinking he'd never get enough of his men.

His men. *Wow. Men.*

Ric linked his fingers behind his head and let Blair be his slut. He moaned when Blair sucked hickeys onto his stiff nipples.

"That mouth of yours is going to get you in trouble, boy."

"Mmmm.'Boy.' Yes, sir. I like it." Blair buried his nose in Ric's armpit and inhaled deeply. "When I get you alone, I'm going to lick you every-fucking-where, including here." Blair dove deeper into his underarms.

"Promises, promises, boy." Ric and Blair kissed and got familiar as they waited for their third to finish his test.

"Hey."

"Yeah?" Ric responded lazily, feeling like he wanted to nap.

"Our Strawberry can see now."

"Yeah." Ric beamed. They looked at each other and laughed like maniacs.

Life was good.

YOU CAN SEE ME

## Chapter Thirty-Six

It was day seven of Pres being in the hospital, and he was scheduled for discharge this afternoon. Ric was finishing his rounds and praying that he'd be able to get his next two days off to get Pres settled back in his place. He whistled as he made the last few notes in his charts.

"Well someone sure is happy today," Nurse Maggie crooned from behind him, making Ric smile wider.

"Mmm hmm," he hummed.

"Does it have anything to do with those hotties you're getting ready to go home with in a couple hours?" she dug, obviously wanting more of a response.

"Get your mind off my men, Maggie," Ric teased her.

He'd come to really like and respect the caring nurse. She took care of every need and want that Pres had during his admittance. Pres even had her cell phone number if he didn't want to use the call button. However, Ric thought the woman just liked bathing his man more than anything, but he didn't care. She didn't have a chance in hell of wooing Prescott.

He, Pres, and Blair were so damn excited to get home and explore their new relationship. They'd barely been able to behave themselves in Pres's hospital room, getting a little too carried away several times. Ric thought back to last night.

It was quiet and peaceful in Pres's room at nine o'clock at night. Pres was lying on his bed reading one of the hundreds of *Food & Cuisine* magazines that Blair had bought him, while Ric reclined in the chair watching the game.

Blair came into the room without a word and jumped onto Ric's lap like he was riding a horse. He hungrily maneuvered Ric's cock out of his scrubs and began jerking him in tandem with his wayward hips.

"Fuck, baby. Hi, how are you?" Ric gasped as Blair slithered to his knees and engulfed his cock. Blair didn't speak. He didn't want conversation. He showed Ric exactly what he wanted…cock. Of course, Ric gave it up without a fight. His eyes squeezed shut at the speed and intensity of his building orgasm. Ric heard Pres moaning in his bed at the live sex show they were putting on.

With Blair's talents and Pres's moaning, Ric came faster than he'd ever come in his life. Blair didn't miss a beat. He gulped Ric's last spurt, stood, went to Pres, leaned over his bed, yanked his covers out of the way, pulled down his thin sweats, and swallowed Pres's already extremely erect cock.

"Take what you need, honey," Pres whispered.

Ric was recovered enough to stand and drape his body over Blair's, giving the pretty Texan his weight. He placed wet, lazy kisses along Blair's neck as he ravished Pres. Ric had discovered how needy Blair was during their few short days together. He was just like his Pres—he needed constant touch and attention.

Their deep conversations had been limited because of the lack of privacy in the hospital, but that would change when they were back in Pres's condo. They'd talk, they'd learn, they'd fuck each other until they knew each other's every habit.

Pres came with a hoarse shout, and Blair laid his head on Pres's thigh, panting to catch his breath.

Ric scooped Blair into his arms and sat them both down in the recliner. Blair still hadn't said a word. He just buried his head in Ric's neck and went to sleep. Pres and Ric exchanged concerned glances as Blair held on to Ric for dear life. They sat like that for an hour before Ric had to get up to make his hospital rounds.

"Give him here, Sunshine."

Ric cradled Blair's sleeping form and got up to gently place him in bed with Pres.

"Is he all right?" Ric whispered to Pres, not wanting to wake Blair. He was concerned, to say the least. Blair was a sexual spitfire, but that display was something else.

"Yeah. Sometimes he just needs to vent," Pres whispered against Blair's soft hair and kissed him tenderly.

"That's how he vents?" Ric frowned. "We'll be talking about this soon."

He bent and kissed his men, Pres on his soft lips and Blair on the top of his head, before leaving to go check in at the ER.

"What time are you leaving?" Nurse Maggie interrupted his thoughts, bringing him back to the present.

"Right now." He got up and put the chart back in the bin. He kissed Maggie on her cheek and bid her a good weekend. He watched the girl blush a brilliant shade of rose. He winked and left out of the double-bay doors toward level five.

YOU CAN SEE ME

## Chapter Thirty-Seven

Scott, Pres's driver, was waiting for them at the entrance with Pres's brand-new, darkly tinted Suburban. Pres had on the medically prescribed UV-shield glasses, making him look seventy years old. Although they were not as stylish as his Kenneth Coles, they were necessary until he got better with the light sensitivity.

When they got outside, Pres was relieved that there were no cameras or lingering medical journal reporters asking for interviews. He didn't want to answer any questions or stop anywhere. He just wanted to go home with his men and be alone and loved on for the next few days, until Ric had to go back to work.

"Okay, Pres honey, we'll meet you at your house," his mom yelled on their way to their car.

"No, Mom, that's okay. You don't ha—" Pres was cut off with a flick of his mother's wrist as she continued walking to her car.

He sighed and looked at his father. His father winked at him on his way by. "I'll handle it, son. Go on home with your fellas." His dad looked at him knowingly.

*What the hell?*

Pres just shook his head in a silly attempt at denial, not really knowing what else to do. He wasn't ready to discuss his ménage relationship with his folks yet. Had his father figured it out? He thought they'd been careful. He knew his folks were accepting of Ric, but how far did their conservatism extend to?

His father had let him off the hook, for now.

"See you next week, son." His dad caught up with his mom in time to open her door for her. His father never ceased to amaze him. His twenty-five years as a white-collar crime detective had left the man sharp as a tack. Pres should've known he couldn't pull one over on him.

"You feeling all right, baby? Is the sun too much?" Ric fussed, trying to usher him into the SUV.

"No, I'm good. Just feeling a little tired is all," Pres confessed.

"Well, let's get you home, Strawberry, so you can rest." Blair got in behind him, while Ric got in on the other side, putting Pres in the middle.

When Scott pulled up, Ric didn't waste time ushering Pres through the lobby quickly. Pres needed to remember to talk with the management staff later. He'd limited his conversations on his sight recovery to his staff only.

They rode the elevator in silence, his men probably wondering how he felt to be looking at his familiar—and yet not-so-familiar—surroundings. He knew these halls, the elevator, the lounge…and then he didn't. It was hard to understand and put an exact word as to how he felt about it. In all honesty, Pres didn't give a damn about the lobby. He wanted to see his kitchen.

Pres paused at his front door, his men at his side.

"You sure you're ready to—"

"Ric, open the goddamn door," Pres gruffed. Jesus, his Sunshine could fuss.

"Don't get your ass spanked as soon as you get inside," Ric growled.

Pres snorted indignantly. "Save that for Blair. He likes that kinky shit."

"Sure as fuck do," Blair chimed in shamelessly.

They laughed as Ric opened Pres's front door. He stepped into his condo, laying eyes on it for the first time in five years, his men close behind him. No one spoke. The silence was too much.

"Guys?"

"Yes?" they both hurriedly responded in unison.

Pres laughed at their nervousness. "Relax, babes. I'm all right. You don't have to be so quiet, is all." He looked around as he continued to make his way into his kitchen. Everything was pretty much the same in his den and living room as when he'd had it done seven years ago. He stopped suddenly when he entered his kitchen.

Everything was earth toned and stainless steel, and the sight—oh my God, the sight of it all—took his breath away, and his legs gave out, but Ric was right there.

"It's okay, baby. I got you." Ric hugged him close as Pres continued surveying the immaculate room…his sanctuary. He could see it again.

He was going to cook again with sight, and he'd be able to cook in someone else's kitchen, too, if he wanted. So many opportunities were opening up right before his very new eyes. He didn't think he would…but he lost it.

A guttural cry left his mouth right before he dropped all his weight onto Ric, no longer able to support himself. Harsh sobs racked his body while Ric struggled to keep him upright.

"Pres, it's all right," Ric tried to assure him.

Blair looked like he was hurting as much as he was. His beautiful hazel eyes were glossy with tears as he ran his hands through his hair repeatedly at watching Ric try to calm him down. Pres stared at his beautiful men, his home, and couldn't help but reflect back on where he was two months ago. Next thing he realized, he was being lifted by strong arms and moved to the back of his home.

Ric gently laid him on the bed and crowded in behind him, keeping him wrapped tight. He rubbed his face against the back of Pres's neck, giving him his wonderful scent as well as his warmth. Blair closed the drapes and turned down the lights in the room. He removed his light jacket and shoes, molded himself perfectly against the front of Pres's body, and began to warmly stroke his cheek, his neck, his chest, and anywhere else he could reach, until his breathing was back to normal.

"That's better, Strawberry. Ric and I are right here, and always will be. Hold on to me." Blair spoke softly.

Pres squeezed his eyes shut and shivered. "I need you so much. God, I need you both. Show me this is real. Show me I'm not dreaming. Blair, Ric, please, make me know this is real."

Blair didn't wait. He pulled Pres in close to him and began to make slow, sensual licks to his face with his silky tongue. Pres was smothered with Blair's clean, sexy scent. He rolled his head back on his shoulders only to be overwhelmed with Ric's spicy scent. It was enough to make his head buzz.

Pres felt Ric thrusting his strong hips into his ass, and he automatically began to rock back into it.

"Yes, Sunshine. Fuck. Like that. Make me feel you." He cupped the back of Blair's head when he felt him sucking hard enough to leave marks on his neck. "Ugh. Take this shirt off," Pres growled, needing more of Blair's mouth.

Ric helped Pres out of his shirt and relieved himself of his own.

Ric was so warm. The body heat he gave off was amazing. It made Pres feel safe, like nothing would harm him ever again. He'd already begun to trust Ric with his heart again. Their time in the hospital was not only time for them to learn and connect with each other, but also time to mend any rifts between them. However, as of right now, this was what Pres needed most from his men.

"Ric?" Pres whispered.

"Right here, baby," Ric responded between thrusts.

"Let me make love to you again. Need to be inside you," Pres pleaded. He was being deliciously assaulted from all angles, and he didn't know if he was coming or going.

Right when he'd decided he needed more, Blair began to undo his jeans button and inch them over his hips. While his pants went down lower, so did Blair.

"My sweet Blair." Pres gripped a handful of Blair's soft hair while the talented man engulfed his entire cock. "Oh my God!" Pres yelled into the dim room. Blair was doing it again, sucking him hard and long with the strongest jaws in the fucking world. "Jesus Christ, baby."

Blair pulled off with a loud pop, making Pres's hips jerk back into Ric's gyrating hips.

"This real enough, Strawberry? We're right here, darlin'. Always will be." Blair went back to work. Pres was going to have to stop Blair soon if he planned on fucking Ric.

"That's good, honey. That hot fuckin' mouth of yours, you make me wanna come deep down your throat. Get up here." Pres pulled Blair back up to his chest and kissed him with passion and fury. "Want you to suck our Sunshine while I fuck his sexy ass, honey. Can you do that for me?" Pres asked, breathless, while peppering kisses on Blair's collarbone.

"Mmmmm. Fuck yeah." Blair rose up and peered over Pres's shoulder. "Come here, my sexy Bear."

Pres felt Ric shiver behind him as he made his way over to Blair. Pres lay on his side and settled in behind Ric, making quick work of getting him out of those tight jeans. With Ric in the middle now, he watched him and Blair kiss like horny teenagers, and it made his cock leak onto his thick tan comforter.

He reached into his nightstand drawer and pulled out a tube of slick and couldn't help but notice the lamp on it that was given to him by his mom last year. She told him it was a rusty wrought-iron color, but actually it had a more mahogany, russet look.

Pres smiled hard at noting that difference.

*This is real. This is my life now. In bold, live color.*

He fully relaxed his mind and let himself bask in his happiness, knowing it wasn't going to be ripped away from him.

Pres focused his line of sight on the details of Ric's defined back muscles. He ran his hand up and down those ridges, relishing the sensation of being able to feel and see this man. He had studied Ric—both his men—from the first day he'd opened his eyes and saw them. He couldn't look away. They were fascinating, and even more fascinating to watch together.

Blair was assaulting Ric's hard nipples, pulling and tugging on them like they held nourishment.

"Blair, fuck! Don't tear 'em off, baby." Ric stroked Blair's back in slow circles. "Shhh. That's it, sexy boy. Gently. Mmmm. That feels good."

The two of them were gorgeous together. Pres popped the cap on the lube and squeezed a generous amount onto two fingers. He felt Ric begin to shake with anticipation.

"Want me to fill you up, honey? Tell me how much you missed my cock." Pres whispered into Ric's ear. He didn't need him to answer with words. The way Ric was moaning and pushing his ass back into his probing fingers was answer enough. Pres propped himself up higher to study Ric's facial expressions as he pushed one finger in halfway and hooked it.

"Augh. Pres. Yeah, right there. More, give me more," Ric moaned.

Pres watched Ric grip Blair's ass hard and grind their weeping cocks together. Blair licked his neck, his lips, and nibbled his way to Ric's cheek, then leaned in to lick Pres's lips too. The three of them on Pres's huge bed, together, in a mass of long limbs, sweaty chests, and hard dicks, was too damn erotic for words.

"Suck him off, honey, while I get him ready," Pres told Blair.

Once Ric's cock disappeared into heaven and Blair's nose was buried in Ric's bush, Pres pushed a second finger in as deep as it could go.

"Fuck! Fuck!" Ric yelled, and Pres didn't know if he was hollering at the feel of his long fingers in his ass or Blair's talented figure eights he was doing on his cock. All he did know was he was ready to fuck Ric again. He'd waited long enough.

Pres lifted one of Ric's thighs and hooked it over Blair's hip, opening him up all the way, and he was rewarded with a beautiful view of Ric's budding star. It was shiny and wet and appeared to wink at him as he stared at it.

*Fuck me.*

He wanted to take his dick and bury it into this man, but he didn't just yet. "Condom or no?" Pres hissed at Ric, silently hopping for him to agree to the latter. They knew they were clean. Since they were in the hospital for days, Ric had decided to get them retested just as a precaution.

"Don't you fuckin' dare. Want to feel only you," Ric answered.

*Oh, thank you, kind and generous God.*

Pres placed his lips against Ric's ear. "You ready, honey?"

"Yes. Need you now," said Ric, his body still jerking at Blair's skills.

"Ima fill you up, baby." Pres twisted three fingers around in Ric's ass, stretching him good and pegging his gland every few pumps. "I want you to come in our sexy boy's mouth. Make him swallow all of you while I fuck your tight ass." Pres moaned, and so did Blair. Pres was going to burst right there if he didn't stop with all the nasty talk.

While lying on their sides, Ric continued to fuck Blair's mouth as Pres placed the head of his cock at that hot entrance. He felt Ric slow down his thrusting, and he took that as his cue to get inside. Pres pushed in and immediately gasped at the tightness.

*Baby, it's been too long.*

Pres felt like he was home again. He pushed in a little more, trying to give Ric time to accept the fullness. It was so goddamn good, and hot, and oh so snug around his cock that he wanted to bless the man who had discovered this blissful act and unselfishly passed it along to others.

Pres pushed in another inch and was met with resistance. He felt Ric tense up. Pres rubbed Ric's thigh while he kissed his wide shoulders, working his way up to his ear. "Open up for me, honey. Let me in. All the way." Pres pushed a little deeper, but Ric's ass was clenched tight. "Stop fighting your orgasm. Come in his mouth. Give Blair what he wants." Pres knew that there was nothing more wonderful to Blair than one of their warm loads shooting down his throat.

He felt Ric relax, and he took the opportunity to slide the rest of the way in. He had the urge to squeeze his eyes shut at the pleasure, but he'd had his eyes closed for five years. He needed to see it all.

"You are so damn tight. This ass belongs to us and only us," Pres said, referring to him and Blair.

"Fuck yeah, claim my ass, Pres," Ric moaned.

Pres pulled out halfway and slammed back into Ric, his self-control snapping at Ric asking him to claim him. He did it again, only this time aimed his stroke to the right and nailed Ric's gland.

Ric bucked hard, almost throwing all of them off the bed. "Pres! Fuck! Aughhh, you're gonna—aughhh—make me come. You're gonna make me come right fucking now!"

Pres found a good rhythm and rammed his man's ass with short, hard thrusts, claiming him the way he needed. Pres wasn't going to last long either. They'd all waited forever to be with each other, and now that they'd come together, it was too much passion unleashed all at once.

"Suck on my balls, Blair. Get 'em in your mouth," Ric ordered.

Pres leaned over to watch Blair. For the life of him, he couldn't stop. He needed to watch it all. Blair was so beautiful when in the throes of ecstasy. Pres saw that long pink tongue lick around the base of Ric's cock and snake down to his balls, tonguing and gnawing at them greedily.

"Such a gorgeous slut," Pres purred in Ric's ear while watching Blair. He reached his hand around and gave Ric's cock a few good strokes before tucking his hand under Blair's chin. Lust-filled hazel eyes stared up at him.

Pres pumped Ric's ass harder, making him cry out to God, but he kept his eyes on Blair over Ric's shoulder. "You ready to take his load, sexy boy?"

Blair's mouth was too full to answer.

Pres had a vise grip on Ric's dick, while Blair's face was full of Ric's large sac. "Suck his balls, honey. Yeah, you like his balls in your mouth, 'cause you're a nasty slut, ain't you?"

Right then the room was filled with a long, deep moan from Blair's throat as his seed spread across Ric's thigh.

The heady scent flooded Pres's nose. "Yeah, that's our pretty slut. Made you come so hard with those balls in your sexy mouth."

"Pres, the things you say," Ric hissed. "Shit, fuck me hard. I'm coming, baby." His voice rose.

Pres fisted Ric's thick cock in time with his firing hips. Ric's channel clamped down on him during his orgasm, and Pres felt his dick get locked into that hot hole. Ric jolted and convulsed in Pres's arms as ropes of hot, salty come shot out of him and into Blair's waiting mouth.

"Ric, fuck!" Pres growled through clenched teeth. He couldn't thrust. He couldn't push in any deeper. While his orgasm raged in his balls, all he could do was stay clamped in place within Ric's spasming hole.

*What the—? Too tight. Fuck.*

Pres couldn't believe the grip Ric had on his dick while he rode out the last of his orgasm, his sated dick still deep down Blair's throat.

Pres's orgasm was coming fast and furious, and Ric would only get a crude warning. "You sexy bastard, make me come inside you," Pres moaned in delicious agony. He gripped Ric's massive shoulders and buried his face into the back of his neck. He was coming…hard.

"Fill me up, lover…I'm yours now," Ric whispered.

Blair scrambled up the bed, leaned over Ric's chest, and gripped the back of Pres's neck to pull him in for a kiss. He shared Ric's flavor with him, making his orgasm rocket up his shaft and fill Ric's tight ass with copious amounts of come, warming his man from the inside out. It was never ending and glorious.

The three of them lay there together in post-sexual bliss, neither wanting to move.

# Chapter Thirty-Eight

"You have to be shitting me! Why the hell am I being fired?" Ric yelled into the phone. He paced back and forth on Pres's balcony trying not to take one of the plush lawn chairs and sling it over the railing in anger. Ric listened to the chief of surgery carry on about his "inappropriate behavior in the hospital with two men," his "using hospital resources for personal means," "excessive days off," blah, blah. It was all bull.

This was because he'd come out, again. He'd had every right to use his personal days, just like anyone else. Pres had only been home for a week. He'd been having frequent migraines, trouble adjusting to his contact lenses, and if all the lights were off, he'd oftentimes have terrifying nightmares that he was still blind, so Ric thought he'd take his personal time.

"That's highly illegal. I don't think this hospital's administrative board will tolerate a blatant violation of dismissal because of sexual orientation. I'll be speaking to my lawyers about this, because my surgeries speak for themselves." Ric hung up the phone, refusing to listen to any more.

He dropped down in one of the chairs. He wished he had a beer out here with him—or better yet, a shot of tequila.

"How the hell am I going to tell my men I've lost my fucking job?" he snapped.

*Damn it. Blair starts his new executive chef job in a few weeks, and Pres has one of the most successful food-critiquing businesses in the country, but is still being bombarded with job offers since he's regained his sight. So am I going to be the bitch in this relationship and let my guys support me? Fuck.*

He'd have to find something before Pres and Blair realized he'd been fired. Then he could say that he chose to move to a better job or something with better hours. Ric didn't know exactly what he'd say just yet, but he'd think of something.

**R**ic had just come back from working out in their building and opened the door to find Pres and Blair going on about the proper techniques of a creamy risotto. He rolled his eyes and quietly made his way to the kitchen.

*Here they go again.*

It seemed not a day went by in the last few weeks that the three of them had been practically living together that Pres and Blair didn't disagree about a cooking technique or a dish. It always ended in Pres insisting he was right and Blair on his knees in awe of Pres's skill.

"You should use a more savory broth if you're adding seafood to the risotto," Pres chastised Blair. Blair shook his head and continued stirring the creamy rice dish on the large stove.

Pres had his back to Blair and was completely oblivious to Blair's reaction going on behind him while he went about prepping his vegetables on the kitchen island. Ric chuckled softly when Blair huffed an exasperated breath at Pres's micromanaging.

"Are you serious, Strawberry? I'm an executive chef, and you think I don't know what broth to use in a simple lobster risotto. Jeez, gimme a fuckin' break," Blair said.

"I'm just saying, honey. It'd be better if you used a dry Sauvignon Blanc, coupled with a seafood broth, instead of chicken broth."

"I did use a white wine, smartass," Blair replied.

"I know you did, but it was Chardonnay."

"How the hell—" Blair's mouth gaped open.

"I could smell it," Pres replied, never turning around to look at Blair's ingredients.

Ric watched Blair abandon his dish and throw himself onto Pres's back. "You fantastic fucker." Blair squeezed Pres's ass. Pres laughed at Blair's enthusiasm and returned his frantic touches.

"You two are something else." Ric grinned at them.

The two of them turned to face him, surprise showing on their faces that he was standing there watching.

"When did you get back, Bear?" Blair let Pres get back to his cutting and came over to kiss him. He closed his eyes and moaned at the shared flavor of the three of them.

"Hey, sweet boy. I just walked in." Ric gently touched Blair's flushed cheek. "Don't let him rile you about your risotto, baby. I think it's delicious." He squeezed the sexy Texan to him and saw Pres cut his eyes at him. Pres threw him a wink and went back to masterfully cutting his vegetables for the lamb dish he was making.

Ric had had to double up on his workout regimen. Living with two masterfully trained chefs could wreak havoc on his midsection, but there was no way he could deny the food, especially Blair's French pastries.

"You smell so manly. How long did you work those fine muscles today?" Blair drawled in his deep voice that drove Ric mad.

Ric let Blair feel him up before taking his mouth in another long kiss. "Just a few hours. Now I'm starved," he replied breathlessly.

Blair popped him on his ass and told Ric to go shower, that dinner would be ready in an hour.

"All right, sounds good." Ric walked over and slouched against the island, pressing his forehead against Pres's cheek. "Hi, love," he whispered.

"Hi, Sunshine." Pres kept his eyes on his vegetables, but leaned into Ric's touch.

"I missed you." Ric's lips wisped gently against Pres's trimmed sideburns.

"Me too." Pres turned slightly and licked Ric's soft lips.

Ric let Pres's tongue glide over his mouth. His man did everything so damn seductively. All he could think about was eating a good meal and getting into bed with his men.

"Everything smells so good. I'm gonna go shower." Ric turned to leave and saw that Blair was watching their romantic exchange and letting his risotto burn. He wasn't sure what he saw reflected back at him in Blair's eyes…longing or sadness. Blair turned around quickly, and Ric hoped he saw wrong. He wouldn't have his men hurting. He made a mental note to talk to Blair later.

# Chapter Thirty-Nine

**P**res and Ric lay shirtless in each other's arms on the spacious couch, watching a documentary on endangered wildlife in South America. Neither was overly interested in the long-tailed otter, but both were too lazy from the large dinner to channel-surf for something different. Ric tightened his arms around Pres's chest and squeezed him tighter to him. He felt Pres's deep moan vibrate through him, causing a good tingling sensation down in his balls.

"Where's the Texan?" Pres asked over a yawn.

"Still in the bedroom," Ric answered.

"He's been in there ever since we finished dinner."

Ric looked at his watch. *That's been five hours.*

"Maybe he was tired," Pres reasoned.

Ric thought back to the look Blair gave him in the kitchen. *I wonder if he's still upset. He didn't look upset at dinner.*

Actually, after Ric thought about it a little more, Blair didn't really say much of anything at dinner. He just thanked Ric for the compliments on his dishes and ate silently. As soon as he finished his dinner, he got up, cleaned the kitchen, then closed himself in the room.

"You ready for bed?" Ric asked Pres.

Pres turned over, positioning himself on top of Ric, and braced both arms on either side of his head. "Yeah, I'm gonna go on to bed. I'm exhausted. I have a restaurant to critique in Williamsburg, so that's an hour drive I have in the morning, two if we hit traffic. Scott will be here to pick me up early."

"When are you going to get your driver's license?" Ric asked curiously, staring deep into Pres's bright blue eyes despite his tiredness.

"I don't know. It's not top priority right now. Besides, that would put Scott out of a job, and his wife just had a baby three months ago. I never missed driving. I just missed being able to see the scenery while I rode. Besides, the therapist said I should take my time with that anyway. So no rush, all right, babe?" Pres leaned in and kissed Ric on his cheek.

"Not rushing you, was just asking," Ric said.

Pres stared at him a few more minutes before leaning in and kissing Ric with so much passion and tongue that it made his toes curl. Ric kissed him back with everything he had, running his hands up and down Pres's back. They made out like lovesick teenagers before Ric finally had to pull back to take a breath.

"Ric," Pres moaned.

"Pres," Ric replied back, his chest rising and falling rapidly.

The kiss had them both completely spellbound. They looked at each other with want and need so deep, Ric could feel the tears pooling in the corners of his eyes. Pres had just told him with the kiss what Ric had longed to feel every day since Aaron's death. He let one tear fall down the side of his face, refusing to wipe at it in fear that he'd break their eye contact.

Pres leaned back in. Ric thought he was going to kiss him again, but Pres passed his mouth and his cheek and pressed his velvety lips behind his ear. "Ric," he whispered.

Ric shivered at the location of Pres's mouth on his body. So damn seductive.

"Ric," Pres whispered again while hypnotically grinding his hard cock against him.

Ric thrust his hips up into Pres's pelvis and hissed, "Yes, baby?"

Pres slowed his hips to the slowest grind ever and continued to speak in a ghostly whisper behind Ric's ear. "I love you so much. You are everything to me. Without you, I couldn't handle this. Thank you for being what I need. Thank you for coming back to me." He licked and sucked the fleshy lobe of Ric's ear into his mouth, and Ric thought he was going to come right there in his thin sweats. His cock leaked and jerked against Pres's leisurely thrust.

"Jesus, Pres. I love you, too. So fuckin' much that it hurts, baby," Ric moaned against the side of Pres's face while his man made him feel a million different kinds of good.

Pres rubbed his face against the tears that fell from Ric's eyes.

"Baby, please." Ric shuddered.

"Shhh. I got you, honey," Pres said while pulling both of their throbbing cocks from their confinement.

Pres braced one arm on the side of Ric's head and stared into his damp eyes as he stroked both their dicks with one hand. Ric felt him struggle at first to hold both of them together, but once he found his rhythm…Pres made him soar.

"Oh God. Yes, baby. Fuck, feels so damn good. Harder," Ric groaned, his release already building. He'd been stimulated, mind, body, and soul, and it was all about to come to an explosive end.

"I'm so close, Pres. Make me come hard," Ric pleaded.

Pres's tight fist moved up and down their cocks with long, rapid strokes. He took his nail and pressed it into Ric's piss slit, making Ric jerk hard and cry out at the pleasure.

"Love you so much, my angel. Come for me," Pres said, then captured Ric's open mouth in an earth-shattering kiss, and Ric let his orgasm take over his body.

Ric couldn't have kept his eyes open if he'd wanted to. "Fuuuckkk. Shit." Ric shot creamy white come all over his man's hand. Pres's mouth swallowed every one of his curses. Ric was still shooting when he heard Pres's familiar gut-twisting groan, his orgasm right on the edge and riding him hard, insisting on relief.

Ric put his index finger in his mouth and licked it, coating it with his saliva before reaching around to Pres's smooth ass and parting his seam, seeking out that tight bud. He felt Pres open his legs wider, granting Ric permission.

"Yes. Fucking do it," Pres groaned.

Ric pressed his fingertip against the opening and massaged it for a second before pushing all the way inside, immediately seeking out the special spot that would make Pres lose himself. He felt every muscle in Pres's body tense as tight as piano wire.

"Fuck! Gawwwd, Ric."

Ric buried his one finger in deeper and applied firm, constant pressure to Pres's gland. Pres bit the juncture of Ric's neck and shoulder to stifle his loud cry.

"Ric!" he shouted and painted Ric's stomach with his seed, his ass clamped tight on Ric's finger. Pres's hips bucked while he milked the last of his load. His one arm shook with effort to continue to hold him up. "Mine," Pres whispered against Ric's mouth, and he took the head of his cock and rubbed his warm come into Ric's skin, marking him as his.

They lay there catching their breath while dropping sleepy kisses all over each other's faces.

"Sleep," Ric moaned.

"Of course." Pres laughed at Ric's typical laziness after coming.

"Don't laugh at me. You jerked all the energy right out of me."

Pres picked up one of their long-ago-discarded shirts and wiped some of the cooling come off them. "Let's take a quick shower and go to bed."

"Can't we shower in the morning?" Ric whined as Pres pulled at him to stand.

"You're pathetic." Pres chuckled.

"But you love me, though."
"Yes, I do. More than life, Sunshine."

YOU CAN SEE ME

## Chapter Forty

When they'd come into the bedroom, Ric could see that Blair was feigning sleep. His chest was rising and falling too fast, and his cheeks were flushed red. Ric didn't say anything. He just let Pres wrap him up, and Ric got into his usual position.

It was the middle of the night, and Ric jerked awake at the sound of something dropping in the living room. He rose up to look at Pres and saw he was still asleep. However, Blair was gone. Ric figured he was probably getting a drink or something and lay back down.

When he heard the alarm beeping that the door was being opened, he jumped out of bed and shot out of the bedroom door so fast that he almost kicked Josey in his haste. He just caught up to Blair and jumped in front of him to slam the door back closed before he could leave.

"Where the hell do you think you're going? It's three in the morning." Ric took in Blair's appearance.

*Oh no.*

Blair's usually bright hazel-brown eyes were bloodshot red.

*He's been crying.*

His hair was sticking up in several directions, like he'd run his fingers through it a thousand times. His jeans were unbuttoned, and his T-shirt was wrinkled as if he'd really been trying to make a fast exit. What Ric noticed most was the large duffel bag on Blair's shoulder.

"What the hell, Blair? What is this?" Ric's eyes darted to Blair's bag and back to his eyes.

"I'm going home, Rickson."

*He called me Rickson, not Bear. Fuck.*

Ric had to take a deep breath before responding to Blair's answer. "What do you mean? You are home. Your home is with us, baby. What's the matter?"

Ric stepped in to put his hands around Blair's waist, but was pushed back hard.

"Don't fucking touch me," Blair hissed.

"Jesus Christ. What is going on, Blair? I'm sorry if I missed something huge here, but you're gonna have to explain what the hell I did."

"You don't need me, Ric. Neither of you do. I'm just the cocksucker in this trio." Blair's tears were falling so fast that he stopped trying to wipe at them.

"Cocksu…" Ric couldn't even finish saying the derogatory word. He was completely taken aback at the term Blair had just called himself. "You're wrong. Don't say that."

"I see you two. When you're together, I don't even fucking exist! Yeah, Ric, you'll come in and give me a quick kiss and pat me on the ass, but when you turn your eyes on Prescott…" Blair's sob burst from his chest, and it made Ric's heart seize. "When you look at him…Christ…I know that neither one of you will ever look at me like that. You look at me as the whore that y'all have at your disposal, or your play toy when you want to get kinky, and you save the love for your own private moments."

"Blair, baby, you're wrong. You know how we feel about you. You're everything to us. This whole thing doesn't even work without you," Ric said loudly, hoping that Pres would hear this and come to help him.

"That's bullshit!" Blair yelled, his anger slamming to the surface. "I saw the two of you tonight. I saw you…God…I saw you. Neither one of you gave a fuckin' second thought about your whore." Blair pointed at the bedroom, spittle flying out of his mouth as he yelled. "I'd been closed up in that goddamn room all evening crying to myself, hoping that one of you would think of me, come and get me." Blair's voice dropped dangerously low, and Ric felt chill bumps break out on his arms. "But y'all just lay there in each other's arms perfectly content. I know I like to get off on being nasty and you calling me your slut, but I never thought you all really considered me as just that."

Ric could only shake his head. He hadn't realized what they'd done to Blair by excluding him tonight, but was it reasonable to think that neither one could touch or love on the other without the third being present? He had to somehow show Blair that him making love to Pres didn't mean that he didn't love him as well.

*I love him, too.*

Ric loved Blair, too. He really did. He'd have to show him that he loved them both, but right now Blair was so angry, Ric wasn't sure he could get through to him.

"I know we've been together only a few weeks, but no one's even tried to make love to me." Blair poked his finger at his heart. "I have wants and needs, too. All you want me to do is suck your motherfuckin' cocks while y'all make love to each other. Well forget about it. If you want a whore, then you'll have to rent one, because that's not what I'll be for you anymore."

Blair moved to go for the door handle, but Ric stopped him, again, bumping him in the process. Ric's large chest muscles were on full display since he didn't sleep in a shirt.

"Your muscles don't scare me, Ric. If you keep trying to stop me from leaving, I'm going to show you how big of a mistake you're making," Blair growled. He lowered his head and glared up at Ric through wet, spiky lashes. "Now. Let. Me. Go." He snapped each word and stepped forward, teeth clenched as he spoke. "Because a kick in the nuts will drop even the biggest motherfucker to the ground."

Ric was damned if he wasn't turned on to no end. His sexy Texan's composure was nonexistent, and in its place was a hissing rattlesnake daring Ric to make another move. Blair's cool, placid demeanor was one of the man's most attractive qualities, but when he was in full-on rage mode, it made Ric's dick hard enough to pound nails.

*Holy hell.*

Ric knew he had to get his wayward libido under control. He needed to calm Blair down and show him the love that he wanted…no, deserved.

Ric slowly put both hands up in a placating gesture, in hopes to ward off Blair's threat at kicking his ass. Ric was a big man, and he had about eighty pounds on Blair's sinewy frame, but Blair was just as tall as Ric and could no doubt give him a good bout if he had to. Ric would be damned if it was going to come to that. His Tex was mad, and he had a right to be, but Ric would never lay a hand on him to hurt him physically. If he had to, he'd gladly take every blow Blair dished out if it'd make him stay.

"Five minutes, baby?" Ric asked.

"No," said Blair.

"Why? I don't deserve five minutes before you walk out on us?" Ric glared back.

"You don't deserve shit, Rickson. You know why? Do you fuckin' know why?" Blair shoved his finger into Ric's bare chest.

"Why, honey?" Ric whispered, closing his eyes at the hurt radiating off his beautiful man.

"You took Prescott to his first movie in over five years the other day. Just the damn two of you. That was major for him. That was major in this relationship. I was stupid enough to think we'd be doing things like that together, but no. You two decided you didn't need your slut tagging along, and y'all went on to enjoy your evening."

"You were at work, Blair," Ric tried to reason.

"So the fuck what, Ric! It doesn't matter where I was. Did it ever occur to you selfish assholes that I'd come back home?" Blair yelled while violently shaking his head back and forth. "No. I'm not doing this. I'm not going to point out every time you jerks have hurt me. I'm done. I'm sure once I'm gone, you will have no problem going back and climbing in that bed to have a long, peaceful sleep beside the only man you want and will ever love."

"God, Blair, I'm so sorry. Please let me make this right. I can't lose you. I'm not lying when I say this doesn't work without you. I'd be heartbroken if you left, and Pres would be, too." Ric thought he saw a little crack in Blair's anger, so he hurried to keep talking. "I never meant to hurt you. I swear on everything I know that I didn't realize what I was doing to you. If you just come back in and give me a few minutes to talk to you, I just want to clarify some things…please."

Ric watched Blair take his fists and dig them into his eyes, blowing out a deep breath.

*He doesn't want to leave.*

He took the chance and hesitantly stepped into Blair's space.

"Come here, please." Ric pulled Blair into him. Blair stayed stiff in his arms as Ric hugged him tightly. "I'm so sorry. I didn't know. I promise, I didn't. Just give us a chance to fix it. I need you just as much as I need him." Ric felt Blair suck in a breath and start to fight his hold. "Don't fight, baby. I would never lie to you."

Ric had to go for broke now. He pressed his lips to the shell of Blair's ear and spoke in a hushed tone. "When I first saw you at Pres's door all those months ago, I was so angry. Not only because Pres was moving on"—Ric lifted Blair's chin to look in his eyes—"but because you were so gorgeous and I wanted you for myself."

Blair's bottom lip trembled.

"I'd see you and him together, happy and smiling. God, I was so miserable back then. I didn't even realize how much I wanted to be a part of what y'all had. The love I feel did start with just Prescott, but it ends with you, baby. I don't want to do this without you." Ric leaned in and pressed the tenderest kiss to Blair's mouth. He took the duffel bag off Blair's shoulder, gripped his hand, and pulled him into the den. Ric sat down on the wide couch and pulled him onto his lap.

He hooked his arms around Blair's waist and looked him in his eyes before he continued to speak. "You're crazy if you think that Pres and I want a whore in our bed. I don't want one, and I'll never have one, in my bed. When I call you my slut, it's just getting a little nasty talk in for excitement…and only talk. You are not a play toy. You are a talented, smart, gorgeous man…my man." Ric leaned in again to kiss Blair, and this time, to Ric's relief, Blair returned the kiss.

A moan tore from Ric's throat, and he trembled with relief. He buried his face in Blair's neck, inhaling his clean, cool scent.

"Honey, please don't leave me. I can't be without you. I need you so fucking much." Ric paused and picked up Blair's head to stare into his hopeful eyes. He took Blair's face in his hands and pressed their foreheads together, their mouths only inches apart. Ric placed his lips against Blair's and spoke into his mouth. "I love you so much. Don't leave me. I promise that I will show you every day just how much you mean to me…and if you give him a chance, Pres will, too."

Blair broke down in his arms, and Ric laid him back on the couch and settled over top of him.

"Ric," Blair cried into the side of his face.

"Shhh, honey. Let me make love to you like you deserve." Ric kissed Blair's pouty mouth, putting as much love into the kiss as he could. Regardless that he had already come tonight, he still had plenty left for his sexy Texan.

By the time he was done kissing and licking Blair, he was writhing beneath him and pulling on his briefs. Ric raised Blair's arms to rid him of his T-shirt. He feasted his eyes on Blair's firm chest. He may not have been packed with muscles, but he had firm pecs and washboard abs. His orange-sized biceps flexed as he gripped Ric's shoulders.

Ric licked a path from Blair's chin down to his left nipple, leaving a moist trail in the process. He felt Blair grip the back of his head as he latched on to that perky bud and sucked on it hard, giving Blair back a little of what he dished out.

"Mmmm." Blair moaned low in his throat. His hips rose up off the couch, lifting Ric with him. Ric knew Blair wanted more friction on his dripping cock by the way he tried to grind into him, but he wasn't going to give him what he wanted yet, refusing to let this be over quickly.

Ric released Blair's red, swollen nipple and moved over to the other one. He swirled his tongue around the hard nub, raising pretty goose bumps all over Blair's chest and arms.

"Ric, please," Blair begged.

Ric ignored Blair's pleading and took his time. He rose back up and placed a quick kiss on Blair's slack mouth before moving back down his chest to dip his tongue into the crevices and valleys on his stomach. A delicious treasure trail guided Ric exactly where he wanted to be. He pulled down Blair's jeans and briefs and threw them onto the floor.

*Fuck, he is beautiful. Different from Pres's regal beauty. Blair is fuckin' sex on a stick.*

"You're wonderful." Ric placed a wet kiss on the head of Blair's dick and whispered, "And you're all mine, damn it."

Ric opened his mouth wide and buried as much of Blair's cock as he could. Blair didn't have a lot of girth, but he had some length, and Ric had to fight his gag reflex.

"Ric. Oh, fuck. Yeah, suck my dick," Blair moaned.

Ric gave Blair everything he had. He licked and sucked aggressively on that warm cock, loving the weight of it on his tongue. Blair tasted so fucking good, like the best French pastry he could ever eat.

He let Blair grip his head and fuck his mouth. Blair was losing himself to the ecstasy, and Ric loved the fact that he was the one doing it. He felt a large drop of pre-come fall and explode on his tongue, making Ric groan hard, vibrating Blair's cock.

"Growl for me, Bear. Fuck yeah." Blair pistoned his hips as Ric complied with his order.

Ric felt Blair's dick harden to granite right before he was rewarded with the first burst of his man's jizz. He barely had time to savor the sweet-salty flavor that was Blair before his mouth was flooded with more…and more…and more. Warm come dripped out of the side of Ric's mouth as he greedily tried to swallow all that Blair gave him.

Blair was a shivering mess. His dick was sated, and Ric let it ease out of his mouth, but Ric was far from done. He didn't let Blair catch his breath from his powerful orgasm before he gripped Blair's legs under his knees and pulled them up to his chest.

"Ric, Gawd," Blair groaned.

Ric ignored him and took a long, slow swipe over Blair's hole with his tongue. Blair vaulted at the sensation, almost throwing Ric off the couch.

"Oh no you don't," Ric growled. He practically folded Blair in half and hooked his large arms around his middle, holding Blair in place and putting that bubble ass in perfect position for the rimming of its life.

Ric didn't rush it. He took another long swipe along Blair's seam, pausing to make a couple circles around that wrinkled star before continuing up his ass. Ric got to his knees and crowded in behind Blair, keeping him folded up but letting his spine rest on his chest. He spread Blair's cheeks and placed sultry kisses all over before delving back in to stretch that tight, pretty hole.

Ric lapped at the rigid skin until it started to give. He inched the tip of his tongue inside and felt Blair jerk in his arms. Ric gave Blair's thighs a few calming strokes before he continued. Ric's own dick was screaming at him for some attention, but this wasn't about him.

"Relax, baby. Let me take care of you. Gonna give you exactly what you need." Ric puffed warm air over Blair's quivering hole.

"Please, now. Need you now, Bear," Blair keened.

Ric stopped briefly to reach over and grab the slick from out of the end table drawer, then quickly got back to work. He lapped, and speared his tongue into Blair's hole, until all he heard was indecipherable nonsense coming from his man.

Once Blair's hole was relaxed, Ric squeezed a large dollop of lube on two fingers and massaged Blair's rim until it was warm and pliant. He lowered Blair's legs and settled over top of him, kissing and biting at his chin while he worked one finger into him. It slid in easily, and Ric's body trembled with the need to be inside Blair's warmth. He quickly added another finger, and Blair's body resisted the extra intrusion.

"Trust me, baby. Gonna make you feel so good. Take deep breaths, love, and let me in," Ric crooned in Blair's ear and felt him relax and open himself up.

Ric pushed in the second digit and let Blair work himself on his fingers.

"Take what you need, love. So fuckin' sexy."

After Blair's hole easily accommodated his second finger, he added the third. He gave Blair a deep, mind-blowing kiss to distract him while he worked his fingers in and out of his hot channel. He had to make sure that Blair was fully ready for him. Ric wasn't a small man, and he refused to hurt his lover.

"Please," Blair begged.

Blair was clawing at his back, and Ric couldn't wait anymore, either. He removed his fingers and lined up the head of his blushing cock against Blair's opening. Ric wanted inside so damn bad, his hands shook violently as he slathered more lube on his length.

Ric braced his forearms on either side of Blair's head and slowly began to inch inside. Blair's eyes flew open, and Ric paused. "You're okay, baby. Breathe through it," he instructed. He waited for Blair to control his breathing before he began to ease in, inch by inch, until he was fully seated.

"So fuckin' full, Bear," Blair groaned.

Ric's body was firing on all cylinders. Blair was so hot and tight around his cock, and he wanted nothing more than to pound his sweet ass, but he remained still until he saw the moment that the stretching and burn turned into pure sexual heaven.

"Move, Ric," Blair said. His eyes closed tight, and Ric could see the wetness building.

"Look at me, Blair." Ric kissed Blair's eyelids and licked at the corners. "Open and let me see those beautiful eyes."

Ric watched Blair ease his eyes open, and Ric's breath caught in his throat. "God, I love you so much, Blair McKenzie."

Ric felt Blair's cock go from semi-erect to instantly hard.

"I love you, too, Rickson. Make love to me. Make me yours," Blair drawled sensually, his voice going even deeper than normal, and it made Ric have to pinch the base of his cock to keep from coming right then.

"Fuuuck," Ric growled.

"Bear, augh, fucking move," Blair hissed.

Ric pulled almost all the way out before gently easing back in. He was determined not to rush them. He hooked one of Blair's thighs over his shoulder and lowered himself all the way down on top of him, using his weight to make Blair feel secure. Ric kept their bodies fully connected from head to toe, only moving his ass up and down in short, deep thrusts.

They stared into each other's eyes as Ric made slow, sweet love to his man. After several thrusts, Ric angled his hips to the right and buried himself in deep. He pulled out only a couple inches before slamming back into Blair's tight ass—and holy fuck was it hot.

"Ric!" Blair yelled.

Ric kept his thrusts short and deep and watched the gorgeous fucker give him one of the most erotically beautiful sights he'd ever seen.

Ric buried himself inside and applied steady pressure to Blair's prostate. Blair's eyes rolled back in his head as he threw his head back and bared his throat to Ric. Blair's warm come spread in between them.

Ric slammed his mouth down over Blair's rapidly beating pulse and bit him hard. "Mine," he growled.

Blair's body thrashed beneath him, and Ric unleashed the pent-up sexual fervor that he'd been holding since sinking inside of Blair's heat. He lifted Blair's other leg, spreading him wide. Ric pulled his cock almost completely out before shoving back in forcefully.

"Yes, Ric. Fuck me. Fuck me hard. Make me feel you forever." Blair's deep voice in his ear was like throwing fuel on Ric's erotic fire.

Ric lost all reason and sanity and commenced reaming Blair's stretched opening, trying to fuck him through the couch. Ric spread his own legs wide for full leverage and plowed in and out of Blair with unleashed need.

Ric grunted like an animal, and the more Blair screamed his name, the harder he fucked him. Ric wanted to make sure that Blair never doubted his love or need for him ever again, and he sure as fuck wanted Blair to understand that under no circumstances was he allowed to leave their bed in the middle of the night.

"Say you're mine," Ric ordered. He pulled out, until only the tip of his head was inside, and paused, waiting for Blair to obey. When Blair's head lolled back and forth, Ric thrust hard into him, making Blair yell loud enough to wake the second floor. He didn't give a fuck. He pulled almost completely out again. "Say your mine," he commanded again. Blair's eyes were rolling in their sockets, and he opened his mouth, but not fast enough. Ric plowed his full length back in again, nailing Blair's gland.

"Yours, yours, yours. I'm yours, Bear. Always." Blair scrambled to satisfy Ric's demands.

Ric continued to pound Blair's tender ass. "Goddamn right you're mine," he snarled in Blair's ear. "Don't you ever try to leave my bed in the middle of the night ever again."

All Blair could do was hang on to Ric's wide shoulders and nod his head vigorously in agreement.

"Say the words, sexy boy," Ric growled.

"Yes, sir. Oh my God, Ric. I'll never try to leave again. Fuck. Mmmm." Blair mewled like a scared kitten, and Ric loved it.

Blair's complete submission to Ric was like cocaine to a crack addict. Ric had to have it, and he'd never be able to get enough. He ground his dick against that supple ass and fully filled Blair's passage with his warm seed. He held Blair close to his sweaty chest and panted over and over in Blair's ear, "Mine, mine, mine."

"Yours," Blair whispered.

Ric didn't know how long they lay there in postcoital paradise, but it'd been long enough, and he needed to get his heavy weight off his lover now. He wanted nothing more than to lie there on top of Blair's beautiful body, still seated inside him, and take a long nap, but he doubted that would feel good to Blair.

"Shower with me, love."

"Okay," Blair agreed easily. He rose up and placed another loving but short kiss on Ric's mouth—saying thank you, without words—before letting Ric pull him off the couch.

Ric couldn't help but smile at Blair's wide-legged walk as they made their way back to their bedroom.

YOU CAN SEE ME

## Chapter Forty-One

Pres paced back and forth in the bedroom. His tracks had probably worn the plush carpet down to bare fibers. He stopped and snapped his head up at the door opening. Ric walked in holding Blair's hand, and Pres's eyes filled with tears.

He took quick steps over to his stunning man and wrapped him in his arms. "Oh my God. I thought he wouldn't be able to stop you from leaving. Jesus, baby. I'm so sorry we hurt you...I'm sorry I hurt you." Pres lifted his tear-filled blue eyes and gazed into Blair's hazel ones. "I love you so fuckin' much. Don't you ever try to leave again, because you think we don't need you or love you, honey." Pres didn't let Blair respond. He kissed him passionately and gave him another tight hug.

Pres stared at Ric over Blair's shoulder. "If you would've let him walk out that door, I would've pushed you out there too, and you wouldn't have been allowed back in until he was with you."

"He would've had to kick my ass before he got out that door," Ric confessed.

Pres felt Blair release a relieved sigh of contentment.

"You heard us, Strawberry?" Blair asked.

"Yes, I heard you. I didn't come out, because I felt it was something that Ric needed to handle. I couldn't hear everything...well, until the end." Pres raised one eyebrow at Ric.

"Sorry." Ric chuckled.

"Don't be sorry. It's what he needed. But, when he's able to walk again, that sexy ass is all mine," Pres purred in his typical seductive way, and he thought Blair was going to try to give it a go regardless of his already tender ass. He gave a throaty laugh and stilled Blair's hips. "Later, honey. I ain't going nowhere…and neither are you. You go on in the bathroom and wash up. Then we'll sleep in, since it's about daybreak, and we'll talk more later."

"Okay," Blair whispered and kissed Pres on his cheek.

Ric waited until Blair was in the shower before speaking to Pres. "How much did you hear?"

"Just about all of it," Pres answered. "I had no idea he felt like that. I wanted to run out there so many times, but I knew you'd fix it. It was torture staying in here and listening to his hurt and yelling. I hope you don't think I was being a coward and not wanting to deal with it. I just thought he needed your reinforcement more than mine right then."

"I agree. I figured you heard." Ric gave Pres a quick peck. "Thank you for letting me do it on my own. We're good now. He knows I love him."

"I'm sure he does." Pres winked. "So how was he?"

"Fucking unbelievable…you'll see." Ric winked back and went to join Blair in the shower.

*Can't fucking wait.*

They ended up sleeping until noon. All three of them were huddled together on Pres's bed when his cleaning lady came through the door and screamed loud enough to make each of them jerk upright. Blair's naked body flailed comically before falling off the edge of the bed, hitting the floor with a loud thud.

Pres leaned over the side and busted out laughing at Blair rubbing his still very sore ass that he'd just painfully fallen on. "Are you okay, honey?" Pres asked, still grinning.

"You're supposed to ask that before you laugh," Blair scolded.

"My poor baby. Come here. Get back up here and let me kiss it better," Pres said, pulling out his provocative voice already.

Pres heard Ric clear his throat. He looked back after helping Blair get back in the bed and cover himself. His maid was now covering her eyes and facing the wall, frantically apologizing in broken Spanish and English.

"*Lo siento, senor.* So sorry. So, so, sorry. Pardon." She repeated apologies over and over.

"It's okay, Nina. I know you thought I'd be on assignment today, but there was a little change in plans." Pres spoke with humor in his voice. "Can you just give us a few minutes—*un momento, por favor*—and we'll be out of your way."

"*Si. Primero*, I clean *la cocina.*" She hurried out of the bedroom and closed the door.

"Yes, start with the kitchen first." Pres laughed and sank back into the mattress.

"I think too many people have a key to your condo," Ric admonished while pulling the covers off his huge chest.

Ric and Blair both turned over and began smothering Pres's chest and stomach with wet, languid kisses.

"Mmmm," Pres moaned. He gripped the back of Blair's head while he licked his nipples and stroked Ric's cheek as he raised light marks on his neck. "Fuck. Feels good."

Blair's hand snaked down to his rising cock and stroked him a couple times before cupping his balls and slowly rolling them around their sac.

"Need more." Pres raised his hips. "How's your pretty ass feeling, honey?" He rubbed Blair's tight bubble ass and dipped his finger in his seam to graze over his hole.

"I'm fine, just a little tender. Our Bear made sure he staked his claim good," Blair said.

Ric reached over, cupped the back of Blair's head, and kissed him hard on the mouth. "Damn right I did." Ric squeezed one of Blair's soft ass cheeks. "Mine," he growled.

"Yours, baby." Blair kissed Ric back. He looked at Pres. "And yours, too."

"Yes, honey," Pres whispered. "How about a little TLC for that well-fucked ass, huh?" Pres smiled wickedly. He didn't wait for Blair to answer. He crawled over and got behind him. "You and Bear suck each other off while I take care of you back here, baby." Pres was telling them more than asking them. He liked to run the show, and he had a lot of different ways that he saw them making love and pleasuring each other. This was one of his favorites.

Ric smiled wide and turned his long body around to get into the sixty-nine position with Blair. Lying on their sides, they both propped one leg up to give each other full access and began to slowly lick each other's cocks. Pres watched them swallow each other's rock-hard dicks, and his own got so hard he felt dizzy from the instant rush of blood to that organ. Blair's cheeks hollowed as he sucked Ric hard and buried his face down in his bristly pubic hairs. Ric's body jerked violently, and his mouth popped off of Blair's long cock.

"Blair! Fuck!" Ric gripped both of Blair's cheeks and spread his ass open for Pres.

Pres was mesmerized by his beautiful men. He buried his face in Blair's seam and licked him in his most sensitive spot. He didn't try to breach his delicate hole. He wanted to make Blair feel loved and taken care of. The pucker quivered under his tongue, and it made Pres's dick leak a large drop of pearly fluid. He used it to ease the friction as he stroked himself in time with their grunts.

They were fully into it now, the sounds of slurping, sucking, moaning, and swearing filling the large room. He heard Ric cry out first, his orgasm hitting him so hard he shook the entire bed. Blair moaned and consumed every drop of Ric's seed.

Pres tripled his efforts on Blair's pleasure and felt his ass clenching around the tip of his tongue. He knew he was about to blow, and Pres was going blow with him. "Come hard for me, baby. Let me feel it."

Blair's body shook in their arms as he cried out both their names.

"That's it, baby." Pres continued to lick and kiss Blair's pulsating bud. "Love you so fucking much," he whispered against the soft ass cheek as he jerked his load into his hand, groaning low in his throat.

Again, they lay in a heap of tangled limbs and sated cocks. Pres inhaled deeply, loving the smell of his men.

"Come on, gentlemen. Let's get cleaned up and get something to eat. I'm starved," Pres said, breaking into the still-heavy pants coming from his lovers.

"Thirty more minutes," Ric requested and pulled the cover up over his head.

Pres exchanged a knowing look with Blair, and both of them yanked the covers off Ric's naked form.

"Oh, that's not right at all," Ric whined.

They laughed and jumped on top of their big, grumpy Bear, knowing how much he liked to be lazy after sex. They pulled him out of the bed, both of them struggling with his bulk on top of his resistance.

"Just ten minutes, I promise," Ric said, trying to fight their holds and inch back to the bed.

"Nope. I'm hungry, too," Blair said, slapping Ric on his ass to get him moving back in the direction of the bathroom.

"Damn it. All right, fine, but when I get back, I'm taking a nap, and anyone who wakes me will feel my wrath," Ric growled.

Ric let Pres and Blair pull him into their shower, which was large enough for five people. At Pres's instruction, Ric propped both arms up on the warm tiles as they lovingly washed every muscle on his six-foot, two-inch frame.

# YOU CAN SEE ME

## Chapter Forty-Two

"So my parents want to come over this weekend," Pres said as he forked his eggs Benedict and popped a large helping into his mouth.

Ric and Blair stopped eating and stared at him, both probably thinking the same question, so he'd figured he'd go ahead and answer.

"Yes, I'm telling them that I'm in a relationship with two of the most loving, talented, and sexiest men I've ever met. Okay, maybe I'll leave off the sexy." Pres laughed.

"I know they like Ric, I already saw that at the hospital, but do you think they'll like me?" Blair asked, worrying his bottom lip.

Ric leaned over and kissed Blair's cheek, nuzzling the side of his face in the small booth. "Who wouldn't love you, sweet boy?"

"My parents are not judgmental, and even more so, they're not homophobic," Pres said.

"Yeah, but you're in a ménage. That's a lot for any parent to accept," Blair said, still looking worried, and it broke Pres's heart.

"Your parents have known all along, and they're fine with it," Pres argued.

"Because they've known for years that I've always wanted to be in a ménage, and I'll love whoever I damn well want to love. My parents have had swingers' parties for as long as I can remember, for Pete's sake. It's different with my folks. They're the epitome of mature sexual liberation. Your folks are like June and Ward Cleaver." Blair laughed.

"Oh, come on. They're not that bad. Hey, they vote Democrat." Pres smiled, making them both laugh at his weak argument. "I'm telling you it will be fine, but even if they don't accept it, you aren't going anywhere. Do you understand that?" Pres took Blair's hand off the tabletop and kissed each knuckle, looking up at him through his long lashes, until Blair smiled again. "Better?"

Ric leaned back in the booth and draped his arm around Blair. "So when are we officially meeting the parents?" He smiled slyly.

"Well, I was thinking that we could maybe have a dinner party or something. Let everyone see how talented our baby boy is in the kitchen, and just keep it light and casual. Ric, you can ask Dr. Brown to come, since he seems to be a good friend of yours. I'll invite Scott and his wife and probably Janice and her current flavor of the month. Blair, you ask your folks, okay?" Pres looked at them expectantly.

"Wow, don't tell me we're gonna be the gay guys that have dinner parties every other weekend where we have themes and costumes and shit." Ric balked.

Blair laughed hysterically.

"You're ridiculous." Pres threw a piece of toast at Ric. "No, we're having a dinner party because we're chefs...not gay. Dumbass."

Ric threw the piece of toast back at him.

"Okay, okay, cease fire." Blair put both hands up. "Sure. I'll ask them. I know they'll come. They always ask a million questions when I talk to them on the phone. They've been dying to meet y'all. I will warn you that my dad has a pretty intense protective streak, so you will most likely get the whole 'what are your intentions with my son' speech," he said smugly before finishing off his coffee.

"Wonderful," Ric grumbled. "So this is our official coming out party." He rolled his eyes. "I don't see why we need to make some huge announcement. We're dating…and we're in love. We're not inventing something new."

"It's okay, Ric. Like I said, we'll keep it light. However, I do think we need to do this so that our friends and family can meet. In the future, there will be holiday gatherings and family dinners. I don't want everyone to be strangers, you understand," Pres reasoned.

Ric nodded once.

"Let's get out of here." Pres stood and grabbed the check.

**R**ic hauled in the two large bags of ice his men had requested and dropped them in the deep sink in the kitchen.

"I hope everyone's on time," Blair said as he stirred a large pot of French onion soup.

After Pres and Blair carefully planned the menu, it was suggested a warm soup would make people feel toasty and like conversing, since it was a brisk fifty degrees outside.

"I'd hate to have to reheat some of the food." Blair scurried around frantically.

Blair wiped his hand across the sweat that had popped up on his forehead, and Ric knew it wasn't from the heat in the kitchen. No matter how many times he and Pres made Blair come last night, he still remained nervous at meeting Pres's parents as their third.

Ric came up behind him and put his arms around his narrow waist, and Blair immediately sank back into him as if he had the weight of the world on him.

"Mmmm. My sexy boy." Ric nibbled on Blair's earlobe and inched his large hands inside his checkered chef's pants. He cupped his soft cock and gave it a couple awakening pulls. "You are still stressing, baby, and I told you to stop it." Ric pulled his hand out and made a seductive show of licking his entire palm before burying it back in Blair's pants, giving his long cock some much-needed moisture to make his stroking smoother. He made slow pulls on Blair's length and whispered in his ear, "Who do you belong to, baby?"

Blair rubbed his cheek across Ric's and answered with a breathless whisper, "Yours, Bear. I'm all yours and Pres's."

Ric bit the sensitive skin over Blair's pulse, feeling him release some of his tension while in his arms. Ric's other arm held him snug against his chest. "Yes, mine. So, I don't want you worrying your pretty little head about anyone not accepting or liking you. You just be yourself, okay?"

"Okay, Bear." Blair pumped his hips back and forth, fucking his cock into Ric's smooth hand.

"Need me to make you come again, gorgeous?" Ric said, licking the side of Blair's face while his hand continued to stroke a now extremely hard dick.

"No, I'm fine. I need to constantly stir this soup so it doesn't scorch on the bottom, but thank you." Blair turned around in his arms and gripped Ric's long hair. It'd grown out significantly in the past few weeks and was now to his shoulders. He let Blair caress his full, thick, wavy locks.

He had it pulled back and held off his face with a thin elastic band. He'd wanted to cut it a long time ago, but Blair was crazy about it…so he left it alone. He tucked it behind his ear and let Blair kiss him long and passionately before pulling back.

"I'm gonna go shower and change for this evening. If you guys make me go to the store again, I'm gonna strangle ya." Ric popped Blair hard on the ass on his way out of the kitchen. "What time is Pres coming back?" he yelled over his shoulder.

"He'll be back by four," Blair yelled back.

Ric closed himself in their bedroom. The gathering was at six, and it was already a quarter till four. Ric went in the bathroom and commenced with his usual routine. After showering, he trimmed his goatee and plucked the few hairs that had popped up in places men didn't want them to be, like his nose and ears. Some men didn't give a fuck, and Ric was probably one, too, but unfortunately, Pres and Blair weren't having it. Ric blow-dried his long hair, combed it back loosely, and simply tucked it behind his ears.

Ric was tucking his white wifebeater into his charcoal-gray slacks when Pres walked into the room. Ric smiled warmly. "Hey, baby, what took you so long?" Ric stopped short at the sheer lust he saw burning in Pres's eyes. "Oh, fuck." Ric knew that damn look. He stepped behind the ironing board and put both hands up when Pres advanced on him.

"You smell so fucking good," Pres growled, trying to wrap himself around Ric's huge form.

"Aren't you supposed to be watching the food or something?" Ric stammered as he tried to pry Pres off of him.

"Everything's done, and the kitchen staff we hired is here now finishing up everything," Pres said while struggling to get a hold of Ric's dick.

"Thank you for the compliment, but we are behaving right now. We only have a half hour before people will start to arrive." Ric laughed as he unsuccessfully gripped at Pres's groping hands. It was like the man had eight fuckin' arms. He was touching and clawing Ric everywhere. "Baby, I'd love nothing more than to turn around and spread my ass for you and let you fuck me against this wall, but I sure as fuck don't want to iron these clothes again, and those sexy black pants you have on wouldn't look good with come stains on them...would they?" Ric stilled Pres's erratic hips.

"Okay, you're right." Pres stepped back.

Ric got a good look at him as he did. Goddamn, he looked fuckin' hot.

Pres had on black suit pants and black dress shoes. The top two buttons of his starched white collar shirt were undone, and his sleeves were rolled, giving him a look that said "I'm a hotshot and can get away with this look." He appeared comfortable but still dressed up at the same time. His perfectly spiked, coiffed hair had obviously been done by Janice because there wasn't one strand out of place. Pres's jewelry was modest. He wore his large white-gold class ring on one hand and his Cartier watch on the same wrist, and he had two small diamond studs in both ears.

"You look great. How the hell am I going to be able to keep my hands off of you?" Ric asked as he slipped on his black shoes.

"If you think you're going to have a problem with me, wait until you see Blair. I tried to attack him, too, but he threatened me." Pres winked.

"When did he get dressed?" Ric asked, thinking that Blair hadn't come in the bedroom yet.

"He got dressed in the guest room," Pres answered.

As if on cue, Blair walked into the bedroom right at that moment, and Ric's mouth dropped open. If his mouth had had any saliva in it, it would've been dripping out and pooling on the floor at his feet. Blair looked like he'd just stepped off the motherfucking runway for *GQ*.

He heard Pres chuckle. "I told you," he said simply.

Blair's eyes got wide at their staring, and he frantically looked all over his outfit. "What? What is it? Do I have something on me?" he asked nervously.

"Jesus fucking Christ, Blair. You look…fuck," Ric panted.

Blair's eyes glazed over. He had on chocolate-brown pin-striped slacks that hugged his ass so deliciously it made Ric want to drop to his knees and worship it. He had on a cream-colored collar shirt underneath a deep brown cashmere-silk vest, but what really set the entire outfit off was the brown snakeskin shoes he wore with it. Blair's honey-brown hair was fingered back, but he'd used a little product to keep it in place.

Blair stepped in to embrace Ric, and Ric instantly tucked his face into that clean, fresh scent that always clung to his man.

"You look amazing, too, lover. Both of you do." Blair laughed. "This is our first time getting dressed up together, huh?"

"Yep," Pres answered. "I must say, we look pretty good together." He came up behind Blair and wrapped his arms around him.

They held each other and whispered a string of "I love yous," "I need yous," and "I want yous" until they heard a light tapping at the door, telling them that Dr. Brown and his guest had arrived.

"Leave it to the anal neurosurgeon to be exactly on time." Ric looked at his watch, and it read 5:58 p.m.

"Well, let's go have a good time tonight and enjoy our families and friends with no worries, okay?" Pres said before kissing them both on the lips.

Ric and Blair agreed and followed Pres out into the beautifully decorated condo.

YOU CAN SEE ME

# Chapter Forty-Three

After everyone arrived, Pres decided to let people mingle and introduce themselves casually as he, Ric, and Blair circled around the spacious rooms. The food was prepared wonderfully, of course. They had a variety of hor d'oeuvres located in the rooms, and the servers kept everyone's drinks filled with whatever spirits they preferred.

Ric was by the balcony drinking a rum and Coke with Pres's father, talking about Pres's progress on his recovery. Ric kept his eye on Blair at all times, making sure he didn't look edgy or tense, but he appeared to be fine standing there talking with Pres and Janice. Ric felt that Pres should have his arm around Blair, providing him with comfort, but they'd yet to make their little announcement, so it may have seemed a little odd.

Ric saw Dr. Brown walking over with a tall, tan-skinned man who looked to be in his early fifties. His eyes told his age, but Ric could tell the man took care of his body, and he had a full head of black hair that had a few gray strands around his sideburns.

He hadn't had the chance to talk to Dr. Brown yet, so when he approached Ric, he greeted him with a firm handshake. No introduction was needed for Pres's father, because he and Dr. Brown had become very familiar while Pres was in the hospital under his care.

Dr. Brown put his hand in the small of his guest's back and gestured him forward. Ric caught the act and knew what it was.

"Rickson, this is my life partner, Dr. Jacob Strauss. He's a doctor of literature at the university I work out of. Jacob, this is the brilliant young doctor I was telling you about, Dr. Rickson Edwards."

Ric gripped the man's hand and told him he was glad to meet him, but he was desperately trying to keep his shock in check. He'd had no idea that Dr. Brown was gay. *Well hell.* At that precise moment, someone could've knocked him over with a feather. Dr. Brown just gave him a knowing smile.

After the surprise wore off, the four of them settled into easy conversation about authors, literature, and the ways social media has affected young adults and the learning system. Dr. Strauss was a brilliant man, and Ric found him very easy to talk to, and it looked like Mr. Vaughan did as well.

After an hour of socializing, Ric was ready to eat and get this show on the road so he could get tipsy and take advantage of his men. As if they'd had the same thought at the same time, Ric locked eyes on Blair and shot him a very discreet wink, making his boy blush beautifully. Ric's cock liked it, and he had to take a couple deep breaths to make his dick stand down, but the way Blair was staring at him, Ric mentally prepared himself for a hard evening…literally.

"Can everyone gather around, please? There are a few things I'd like to say before dinner is served." Pres stood in the middle of the large den and spoke with determination and courage. At that moment, Ric was glad that Pres would be his and Blair's forever.

Everyone moved closer together and focused their attention on Pres. Blair and Ric stood off to the side. Ric desperately wanted to wrap his arms around Blair, but he didn't…yet.

"I want to thank everyone for coming tonight. I'm having such a wonderful time, I almost forgot why we wanted to host this dinner in the first place." Pres cleared his throat, and his look turned serious as he made eye contact with everyone, his beautiful blue gaze lingering on him and Blair.

"The people here tonight are who we consider to be close friends and, of course, our family. A couple months ago, God saw fit to bless me with my sight again, and at the time, I didn't know what I'd done to be in his good graces. I was, however, told by a very wise woman—my mother—to not question God's blessings, but to just say thank you." Pres smiled at his mom. "When I came out of the darkness, there was brightness everywhere, but nothing shone brighter than the beautiful face of Dr. Rickson Edwards. I called him my 'Sunshine' way before I was able to see light again."

Ric blushed terribly at Pres's compliment, but he was also full of pride. He cut his eyes to Blair and saw the moisture building in his eyes, too. Ric moved closer to him and put his arm around his shoulder, pulling him into his chest. He'd be damned if he kept his hands off his man when he needed his comfort.

Ric didn't look around at the reactions of their guests. He and Blair kept their attention on Pres. When Pres saw them connected, he smiled so brightly that they no longer needed the artificial lights that were on over their heads.

"Ric and I weathered a tough storm at the beginning of our relationship." Pres looked at Ric and lowered his head, his sparkling eyes clouding over at obviously remembering their painful breakup. Then he smiled that fucking sexy smile, and Ric shook his head in awe at the man that was Prescott Vaughan.

Blair's hands were covering his mouth, and tears were falling down his cheeks. Ric hugged him tighter and kissed him on his temple.

"But, eventually, the storm passed, and the dark clouds disappeared. The skies cleared, and that's when we both saw a rainbow so bright and brilliant in color that it stole our breath away." Pres moved closer until he was right in front of his men. He slowly brought his hand up and gently wiped the salty tears from Blair's eyes before he spoke again, this time in a hoarse whisper as his emotions slammed to the surface. "Our rainbow has a name." Pres winked at Blair. "Blair McKenzie."

There were a couple gasps and aws around the room as Pres continued.

"There was so much feeling and passion that swarmed around between us that at first we didn't know what the hell to do with it." Pres let out a humorless laugh. "But our Blair knew exactly what to do. He told us that we belonged together. Regardless of what society says, we shouldn't have to deny who we love…or limit it to only one." Pres put his arm around Blair's waist and hung on to his other side, both of them supporting him as he broke down in their arms.

Ric finally surveyed the faces of their friends and family, and there wasn't a judgmental eye in the room. Ric let out a huge sigh of relief, glad that they weren't going to meet any resistance or bigotry from the people they cared about the most.

"So, we called you here to tell you that we—the three of us—are in a committed relationship. We are in love with each other, and none of us will deny the other because being in a threesome is still so taboo. All that matters to us is our family and friends. Everyone else can go to hell. We love all of you and hope you can be happy for us."

Pres placed his palm on the side of Blair's face and brought his lips to his and kissed him with an overwhelming amount love and emotion. Ric buried his face in the back of Blair's neck and placed soft kisses there. He pulled back, not wanting to put on a full show, complete with raging hard-ons.

Janice, Scott's wife, and Pres's mom clapped and squealed like schoolgirls at the public display of affection, while the men discreetly turned their heads and stifled fake coughs. Pres broke their kiss, and Ric heard him whisper, "I love you," into Blair's mouth before he put his hands up and told everyone to make their way into the dining room for dinner.

"Let's eat this wonderful meal that my extremely talented man has spent all day preparing. When I say man, I mean Blair. We don't allow Ric into the kitchen. The condo association will cancel my insurance if he's going to be cooking."

Pres took off running as Ric tried to grab him at making fun of his lack of culinary skills. Everyone laughed at their playfulness and made their way to the table.

# YOU CAN SEE ME

## Chapter Forty-Four

Pres sat at the head of the long dining room table with Ric and Blair on either side of him. He had to admit he felt like a king. His men were so smart and sexy, he felt like they could conquer the world—okay, well, maybe that was taking it a little far, but he knew life with these men would be wonderful and filled with love.

The conversation at the table bounced from Blair's new job as executive chef at the new five-star restaurant attached to the monstrosity of a hotel on the oceanfront, to Pres's new ventures, and finally to Ric's exciting job as an ER trauma surgeon.

Pres didn't miss the fact that Ric avoided several questions and exchanged an undecipherable look with his mentor, Dr. Brown, when talking about his job.

When conversations got lighter and more jokes began to fly, Ric went into stories of Pres and Blair's frequent comedy acts in the kitchen. Ric really had the table laughing on how bad Blair would pout when Pres was always right while they cooked. He told them about their cook-offs and that Blair officially had dishpan hands now that he'd lost so many times. They all knew that Blair was just out of the academy and Pres had ten years of professional cooking on him, but it didn't stop the ribbing. When Blair pouted at the table, his mom smothered him with kisses, only making everyone laugh harder.

"Well now you know who the dramatic one is in this relationship," Pres joked, and reached over to pinch Blair's red cheeks. Even Blair had to laugh at that one, because he was indeed dramatic.

Pres's mom spoke up. "All jokes aside, dear, this meal is fantastic. You've obviously trained well, and it has shown here tonight in this magnificent dinner. I would love to have you come over and cook with me sometimes, just like I do with Prescott."

Blair was stunned but smiled broadly and told Pres's mom that he'd love that as well.

Pres winked at his mom. Coming together like this was the best idea they could've had. Now neither man had to ever question what role they had in the relationship… They were all equal.

It was going on eight thirty, and the staff had begun cleaning up in the kitchen. The dinner table broke off into individual conversations as they sipped on after-dinner drinks. Ric was talking with Dr. Brown and his partner about modern science, Pres's parents were talking with Blair's parents about getting together for Christmas, and Janice and her date laughed with Scott and his wife about the adventures of being new parents.

Pres was beyond elated. He patted Josey's head and fed him little scraps of beef Wellington from his plate.

Pres heard Dr. Brown ask Ric to talk with him out on the balcony in private before he had to leave. Ric agreed. He picked up his drink and leaned over to kiss Pres on the cheek and threw a wink to Blair before leaving the table.

# Chapter Forty-Five

Ric looked over the balcony at the hustle and bustle going on down on the street below. Their building was on a major artery in the city, and there was always something to look at when he came out here. He slowly raised his eyes to study his mentor and saw Dr. Brown's knowing eyes were already focused on him.

"You want to talk to me about my termination from the hospital, don't you?" Ric asked, lowering his head.

"Of course. I figured you hadn't told your boyfriends since they were talking about your job in the present tense," Dr. Brown said.

Ric snorted a laugh at the word "boyfriends" and that it was just used by his mentor. "Knew I wouldn't get one past you, sir," he confessed.

"Have you ever?" Dr. Brown said and turned to face Ric, so he did the same.

"No, sir. I haven't. I would never try either, for that matter."

Dr. Brown smiled. "I thought of going to the board and giving them a good piece of my mind regarding their decision and threatening them with a few of my resources that I have at my disposal." He stopped and rubbed his neatly trimmed, graying beard. "Then I thought of something even better."

"And what might that be?" Ric asked, intrigued.

"Well, I figured that their loss is my gain. I'm going to be opening a practice here in the Virginia Beach area and am looking for a partner to take on. I have three practices and no one I trust to help me run them. I have a great staff of doctors and managers that keep things running smoothly, but I'd like a partner so that I could focus on a new clinical trial I've got coming up at the beginning of the year."

Ric was in complete shock at what he was being offered. Dr. Clark Brown was famous all over the world for his breakthrough science on offsetting first-stage Alzheimer's disease. The man had single-handedly designed a practice to combine MRI techniques with EEG signals to simultaneously record and monitor blood flow and electrical activity in the brain. The man was an absolute genius, and he'd just asked Ric to partner with him—not work with, but partner with.

"Clark, I don't know what the hell to say." Ric gaped at him.

"I was hoping you'd say yes, son," he laughed. "Now, I know your termination is still fresh, but you can imagine that I'd been considering this for a while. That's why I didn't hesitate to come and help your partner when he got hurt. I've always respected you as a physician and as a man. Of all the doctors and so-called hotshot surgeons I've worked with, none of them were more humble to work with than you. You were in it for the science, not the recognition, and I've always admired that. I need someone to run my offices while I work on this new study.

"You will have a full staff that you will hire and more stable hours that you can be home, too. You will still be able to perform surgeries and delegate them, if need be. Most importantly, son, you'll never again have to worry about your personal life interfering with you practicing medicine. If any member of your staff shows distaste in your lifestyle…fire them." Dr. Brown stepped back from the railing and stuck both hands in his pockets. "So what do you say, Rickson? How does Brown and Edwards, PLC, sound to you?" he smirked.

"Sounds damn good to me, Clark. I accept." Ric laughed and shook Dr. Brown's extended hand. "You know what? I'm sorry, but I have to do this." Ric rushed in and grabbed Dr.

Brown in a bone-crushing hug. His large biceps gripped the man so hard that he had to suck in a large breath after Ric released him. Dr. Brown laughed hard and told Ric that it was all right, he understood.

"We'll get together for a business lunch next week with our lawyers and iron out some details. How's that sound?"

"That sounds more than fine. I look forward to it. Now I can tell Pres and Blair what's going on. I couldn't tell them I was fired," Ric said, feeling frustrated.

"Let me give you a little advice, son. If you want what you have to last, you have to be honest and forthcoming with your men. They're sharp and intelligent, and they'd probably understand just about anything you dished out. A relationship takes work, and you, my dear boy, have two relationships. It's going to take a lot of dedication, communication, and, more than anything, honesty."

"What about, love?" Ric smiled.

"Well, it's obvious to anyone that love overflows with abundance between the three of you." He smiled back. "I've been with my partner for fifteen years, and we have seen our storms too, my friend, but honesty will get you through them all. Always tell your guys the truth."

"Thank you, Clark. I always take what you say to heart, and always will. Anytime you've talked, I've listened, and you've never steered me wrong."

"I'm looking forward to a long, prosperous working relationship with you, Dr. Edwards."

"Likewise, Dr. Brown."

Dr. Brown turned and looked back at the party through the glass patio doors. It had thinned out, most of the company having already left. Ric saw only Pres's parents and Dr. Brown's partner talking in the foyer. When he looked at Dr. Brown, he gave a slight nod of his head.

"Well, I'm going to let you get back to your guys," Dr. Brown said and then looked around inconspicuously. He stepped in closer to Ric and whispered to him. What for, Ric didn't know. They were out there alone. "You are one lucky son of a gun to have not one but two fine men like that, Dr. Edwards. I think I'm gonna take Jacob home now. Your little three-way kiss earlier had him feeling pretty anxious. I think I'm going to reap the rewards from that tonight." He slapped Ric on the shoulder and walked inside.

Ric could only shake his head and laugh at Dr. Brown's admittance of being turned on by them. He was looking forward to their new partnership already. While the last of their company said their good-byes, Ric stayed out on the balcony thinking about how much his life had changed in the last year.

## Chapter Forty-Six

**R**ic was gazing up at the starry night when he heard the sliding glass door open. Pres's calm tone floated to him over the brisk air.

"Everyone's gone home, and they told me to tell you good night since you and Dr. Brown were in deep conversation." Pres wrapped his arms around Ric's waist and puffed warm air against his neck as he spoke. "We've all made some type of plans to meet up soon. Scott, his wife, and Janice want to get together for dinner and dancing in a couple weeks. Of course, Blair agreed to that right away. Tomorrow, my mom and Blair's mom are going to lunch and then shopping at that new flea market that opened last month in downtown. And get this, honey. Blair's dad has season tickets to the Redskins home games, and he's taking my dad next time they play at home. I've never seen my dad that excited." He turned Ric around to look at him, looking confused by his silence. "You okay, honey? What were you out here talking about for so long? You don't have to tell me if it's private," Pres hurriedly admitted.

Ric laid a soft kiss on Pres's perfect lips. He moaned and pulled Pres in closer, needing more body heat. "Nothing will ever be private between us. I will always tell you the truth," Ric said. "Where's Blair?"

"He's paying the kitchen staff. He should be done now. Let's go inside. It's chilly out here." Pres turned and went inside.

Blair locked up the condo and trudged back into the den looking exhausted. Pres and Ric sat side by side on the large couch and waited for him to remove his vest and shoes. He came over and sat on Ric's lap and curled up his legs to rest over Pres's.

"Why's everyone looking so serious?" he asked over a yawn.

"'Cause Ric has something serious to tell us," Pres answered.

Ric felt Blair stiffen in his arms, and he immediately pulled him to his chest and rubbed his back. "Calm down, baby boy. It's really good news."

"Oh. Sorry," Blair replied sheepishly.

Ric explained everything to his men, from his termination to Dr. Brown's miraculous offer to partner with him. When he was done, they were all grinning from ear to ear.

"Holy shit! You're going to be a neurosurgeon?" Blair gaped at him.

Ric laughed. They still had so much to learn about each other. "Yes, baby. I have an MD, but I also have an MBBS, which is a bachelor of surgery in neurology. Neurosurgeon was the position I held at my previous job before I was blackballed for being gay, and so I took the first thing readily available at Chesapeake General, which was trauma surgeon. I always liked working with Dr. Brown, and I know this is going to be really good for me...for us."

"I'm so proud of you. That's really awesome," Pres said and kissed him on the mouth.

"Oh my God, I'm fucking the hottest chef in the world and a neurosurgeon. Damn, it doesn't get any better," Blair said, moving his legs to fully straddle Ric's lap.

"You are hopeless." Pres laughed.

"But you love me." Blair winked while grinding his rising cock into Ric's stomach.

"I most certainly do." Pres rose up and cupped the back of Blair's neck to pull him in for a hard kiss. "I want this sexy ass tonight," he hissed in his face, and it made Blair shudder. Blair let Pres control his mouth as he massaged Ric's chest and continued to work his hips. Ric let his head fall back on the couch.

"Fuck, baby. So fucking hot," Ric groaned as he worked to free Blair's cock.

"Let's take this to the bedroom," Pres ordered.

Pres was moving fast across the hardwood floor. Ric threw Blair over his shoulder and slapped his ass hard as he fireman-carried him into the room.

"Put his hot ass in the middle of the bed, honey," Pres told Ric while he made quick work of his clothes.

Ric tossed Blair onto the bed, making him release a shocked yelp.

"Oh God, Strawberry. I need you so bad. Need you to claim me," Blair whined and pressed his hands onto his aching cock.

"I'm gonna give you my dick, honey, but not until you fucking beg for it," Pres commanded. He turned around and walked his bare-naked ass into the bathroom without even a backward glance.

Damn, Pres was a sight to behold when he turned on his domineering side. Ric's cock was large and weeping as he circled the bed, watching Blair writhe and twist in the sheets as if the want and need for Pres's cock was too painful to take.

Ric quickly removed his clothes, dimmed the lights, and got on the bed with Blair. Blair's half-lidded eyes popped open, and Ric was instantly attacked by Blair's mouth. He licked and sucked his chest, his nipples, his throat, everywhere and anywhere all at the same time. Ric interlaced his fingers behind his head and let Blair have his way. He felt Blair bury his nose in his armpit and inhale deeply.

"Love the way you smell, darlin'." Blair spoke in his roughed honey drawl, and it made Ric growl with need. He put his hands around Blair's thin frame and slapped both palms down on his ass, making him jerk.

"Augh, yeah, baby. More," Blair keened.

Ric buried his tongue in Blair's mouth, stealing his moans and curses. He spread his legs wide, letting Blair settle in between them, and slapped his ass again, pulling him in hard against his cock and thrusting his pelvis up into him.

"Yes, Bear. That's it. I want it fuckin' rough tonight," Blair said while meeting Ric's thrusts.

"You're going to get it rough," Pres whispered.

Ric and Blair both stilled their hips and turned to look at Pres. He stood at the foot of their bed, his head bowed slightly, sapphire-blue eyes staring at them provocatively through long, dark lashes. He must've splashed water on his face because his bare torso had small rivulets of water, and it made Ric want to lick off every damn drop. Pres's dark hair was spiky and wild. His diamond earrings were still in his ears, and it made him look like a delicious bad boy…the one you didn't bring home to Mom. The overhead lights cast a warm, celestial glow across Pres's evenly tanned skin. His dick was fully erect, and a large dollop of pre-come was forming on his slit. Pres took two fingers, swiped the large, pearly bead off his blushing cock head, and oh so slowly brought it up to his still-kiss-swollen lips. He stuck the two fingers in his mouth, moaning at the taste of himself, and used his other hand to pinch his nipple, making his chest jerk at the self-inflicted sensation.

Pres let out a throaty groan and left his nipples alone. He brought his hand down to gently graze his dick before giving it a couple of torturously slow pulls. Pres's cock looked painfully hard, and his balls hung low with seed. With his fingers still in his mouth, he let his head fall back while his tight fist squeezed more natural lubricant from his slit. Ric and Blair were perfectly still watching this Greek god put on the most erotic show they'd ever witnessed.

"Fuckin' Christ, Pres," Ric growled, his voice so raw with passion he barely recognized it.

"Pres," Blair mewled.

"Look at me, Blair." Pres ran his hand down his cut abs. "You want this?" Pres pulled hard on his cock.

"Yes!" Blair practically shouted.

Pres gave the most devilishly seductive grin ever and simply replied, "Beg."

"Fuck," Ric whispered into the dim room and watched Blair get to his knees and crawl to the end of the bed and kneel in front of Pres.

Hell, Blair hadn't been fucked by Pres yet, but Ric sure as hell had, and if Pres told him to beg for his cock, he'd beg like a bitch in heat. Ric didn't want to blink, in fear he'd miss even a millisecond of Pres's show.

# YOU CAN SEE ME

## Chapter Forty-Seven

**P**res had to grind his teeth together to keep from shooting his load all over Blair's beautiful face. Blair had crawled to him on his hands and knees, kneeled in front of him, and pleaded with his eyes before uttering one word.

"Please, darlin'," Blair pronounced slowly.

Pres moved closer to the footboard of his king-sized sleigh bed and cupped Blair's chin, making him look him in the eye. "Please what?" he asked.

"Please fuck me, love. Fuck me hard. Fuck me till I scream your name. Fuck me until I can't walk," Blair begged him.

"Mmmm. I like that. That's more like it, honey. Begging like a good little slut." Pres rubbed Blair's cheek affectionately.

Pres watched Blair's eyes drop closed, and his cock leaked a clear trail of pre-come onto the bed. Pres knew what his dirty talk did to his men. Both of them loved to be handled, and the nastier tPres talked, the harder they got off.

"God yes. Fuck me like the slut I am," Blair moaned.

Pres climbed onto the bed, leaned in, and covered Blair's mouth with his, licking and tasting his lust. He worked his way to his smooth cheek, into his ear, and down his neck, nipping and biting hard enough to leave imprints.

"Gonna mark you good so everyone knows that you're my slut," Pres whispered in his ear, making Blair's body slump down, but Pres held him tight against him.

Blair's body shivered violently in his arms, and Pres felt like a Dom, mastering his sub's body. Blair was under his complete control, and it gave him a serious head rush.

"I want you to climb back on top of Ric and lie between his legs. He's going to hold you down while I fuck you. I'm going to pound your slutty ass until you can't take any more." Pres roughly grabbed a handful of Blair's hair with one hand, wrapped his other hand around his throat, and slammed Blair into his chest. "And when you beg me to stop, I'm just gonna fuck you harder," Pres growled.

Blair's body jolted, and Pres released the grip on Blair's hair but not his throat. Pres's long fingers squeezed Blair's throat harder, and again Blair's body wrenched violently. Blair released a keening moan so low in octave that it vibrated Pres's chest. He wrapped his arm around Blair's waist to hold him up before Pres's eyes widened at the realization that Blair had just come all over himself.

*Oh. My. Fucking. God. He just came from my words.*

Blair's face was buried in the crook of Pres's neck. His breathing was erratic and labored as he came down from his orgasm. Pres didn't let Blair go. Otherwise he would have melted into a puddle on the mattress.

Pres stole a glance at Ric and saw that he'd risen up on his elbows and was watching them intently with a shocked expression on his handsome face and his cock jutting straight out and resting on his stomach. He shook his head at Pres and mouthed, *What the fuck?*

"My, my, my. You are something else, honey." Pres rubbed Blair's back. He was still trembling in his arms, but his breathing was slowing.

Blair didn't raise his head, and his hot breath gusted onto Pres's neck. "I've always wanted to be talked to like that, and handled rough, but never found someone I trusted enough to do it and not hurt me. When you grabbed my throat and…" Blair shivered again. "Shit. It was so damn exciting, and I fuckin' lost it."

"Baby, that was the sexiest thing I've ever seen. You were beautiful just now, and I got to hold you and feel your body's response to me, and I loved every damn minute of it," Pres said and nuzzled Blair's cheek until he lifted his face. "Kiss me."

Blair and Pres kissed until the heat turned back up. They touched and groped and licked until Blair was almost hard again.

Ric was so damn quiet. His hands were behind his head, and his lust-lazy eyes were feasting on their every move.

Pres winked at Ric seductively while he stroked his hard cock, which was now screaming for release after what Blair had just done. Pres dropped his head back and let Blair mark him on his neck.

"Come on, honey. I'm not nearly done with you yet." Pres gripped Blair behind his neck, making him pull his mouth fromwhere he'd clamped on to his throat. "Get up there on top of him and let him hold you."

Blair followed his instructions and climbed on top of Ric's large chest and settled down between his thickly muscled thighs. He immediately buried his face in Ric's scent.

"So gorgeous," Ric whispered into Blair's hair while massaging his back. "You ready for him, baby?" He thrust his hard cock into Blair's stomach.

"I'm more than ready," Blair groaned.

"Good," Pres said and smacked Blair hard on his ass, the sound loud in the quiet room.

"Fuck," Blair hissed in Ric's ear.

Ric rubbed Blair's stinging ass and licked his neck. "Feels good, doesn't it, baby?" Ric crooned.

"Spread 'em open, Sunshine," Pres said and dropped down to put his mouth at Blair's tight hole.

"Oh God," Blair groaned as Ric spread his cheeks as wide as they could go. Then, Pres's tongue was there, not wasting an ounce of time on gentility or grace. He delved in and speared

Blair's hole, forcing it to give. He tried to shove as much of his warm saliva into that tight channel as he could.

Blair tried to thrash, but Ric did his job. He held Blair tight in his arms and hooked his legs over top of his—spreading him wide and keeping him open for Pres's assault. Pres thought Ric liked this just as much as Blair, because Blair's bucking was driving his hard cock directly into Ric's.

After Pres licked and prodded Blair's sweet hole, he clicked the top on the lube and coated three fingers. He saw Ric massaging Blair's ass cheeks while whispering sweet nothings in his ear. Pres easily pushed one finger in and used his tongue to lick around Blair's stretching hole. He waited until he heard Blair's bawling in Ric's neck and quickly added a second.

Pres's reserve was slipping. He knew it wouldn't be long before his dominating instinct kicked in and he ravished Blair's ass.

"Fuck, need you so bad. You're so fuckin' tight." Pres pumped Blair's ass with two fingers. "Gonna live in this heat of yours, babe." He hooked his middle finger on his next thrust and felt Blair jerk hard in Ric's hold.

"Fuck. Do it again, Pres. Do it again," Blair begged.

Pres hooked his finger again and pressed against Blair's sweet spot on every thrust. Blair thrust his ass higher in the air, and Pres took his other hand and rewarded him with another hard slap.

"That's right. Put that greedy ass in the air for me." Pres finger-fucked him until his hole was anxiously sucking in his three fingers. "You got a hungry hole, don't you, slut? Ready for my cock to make you scream."

"Augghhh. Gawwwdd. Pres, don't make me come again. Not yet, not yet. Stop talking. Can't come until you're inside me. Fuckin' get inside me, Pres!" Blair yelled and bit into Ric's hard chest.

"Fuck!" Ric hollered and squeezed Blair tighter.

"Oh, you're being a naughty boy." Pres spoke gravely low. "Do you want to know what happens to bad sluts that bark orders, my sweet Blair?" Pres lathered his cock with way more lube than necessary and settled his weight over Blair's back.

He knew Ric could take all their weight. Pres positioned his cock at Blair's hole and gave him a couple warning knocks at his back door. He leaned in to whisper in Blair's ear. "I'm gonna make you mine, baby. So hang on." Pres made eye contact with Ric before breeching Blair's outer ring.

He paused only for a couple seconds, enough time for Ric to quietly encourage Blair to breathe and push out, before he slid all the way in until his balls were snug up against Blair's now-red ass.

It was the most spectacular sight. Pres never forgot how fortunate he was to be able to see his men in unbridled ecstasy.

Blair let out a low, husky moan and clamped his ass tight around Pres's cock.

*Damn it, his ass is just like his goddamn mouth.*

"Fuckin' hell." Pres gritted his teeth. "Fuuuuck, you are fucking tight."

"Pres, move now. Please. Need you to move. So full," Blair said in a throaty whisper.

Pres kept his face close to Blair's mouth so he could hear every curse, praise, and promise he made while he fucked him. He drew his cock out halfway and eased it back in, trying to let Blair get used to being full.

Blair let loose another rasping cry, and Pres was having a hard time keeping his hips under control. He wanted to pound him, he wanted to make him scream, and he wanted to make him come.

Blair shivered in between them even though the room felt like it was one hundred degrees.
"Oh…my…So…Goddamn…Pres, what are you doi—" Blair couldn't finish either sentence.

Ric's legs were wide enough that Pres could open Blair's legs wider and give himself more room to thrust.

"Ready?" He licked the shell of Blair's ear.

"I'm yours, lover." Blair laid his head on Ric's chest and hooked his arms under those large biceps. "Take me."

Pres snapped. His beautiful man was laid out all needy and shameless, begging to be claimed. This was what Pres lived for. This was who he truly was.

Pres rose up and braced his arms on either of side of them, pulled out almost to the tip, and slammed back into Blair's tight channel, making Blair thrust his hard cock into Ric's. Pres saw Blair latch his mouth on to the fleshy part of Ric's muscled pec, muffling his cry.

*Oh no you don't.*

Pres pulled out again and left his cock head on the rim of Blair's hole. He grabbed a fistful of Blair's hair and yanked, making Blair's mouth unlatch from Ric's chest.

He tilted Blair's head to the side and snarled in his ear, "I want to hear every fuckin' cry and scream you make." He bit Blair on his neck and slammed back into that hot tunnel at the perfect angle.

This time Blair didn't hesitate to scream out into the dim room.

"Better." Pres released the grip on his hair and slowly eased his fingers around Blair's throat and clamped on tightly, still mindful of Blair's need to breathe through his pounding. Blair and Pres were cheek to cheek, and Pres battered that tight bubble ass with every ounce of energy he had.

The grunting and panting was an aphrodisiac to Pres, and it drove him up the wall to know that his thrusting was causing both of his men so much pleasure at the same time. Ric's dick was deliciously trapped between his and Blair's muscled stomachs.

He watched Ric's expression change to pure pleasure, and his hips lost their rhythm. Ric clenched his teeth and pressed his forehead to Blair's, letting his orgasm flow. Ric grunted through it, releasing ropes of luscious come in between him and Blair.

"Pres, Jesus," Ric panted.

Pres momentarily slowed his hips and bent down to kiss Ric on his slack mouth. "I ain't done, honey."

"You fantastic bastard," Ric panted into Pres's mouth

Pres grinned slyly and braced himself back on his arms. His cock was still hard as stone, and he wasn't ready to come yet. He took Blair's bent leg and slid it up Ric's side, letting Ric keep it pinned with his arm. Blair was spread wide, his hole pulsating and calling to Pres for more.

Blair let out a sexy whimper, and Pres ate it up. He slammed back in, going balls deep, then keeping his thrusts shallow and deep.

"Cry for me, sweet boy. Tell me how much it hurts," Pres murmured against the side of Blair's face. "Hurts so good, don't it?"

Blair's body rocked on top of Ric's with every deep-seated thrust Pres gave him. His eyes crossed as Pres pounded steady pressure to his prostate. His body shook violently, and he screamed to whoever would listen that he was coming.

Pres rose off Blair and watched his boy's back arch like a feline. Blair let out a startled sob when the first spurt of jizz landed on Ric's chest. He dropped his chin to his chest and choked on his own breath as jet after jet of come mixed with Ric's, again filling the room with the pungent smell of come and sweat.

"Oh baby. Squeezing the fuck out of my dick," Pres groaned. "Keep coming, baby. Ima fuck you right through it."

"Pres, what the hell are you doing to me?" Blair groaned.

"Claiming you."

Pres rose to his knees and went back on his haunches. He refused to give Blair any recovery time. He gripped Blair's hips and pulled him back onto his cock with enough force to make them both cry out. With Blair seated firmly on his lap, his limp body fell back against Pres's chest, and his head tilted back and landed on his shoulder. Pres turned and kissed Blair's sweat-drenched hair. His lips whisked over Blair's flushed cheek as he spoke.

"I told you I'd fuck you until you begged me to stop," Pres reminded him.

"Darlin', stop. Please. Can't take any more."

"Oh fuck," Ric whispered from the other side of the bed.

"And I told you when you begged me to stop"—Pres wrapped one arm around Blair's middle to keep him from getting away, and got in position—"I said I would fuck you harder." Pres bared his teeth and annihilated Blair's ass again. The sound of skin slapping skin echoed loudly throughout the dark room.

Blair was like a rag doll in Pres's arms, and he loved it. Blair's body was his for whatever he wanted to do with it, and the knowledge of that power was fueling Pres's pending orgasm.

Blair's eyes were shut tight, the veins in his neck bulged, and his teeth clenched. Pres knew Blair's body was overwhelmed with sensations, surrendering to his assault as he dangled him from the shallow precipice of exquisite pleasure and blissful pain.

Pres felt the familiar stirring in his balls, but it was still a ways off. He practically threw Blair off his lap and pounced on top of him before he could scurry away, because he sure as hell tried.

Pres held Blair down on the bed and slowly eased back inside him this time, savoring the spine-prickling feeling of entering his man. He gently moved the wet hair off Blair's forehead and tenderly kissed him there, licking out his tongue to taste the sweat that ran down his temple.

"So pretty," Pres whispered.

"Can't take no more, Strawberry," Blair rasped in his rough-hewn drawl, and Pres thought it was beyond hypnotic. But just like that, his angelic kindness was soon replaced with the little devil man on his shoulder, and Pres tilted his hips and drove in hard, seeking out that spot to make Blair beg him to stop again.

Pres had his eyes locked on Ric now, teasing him with the show of pounding Blair's ass while licking his lips at him. Ric's cock was growing while he lay there stroking himself.

Blair looked up at Ric, and in a throaty whisper he moaned, "Bear, please."

Pres watched Ric crawl over to Blair and whisper something that Pres couldn't hear. He'd slowed his hips but was still driving in deep, his orgasm getting closer and closer with every cry Blair made. When Ric moved around and settled in behind Pres, he knew exactly what Ric was up to. He heard the familiar sound of the lube bottle click open.

"Ric, you motherfucker," Pres snarled and pushed deep into Blair's warm ass.

"Augh!" Blair yelled.

Ric's strong arms slammed Pres down on top of Blair. He straddled Pres's lower legs, making it impossible for Pres to thrust with Ric's heavily muscled body pressing him down.

"Who's being naughty now, huh?" Ric teased while sucking on Pres's ear.

"Get off me. He's mine." Pres raised his head and snapped at Ric.

"I love it when you get like this, baby. All crazy with power. Fucking turns me on," Ric said, still holding Pres down.

"Bear," Blair whined.

"I got you, sweet boy," Ric answered.

Ric lathered one finger with lube.

"His sweet ass is mine tonight." Pres tried to inject some anger into his voice, but it came out as a pathetic whine. With Ric on top controlling him, his own throbbing cock still buried in Blair, and Blair still crying for relief, Pres's orgasm was barreling to the surface at a rapid speed, and there wasn't a damn thing that could stop it.

"Face. Down. Ass. Up." Ric snapped those words into Pres's ear right before driving one thick finger deep inside Pres's ass.

Pres instinctively clenched his ass around the imposing digit and hugged Blair hard from behind. "I'm coming, lover. I'm coming."

"Pres, goddamn it, come! Fuckin' fill me up!" Blair yelled.

Ric twisted his finger and pushed hard on Pres's spot. Pres's asshole spasmed around that thick digit, and he let his orgasm break through.

"Fuuuuck." Pres's hips didn't move. He just let the eruption pump his hot come into Blair's ass.

Ric kept rotating his finger and slowly pumping in and out of Pres's tight ass as his orgasm eased to an end. Pres felt Ric rub his back before pulling him off of Blair's limp body. Blair flipped over on his back and splayed his arms out, letting his chest rise and fall.

"I'll never walk again," Blair gasped. "Jesus Christ, Strawberry. How the hell do you have the stamina of a high school football star?"

"Many years of jacking off alone in the dark," Pres whispered. "So now, when I'm inside you—both of you—and I can see your gorgeous faces, something in me snaps, and I don't want it to ever end."

Blair and Ric surrounded their lover. They hugged him, kissed him, and whispered "I love yous" until Pres was clawing at them again.

# Epilogue

*Six months later*

"Honey, how the hell can you watch that shit? Turn it off," Pres said, removing his glasses since he'd taken his contacts out. He closed his laptop and reached across the wide bed to turn the lamp off.

"It's funny. That's why I watch it," Blair replied and swiped the remote before Pres could grab it and turn the station on the sixty-inch television mounted on their bedroom wall.

"What moronic reality show is this anyway? Desperate housewives swap husbands while driving a food truck through the wilderness on a scavenger hunt to win your dream wedding?" Pres mumbled.

"Oh, real funny. Why have you been grumpy all evening? How did your review go? I saw the grand opening for the restaurant in the paper, and it sounded real nice." Blair moved up Pres's body and laid his head on his chest.

Pres let out a soft sigh. "The review went well. I'll give it four stars. The owner was so happy he'll probably give us free dinners for a year. Want to go to there and eat this weekend?" Pres kissed Blair's forehead.

"Yeah. Sounds good," Blair said around a yawn. "Saturday works best, because I'm going over to your mom's on Sunday to show her how to bake chouquettes for her book club."

"That's sweet," Pres said and pulled Blair all the way on top of him. For several minutes they just stared at each other. "I love you all the way to the moon and back, honey."

"I know, Strawberry." Blair leaned in and kissed Pres with so much love that it made his toes curls and his dick harden. The kiss went on for several minutes until they heard the beeping of the front door alarm to their condo.

"He's home," Blair whispered into Pres's mouth. "Be nice to him, please."

"I make no promises." Pres looked at Blair seriously.

Ric walked into their bedroom and dropped his bag on the desk in the corner. The bottom half of his long brown hair hung past his shoulders, while the front was pulled back into a ponytail.

Ric let out a tired sigh. "Hey, guys," he said while undressing to take a quick shower.

"Hi, Bear. How'd your surgery go?" Blair asked from Pres's arms.

Ric smiled. "The tumor was removed successfully. Little Katie will grow up to live a full and active life."

Blair tried to get up to hug Ric, but Pres held him to him, not letting him move.

"What is it, Pres?" Ric stared at him.

"You know what it is." Pres stared back.

"It better not be what I think it is, because I'm not going into that shit again, and I'm too fuckin' tired anyway." Ric huffed, turning to go into the bathroom.

"I thought the partnership with Dr. Brown would allow you to have better home hours, but in the last couple of months, we've barely seen you, Ric," Pres fussed and jumped up to follow Ric into the bathroom.

Blair sat up in the bed, pulled his legs up, and draped his arms over his knees. He dropped his chin to his chest and let out a depressed sigh.

Ric turned on the taps in the shower, not bothering to respond to Pres's ranting.

"Are you going to fucking ignore me, Ric? Like I'm bothering you, or don't you give a damn about me...or Blair's feelings? Every fucking day you leave before either of us, and you drag your ass back in here after eleven or later at night. Hell, sometimes you don't even come home. You're tired all the time. Are you not in this relationship anymore?" Pres yelled through the glass doors of the shower while watching the hot water cascade over Ric's head, making his long, beautiful hair lay tantalizingly on his rippled back.

"Guys, don't fight, please!" Blair yelled from the room. "Strawberry, leave him alone. He's exhausted."

"Quiet, Blair!" Pres slammed the bathroom door so he didn't have to hear his reasonable cut-him-some-slack attitude.

"I know that you're exhausted, and it's killing me." Pres lowered his voice and stood right outside of the shower doors. "I can't stand to see you so tired, Sunshine. I need you... We need you. I know you are an amazing surgeon and you save lives. All I'm asking is that you let your men give you the love you need sometimes." Pres watched Ric brace both arms on the tile and let the water beat on his tense neck.

"I'm sorry," he finally heard Ric say softly.

Pres's heart cracked. He removed his black briefs, stepped into the warm shower, and began to massage Ric's shoulders. He heard him let out a satisfied groan and press his forehead against the wall, letting Pres love on him.

"God, baby. You have knots everywhere," Pres said, kissing Ric's shoulder. "This is hurting me, Sunshine."

"I know," Ric rasped. He turned around and pulled Pres into him and crushed his lips over his. They kissed so long that the water began to turn lukewarm. "I'm so sorry, baby. God, I miss the hell out of both of you. I swear I do. I guess I was trying to prove something to Dr. Brown that didn't need proving in the first place. Tonight he told me to go home and not to come back until next week. We are changing the surgery rotations, too." Ric buried his neck into Pres's throat. "So I'll be home a lot more."

Pres smiled wide and licked Ric's mouth seductively. He was sure his man wasn't up for a hard fuck, but he knew what would help him relax. He hugged Ric close to him and licked him behind his ear before whispering, "I love you, baby, and when I'm missing you, I don't know how to function." He licked and kissed Ric some more. "Forgive me for bitching these last few days."

"Don't apologize. You were right. It's not just you and Blair in a relationship. I need to be here for y'all, too. These last couple months have been hard, and I miss you so damn much, baby." Ric squeezed Pres to him.

"Let me take care of you," said Pres.

It was an order, not a request. Pres lowered to his knees and gently caressed Ric's thighs. He nuzzled his face into Ric's balls and lapped at the fleshy sac, letting them roll around on his face before sucking one into his mouth and then the other.

Ric spread his legs wider so Pres could get to a better angle. He gripped the back of Pres's head and lazily stroked his hair.

Ric let his head fall back against the hot shower wall. "Damn, baby. Fuckin' needed this so much."

Pres's own cock was hard and aching. He took one hand and began to jerk his own dick with hard, fast strokes, not wanting to prolong it. He wanted to come with Ric.

Pres knew Ric hadn't had any sexual release in several days, and by the way his thighs trembled at his touch, it wasn't going to take long.

Pres bobbed up and down on Ric's hot length, swallowing every inch he had. The water ran down Ric's chest and landed on his cock, making Pres thirsty and needing to lick off every drop. He could see Ric fighting to hold off his orgasm, but Pres wasn't having it. He took his wet finger and circled the tip of it around Ric's hole.

Ric bucked hard. "Mmmmm. Fuck. Feels good. Give me more. Make me come in your mouth," he moaned.

Pres kept Ric's dick planted firmly in his throat and pushed his finger in that sweet hole, immediately aiming for Ric's gland. Ric let out a long growl from deep down in his chest as his dick exploded in Pres's warm mouth. Pres rapidly swallowed all of his lover.

Pres's tight fist flew over his own cock. He pressed his thumbnail into his piss slit and bucked hard, spraying his come over his hand, letting some of it wash away with the running water.

He felt Rick pulling on his arms. "Let me taste," Ric moaned.

Pres took his hand and wiped some of his remaining come onto Ric's parted lips and stuck his come-coated tongue deep into Ric's mouth.

Ric sucked hard and chased all of their mingling flavors that Pres had clinging to his lips, teeth, and tongue. "Thank you," he whispered against Pres's cheek. "It hurts so much when you're upset with me. I'm going to do better, I promise."

"I know, Sunshine. I love you, too." Pres stepped out of the shower. "Now let's get you into bed. I'm sure Blair wants us back in there with him now."

"How's he been?" Ric asked while toweling off.

"Missing you too. But you know he's your biggest fan. He's been giving me hell for coming down on you this week."

Ric conceitedly smirked at Pres. Pres grabbed the hand towel, rolled it up, and popped Ric on the ass with it, making him jump and run out of the bathroom laughing. He ran after him and saw Ric jump onto the bed and grab Blair, throwing him in front of him as a shield.

"Oh, that's not fair." Pres smiled.

"You know he'll protect me. You better back off." Ric chuckled.

Pres and Ric cracked up laughing at Blair's perplexed expression. He'd probably expected them to come out of the bathroom still cursing up a storm.

"Turn off the lights, and get your sexy ass in this bed, Prescott," Ric ordered.

Ric pulled Blair to him and tenderly kissed him. He explained to him that he was on vacation and going to cut back on the surgeries to spend more time with them at home. Ric apologized in between kisses while lowering their bodies into the warmth of their California king-sized bed.

"I'm so glad, Bear. I was worried about you, and I was worried about Pres," Blair said as he snuggled under Ric's armpit and twirled his finger around one of Ric's long, wet locks hanging over his shoulder.

Pres slid under the covers and nestled in close to Blair. He draped his long leg over Blair's hip and pressed a soft kiss to his temple. The three of them always fit so wonderfully together.

"We're going to be just fine, sweet boy. I'm gonna be hanging around here so much, y'all are going to get sick of me," Ric laughed.

"Impossible. That'll never happen," said Blair. "I don't know what I would've done if you had continued being gone from home all the time."

"Sometimes I'll need my head pulled out of my ass. That's what Pres is for. He wages havoc in my heart like a storm on the sea," Ric said quietly.

"With every storm, there'll be sunshine after," Pres responded.

Blair laughed in between them. "Storm and sunshine…so what does that make me?" asked Blair.

"The rainbow," Ric and Pres responded in unison.

## The End

# COMING SOON

**Nothing Special**
**The Story of Det. Leonidis Day & Det. Cashel Godfrey**

## PROLOGUE

"I expect my officers to be diligent, dedicated, focused, and work together as one unit. But most importantly, I expect my officers not to get themselves killed."

Cashel "Cash" Godfrey groaned and rolled his eyes at the Captain's obvious goals. He was pretty sure all of the officers just coming out of the academy didn't want to die anytime soon. Fifteen new recruits were squeezed in the small meeting room, eagerly anticipating who they were going to be partnered with and how soon they were going to be able to get out onto the streets. The ever-present hero complex shinning in their eyes.

Cashel tried to inconspicuously survey the freshly shaven faces. He didn't recognize any of them from the academy class he'd graduated from. Most of the cliché rookies were sporting gelled hair, large tattooed biceps, and sports Ray bans turned backward and resting on their thick necks. He tried not to be too obvious while looking into their eyes—seeing if he could make any kind of a connection with his future partner. He wasn't prepared for the light brown eyes that were unblinking and locked onto him.

Cash quickly took in the man's lithe but strong physique. Although the man was sitting he knew he couldn't be any taller than five foot ten, five eleven. His hair was a dirty blond color, free of product and longer than he'd expect for a rookie to wear it. His trendy five o'clock shadow was already present at eight in the morning. Cash unconsciously fingered his own neatly trimmed goatee, and saw the man quirk up one side of his mouth, his gaze still steady on him.

His arms were crossed over his chest, and the shortsleeved blue polyester uniform shirt showed the peeking of a skull and crossbones on his left bicep. Cash had to squint his eyes to see the simple lettering on the five inch name tag that sat just above his right pocket. 'DAY.' When he brought his eyes back up, he could see Day's intelligent eyes were sizing him up just as hard.

Cash heard the Captain clap his hands together once, breaking their stare-off.

"All right, officers, today you'll spend most of your time in admin getting your logins and IDs for the database. There will also be a few uniforms standing by to do the tour of the station: interrogation rooms, holding tanks, records room, gym, locker rooms, blah, blah." He trailed off. The Captain looked hard at everyone in the room. "When you're finished today, I want you all to go home, fuck your wives and kiss your kids, because from the next day forward, I don't give a fuck about office hours. You're here until I tell you you can leave. I own your rookie asses until you prove otherwise. Got it? Any questions?" His voice boomed in the large room.

Cash watched Day raise two fingers.

"What is it, Officer Day?" The Captain looked hard dark eyes at the man that was already showing a sarcastic smirk.

"What if you don't have a wife to fuck, sir?" Day quipped, his mouth twitching at trying to hide his amusement.

"Then fuck your boyfriend, Day. I don't give a shit. Just make sure you can still drag your ass back in here at o'dark thirty tomorrow, smart-mouth." The Captain snatched his paperwork off the small wooden podium and left the room.

"Yes, sir," Day whispered after the Captain slammed the door.

The men started to gather their papers and bags getting ready to file out of the room. Cash lingered while watching Officer Day pull out his cell phone and use a thin stylus to manipulate the small screen.

"Well at least we've spotted the faggot cop early on, so we know who to protect our junk from in the locker room."

Laughter rang throughout the room.

Day's head eased up slowly and revealed what Cash assumed was his annoyed face at the wannabe 21 Jump Street cop that'd stopped to see if he could push a couple of Day's buttons while securing his reputation as the homophobic, asshole cop.

Cash slowly eased around the table, approaching the cop from behind, and Day immediately locked on to Cash's eyes over the assholes's shoulder.

Day looked at the man's nametag. "I think your pencil-dick is safe, Ronowski. You're not my type anyway. I have a strict no-bastards rule. Now move on."

"Oh so you're a selective faggot. I thought you guys fucked the first dick available." Asshole cop sneered.

"I wouldn't fuck you if your dick jizzed liquid gold." Day smirked while a few of the other officers laughed.

Ronowski took a couple steps closer to Day, and things all-of-a-sudden turned real serious, making several of the officers in the room move in closer too.

"Just make sure you stay the fuck away from me, ass licker."

Cash was moving up the row when he saw Day pocket his cell, snort, and flick the side of his nose with his thumb, the telltale sign that he was getting ready to knock this asshole out.

"I said to move on," Day growled, his furious hazel eyes now the color of burning amber as he closed the small distance between him and his bully. Cash was now directly behind the asshole, who was completely oblivious that he was sandwiched between fury and disgust. Cash was actually beyond disgusted. He couldn't believe there were still people that had this type of hicktown mentality. He'd had to deal with prejudices and bigotry all his life growing up in Clayhatchee, Alabama, and just when he thought he'd escaped it, it reared its ugly head again.

The asshole spun around and ran into Cash's large chest. The man rubbed his forehead as if he'd run into a brick wall. His eyes traveled up the rest of the way until he reached Cash's green eyes that now glowed with intensity.

"Who are you, his bodyguard? You gonna make me leave him alone?" Ronowski sneered and went to move around him.

Cash reached out at lightning speed and gripped the man around his throat leaving him zero time to react. His knees buckled, and his eyes bulged as he scrambled to get a grip on Cash's large forearm. He dragged the man in close and snarled in his face.

"No, I'm not his bodyguard. But if you don't shut your fucking mouth, I will make you his bitch."

"That depends… Does he swallow?" Day asked casually.

"What the fuck is going on in here!" The Captain's loud voice made Cash release the small throat in his hand, but not before glaring hard at the asshole daring him to say a word.

"Just getting to know each other, Cap," Day answered. "Officer Ronowski was just showing my partner the correct technique on chocking the shit out of a suspect." Day grinned. "Isn't that right, Officer Ronowski?"

Day gave the still coughing officer a hard smack on his back, while Cash gave him the look of death.

"Yeah. We're just fucking around, sir," Ronowski barely huffed out while still rubbing his red throat.

"Well knock that shit off and get your asses down to admin, now," the Captain barked then walked off mumbling something about them slacking off already as he made his way back to his office.

Cash and Day looked at each other for a few minutes before Cash quirked one eyebrow up at him. "Partner, huh?"

"Yep," Day said with confidence. He stuck out one hand, "Leonidis Day, most people call me Leo or Day."

Cash shook his future partner's hand in a strong grip and gave it a couple small pumps. "Cashel Godfrey, call me Cash or God," he said back in his deep baritone drawl.

"Cash, huh." Day gave him a knowing smirk.

Cash shrugged. "Works for me."

The other officers moved out of their way as Cash made a hole for him and his new partner.

## CHAPTER ONE

*Four years later.*

"Atlanta PD! I said freeze! Don't you fucking make me chase you," Day yelled as he pushed his legs to move faster. He shrugged out of his leather coat and easily hopped the car in the intersection while keeping his weapon trained on the man that was currently thirty feet in front of him.

"*Stop,*" he yelled again.

His suspect turned to see how close he was, and Day took the opportunity to leap, successfully knocking the large man to the ground and rolling with him. Day immediately scrambled to get on top and kneed the man as hard as he could in his kidneys, immensely satisfied at the loud wail that burst out of him. Day looked around first before dropping another knee onto the man's other kidney. "That's for making me run, asshole. I just had a bean burrito. You do not want to know what's going on in my fucking stomach right now." Day removed his set of handcuffs from his back pocket. He looked up and saw Cash smiling down at him from the driver's side of his truck.

"Are you gonna fuck him or arrest him, Day?" Cash smirked at him.

"Fuck you, Cash." Day grunted as he pulled his suspect up off the ground. "Why do I always have to chase the runner?" He huffed, and threw their suspect non-to-gently into the police cruiser that'd pulled up too.

"My suspects are always too scared to run," Cash said with a shrug.

"I can't wait to get back to the station. I'm going to kick James' ass. There were twice as many guys in that drug house as he said there'd be."

Day took his leather coat the uniformed officer picked up for him and jumped up into the big F350's passenger seat.

"Yeah, I definitely think we need a new snitch," Cash responded while pulling smoothly into traffic and then flooring it down the boulevard.

"So, good cop bad cop?" Cash smiled at Day.

"We're both bad cops, Cash." Day smiled back.

"This is true, but you're more convincing as good cop." Cash stroked his goatee. "Hey, uh. You know Cap is gonna chew our asses out for not calling in back up."

"Which is whose fault? I told you to call it in, Cash, but no, you gotta be Billy Badass and kick the door in before we even got the plan down good," Day argued. He tried to stretch his legs in the huge truck and hissed at the pain in his knees. "Cash, I swear you're chasing the next one. Man, my knees are killing me."

"If you stopped dropping down on them in back alleys, they'd be fine when you're at work," Cash replied easily, taking the toothpick from his mouth and flicking it out the window.

"Oh wow, aren't you just full of shits and giggles today." Day pulled one of his 9mm handguns from his holster and checked the safety before locking it back in place and putting his leather coat back on. He held on to the "oh-shit bar" as Cash made a hard right turn into the station's parking lot. They saw the squad cars pulling into the underground tunnel with their four new arrests and the evidence van backing in to unload the fifty pounds of marijuana they'd just secured from their raid.

Day dropped down to the pavement and winced again at his knees.

"There's no way those idiots we just busted could bring that kind of weight into the city on their own, Cash. We're getting closer to the kingpin. I can feel it."

"Well, let someone else feel it, princess. Long as we get the drugs off the streets, I'm good," Cash replied and turned the key fob toward his truck, activating the alarm.

Cashel Godfrey was primarily known as God on the streets, but Day and most of the officers liked to call him, Cash. His partner fell in line with him and strolled through the precinct's bull pen like they hadn't a care in the world. But Day knew they'd fucked up. They should've had back up with them when going to make that kind of an arrest, but their snitch had lied to them about how many dealers worked out of that house. Although he and Cash were able to get four of them into custody, three of the men had gotten away…and there was also a little gunfire in there too.

Cash's tight black T-shirt clung to his body while his gold detective's badge that hung from a sterling silver link chain around his neck swayed methodically as he walked. His dark denim jeans fit snuggly but comfortably. His gun holster held his Desert Eagle on one side and his 9mm handgun on the other. His thigh length black leather coat barley concealed the large firearms or the six inch serrated blade with pearl handle grip he kept secured under his left arm.

Day was about five inches shorter than him, but they complimented each other perfectly. Day was quick, witty, smart, skilled, and very dangerous. He'd graduated at the top of his class in the academy and already had accommodations for marksmanship. It'd only taken four years for the two of them to make detective and get promoted to the Tactical Narcotics Team after overseeing several of the city's most successful drug bust. Cash and Day were known on the street. They were respected, revered even. When drug kings saw the two of them bursting through their front door, they knew their reign was over.

Everyone also knew Day was gay and out, but ever since that first day in the conference room when Cash choked Ronowski without a second thought, no one bothered Day about it, because no one wanted to face Cash about it.

"So we hear you two busted up that cartel over on thirty-third street." Detective Seasel strolled up beside Cash as he sat at his desk with his boots propped up on the edge. Day was perched on the corner looking down at Cash silently communicating with him like always.

"That's right, sweetheart, another righteous bust for us," Day bragged. He looked around Seasel to her partner whose electrifying blue eyes were shooting daggers at both of them. "You got a problem with that, Ronowski? You look like you're dying to get something off your chest."

"I don't have a goddamn word to say to you, Day. Come on, Vikki. Let's get out of here. We have a planning session to get to. Unlike you fuck-ups, there are some of us that believe in working together as a team to get the job done right."

"Tsk,tsk,tsk." Day shook his head sadly and sucked his teeth at the angry man. "Mad 'cause we didn't invite you to come along, Ronowski?"

Ronowski gritted his teeth. "What-the-fuck-ever. This unit is about working as a team. Every time you jackasses go off half-cocked, someone has to come behind you and clean up your fucking mess."

Cash just shook his head watching the angry exchange. There was no love lost between Day and Ronowski, obviously. Ronowski's partner, Vikki Seasel, was cool though. She was a pretty woman with an even hotter body. She had plump lips and long sandy brown hair she kept pulled into a tight ponytail at the base of her neck. Her warm brown eyes were beautiful, and although she was tough as nails, she knew how to bat her eyes to throw a suspect off during an interrogation. Her hips were nicely proportioned with her small waistline, and Day didn't miss Cash's lustful stare whenever she approached.

"Alright, let's go, Ro. I'll see you guys later." She gave Cash an extra long stare before turning and following her partner through the bull pen.

Day waited until they were almost to the other side of the room before standing up.

"So, Ronowski, same time as last night…my place, right? I bought the extra large condoms this time, so we don't have that little problem again." Day yelled for all to hear.

Ronowski spun around, his face a bright shade of red, and Day thought the man was going to burst a blood vessel in his neck.

"Fuck you, Day," Ronowski yelled back at him, his fist clenched at his side.

"So you want to do me this time. That's cool. I'll let that tight ass of yours have a break tonight." Day feigned a confused look on his face before adding, "I guess we won't need those extra-large condoms after all, huh?"

The room was buzzing, and many of the officers had turned their attention on a livid Ronowski laughing hysterically. Even Cash had a hard time concealing his smile.

Ronowski looked like he was about to charge back across the floor until Cash stood slowly.

"Alright, knock it off out here! Get back to fucking work," the Captain bellowed out into the office from his open door. He turned his sharp eyes on them.

Cash looked at Day and shook his head. "You just can't get enough, can you?"

"That's the same thing Ronowski said last night." Day winked.

You sonofabitch," Ronowki growled as he was dragged out of the bullpen by Vikki, while the other officers laughed at Day's last jib.

"I said knock it off!" Their Captain looked around the large office, daring anyone else to keep laughing. "Day, God. In my office now."

They got the scolding of their life and a threat of demotion if they ever pulled a stunt like that again. Day gripped his coat in his hand and exited the Captain's office thirty minutes later.

"Thanks a lot, Cash. I really enjoyed that." Day shoved his partner hard in his arm, barely moving him at all. "Just because the Captain was best friends with my dad doesn't mean he's going to go easy on us."

"Alright, sissy-queen, you don't have to be so dramatic," Cash teased.

Day didn't care about Cash calling him names because he knew the big man was crazy about him and would kill anyone else that insulted him for real.

"I don't like getting my ass chewed out, man." Day plopped back down in his chair at his desk and let out a long sigh.

Cash leaned against the desk and starred at him. "I thought you did like getting your ass chewed. Umm, what do ya'll call it?" Cash snapped his fingers. "Oh yeah…tossing salad."

"Fuck you." Day laughed.

"Not even on your best day." Cash winked and removed his large frame from leaning on Day's desk and sat back in his own chair facing him.

Day picked up his favorite coffee mug and told Cash he'd be back.

"Yeah, yeah, I know. You're a damn addict, dude. What would you do if there was ever a shortage of coffee beans in the United States?" Cash shook his head at him.

"What do you think I'd do? I'd move to a country that didn't have a shortage, dumbass. I swear, Cash, to be as smart as you are, you sure do ask some stupid shit." Day dodged the paperclip Cash threw at him and started toward the station's kitchen.

Day made quick work of starting his expensive Keurig coffee maker. It was the best one on the market, and he had multiple carousels with a variety of coffee flavors. The kitchen had other coffee makers too, industrial size ones, but Day had to have a freshly brewed cup each time. Cash was right about Day being addicted to coffee. He drank at least ten to twelve cups per day. Although he griped about his lack of sleep at night, he refused to sacrifice his coffee, or switch to godforsaken decaf.

Day hummed while he took inventory of what was left and saw that someone had brought in Vanilla Biscotti flavored cups. *Yes, been meaning to get some of those.* Everyone knew the elaborate coffee machine was his. Other officers were more than welcome to use it as long as they kept it clean and made contributions to the stash.

"Well hello there, handsome," a richly deep voice crawled up Day's spine. *Great...of all the precinct kitchens in the world...he had to walk into mine.*

Day turned around slowly with his steaming cup of coffee held right under his nose letting the bold aroma calm him.

"Detective Johnson, it's such a pleasu— It's nice to—" Day stuttered sarcastically "Well, let me just say hi."

"Ouch. You hurt my heart when you say things like that." The tall detective rubbed his hand over his ample chest, like he really felt an ache. "You're way too beautiful to act like that."

Who said I'm acting?"

Day watched him crowd into his space, using his height to try to smother him, but all he was doing was overpowering the smell of his coffee with all the cologne the man had on. Day refused to look up into the detectives eyes. The man was an arrogant prick, and he didn't deserve Day's respect.

Just because the detective was out and proud too, he somehow thought that made them a great couple. But Detective Johnson was a spoiled rich kid. His father was the police commissioner, and what made that irritating was the man wasn't ashamed to throw big daddy's weight around, and Day and Cash hated that. There was no way in hell Day would ever consider dating him, no matter how handsome the bastard was.

"Where you been hiding yourself, Day? I called that number you gave me, but it was to an adult video shop. I really didn't like that. It was rude and childish, don't you think? If you didn't want me to have your number, all you had to do was say so."

*I did, shit-dick, but someone can't take no for an answer.*

Day didn't bother voicing his response as he took a long sip of his hot coffee, refusing to let this man ruin his zin feeling. Detective Johnson by far wasn't an ugly man. Actually, he was fucking stunning, but he was also pompous and not Day's type. The man really thought he could have whatever he wanted because he had a substantial trust fund.

"You gave me that number and said you didn't mind me calling you." He propped one arm up on the cabinet next to Day's head. His cinnamon breath wafted down on top of him…and into Day's motherfucking cup of coffee.

"I know I said you could call me, but there are two explanations for that. Now either I was lying, or I was wrong about the number of explanations." Day smirked and took another sip.

"That slick mouth of yours is going to get you in trouble." Detective Johnson turned his lip up at him. The man really couldn't take a damn hint.

He had Day up against the counter with only an ounce of breathing room between them. Day could've easily gotten out of the corner, but he personally liked fucking with the smug detective. Detective Johnson was a ballistics expert, and he went from precinct to precinct assisting with cases. Obviously, Cap called him in to assist with the guns that were recovered from their recent bust.

"Well umm, I got to get back to the grind. Wouldn't want you to tell Daddy I'm slacking off." Day gently set his cup of coffee on the counter, spun, and ducked under the detective's arm before the man could blink twice. Day grabbed his mug and made his way to the other side of the room.

"So me and you, dinner this weekend?" Detective Johnson said to his back.

Day snorted, while grabbing a muffin off one of the tables for Cash.

"So is that a no, Day?"

"That's a fuck no." Day opened the door and left the room. He could hear Detective Johnson's curses as he walked away.

Day made his way through the office, and when he was only a few feet away from their desk he tossed God the blueberry muffin. Cash looked at him for a few seconds, using their soundless communication."

"You're welcome," Day said, dropping down in his black leather chair. He took another long gulp before releasing a long deep breath. He cracked his neck on both sides and leveled his hazel eyes on his partner. "So you ready to do the nasty with me, Cash?" he asked him with complete seriousness.

"As ready as I'm gonna be. Give it to me, baby," Cash replied with a frustrated huff.

Day began downloading the multitude of forms one by one and printing them out for them to complete. Cash groaned at all the papers repeatedly printing out from their small desktop printer. "Uhhh, fuckin' paperwork...shit! Hate it!" Cash all but yelled.

# About the Author

A. E. Via lives in Virginia Beach, Virginia with her beautiful husband and four very patient children. She's the baby of five older brothers and sisters. She's lived in Virginia her entire life…and believe it or not hates the beach.

When not writing about male/male romance, you will most likely find her curled up with a blanket and a large glass of sweet tea, reading it. That is until football season starts. (She no longer has a favorite team, but still loves the sport).

Although she is new to writing, she is constantly creating new characters and stories in her head. It doesn't matter if she's grocery shopping, working out, eating dinner, pumping gas, or driving (uh-oh), her creative mind never turns off.

She graduated in May of 2008 with a Bachelor's Degree in Sociology from Virginia Wesleyan College and currently owns and operates a successful paralegal-for-hire business.

# Also by A.E. Via

Blue Moon I: Too Good to be True

Blue Moon II: This is Reality

Blue Moon III: Call of the Alpha

# A.E. VIA

You Can See Me

Nothing Special (Nothing Special Book 1)

Embracing His Syn (Nothing Special Book 2)

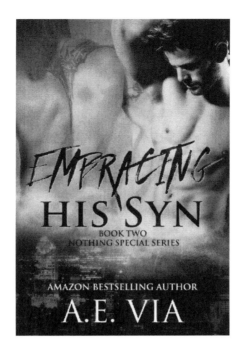

Here Comes Trouble (Nothing Special Book 3)

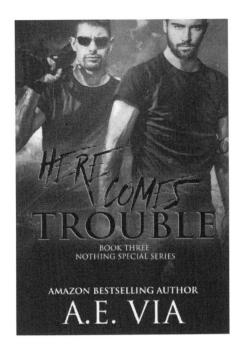

Don't Judge (Nothing Special Book 4)

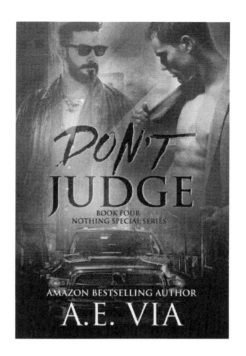

Promises

# A.E. VIA

Promises 2

Defined By Deceit

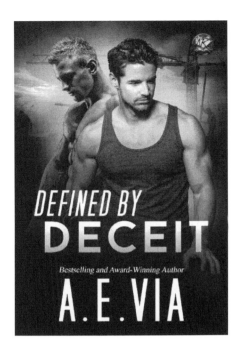

The Secrets in My Scowl

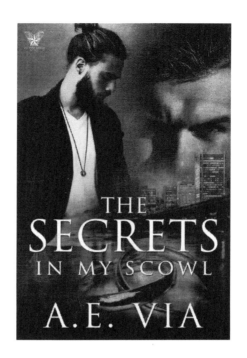